Jeff Abbott is the author of thirteen previous novels, published in twenty languages. His books *Panic* and *Run* have been optioned for film and are in script development. Jeff graduated from university with a degree in History and English, and worked as a creative director at an advertising agency before writing full-time. He lives in Texas with his wife and two sons.

THE
LAST MINUTE
JEFF ABBOTT

sphere

SPHERE

First published in Great Britain in 2011 by Sphere

A CIP catalogue record for this book
is available from the British Library.

ISBN 978-0-7515-4328-5

Typeset in Garamond by M Rules
Printed and bound in Great Britain by
Clays Ltd, St Ives plc

Sphere
An imprint of
Little, Brown Book Group
100 Victoria Embankment
London EC4Y 0DY

An Hachette UK Company
www.hachette.co.uk

www.littlebrown.co.uk

For Shirley Stewart

PART ONE

A VERY PRIVATE WAR

1

Manhattan, Upper West Side

I knocked on the green door and knew that in the next five minutes I'd either be dead or I'd have the truth I needed.

The man opened the apartment door just as I raised my fist for the second, impatient knock. He did not look like a man who traded in human lives. He looked like an accountant. He wore a dark suit, a loosened tie with bands of silver and pink and a slight air of exhaustion and impatience. His glasses were steel-framed and rectangular. His lips were greasy with takeout Thai, and the remains of a meal – maybe his last – scented the air.

He looked at me, he looked at the pixie of a woman standing next to me, then he looked at his watch.

'You and your wife are late, Mr Derwatt,' he said. 'One minute late.'

There were several misconceptions in his statement. First, my name was not Derwatt. Second, the woman standing next to me, Mila, was not my wife. Third, we were exactly on time; I'd even waited for the second hand to sweep past the twelve before I knocked. But I shrugged, full of graciousness, and he opened the door and Mila and I stepped inside. He looked her over. He did it all in a second but I saw it. She was glancing at the two thick-necked thugs who stood by the apartment's dinner table. Then she cast her gaze down, as if intimidated.

Nice bit of acting, that. Mila could stare down a great white shark.

I offered the accountant a handshake. 'Frank Derwatt. This is my wife, Lilia.'

'Mr Bell.' He didn't shake my hand and I let it drop down to my side. I threw in an awkward laugh for effect. I was wearing jeans and a navy blazer with a pink polo underneath. Mila had found a horrible floral skirt that I suppose approximated her bizarre idea of what an American suburban housewife would wear. She clutched her pink purse. We looked like we were more interested in country club membership than an illegal adoption.

'I thought we were meeting alone,' I said. Mila stepped close to me, like she was afraid.

The accountant dabbed a napkin at the Thai sauce smearing his mouth. I wanted to seize him by the throat, throw him against the wall and force him to tell me where my son was. But that would only get my son killed, so I stood there like I was the nervous suburban wannabe dad that I was playing.

'Face the wall,' one of the big men said. He was a redhead, with his hair sliced into a burr and freckles the size of pebbles on his face. 'Both of you.'

We both did. I set down the small canvas briefcase I was carrying.

I didn't argue. I was supposed to be a nervous, law-abiding citizen and, although I have been those things in the distant past, I wasn't right now. No wire, no weapons. Just me and my shining personality and a rage I kept caged up in my chest. The redhead searched me thoroughly. Then he did the same to Mila.

'Frank,' she said, about halfway through, a tinge of fear in her voice. She was selling it.

'Just be patient, honey, it'll be over in a minute,' I said. 'And then we can get our baby.'

Mila made this soft hiss of assent, the patient sigh of a woman who wanted this deal to be her gateway to happiness.

'Mr and Mrs Derwatt are clean, Mr Bell,' the redhead said. He stepped back from us. I took Mila's hand for just a moment.

'Sit down, Mr Derwatt,' the accountant said. 'Excuse the mess. We decided on an early dinner. I don't usually meet with clients at night.'

I knew that normally the accountant would now be on a commuter train back to New Jersey. I had checked into every nook of his life: a wife, two sons, a mortgage on a cozy little place to live, a life full of promise.

All the sweet elements I'd once had, and had lost.

The accountant and his toughs studied me. Let them, I thought. I'd been careful.

One opened the briefcase. He dumped the bricks of cash out onto the table and began to sort them.

Mr Bell glanced at me.

'My wife and I,' I lied, 'we've failed to conceive after three years of trying. It has nearly destroyed our marriage. I'm eager to give my wife a healthy, happy baby.'

'You could adopt through legit channels.'

'Yes. But, um, some of my business practices, I don't care to have them scrutinized by well-meaning social workers. We simply wish to acquire a child.'

Mila moved close to me. 'You have done our background checks, yes? We wish to make our selection and get a child.'

'It's not that easy, Mrs Derwatt.'

'I've brought the down payment. We select our child and then we go get him or her.'

He blinked at me.

'That was what was agreed,' I said.

3

'The money's all here, Mr Bell,' the redhead had counted with the precise quickness of a man used to handling banded stacks of cash. 'Twenty thousand dollars.'

'There were some anomalies in your background checks,' Mr Bell said.

'Anomalies. I do not know this word,' Mila said. She'd thickened up her eastern European accent.

'Um, questions, Mrs Derwatt.'

I held my breath. We had been very, very careful in setting up these identities. Mila had worked on them while we tried our best to find any link to the one clue we had to my son's whereabouts: a photo of a woman leaving a private clinic in Strasbourg, France, soon after my son's birth. I had been told she'd sold my son. We still did not know who the woman was, but using Mila's considerable resources we'd found a surveillance photo of her arriving in New York, a week after my son's birth, walking out of the terminal with this man. Mr Bell, whose face was in a criminal database maintained by the state of New York for having been convicted of embezzlement six years ago and had gotten parole. We matched him to the airport photo. Found out where he lived, where he worked and who his associates were. Slow, plodding detective work but it had paid off. We had sent out feelers as potential adopters of a child, provided background, gotten this meeting to pick out a son or daughter.

But now.

'We could not find a complete enough history for Mrs Derwatt before she came over from Romania.'

Mila was from Moldova, but the languages are identical. She turned to me and said in Moldovan, 'We will have to kill them.'

I forced a smile. 'She doesn't understand what you mean,' I said to Mr Bell in English.

4

'You said you met Mrs Derwatt through an online dating service that matches Western men with eastern European brides.'

'Yes. What does this matter? We've brought the money. We want a child.'

'She's Romanian, why not adopt there?' Mr Bell said. 'You could just go to eastern Europe and buy yourself a kid like you bought yourself a wife.' Nice sneer at the end.

Somewhere, we'd left a hole in our story. Or, conversely, this was a test. I put on my outraged face. 'We don't care where the child comes from. I told you, I cannot use normal channels.'

'As many of our clients can't, Mr Derwatt. So you understand why we must be so cautious. Our potential parents are . . . dangerous people.'

'My business is my business. I've provided you with what you need to know about me. Anything more could be compromising.'

'For me or for you?' Mr Bell asked.

'Darling, let's gather up our money,' I said to Mila. 'We're leaving.' I continued to play the outrage card.

'Don't touch the money, Mrs Derwatt,' Bell said.

'We had a deal.' I pointed at the laptop on the table. 'Pay a deposit, pick a baby from the list, pick him up and pay the rest.'

'We can decline to do business with anyone who makes us uncomfortable.'

'What is problem?' Mila said. 'Maybe you make misunderstanding, and this is easy to fix.' She tried a bright smile with him.

'You claim to be Lilia Rozan, from Bucharest, immigrated here three years ago.'

'No claim. Am.'

'That particular Lilia Rozan is currently in a cancer ward in New Jersey.'

Misstep. We'd used a bad identity. Mr Bell stood a little straighter. He was nervous but he had the muscle here. 'So, Mr Derwatt, we want to know who you and the lovely missus are.'

'We're wanted by the police,' I said. 'We had to lie.'

Mr Bell smiled. 'Details, please.' The two men were on each side of him. They didn't have their guns out but they thought they didn't need to; we were unarmed.

I looked at Mila. 'Look, our money's good as anyone else's. Please.'

The bald man moved behind Mila. She clasped a hand over her wristwatch.

'We want to know who you are. Right now. Or he starts in on your wife.'

Mila turned, hands clasped together as if in prayer. 'Oh no, please, don't hurt me. We just want a baby. Please. That's all we want.'

He shoved her into the wall. She kept her footing but tears sprang to her eyes. 'Oh, please.'

I stayed very still. The bald man glanced back at me, frowning with disgust that I would let him manhandle my woman, and in that second Mila pulled the watch from its band. Connecting them was a thin steel wire. She leapt onto his back and looped the garrote over his neck, the watch and the band serving as handles so that she didn't slice her fingers off. His yell became a gurgle in an instant.

I hammered a fist into Mr Bell's chest and he went heaving into the air and landed on my money. The redhead started to draw but he couldn't decide, for one crucial second, whether to shoot me or save his buddy, now purpling under Mila's wire. As

6

he swung the silencer-capped Beretta 92FS back toward me – hello, self-preservation – I launched into him. I levered the gun down as he fired and he hit his own foot. He howled and I slammed a fist into his solar plexus and then into his throat. He staggered back and we fought for control of the gun. He was bigger than me. I wrenched the gun, pushing it back toward his chest. His eyes widened as he realized the barrel was going to slip under his chin. It did and I squeezed his hand and his own finger pulled the trigger. A spray of blood and flesh fountained as it carved a path into his face. He looked surprised before the bullet distorted his flesh.

I freed the gun from his fingers and whirled, aiming at Mila's opponent. But that guy was already gone. She's not big but still a hundred pounds, hanging onto a wire; a throat can't survive the trauma. The bald man lay in a sprawl at her feet; she hovered over Mr Bell, panting.

'You all right?' I asked her. She nodded. I felt a tickle of bile at the back of my throat and I swallowed it down.

'You killed them,' Mr Bell said, gasping. People say the most obvious things when they're in a daze.

'They sell people,' I said. 'They're worse than I'll ever be.'

'Who are you?'

I didn't answer. I'm just a man who wants his stolen child back. My son I've never seen, except on this video, being carried by a woman who sells human beings for profit. My child. I was much closer to finding my kid than I'd ever been. And I thought of the times I rested my hand on my wife's pregnant swell, feeling the bubble of movement beneath the skin, knowing it was a baby but not knowing it was going to be Daniel, this unique and special person who I'd never gotten to see with my own eyes, hold with my own arms.

I'm coming, I told him, my breath like a prayer on the air.

Mr Bell swallowed; his mouth quivered as he looked at the dead men. 'Okay, you can have a baby. Whichever one you want.'

'I want one born on January 10th at a private clinic in Strasbourg called Les Saintes. His birth name on the certificate was Julien Daniel Besson but his real name is Daniel Capra. This woman took him from the clinic. All we've been able to find out is that she travels on a Belgian passport under the name of Anna Tremaine. Now, I asked around, and I found out that you work with Anna Tremaine.'

He gave a half-nod. He was scared to death, blinking at the bodies of the muscles.

'Where is my son?' I asked, very quietly.

'I didn't handle that placement. Anna would know. Oh, God, please don't hurt me.'

'Don't lie to us.' Mila held up the watch-garrote, slicked with blood.

'I'm not lying. I'm not.'

I squatted by him, put the silencer – still warm – against his modishly unshaven cheek. 'Did Anna know you were suspicious of me?'

'Um, no. We initially reject every adopter – we claim they aren't suitable, that there's a hole in their story. Our clients are normally so desperate, they will do almost anything not to be rejected. Usually we can pressure them into "qualifying" by sharing information that is valuable – you know, insider info on a company, or they can render services to us that can be useful later.'

Extortion and blackmail, as if illegal adoption wasn't enough. What charming people.

'So you meet us. We pass your test. Then what?'

'I call Anna. We set up a meeting. You give her the rest of the money. Then she makes a phone call and the child is brought to you.'

'Has my son been sold?'

'I told you, I don't know. Please. Please!'

'Watch him,' I said to Mila. I opened the laptop. On the screen was a catalog in PDF format. Pictures of babies. Countries of origin. Description of parents, if known – but no names. The spring catalog featured over two dozen children. Beautiful kids on the auction block. I scanned it quickly. None were listed as being born in France and I didn't see what the point of lying in the catalog would be.

'You're going to call Anna Tremaine, and you're going to set up a meeting.'

Mr Bell's lip trembled.

'Where is she based?'

'Her cell phone has a Las Vegas area code. But that's not where she necessarily meets people,' he added in a little rushed lie.

'Las Vegas will be just fine.' I decided I'd make it extra easy for Anna Tremaine. 'You tell her that Mr and Mrs Derwatt have checked out and that we'll be in Vegas tomorrow night to collect our child and pay the money.'

'You have to pick one, then.'

'What?'

'A child. You have to pick a child.'

'This one.' I just pointed to the infant whose picture was on the current page of the digital catalog.

'Okay.' His breathing slowed. 'I'll do it, please don't kill me.'

'Call her. Now. And if you say a single syllable that I don't like, I *will* kill you.' And I slipped Mila's garrote around his throat.

The bloodied wire lay against his shirt and I tightened it enough so that the steel lay against his soft throat. I gave him an address in Las Vegas to suggest as a meeting place. He nodded.

He dialed. He waited. I leaned close enough to hear.

'Yes?'

'Anna. It's Bell. The couple today, the Derwatts, they checked out okay. They've made their selection.'

'Which one?'

'Number fourteen.'

I could hear the barest scratch of pen and ink. 'All right.'

'They don't want to meet in New York. I think they would be willing to come to Las Vegas.'

A pause. 'All right.'

'Do you know a place called The Canyon Bar, just off the Strip?'

'Oh, wonderful,' she said. 'Hipster parents.'

'They suggested meeting there. Tomorrow evening at nine.'

I thought she might suggest her own choice. But any public spot could be put under surveillance. Our locale was as good as any other. 'That's fine,' she said.

'All right, I'll tell them.'

'Thanks.'

'You're welcome.' The conversation felt off. Tense. But he hadn't said anything I could pinpoint as a signal to her.

'The wife and kids all right?'

'Yes, Anna, thanks for asking.' He swallowed against the wire. 'Brent starts flag football this weekend. Jared's joined swim team.'

'Oh, that's nice. All right, I'll see the Derwatts tomorrow. How will I know them?'

'She's very petite, dark-haired. He's about six foot, wiry, dark blond hair, green eyes. Nice looking couple.'

'Tell them to get a table, preferably in the back. Order me a martini, three olives, and leave it at the table with a seat for me. I don't like the look of anything in the bar, I skip the meeting, and no baby.'

'I'll tell them.'

'Very well,' Anna said. 'Bye.'

He hung up the phone and dropped it to the floor. Shivering under the wire, waiting for me to kill him.

Mila knelt to meet his gaze. 'You're not going to die. You're going to talk. You're going to tell me everything you know about Novem Soles.'

'Who?'

'Novem Soles, also called Nine Suns.'

'What? I don't know what you mean.'

'I mean the criminal ring that Anna works for.'

'I only know Anna. She's self-employed.'

I pushed up the sleeves on his shirt. There was no marking tattoo, a fiery nine transformed into a blazing sun. Novem Soles's mark of ownership; I'd seen it on too many arms back in Amsterdam. I checked the arms of the two muscles. One had a tattoo, but it was the Chinese symbol for luck. Hadn't worked.

'She's not working for herself,' I said. 'She works for an incredibly dangerous group of people. They were plotting a mass assassination a month ago. You screw them over, you die.'

Mr Bell's lip trembled. He was trying to find his bravery but failing.

'You see them?' Mila pointed at the bodies.

He nodded.

'You're not going to be like them unless you make trouble. You're going to be locked up in a room and wait until we've

11

taken care of Anna. And you tell my people all you know about Anna Tremaine and her operation,' Mila said. 'Everything. And then you're going to go back and live with your family and you're going to stay the hell out of illegal activities.'

He nodded.

'Call your wife. Tell her you need to go out of town for a few days. Then call your office.'

He nodded, eager, hopeful he would live.

When he was done, he handed her back the phone. She took a pair of handcuffs off one of the dead men and cuffed Bell. I almost saw him shiver in relief. If she was cuffing him, she wasn't killing him.

I had the information I needed, finally. I was going to find my son.

2

Cable Beach, the Bahamas

It was a breaking of the rules, punishable by death. His project; his failure. His only shield was that he controlled access to many secrets that made their work and their profits possible. He smoothed out the thin strip of blond hair that bisected his scalp, a low-cut mohawk, and tugged at the jacket of his Armani suit. He stood on the porch of the large house and waited for the other eight to arrive in the darkening evening.

Rain slashed the beach, wind whipped the waves. Thunder thrummed the sky and the world appeared to have been smeared with gray paint. Alongside the sodden beach ran an equally sodden road, with a sign marking that it had been closed for repairs. Over the course of two hours, eight cars came down the rain-smeared asphalt and went around the wind-buffeted sign without the slightest hesitation. Each of the Lincoln Navigators, with its windows tinted against prying eyes, had been hired out from a local company that usually specialized in transporting film actors and rock stars around the island.

The passengers in each car, in this case, were not famous, and each liked their anonymity.

The house nestled in a private cove. The drivers helped their passengers inside. Each had packed light and carried a single bag. The drivers – all former military, now security for hire, from a variety of English-speaking nations – then took up stations around the house, to ensure that no one approached via boat, or car, or plane. Shortly after the last passenger arrived, the sky began to break, the clouds parting as if a curtain was rising on a stage, the early evening stars as witnesses.

The house smelled of Italian cooking: a heady mix of oregano, garlic, simmering beef and red wine. The host for this gathering of the Nine Suns, or Novem Soles as it was also known, had spent part of his wandering childhood in Rome. He loved food, and his nanny had taught him how to cook. So for dinner there was salad, grilled fish, hearty pastas, and fine wines imported from Tuscany and Piedmont.

The nine men and women ate and sipped wine and chatted about the world's events: a financial crisis in South America, the increasing violence between Muslims and Christians in Nigeria, the latest scandal in the American Congress – and the opportunities for expansion that all three presented.

The man with the blond mohawk accepted compliments on the food; he smiled and encouraged the quieter members of the group – quiet, that is, in the way of cobras, observing, considering when to strike – to join the conversations. He had wanted to arrange prostitutes for the visiting group, but had been sternly warned that, given recent events, this was no time for debauchery. He missed sex; he was reduced to being a spectator nowadays, but even watching, a feeble substitute, was better than nothing.

In these rooms they did not use each other's names. They were known by their responsibilities: the Banker, the General, the Diplomat, the Courier. Titles passed down through long years, or kept by the original members of the nine. The blond mohawk was called the Watcher; it was a role he'd fought hard to get, and he had no intention of losing it now.

The Watcher waited for the Banker and the General to get into their usual bickering, but for once they did not. He heard English spoken, Russian practiced, the silk of Arabic whispered. These gatherings were always a good chance for everyone to practice their foreign language skills. But the meeting would be conducted in English, the group's lingua franca.

After supper, the nine gathered in the large den. The Watcher stood at the head of the long table. He took a calming breath that he camouflaged under a welcoming smile. He was the youngest. *Can't be scared, boy. Be tough.*

'I'm a firm believer in bad news first,' the Watcher said. 'As you know, our recent mass assassination plot in the United States failed.'

Silence among the nine. It seemed like all the goodwill engendered by his fine food and wine evaporated like ice on summer concrete.

'A smuggling ring that we used as a cover to get experimental weapons into the United States was destroyed. The ring was infiltrated by a former CIA operative named Sam Capra. He should have died in our bombing of a clandestine CIA office in London dedicated to stopping illicit transnational activities. His office was part of the Special Projects branch – which, as you know, does the work that even the CIA is not supposed to discuss.' The mention of Special Projects caused a bit of a stir in the room: glances exchanged, water sipped, eyebrows raised. 'These days Special Projects is specifically interested in any criminal, non-terrorist activities that can affect American national security.'

He paused; they stared. Waiting. He tapped on the laptop button and a picture of Sam Capra appeared on the screen. Brownish-blond-haired, green-eyed, the lean face of a runner, mid-twenties, boyish. 'Capra survived only because he walked out of the office before it was bombed, however, and was regarded by the CIA as a likely traitor due to financial irregularities committed by his wife, and the inconvenient fact that his pregnant wife had told him to leave the office right before it was destroyed. Capra escaped from the CIA's custody, went searching for his wife, infiltrated our group in Amsterdam and disrupted the assassination plots.'

The nine waited while the Watcher took a long drink of water. He studied their faces. Most of them would not have been recognized by any government official, any police department, any journalist, any intelligence service. They were, for the most part, so ordinary. Frighteningly ordinary. The person who might sit next to you on the subway, or stand behind you in the grocery store line, or drop off their child at the same time you did at school. They came from around the world, yet they all seemed to have that same suburban sameness. It was, the Watcher thought, a superior camouflage. Yet they had come so close to delivering a history-changing death blow to American stability, to bringing the country to a level of chaos that promised an erosion of the rule of law and, in turn, enormous profit.

Look how far we've come since the early days, the Watcher thought. A tremendous lesson could be learned from a tremendous failure. They were unbloodied and unbowed. 'You will note that we lost our main CIA contact. He was killed in action by Capra. We have since lost two other low-level contacts I ... recruited inside the CIA. They've been arrested. Fortunately we did not deal face to face with them, and they cannot betray us.'

'So right now, we have no eyes inside the CIA?' the Banker asked.

'We have an eye or two that never blinks.' He smiled. Let them know he still had information feeds inside the agency, but not exactly what kinds. 'I do not know if they can see as well, or as far.' The Watcher cleared his throat. He could have shared a file two inches thick on Sam Capra's life with his compatriots, but he'd decided not to play up the man's importance. 'We do, however, have leverage over Sam Capra. We have his infant child.'

'Children,' sniffed the Banker. She was a Chinese woman, petite, thin, with a lovely face that could have sold cosmetics by the tonnage. She made a frown, as though the word held a sourness.

'Control,' countered the General.

'Control of a puppet with no strings for us to pull. While we have control over his kid, there's no way the CIA will let him close to any information that is useful to us,' the Diplomat said. He spoke with a deep baritone, a South African accent, hands tented before his face. 'I say we kill him. Show that we cannot be defied.'

'Sam Capra,' the Watcher said, 'doesn't know that our group

has steered him from six years ago, that we have guided his life as surely as a hand on a rudder. We made him into what he is, not the CIA. The setback with his wife was ... unfortunate. But he only knows us as a name that means nothing, a vague threat. He doesn't know who we are, he doesn't know how we came to be.'

'He has damaged us like no one else has,' the General said. 'I truly prefer that he be dead.'

'We should not be killing CIA agents unless absolutely necessary,' the Historian said. He was a heavy-set Russian, head shaved bald, muscles thick under the black of his tailored suit. 'It provokes attention. It is bad for business. He's no longer with the CIA, he is useless to us. He cannot hurt us. He cannot find us. He dies at our hand, the CIA will be coming to investigate.'

'I agree,' several of the others murmured. The Watcher scanned their faces, taking the temperature of their reactions. The Banker stared at him and he nodded at her and said, 'You have a thought to share?'

'Yes. You wanted us to finance your ability to spy on very specific people. I want to know how much of that ability has been compromised by this failure.'

'The whole reason we were able to attempt a project of this scale was because of me. Because I have made it easy for us to access information that is critically damaging to some of the most vitally placed people in the world and use it to force them to do what we need. We had a failure. It doesn't change the fact that I – I mean we – now own several people in key positions in government and business around the world.'

'So. You want to mount another project, using your resources.' The Banker's tone mocked him. In another time he would have slapped her across the face, torn her silk suit from her body, taught her who was master. His jaw quavered. Those days were done. Instead he nodded gravely. 'Yes. But first I want to clean up the mess that Sam Capra made for us, but I want you to understand why it's a risk.'

The Banker nodded.

'We had an asset in Amsterdam, a computer hacker who had helped me with infiltrating the laptops of our targets so that we had a free view of the classified information that came into their systems. Nic ten Boom. He's dead, killed by Capra. There is a loose end there that we have only now discovered.'

'What? Who?' the General asked.

'A young Chinese graduate student, a computer hacker named Jin Ming, was present at a shootout in a Rotterdam machinists' shop that was owned by the smuggling ring we used in Amsterdam. He was Nic ten Boom's hacking assistant, if you will. Ming is in the hospital, recovering from his wounds.'

'The assistant may know nothing.'

'He may not. I would very much like to know if he is going to be a problem. We know that Nic ten Boom was most ambitious.' He had to be careful here. 'In checking my own computer's logs, I found out that ten Boom was trying to learn more about us, and about our organization when he died. We hired him to spy *for* us, but he was starting to spy *on* us.'

'Then I'm glad he's dead, and you should hire with a more careful eye,' the Banker said.

'Nic was attracted by success. He wanted to move up the ladder.' The Watcher shrugged. 'He didn't seem to realize we require success before promotion.'

'Kids today are lazy,' the General said.

'Everyone else involved in the Amsterdam operation is dead, either killed by Capra or by one of our people, Edward, who

18

sought to minimize our risks by eliminating those who could identify him. Edward is dead.'

There was no sentimentality about the death of a hireling.

'I did not know until now that this young man, Ming, was alive. He was grabbed by the CIA from an internet café, then we assume Ming gave them the Rotterdam address. They took him in when they raided our smuggling operation and Ming was shot. Apparently both our side and the CIA left him for dead. He is in an Amsterdam hospital, under police guard.'

'So have him killed.' The Banker gave a dismissive wave of her hand. 'I can assure you, if there is a surfeit of anything in the world, it's Chinese grad students.'

'I will. But why I've told you all this is because it's all part of a bigger picture. We have shaped Sam Capra, over the years, like he was made of clay. And I don't intend to let that wheel stop spinning until he is molded in just the way we need. The time has come. I have thought of a way in which Mr Capra can be invaluable to us.'

'Because we have his child,' the Banker said. 'You just got a new pawn on your chessboard, darling.' She actually smiled at him.

He did not like her changing his metaphor. 'You have to seize what advantages you can,' the Watcher said. He felt the tension in his chest begin to loosen. At any moment any of the others would have been in their rights to call a vote on his life. They hadn't.

'The CIA will never trust him while we have his child. Ever,' the General said.

'Oh, I know. I intend to take full advantage of that. It's not like there's a surplus of highly trained CIA operatives on the market. And most of them would never consider working for us.'

'But he will,' the Banker said.

The Watcher nodded. 'Yes. He will.' He was going to get to live another day, he decided.

3

Amsterdam, the Netherlands

The woman who was not a nurse but was dressed like one entered the hospital shortly after 11 p.m. Amsterdam time, while a group met and talked in the Bahamas and Sam Capra got the best lead yet on his son. The woman had been most careful to forge her credentials with care; she had stolen a nurse's uniform earlier in the day from the hospital laundry; she'd had to settle for buying shoes that looked good enough to pass. The real trick was getting the passcard for the secure floor where her target slept. That had taken time, to pierce the hospital's security provider database, to imprint a card with the necessary code, to break into the police department's voicemail system and finally find a message that told her which room held Jin Ming. But she had done it.

And when she saw him, she was going to kill him.

Jack Ming was playing the Quiet Game, the one where you tried to see how long you could go without speaking. He was going on three weeks now, three weeks of such careful, cultivated silence that he wondered if his voice would still work. He lay in the hospital bed, the sheets pulled up close to him like a damaged cocoon. His throat bore the raw scar from where a bullet had furrowed across skin and muscle, the giant bruise on his temple from where he'd fallen against a piece of machinery. The injuries had kept him in a coma for nearly two weeks. The doctors and the nurses and the police investigators all called him Jin Ming, which wasn't his real name, and he did not correct their mistake.

Keeping quiet became an exercise – like writing a program with the least possible lines of code, or breaking into a database in the fewest, most elegant steps. How long could you play the Quiet Game? His father and mother had made him do it, when he was a child and playing loudly or asking one of his endless questions about why was the sky blue or why did they fight so much or why couldn't he buy a toy he wanted, and they would flash angry eyes at him, his father looking up from one of the books he always was reading, his mother from her desk where she seemed to live. Be quiet, Jack. You're bothering me. Let's play a game. See how long you can be quiet. But it was never a game; *they* were never quiet. A proper Quiet Game involved a stare down. This was simply a way for his parents to put him on a shelf.

So he stayed quiet.

He had woken up, sure that he must be dead. A bullet had scored along the flesh of his throat; another centimeter and he would have bled out in moments, his carotid artery emptying on the cool concrete floor of the smugglers' den near the Rotterdam port. But the artery went untouched. Three days after he woke up the police moved him from Rotterdam to a hospital in Amsterdam. He slept but it was strange: when he was wheeled inside they put a sheet over him. Like he was a secret they wanted to keep. He had his own room, he didn't have to share. He wondered what this meant; he wanted to ask for a computer, but he

21

didn't want to speak. Not talking was, weirdly, very liberating. He didn't have to tell the truth, he didn't have to lie. After all these months he did not have to keep pretending to be someone he wasn't.

At night he dreamed of the red notebook. Nic, drunk, had told him: 'The people we work for would kill us if they knew I had all their secrets. All bound up. That's my insurance policy. The red notebook.'

'If it's a secret, why tell me? You're drunk.' *And foolish*, Jack thought, but there was no point in stating the obvious.

'Because if something happens to me, I want them to suffer,' Nic had said in a beery slur. 'The red notebook. You find it at my place, hidden. You're smart enough to find it. It will bring the Nine Suns down.'

The Nine Suns. Nic invoked them like they were cartoon boogeymen. Jack didn't do an eye roll. No one wants to kill you, Nic, Jack had said. Stop being so dramatic.

But in the machinists' shop, with the smugglers working for Nine Suns in front of him, and the CIA behind him, he'd seen Nic lying dead on the floor, before all the gunfire erupted.

If he had to protect himself, he needed to find Nic's red notebook. Which was slightly difficult to do from a hospital bed.

Earlier that day they'd sent a new police inspector; as if a variety of interrogators would suddenly get Jack to speak. 'The doctor says that you should be able to talk,' the police inspector said. His name was Van Biezen and he sat at Jack's bedside and he watched Jack Ming watching him. He held a notebook in his lap and Jack could see the words on the paper: *Jin Ming. Graduate student in computer science at Technical University of Delft. Found shot near bodies of known criminals, including hacker Nic ten Boom. Refuses to speak. No medical reason for not talking.*

The writing on the inspector's notebook looked as exact as a computer font. The precision scared him. This was a man like his own father, a man who was going to ferret out truths.

Jack stared at the policeman.

'I understand the wound in your throat was fortunately rather shallow. Your vocal cords are not damaged, Mr Jin.'

Jack didn't speak.

'We need to know your connection to the dead men in the machinists' shop. Nic ten Boom and the Pauder twins.'

Jack stayed quiet.

'I know you've been told ten Boom is a known computer con artist. Did you know he was also a suspected internet pornographer?' Van Biezen let the next two words detonate, a soft bomb in the quiet hum of the room. 'Child pornographer.'

Bile inched into the back of Jack's throat. This was new. He hadn't known that about Nic. It was a most unpleasant surprise. He closed his eyes and he tried not to shiver. When he opened them Van Biezen still sat across from him.

'He specialized in creating custom videos. You want a certain kind of child doing a certain act? He could deliver.'

Jack gritted his teeth. Closed his eyes. No, no, no. He had intended on complete silence but now a sickened moan rose in his throat, like a bubble loosened in a bottle. The first real noise he'd made in weeks.

'Our informants say Nic ten Boom had a rather global clientele. What can you tell me about them?'

Jack wished he could die, snap his fingers, stop his heart. Every time this gets worse, he thought. I think it cannot get worse, and it does. It does. But he kept his mouth shut.

'The Pauder twins are known freelance enforcers for a variety of criminal enterprises. Now, Mr Jin, how does a nice graduate student in computer science get caught in a shootout with such bad people?'

Jack said nothing.

'I think your silence is to keep yourself from lying about who and what you are,' Van Biezen said. 'I think it's been tolerated far too long. You won't even write a note on a pad. But you *are* going to talk to me.'

Jack raised an eyebrow.

Van Biezen opened a file. 'Let's see what's true today, shall we? You are Jin Ming, and you are a Chinese citizen, born in Hong Kong. You speak perfect English, according to your classmates at Delft. That's all we know. I'm waiting for you to explain to me how you ended up in a bullet-ridden shop, full of counterfeit cigarettes and dead criminals.'

Jack had imagined how to answer this during his enforced silence. His false identity – backed by a computer record in the university's database, and inside a distant Beijing database of all students abroad – had held up. He could survive this and vanish again. So he spoke his first words in weeks. 'I was kidnapped.' The words sounded scratchy, like sandpaper grating against wood.

Van Biezen raised an eyebrow at the unexpected sound of Jack's voice. 'He speaks. Very good.' He cleared his own throat. 'Kidnapped.'

'Yes. Grabbed from an internet café over on Singel. The Café Sprong on 12 April. Ask the barista there. Three men came in and they pretended to be with the police. They pulled guns on everyone and ordered us to be still. Then they took me with them, they beat me up and they took me with them to that shop.'

'Why would they kidnap you?'

'I believe because they wanted my computer skills.'

'You're a hacker?'

'I am the opposite.' He injected dignity into his half-lie. 'Check my work in grad school, speak with my adviser.'

'We have.'

'Then you know my thesis subject is computer security. No one knows system weaknesses better than a security expert. I specialize in RFID chip programming – you know, the chips that are placed on products to stop counterfeiting and to facilitate tracking.' He paused. 'May I have some water?'

Van Biezen gave him a glass with a straw sticking out of it. The water tasted like heaven to Jack. 'Check the date. I'm sure there was a police report filed. The barista was mad.'

'I will. And how did all these three men end up dead?'

Jack kept his gaze steady on Van Biezen. The cop had misunderstood; he thought the three dead men – Nic and the twins – were his kidnappers. Jack nearly wept with relief. If he mentioned that a team of three CIA agents, hunting one of their own named Sam Capra, had kidnapped him right now it would be unwise; he preferred to approach the CIA on his own terms.

Because he had already decided that the CIA was going to help him get out of this mess. He swallowed and continued: 'Other men came in and shot them. I don't know why. Except . . .'

'Well?'

'They had crates of cigarettes. I assume they were smuggling them. If the cigarettes were stolen, then they might have wanted me to reprogram the RFID chips in the crates so they could not be tracked.'

Van Biezen said, 'They weren't stolen cigarettes. They were counterfeit brands.'

'Then I guess they wanted me for some other reason.'

Van Biezen did not look impressed. He said, 'So, when we check your phone records, we're not going to find any calls to Nic ten Boom or the Pauder twins. They were strangers to you.'

'Yes. Strangers to me.' He had been careful to use only the pre-paid phones given directly to him by Nic; his own phone and email records were clean.

'I'm going to check your story. I hope for your sake it holds true.'

'It will.'

'So why did you not speak for so long?'

Jack said nothing. He put on his Mona Lisa smile and stared back at the detective. He'd returned to his Quiet Game.

Van Biezen left and Jack leaned back against the pillows. He considered. The CIA had killed Nic and the other men in the warehouse and left him to die. Or maybe they'd thought he was already dead. He had no idea. But . . . he'd been here a while. He had his own hospital room. They'd brought him here, covered, and he was under police protection.

Were the police *hiding* him?

They must be. Which meant maybe Nine Suns and the CIA weren't looking for him. That was buying him time, very precious time he couldn't waste lying in a hospital bed.

He needed that notebook.

He was not going to ask the police for help or for protection. The only protection was the notebook full of Nine Suns' secrets and Nic had hidden it somewhere. He had to get out and he had to find it. The men who had taken him from the internet café would want it. The CIA, who had been hunting this group. Nine Suns must be special, international, if the CIA had an interest. They paid money for information. They protected informants.

He could see his only course of action perfectly clear. He could find Nic's notebook and sell it to August, and then could go into hiding for ever. He could not trust the police. He knew Nic had broken into the police department's servers; even if the police hid him, Nine Suns could find him. He needed the most powerful ally he could muster. It would have to be the CIA.

Jack Ming studied the white purity of the ceiling of his hospital room. All he had to do now was to get the hell out of this hospital and find the red notebook.

The door opened. A nurse stepped inside. She was tall and black-skinned and had a strong face that wore a frown. He blinked. He wasn't dreaming.

She closed the door and turned to him. His eyes widened in shock. A nurse's uniform?

'Well,' Ricki said. She came close to the bed, leaned down to his ear. 'You've been a lot of trouble to find.'

Jack decided to keep his ongoing silence, although he could not believe she stood before him.

'Do you know how worried I've been? I could kill you for not letting me know you're okay.'

Jack made a noise.

'I've had to hack into you don't want to know how many databases, looking for you.' Ricki was originally from Senegal, in West Africa, and her accent, fueled by anger, chopped the words into shards. 'Aren't you going to say anything?'

He shook his head, pointed to the surgical scar on his throat. She can't know what I've been doing, he thought, I can't put her in danger.

'Are you kidding me? I go through hell to find your hidden ass and you aren't going to talk to me?'

His heart felt like it would burst. He let his lips form the beginning of a word: I am so glad you're here, please get me out of this. But then he stopped. Ricki had known Nic, slightly. He couldn't connect her to Novem Soles. He had to keep her away from these lunatics.

So he shook his head: no.

Then she fell onto him, crying softly, putting a kiss in his hair. Not on his lips. They'd broken up weeks ago. She held him and he thought he might cry, he might let out all the emotion penned up inside him out, like a long-echoing wail.

She sat next to the bed.

He pointed at her nurse's uniform and raised his eyebrows. She shrugged. 'I had to wait for the night shift, and if I get caught I'm arrested. I had to sneak down here and talk my way past the guard because he hadn't seen me.'

The door opened, the guard peering in. Ricki had his wrist, as though taking his pulse. Jack gave the guard a nod. The guard shut the door.

'The police have been hiding you.' Ricki leaned close in her whisper.

Hiding him. And yet she'd found him. He loved how smart she was. He wanted to take her hand but they'd broken up, he reminded himself. She kept hold of his wrist.

'Ming' – and it shamed him she didn't know his real first name – 'what have you gotten involved in?'

He shook his head, pointed at the surgical scar.

'You don't fool me. You can talk. God knows most days you never shut up.'

He closed his eyes.

'Don't protect me,' Ricki said. 'Let me help you.'

The police officer outside opened the door and Ricki's voice shifted into a louder tone. 'So, everything looks okay. Sorry to have woken you.' She stood, nodded smartly. She glanced at the police officer.

And she walked out without a backward glance.

Let me help you. No one, though, could help him. Unless he found Nic's red notebook.

4

Upper West Side, Manhattan

It's not easy getting two bodies of heavy-set men out of an apartment. We had to assume the apartment was tied to Bell, and right now we didn't want people looking for him or linking him to two dead guys. We didn't want his name in the papers.

I called Bertrand to help. He showed up an hour later. With a moving van and crates. He brought Mila a moving van uniform and a cap that seemed to cover most of her face. He raised one eyebrow at the bodies, muttered something in his Haitian-accented French and got to work. The bodies were loaded and gone within fifteen minutes. He took Bell, too, now uncuffed from that corpse, shot up with a load of tranquilizer, and put into a crate.

'You're not taking him back to the bar?' I asked.

'You want me to carry an unconscious man past customers?' Mila always seems to assume I'm brain dead. 'I'll stash Bell where he can't be a problem and have a little chat with him. A man with a family to consider, he wants to keep a nice life, he will work with us. You go arrange travel to Las Vegas.'

I waited until they left. I watched the street to see if they were followed. The CIA had left me alone since I'd declined to return to the embrace of their employ, although I thought it likely that they might be checking in on me. I didn't see a sign that anyone was following Mila and the truck.

I walked out onto the street. I glanced at the faces of those near me and committed them to memory. It was eight blocks to Columbus Circle. The early evening breeze felt good against my face. The night was oddly full of music. From the buildings I passed I heard the soft tones of a Mahler symphony, the spice of Cuban salsa, a thunderous beat that drowned out hip-hop lyrics. Music was something people living a normal life got to enjoy.

When your child is missing, you live in a limbo. A purgatory without clocks. A room without windows, without doors, pitched into black, and all you can do is fumble along in the darkness and hope you find the knob to the door, or the sash of the window. That is hope. That you can throw an exit open, let light flood back into your prison, and standing there will be your child, safe and sound.

I had no intention of staying in limbo.

I spotted the first tail boarding the subway one car down from me. A sixtyish woman, hair styled short, dark glasses, delicate blue earrings. She'd been standing on the corner down from Mr Bell's building when I walked out. Looking away from me. I'd walked at a good pace and she'd kept up.

I stayed on the train. So did she.

I got off at the next stop, which was Seventh Avenue. So did she and a moderate sized crowd of people. I slowed, forcing her to get ahead of me. I had to figure she had at least one partner, someone who would stay with me if she peeled off, someone I hadn't seen when I exited the building.

The woman, pushed slightly ahead of me by the crowd, climbed the stairs to street level and she had to choose. She went left with brisk, heel-clicking purpose. I headed right. I didn't look back to see if she'd turned to follow me.

I didn't hurry. I wanted to see if she would backtrack. I also wanted to see who was sticking close to me. I turned into a small convenience store and I browsed. I bought a bottle of red wine, a couple of apples and a wedge of Cheddar cheese. I took my time, waiting to see what fly would stick in the honey. Seven other shoppers in the narrow aisles. I glanced at their faces, their profiles, without them noticing. One was familiar. He'd been on the subway with me. Late twenties, a bit older than me, dark hair, wearing a Yankees cap and a dark T-shirt and a light jacket although it'd been a warm day. Jackets change your appearance to the casual eye, and they're easy to ditch. So are hats.

I paid for my purchases and I headed back toward the subway station. I didn't look back but in the rearview of a parked car I saw the Yankees cap coming behind me. I ducked into a clothing store at the next corner.

At a distance he followed and in one of the mounted security mirrors I saw him enter the store. I grabbed a brightly colored shirt that would have embarrassed a peacock off one of the racks and I asked the clerk where the changing room was. She nodded toward the back and told me I couldn't take my grocery bag in with me, like I'd planned to shoplift some ugly plaid. I gave it to her to keep under the counter and I went into the changing area. Four saloon-style doors, a tailor's stand with a triptych of mirrors. I went inside one of the changing rooms and I waited.

If he'd seen me come with just one shirt he might wait. He

might still think I hadn't spotted him; at no point had I looked at him directly.

So I decided to really, really consider the merits of this kaleidoscope of a shirt.

Five minutes. Ten. The clerk hadn't come back to check on me yet. Then I heard him. I knew it was him because he gently pushed open one saloon door. Then another. If he was just looking for a place to try on clothes he would have stopped with the first one.

If I was wrong I would apologize.

He pushed on the unfastened door to my cubicle and I seized his hand. I levered him forward hard, slammed him in the wall. I smashed his face against the wall and he ooofed. You got to love an oof. Then I cracked his head again.

I wrenched his arm hard against his shoulder blades. Checked the left ear. Empty. Right ear. Oh, there it was, like a tiny beige fleck of wax. The earphones get smaller every year. I reached down, flicked off the lead for his mike under his shirt.

'Who sent you?' I asked.

He didn't answer.

'Special Projects?' That was the secret CIA branch I worked for; they have trouble saying goodbye.

He didn't answer. He tried to lever back and free his arm. I kept my grip above his wrist, on the cloth of his shirt.

I don't believe in giving multiple chances to cooperate. I battered the juncture of neck and shoulder, twice, and he folded. I took the mike, the earplug, and put them on, switched them to live. I searched his pockets. There was a wallet that I left alone, but a telescope, palm-sized. I took it. I put the unconscious shadow up on the small seat in the changing room. He was breathing just fine.

'Gato, respond.' He was being called. I knew the voice. So I answered in Special Projects code.

'He did a four-nine.' I'd heard him speak in the grocery, the barest tinge of a Boston accent, when the cashier asked if he had coupons. So I copied it. It only had to be good enough and I'm a decent mimic. Four-nine meant the subject had cut me loose in a crowd.

'Lucky, respond.' Now the speaker was calling the other agent; I figured this was the older woman from the subway. I looked around for her as I tossed the shirt I hadn't tried on back to the clerk and scooped up my bag of groceries. I hurried back onto the street.

'I don't have visual confirmation,' she said. 'He did not return to subway station.' She had hung close to the subway to pick me up if I doubled back.

'Return to base,' the voice said. 'We'll see if we can pick him on the traffic cameras.'

Yes, please, return to base. I waited. I had nothing more to contribute to class discussion, as Gato, so I stayed quiet. If the unconscious man was found an alarm might be raised. And I had to hope that they were the only two on me. Normally a team of four would have been used. Either I didn't matter or resources were thinner than usual. I didn't care about the reason. This stopped now.

I melded into the constant stream of pedestrians on Seventh and cast my gaze down the street with my palm curved around the telescope, as though shading my eyes. I caught the woman walking away from me, back the way we'd come. She pushed back her hair and in the telescope I could see her blue earrings I'd noticed before. I followed at a distance.

Several blocks later, along West 58th Street, I saw her

approaching a parked van. It advertised a floral delivery service. I thought that was funny because it's an old CIA joke that Langley does more to keep florists and chocolatiers in business because spouses get neglected and we have to make frequent apologies.

I don't have to worry about that any more.

I ran. I caught up with her, put my palm under her ribs, and gently – and rather gentlemanly, I thought – propelled her forward.

'Open the door,' I ordered.

She did. She was smarter than Gato. She tapped on the van door, three times, and it opened.

My best friend sat on the other side. August Holdwine is a smart Minnesota farm boy: big, broad-shouldered, cherub-faced, with a blond burr of hair and ruddy cheeks and eyes of sky-pale blue. I love him like family. He frowned at me. 'Well. You can wipe the Cheshire cat smile off. Where's my guy?'

'Sleeping it off.'

'Don't tell me you actually hurt him.'

'Bruises heal. He's okay and probably awake now. He might be too embarrassed to check in. I left him his cell phone. Call him.'

'You assaulted a CIA officer.'

'And you used the names of your childhood pets for your team. Stupid.' I glanced at the woman. 'Lucky was the nice cat, so August says.'

'Get in the van, Sam,' he said. 'Let's talk.'

'That might be an illegal action. You aren't supposed to be operating on American soil.'

'Go get yourself a coffee,' August Holdwine said to the woman. 'We'll talk later back at the office.'

'Your earrings,' I said to her. 'The blue is a shade too bright against the gray of the street and the buildings. Too memorable. But they do set off your eyes.'

'Don't be a punk,' she said and she turned and vanished into the river of people.

'Get in,' August said. 'Please.'

'That would be stupid if the point of following me is to grab me.'

'It's not. It's to talk to you.'

'You could walk up and say hello.'

'Not while you're with that woman. Mila.' He tossed his headphones on the computer keyboard in the back of the van.

'No one's here, August. Don't lie to me. Are you thinking I'm going to lead you to her?' But I needed to know why August and the CIA were interested in Mila. I needed to know now. So I got into the van. August moved up into the driver's seat.

'Where to?' August said.

'What about your guy?'

'He can find his way home. Where can we go and talk in private?'

'I know a bar.'

5

Amsterdam

Jack Ming couldn't sleep. He watched the clock tick toward midnight. He remembered reading once that there were eighteen million cellular phones in the Netherlands, and it frustrated him that not a single one was within reach. With one call he could be out of the hospital, his bill settled, safe under arms. He should have asked Ricki to leave him hers. But her showing up had surprised him too much, and she'd left before he'd thought to ask.

August. That had been the muttered name of the kind CIA officer who'd grabbed him, the one who stopped the others from beating him further. That was the name he was going to use when he phoned the CIA. He would call and ask for August. That was his ticket to safety, to money, to freedom.

Ten minutes after Ricki left, Van Biezen reappeared in his doorway, looking tired and rumpled, looking ready to go home. 'Your story checked out about being grabbed from the café. I thought you would want to know.' He raised an eyebrow to see if Jack would speak.

'Am I going to be released now?'

'From the hospital or our protective custody?'

'Both.'

'I cannot speak for the doctors. But I think you should be careful. These smugglers were apparently part of a much bigger criminal enterprise.'

'What do you mean?'

'On ten Boom's laptop we found evidence he had been hacking into police databases, downloading classified documents relating to far-ranging investigations. The sort of information that a criminal network would like to buy.'

'I know nothing about whatever this man was doing,' Jack said. 'And if you are going to question me further along these lines, I would like to see someone from the embassy and I would like a lawyer.'

'I wasn't questioning you. I was warning you. These are

dangerous people, Mr Jin.' Van Biezen's voice was measured and careful, sleek as a diplomat's. Just like his mother. 'Are you planning to return to Hong Kong? I understand you have not given the doctors a clear answer.' Just a bit of a sarcasm in his tone.

'I haven't decided. I am already ruined for this semester. I have much work to do.' He paused. 'You said you were giving me a warning. Do you think I'm in danger?'

'We have kept a guard by your room. He's not for show.'

Immediately after Van Biezen stepped out, a polite functionary from the Chinese embassy stepped in, now that he was speaking; to be sure that he was all right, and that there was no issue of embarrassing the motherland with the police. It was frightening to Jack because he had no desire to be shipped off to Hong Kong and the fact that a bureaucrat was here so late at night made him nervous. But his false identity held. Yes, he said as Jin Ming, his parents and his grandparents were dead, he had no family back in China. He had been careful to craft an identity without family. The Chinese diplomat was concerned for his wellbeing and Jack reassured the man he was the innocent victim of a crime. He thanked the embassy visitor and when the man had left Jack stared at the window.

He wondered if his mother was looking for him; he thought not. She didn't want him. He had been lucky, too lucky, and it was time to place a surer hand on the reins of his own fate.

He couldn't sleep. He got up for a walk.

Each day, the doctors had encouraged Jack to walk to stretch his leg muscles, even if it was just around the floor for five tottering orbits, ambling past rooms and equipment in the hallway. His mind full of Ricki and his rapidly unraveling situation, he was walking back to his room and as he turned the final corner he saw, from down the hallway, a man he didn't know in an orderly's uniform enter his room.

His police guard was gone.

Jack stopped. The man looked short, thickly built. He shut Jack's door behind him. He knew the night-shift orderly; he had seen him on the opposite side of the floor, during his walk.

If Ricki could steal a uniform . . .

He can see I'm not in the bed, Jack thought. He must think I'm in the bathroom.

He ducked back behind the corner, keeping one eye focused on the door.

After thirty seconds, the man stepped into the hallway. Heavy eyebrows, pale skin, a soft mess of a mouth, a bottom lip long ago disfigured in a fight.

You're a loose end, Jack thought. And now either someone who knew Nic, or someone who knows Novem Soles has come looking for you. They know you're alive. They've either waited for the guard to go to the bathroom or they've paid the guard off. They want to be sure you can't talk.

And if he was wrong, then no harm done. But if he was right . . .

The man saw Jack. The twisted lip smiled. He raised the eyebrows as if in greeting. Like he was a friend, come by to talk to Jack.

Jack ran.

Or, rather, Jack stumbled in a loping run. He wasn't entirely recovered from the bullet that had grazed arteries and windpipe. He wore a bathrobe and the hospital gown and flimsy slippers the nurses had given him. He saw a stairway and he hit the door, leaning out into the cool slightly stale air of the concrete staircase. His mind moved as fast as it did when he was crafting a software program. If the guy was here to silence Jack he would expect Jack to try and escape.

Most immediate escape meant down, toward the ground floor.

So Jack headed up. He wasn't used to physical exertion and little black clouds dotted his vision. His breath sounded loud in the stairwell. He hit the next floor, opened the door, stepped out into the unit. More recovery rooms but this floor was less crowded. He was on the opposite side of the floor from the main nurses' station.

An old man in a brown bathrobe walked past him, ambling with an insomniac's shuffle, carting an IV feed on a wheeled pole. Jack moved in the other direction. He had to hide. Get to a phone, get Ricki to come and pick him up at a nearby pub or café. He couldn't stay out on the streets of Amsterdam dressed like a patient; even in the world's most laid-back city around midnight, it would attract too much attention. He looked like someone who might have wandered away from the hospital and needed help.

He opened the door of one room, saw an elderly woman sleeping inside. He eased it shut.

Behind him he heard the stairwell door open with a steely crank. As it did he stepped into another patient room, this one holding two beds, both empty. He left the lights off. An IV pole stood on duty by each bed, a drawn curtain dangling between them. He had no real place to hide. He pulled the curtain partway between the beds, and ducked behind its cover, the IV pole clanking into the wall behind him. Next to him was one of the adjustable wheeled tables for patients to use while lying in bed.

He closed his hands around the cool steel of the pole. He heard the door open. Maybe a nurse coming to see why he was trespassing in this room. He couldn't see through the curtain.

He heard two footsteps and then silence.

The nurse wouldn't just stand there, right? he asked himself. He was suddenly consumed by fear and certainty that this man was here to kill him.

Jack pushed the patient table into the curtain.

The two bullets sang out, cut through the fabric, pounded into the wood. The impact was louder than the firing.

Jack moaned, in fear, without thinking that he was baiting a trap.

As the man stepped around the curtain, Jack swung the pole, like a baseball bat, and he caught the man's face between the bushy eyebrows and the tattered mouth.

'Uggghhhh,' the guy grunted.

Jack rocked his feet, swung again in the same vicious arc, hit again and again and then there was an oddly wet noise that sounded . . . final. The guy collapsed onto the floor. Shuddered, shook, gasped. He looked at Jack with blind surprise. Then his head fell back and a sagging shift downwards trembled through his body.

The man's nose was a splintered mess. Jack had not known he had the strength; it was as if all the energy he'd stored in the past few weeks roared out of him when he needed it. The man was very still. Jack knelt by him, dropping the pole with a clank to the tiled floor. He tested for a pulse, found nothing but a warm and sudden silence in the man's throat.

Bone shard, Jack thought. First blow broke the nose, second sent a bullet of bone into the brain.

He clapped his hands over his face in shock. He had killed a man. Killed him.

Because he was going to kill you.

Jack picked up the gun and he stood. He footed the body under the adjustable bed. He picked up the gun and put it into the pocket of his robe.

He stepped back out into the hallway. In the next room the old woman still slept. He went through her bureau and he found ten euros and a mobile phone. He took it, feeling guilty about the theft, and he laughed because he didn't feel guilty about killing the man. He hurried out into the hallway and back down the stairwell. In a few minutes he was in his room, sitting on the edge of the bed.

Who could he call?

Ricki. He could call her. They were still friends. He still kind of liked her even though she'd only really been his girlfriend for five whole minutes after he arrived in Holland, after he'd stepped into the secret life he'd made for himself. And clearly she cared about him, to have gone to so much trouble to find him. He cajoled her into coming and picking him up and bringing him clothes to the hospital. The police had taken the clothes in which he had been shot as evidence, and they were stained with blood anyway. Ricki agreed and said she'd be there within an hour. He told her to meet him at a coffee shop nearby that he knew well.

When he got off the phone he lifted a pair of jeans from a room down the hall where a man lay zonked out on painkillers and grabbed a rugby jersey from the man's closet. He left, sneaking past the nurses, riding the elevator down, stepping out into the cool quiet of the night. There was an old café down on the corner.

He walked out into the street. *They found out you're still alive. They're coming after you. You've got one weapon to fight back. If Nic was lying about that notebook, you're a dead man.*

6

Midtown Manhattan, near Bryant Park

We walked into The Last Minute, my bar near Bryant Park. The Last Minute's a nice bar. Elegant, refined, oriented toward jazz. The bar itself is exquisite Connemara marble. The mirror behind the bar is huge and ancient, a leftover from a New York establishment from before the Civil War. We get a bit of tourist trade – any high-end bar in New York does once good reviews land on Yelp or on the guide sites – but we get a lot of Midtown office people, bored wealthies, regulars who actually know what goes into a proper Old-Fashioned or Sazerac. The post-work crowd had started to melt away. Eloise is at the piano, softly playing a Thelonious Monk arrangement. She's older than God but the sparks of jazz in her body are apparently going to keep her alive forever. When I'd acquired the bar from Mila a few weeks ago, it had been called Bluecut, but I'd renamed it. The Last Minute was my base of operations in searching for my son, and it reflected my sense of urgency and my determination that I would never give up.

I nodded at the bartender and pointed at a stool for August. He sat. Then I went back behind the bar to make our own drinks, which is a statement in itself. I knew I had to let go of some secrets right now to protect others.

August looked like what he is, a Minnesota farm boy of Swedish and German descent. He glanced around at the beautiful people, at the elaborate décor, at the shimmer of lights. He'd met me here for a drink a few weeks before and, five minutes after he left, Mila showed up and gave me ownership of The Last Minute, and of thirty other bars in cities around the world. I hadn't told him because so far he didn't need to know. But as I moved to the other side of the expanse of Connemara marble, he raised an eyebrow at me. 'You bartending now?'

I gestured, open-handed, at the charm and the glory. 'The Last Minute is mine.'

'The bar is yours?'

'Yeah.'

He glanced around at the finery and absorbed the news. 'Well. I was going to order a beer. But if you own the joint, then I'll have a martini made with good gin.'

'All right.'

I crafted his martini, with all the care you would take for your best friend having his first cocktail in your new bar.

I slid a Plymouth English Gin martini in front of August, two olives. Not the most expensive gin but really a strong choice for a martini. August took a sip and nodded in approval. I poured another one for myself.

'Let's go sit in a booth,' he said.

Old banquette-style leather booths lined one wall; they provided a modicum of quiet. August followed me to one.

'Why have you bought a bar?' he asked.

'I need a livelihood to support my search for my son,' I said. There was a lot more to the story, but he didn't need to know how I'd come into possession of The Last Minute and its thirty sisters around the world. Mila's bosses – a group known as the Round Table, who claimed to be a force for good in the shadows – had offered me the bars as a cover to travel the world, to track down my son and to do the odd job for them that required my skills.

'You could have come back to work at the Company.'

'They don't like to accuse you of treason and then backtrack by offering you gainful employment.'

My past with the CIA was a sore spot with him; he almost cringed as I spoke. To camouflage his embarrassment, he glanced around the bar, drinking it in as carefully as he'd sipped his martini. Some spy; he couldn't keep the surprise off his face. 'Really nice place, Sam.'

'So now you know where to find me. Why are you following me?'

He twisted the toothpick holding the olives. 'This woman. Mila. Who helped you fight Novem Soles in Amsterdam. I want to know about her.'

'There's nothing to know.'

'Sam, let's not insult each other.'

Fine, I thought. I'd play. 'You followed us today. Mila, too.'

'Yes.'

I had had an early dinner in a favorite old haunt of mine; that must have been where August's watchers had picked me up. Then Mila and I had met in Central Park, then gone to the apartment address Bell gave us. She hadn't been here at The Last Minute in weeks. And she'd left with Bertrand. And with her cap and sunglasses and moving van uniform the followers must not have spotted her leaving, else they would have followed her, not me.

'Why?'

'I want to know who she is.'

'Stop following her and ask her.'

'I'm not going to kidnap her off the street.'

'Because the CIA isn't supposed to operate on American soil. And yet here you are, tailing people. I guess I should be grateful you haven't set the FBI on me.'

August took an appreciative sip of the martini.

'I don't need to kidnap her when I think you'll tell me what I want to know.'

I slid the olives off the stick with my mouth and dropped the toothpick next to my glass. 'Mouth full,' I said. 'Can't talk.'

'You've really picked your side, haven't you, Sam? You've picked this Mila.'

'I can rely on her.'

'I told you we would help you find your kid.'

'I told you I would handle it myself.'

'Because you think you still have enemies in the Special Projects branch.'

'Yes. Who would use my kid against me.'

'You're paranoid.'

'You get to be after you get framed for treason, August.'

He took another sip of his drink. 'You're trying to find the woman who took Daniel.'

'No luck yet.'

'I'm betting you're close.'

'August. Go home. Let me get my kid back.'

'Have you made progress? Can we help you?'

'I trust you. But if you tracked my kid and there's another traitor inside the Company working for Novem Soles, then, well, maybe my kid is dead. Right now they don't know what I'm doing and I have to keep it that way. I get him back, that's all I care about. I'm not in the revenge business.'

'We don't even know what Novem Soles is,' he said. 'Some of the thinkers at the CIA are arguing that Novem Soles actually stands for "nothing special". They could just have been a few guys who decided to make some cash committing corporate espionage and smuggling weapons. They got a gang of low-level thugs to tattoo themselves and talk like they were part of a big deal and maybe it's all just a grand illusion.'

'I don't think so,' I said. 'I think they're big.'

'I think you're right. My hope is that Mila could tell me exactly what and who they are.'

'If she knew that they'd all be dead.'

'I'm glad Mila and I are on the same page, then. What were the two of you doing today up on the Upper West Side?'

'Meals on Wheels.'

August tapped a finger against the base of the martini glass. 'Look, I want Daniel back for you. More than anything, Sam. But you can't grab him back and just let these people roll on.'

'I am going to do what's best for my kid and me.' I gestured toward his martini. 'I want out, August. I want a normal life again. They took it from me and I'm going to get it back.'

'And, what, run a bar?'

'Yes.'

'Sam. You did us, and the nation, a good turn here in New York.'

'You sound like an award plaque.'

He ignored my sarcasm. 'I won't ever forget it. But I've had to argue, repeatedly, not to pull you back in. I've protected you because we're friends. I did it because I know you want it this way. But Novem Soles is much, much bigger than you. I'm running a task force in Special Projects on finding information about this network, what they want, who they are.' He turned the martini glass. 'They're something new. Different. I would expect a terrorist group to try to do a mass assassination. But not a criminal group. What's the profit in it for them? Who are they? Why are they doing what they're doing? It makes no obvious sense.'

'Good luck.'

'So. Let me help you. We'll find them together.'

I let the piano music wash over me for a moment. 'A few weeks ago I saw a redacted document from a Company file. It claimed that I could be controlled through my son. Inside the Company, August, on your side of the fence. I'm not exactly looking for help.'

He said, 'Where did you get this document?'

'It doesn't matter.'

'Well, I've certainly never seen it, Sam, and documents can be forged.'

'This wasn't. Because it's true. I *can* be controlled through my son. Which is why I and I alone am going to get him back.'

'You're not alone. There is Mila. There's no record of her in any government database we can find. Her name *is* Mila, right?'

'So the only reason you are following me is to find her?'

'Yes.'

'Then you're wasting your time. I don't know where she is now or where she lives. I'm sorry. Would you like another martini before you go?'

'No, thank you. I saw her, I think, in the internet café in Amsterdam, when we grabbed that Chinese hacker that was tied to Novem Soles. I showed her picture to some people in Europe who provide us with information now and then, at a cost.'

'Well, if I wasn't with her, I couldn't say if you saw her or not.' I risked a smile.

The scene was vivid in my head. I'd tried to infiltrate a criminal ring in Amsterdam, and the Chinese hacker was some poor college kid they'd used to research my forged Canadian identity and had gotten caught by August. The hacker had died in a shootout later that day where most of the ring died as well, and I'd barely escaped with my own life. Mila had been watching me from the same internet café across the canal.

'You're scraping the bottom of the barrel,' August said. 'She does not have a nice reputation.'

I said nothing.

'There's a price on her head. Did you know that?' August delivered this with the kind tone of a friend breaking bad news. 'A cool million dollars for your Mila, preferably alive.'

The words hung in the air. I distantly heard the trill of piano jazz, the clink of the crystal, a drunken bray of laughter from a guy who'd had a pint too many.

'I mean, you can have someone killed rather cheaply these days – under ten thousand. There's been a price deflation on hits, what with the economic downturns. But a million on her head, Sam.' August gave out an amused whistle. 'That's trouble. Some very bad people are looking for her to collect that payday. I wonder what she did that's worth a million dollars.'

Maybe he already knew. He had been my one true friend in the CIA, and until he proved otherwise I had to consider him a friend. One of the waitresses passed. I pointed at August's martini and raised two fingers. August's brain needed picking.

'We could protect her, Sam. In exchange we'll find out who has the contract on her and we'll make it go away.'

Once again I said nothing. I couldn't negotiate on Mila's behalf. Someone must truly, truly hate her. It did not surprise me.

'Makes you wonder who she's pissed off.'

'Who put out the hit?'

'We picked it up on chatter online.' He leaned forward. 'You're welcome.'

'You're not helping *me*.'

'Sam. She can tell us what we need to know. Clearly she's connected to movers and shakers. She armed you, she financed you, she got you into the Netherlands and into the UK and into the United States with no trace of entry. She helped you get inside

48

a major criminal ring that was planning the biggest assassination plot in American history.' He shook his head. 'We want to know who she works for and what she knows about Novem Soles, Sam. Give her to me.'

'You have a very vivid imagination. Maybe I did all that hard work.'

'Not on your own. You didn't have the resources, the money.'

'You following me today is no different than when you had me living in Brooklyn, waiting to see if someone from Novem Soles tried to kill me or grab me. I don't work for you, August. I quit the Company. So you worry about your projects and let me worry about mine.'

'Let me talk to Mila, Sam. Please. We can help each other.'

'I'm not going to repay any help I've gotten from her by handing her over to you for interrogation. If she wants to talk to you, she will.'

The silence between us felt like one you'd find at a poker table when the cards still hold every possibility and the only measure you take is in your opponent's face. 'I don't want to play hardball with you.'

'August, you don't even know where the hardball court is located. Now. You've learned you can't follow me, and you've had your most excellent drinks.' I stood. 'I have to go tend to my business.'

'I find it fascinating that you now own a bar. Where'd you get the money?'

'Good night, August.'

'Who are you working for, Sam? What have you gotten yourself into, hanging with a woman who has a million-dollar bounty on her head? You and I both know that only happens when you get down and dirty with the very worst.'

49

'I'm going to find my son. No matter what it takes. Remember that.'

He was silent, staring at his martini glass. I know he wanted to help me. He was my friend. But he couldn't.

'You said you wanted your life back. If that means working for Special Projects again, and it should, then have your lady friend talk to me. Tell me who's been helping you. Give us them and get what you had back.'

'The Company showed me zero loyalty in my hour of need, August. Let me guess: you'll run straight to them and tell them I own this bar now. Although it's none of their business, and I want them to leave me alone.'

He sat silent for ten long seconds. 'I don't need to tell them your business. You may not think it, Sam, but I've always been your friend.' He looked more angry than hurt, and I knew he wasn't playing me. He stared at me. 'In the crazy hours, right after you were accused of killing everyone in London Special Projects, I thought – do I know him? Do I really know him, could what they say be right? You could have fooled me, could have fooled everyone else. You could have been the worst murderer and traitor in CIA history. But then I thought, no, if he killed them he wouldn't have been so stupid about it to be there when the bomb blew. He would have vanished. Because Sam is not stupid. Sam always does a calculatedly good job.'

I missed August. Hated to admit it, but I did. I wanted to trust him. But I couldn't trust Special Projects, not after what they'd done to me. 'A compliment. Thanks. I can encourage Mila to talk to you. But I don't know where to find her, and that's the truth.'

'Getting your kid back, that's huge to me. But I'm going to find Mila, Sam, with or without your help, and if you get in my way the friendship does not trump my duty.' He folded his heavy arms. August played college football at Minnesota, and he's a lot bigger than me. More pure muscle. I am smaller and faster and a little less naïve.

The worst enemy is a one-time friend. I knew that.

'I'm not your enemy, Sam, and I won't be, unless you choose to be mine.' His word choice made me feel like he'd read my mind. He picked up the martini, finished it with a toss.

'It's too warm now, it's no good.'

'Things don't stay good,' he said, and I knew: something had happened. 'I hope you get Daniel back, safe and sound. You know I hope that more than anything else, Sam.'

'I know.'

I used to fight with my brother Danny and the awkward, awful silence between us felt like the one now between me and August. A bitterness that could be sweetened with a word, but neither of us was willing to add that ingredient. He turned and he walked out, and I turned to go upstairs to pack for Las Vegas. The Round Table had a private jet I could use, and I wasn't waiting a moment longer. I would head for Vegas tonight.

7

Amsterdam

Jack and Ricki had met under less than auspicious circumstances: she appeared in a hacker's chat room when he was still in New York City, looking to trade piracy software for counterfeit DVDs. Jack didn't think film piracy was really very cool, he knew it was theft, but in her postings Ricki was funny and charming and she was Dutch and so he thought she was hot. No one on the hacker discussion group knew he was Jack Ming, the guy the New York police wanted to bring in for questioning.

I got to run and hide. My parents are so uncool, he'd written.

Come and hide in Holland, she wrote in answer.

So he had, just on impulse, and he and Ricki had met for coffee in Delft after he arrived on a fake passport a friend back in New York helped him get. Instead of the dainty Dutch girl he imagined, Ricki was half a head taller than him and an immigrant from Senegal. She was funny, smart, pretty, and oddly tough. He was thoroughly overwhelmed and intimidated by her. He didn't know what to say. Their coffee dates became fewer; he figured she was disappointed in him. He was a geek on the run. And he kept too much hidden in himself for her taste. How unappealing was that?

The hacker community tended toward what Jack thought of as a distant tightness. They stayed close online but they didn't hang out much in real life. A person who was socially nimble behind the cocoon of a screen could be one who consistently missed normal interaction cues in a café or a pub. Ricki was one such individual. She arrived at the coffee shop thirty minutes late, stuck a wad of cash into one hand and a bag of cheap clothes into his other hand and said, 'You owe me.'

'Where'd you get the clothes? All the stores are closed.'

She shrugged. 'Old boyfriend before you left them behind, but I think they should fit. You're about the same size.'

He tried to ignore the stab of jealousy he felt. 'Yes, I know. I'm going to owe you more. I need a place to stay. Just for tonight.'

'Please.' Ricki rolled her black-lined eyes. 'Now you've decided to talk?'

'Just one night.' He glanced in the bag; the clothes were a lot more colorful and stylish than he would have selected.

'What kind of trouble are you in?'

'Nothing major, I just need a place to crash.'

'Do the police know you've checked yourself out of hospital?'

Information was currency. 'Look, I'll write a program for you, a Trojan that'll send you back information from the infected computer. Could be valuable.'

Ricki touched the corner of her mouth with her tongue. Please be greedy, Jack thought. Please.

'You don't need to bribe me to help you, Jack!' She looked wounded. 'I took a huge risk to find you.'

'Oh,' he said. 'No. I didn't mean ... I didn't mean that. I was going to give it to you as a gift. For helping me.' His voice trailed off.

She sighed. 'So smart, so clueless. Buy me a coffee with the money I brought you and we'll go back to my place. I'm just glad you're okay.'

'You are?'

'Duh. No, I've often wished you dead. Honestly, you are dumb as a rock.' But Ricki smiled at him. A short, sweet flick of a smile and it nearly made him cry, he was so happy to see a friendly face.

He changed clothes in the tiny bathroom of the café. He bought her a coffee to go. He wanted to put as much distance between him and the hospital as possible. He felt he'd nearly gone insane waiting for her.

The first thing he thought when he saw her apartment was blink and wonder where she actually lived, because there was hardly space for her in the rooms. When they'd dated months ago, she'd never let him come to her place. She was in Amsterdam, he lived in Delft and she came to see him, not the other way around. The apartment was small. One entire wall was full of bookshelves, each holding at least two dozen DVD burners. On the opposite side of the wall he saw neatly packaged DVDs, mostly of films currently playing in theaters. Hundreds of them. He started doing the math in his head.

'It's probably about fifty thousand dollars' worth,' she said.

'Wow. And you sell these on the street?' She had not really talked much about her 'work'.

'I used to. That's how I came here from Senegal. The counterfeiters start you off selling on the streets. I sold DVDs better than anyone. I got promoted. Now I have a street team.'

'Don't you get caught?'

'Not me,' she laughed.

The machines whirred, all creating illicit product. Machines began to beep, completing their copying, and she started to pull the finished discs from the machines.

She tossed him a T-shirt from a freshly opened box, for a new vampire film that wasn't out for another three months, with a still shot of the main characters at a critical moment silk-screened on its chest.

'So. You got shot and had a vacation courtesy of the police,' she said. She glanced at the raw scar on his neck. He would, Jack thought, need a scarf. The thought of wearing the vampire shirt while having a healing neck wound nearly made him laugh.

'Yes.'

'You're a dangerous boy now, Jack.' She touched the skin below his scar. 'Who shot you?' Excitement brightened her dark eyes.

'I was in the wrong place at the wrong time, excuse the cliché, in my case it's apt.'

54

'Nic was shot to death,' she said. 'It was in the news.'

'Yes.'

'When you were shot?'

'No. Before. He was dead before I got there.'

'Well, that wasn't in the papers.' Her voice rose. 'Why not?'

'Because it wasn't.'

'Why?' Her voice sounded accusatory.

'Because I suppose the police were protecting me.'

'And, what, now they're not.'

'Now they're not.' He weighed his choices. He had few. 'I killed a man there tonight, Ricki.'

She laughed. Then she didn't. She sat and stared at him.

He fought down a surge of shivers. 'Maybe some tea?' he asked.

'Yes, but decaf. You don't need any more stimulation. You won't sleep at all tonight.' She got up and microwaved two cups of water and stuck a decaf English Breakfast teabag in each cup. He watched the steam curl and stayed silent while he let her process his confession. She produced a bottle of brandy from her cupboard and raised eyebrows at him and he nodded. Ricki dosed both cups.

He thought she might keep quiet. She would never go to the police, not at all. But now he had to win her sympathy to earn her continued help. She came looking for you, he told himself. She must want to help you. At least, until she finds out how dangerous this could be.

'The man was sent to kill me. I have to vanish for a while. I'm not so scared of the cops but the cops can't protect me, and I'm not going to jail. They won't let people like you and me have a computer in jail. Ever.'

She folded her arms as though his dire prediction made her

cold. She was immediately weighing her options, he could tell. She wasn't easily given to shock.

'Will you help me?' he asked.

'Who wants you dead?'

'Nic got me involved. He did work with a group called Novem Soles. Or Nine Suns?'

She shook her head. 'What, they're Catholic computer hackers?'

'Uh, no. They're afraid I might know more than they think I do. I'm a loose end. I'm a mouth that could talk.'

'Do you really know anything that could hurt them?'

'No,' he said. It wasn't exactly a lie. The notebook – Nic's self-described nuclear weapon – there was no point in mentioning it to Ricki. The less she knew, the safer she was.

'So, what, you run for the rest of your life? This guy you killed, it was self-defense, right?' Her voice rose slightly. 'You won't be able to finish school.'

'I was kind of bored with school. You and me, we're not suited to day jobs.'

She gave him a shy smile and sipped her tea. 'So you run and to begin with I equip you.'

'Well. If you can. I'll pay, of course.'

'What do you need?'

'A laptop. I need to be able to transfer my money to a new account. I need to get documentation so I can get out of the country under a new name. And I know somebody who might be able to hide me from these guys, and I need a way to contact him without him finding me after I give him a call. I want to see him on my own terms.'

'I can spare you a laptop, a year-old MacBook Pro with the latest operating system. I have an anonymiser program on it

56

that can shield you from being easily traced. Is that good enough?'

'Thank you.' To hackers laptops were like racehorses; they always preferred the most muscle. A year-old computer was an antique to Jack; he routinely bought a new system every six months. But it would do.

Ricki tapped her lip. 'A passport and credit cards? I know a guy in Brussels who works wonders, but he's not cheap. He can probably have you a passport in three days, another day to overnight it.'

'All right.'

'Your money, I can ask a guy in Russia. He moves a lot of funds for me. But I can't promise. Could you just withdraw all the cash?'

'Yes, but I'd prefer to keep it electronic, less likely to lose it.' He did not want to add that he didn't care to keep tens of thousands of euros he'd earned hacking for Nic's criminal ring about his person. He wanted the money moved, cleanly, hidden where he could reach it under a new name. And where he wouldn't have to worry about customs, or the police freezing his accounts if they figured out Jin Ming was a lie. He was a potential murderer in their eyes now, everything had changed. He needed to keep as many of his secrets close to him as he could.

'Okay, this guy you need to contact. He doesn't want to be found?'

'He is part of a bureaucracy that can hide me.'

'Government?'

'Yes.'

'Dutch?'

'No. American.'

Ricki stared. 'You want me to penetrate a top-level American

57

government network. Did you go to a smoke bar after you left the hospital?'

'No. I'll do it. But if I run into a wall I will want your expertise.'

Flattery was the most potent currency in the hacker world. That and respect, acknowledgment of skills. She didn't smile until she'd lifted the tea cup and she thought Jack couldn't see her grin. 'I thought you might have some programs to help me chisel my way in.'

'I might. You hungry?'

'Yes. Very.'

'I can cook some pasta, open some wine. Oh, I didn't think about giving you more alcohol, are you on meds?'

'I would very much like a glass of wine. And, no, I have no meds.'

'Now that would be a challenge,' she said. 'Get an online pharmacy to send you what you need, without placing an actual order.' She laughed and so did he, and for a moment the memory that he had killed a man, albeit an assassin, edged from the center of his thoughts. He was always happier when he had a problem with which to play.

'Is that all you need?'

'Yes,' he said. But it was a lie. He knew where Nic lived. And Nic being dead, and the police would have had all his computers confiscated since he was a known con artist and trader in online filth. So had the police found the notebook and taken it? Surely that would be news, if a murdered man's notebook could blow open an international crime ring. But the police could keep the discovery silent, the same way they'd shielded his name and location while he recovered.

Ricki brought him wine and sat down next to him. Close to

58

him. She smiled at him, warmly. Was surviving a shooting . . . was that sexy? He'd avoided most girls at Delft because he didn't want to risk blowing his cover story. Girls always wanted to know about you, to delve into secrets. But Ricki had secrets of her own. She might not ask too many more questions.

They drank the wine and before he knew it, before he could analyse it, he'd taken her wine glass and set it on the coffee table and he was kissing her warm mouth. She kissed him back. He was alive. He'd forgotten how good it could feel. So he did all the things necessary for living; he kissed her, he laughed with her, they ate dinner, they made love. Then they lay in bed and watched a movie she'd stolen from a studio's laptop, a film that wasn't hitting theaters for another three weeks.

When she fell asleep and the movie was over, Jack began to think. He needed a way to figure out where Nic would hide his most potent and powerful secret of all, and he would have to start by breaking into Nic's house tomorrow morning.

8

Las Vegas

I hit the ground wrong.

I rolled too sharply, and felt a pull in my shoulder. I stopped and the early morning desert sky loomed above me. Back in my London days I ran parkour – extreme running, where you vault up walls and use handholds and drop from heights without breaking bones (hopefully). It had been my release from the tension of work, exploring abandoned spaces, turning walls into roads, using precision to power through a space in a more efficient way. But I was out of practice; when your child is missing you don't really want to take the time for exercise. I'd arrived around midnight Las Vegas time last night, and couldn't sleep, too wound with excitement and tension. Today was a waiting game, with the rest of the day to kill before Anna Tremaine arrived for our meeting. So I'd gotten up early to try my luck against gravity. It was 5 a.m. and the quietest hour in Vegas, and no one around to see me run.

I'd decided to run through an unfinished building not far from my bar. The last thing I needed to do before capturing Anna – and I had every intention of taking her prisoner – was to hurt myself so I wouldn't be at peak condition.

But the parkour helped my head. When I had to plan a run, a vault, a leap that I could barely make, only then I didn't think of Daniel. Then I didn't think of Lucy. Distraction is a sure way to break a leg or an arm. I got up, dusted off my butt. Looked at the wall before me, five feet high; beyond its rim was air.

I was tired of the walls around me, the false ones in the shapes of threats and violence. I wanted my son back. That was the only wall to conquer. I ran at the wall, did a *saut de chat* (jump of the cat). I went head first, my hands landed on the wall's top surface. My legs powered past my arms as I flew from the wall. I landed fair and kept running.

I hadn't had a clean run since the bombing, when my wife was taken from me before my eyes in a London street and I did a parkour run through a remodeled building, bomb-damaged scaffolding collapsing around me, running like I never had before to keep her in my sight, to not lose her.

But, of course, I did lose her, and in a worse way than if she had been kidnapped and killed.

I vaulted up a narrow staircase in the unfinished motel, bouncing off the walls, feeling the sweat explode from my skin. Burning off the too many drinks of the middle of the night, the worry about Daniel, the stress over whether I might be arrested or grabbed by August's team to force me to tell them more about Mila and the Round Table.

I reached the roof and the desert early morning sun shone on me. Las Vegas, even at its edges, is never entirely hushed. I wished there were neighboring roofs. I used to run the council housing projects in London, and on a roof I felt like I had wings. I ran in a circle here, staying warm, building up my power, stopping only to study the balconies jutting off the side of the building, wondering if I could navigate the seven stories in a series of controlled jumps and drops from balcony to balcony. Who needs stairs?

Dropping from balcony to balcony might attract attention; the police are rarely parkour fans. I studied the line of movement it would take to do the balcony drops. Part of my mind said too risky, but another part wanted to feel like I'd pushed myself, like I was testing myself for the final stretch of confronting Anna Tremaine and getting my son back. I wanted to be sure I still had my nerve, my daring.

Drop, roll, vault, drop again, roll. I played the run in my head.

I dropped down to the first balcony and from the edge of my eye I saw the car on the facing road brake to a halt.

I should have checked first. I'd needed to be sure that I didn't have a witness, someone who might call 9-1-1 on the crazy guy doing the balcony surfing. I stood up from the balcony.

The road near the unfinished motel was empty. Except for the one car, stopped at a light at a deserted intersection.

Okay, I thought, not me, it stopped for a light. A green light.
I could see the double glint of binoculars past the window.
I dropped back out of sight.

Waited. I heard the purr of the car's engine moving. I glanced over the edge. I could see the driver below, a sleeve of purple jacket, a snug knit hat pulled tight over the head.

The car sped away.

Maybe he just stopped because he saw you jump. That's it. Yes, that's all.

But the run was ruined for me. I dropped down the rest of the balconies and ran back to my car.

Mila would be here this afternoon, and then Anna Tremaine. And, by tonight, I hoped, I would have my son back.

9

Amsterdam

The doorknob to Nic's apartment turned under his hand. Unlocked. But Jack stood and knocked for the fourth time, his heart hammering in his chest. If Nic had a woman or a room-mate still living here, that person was also likely connected to Novem Soles. But he had to know. And he couldn't wait. The police were looking for him. The dead man had been discovered at the hospital. The papers carried a picture of both Jack's face and one of the man he'd killed. The online news site had the most up-to-date information, and by noon Amsterdam time the police had released the man's identity: a Czech immigrant named Davel, who had an arrest record a meter long, mostly as a rented enforcer for eastern Europeans who were muscling into illegal activities in the West.

A hired thug, sent to kill Jack, and he'd ruined Jack's plan to slip out of sight.

Jack remembered Hollywood blockbusters about a man on the run. Being on the run could look like a bit of a lark. You could always outpace and outthink the pursuers. It was not fun. Jack was sick with the thought that even walking on the street he would be seen, noticed, made for the man on the front page of the paper.

He pushed the door open and called out: 'Hello?'

No answer. The apartment was small and not tidy. Old newspapers sat stacked, unread, on a coffee table. He could smell spilled lager. A muted television played in the corner, offering news of the world, ignored.

He had the gun he'd taken from his assassin in his pocket.

He stepped down the hallway to where a door was half closed and inside the room lay an old woman. She slept, a vodka bottle clasped loosely in her hands. Her pose could have been a poster highlighting the blight of alcohol. He glanced at the label: very cheap vodka, the kind the university kids with no money drank, and the room smelled as though she didn't invest much in soap, either. She looked like a female, fragmented version of Nic – strands of red in the graying hair, short, stocky, a fleshy mouth.

Nic lived with his mother, at his age? Jack couldn't imagine. Of course, Jack's mother didn't want him around. He stepped out and made sure the rest of the apartment was empty. He guessed a back bedroom had been Nic's. Large desks with a slight settling of dust, with clean spots where computers and monitors had likely sat.

Naturally the police had taken all of Nic's gear. It was evidence – he was a hacker and a scumball and he'd been murdered. He searched the rest of the room. Nothing electronic remained. He saw no papers, no records. The room had been picked clean except for Nic's computer books.

No sign of a notebook. He didn't even know how big it was, which could affect where it was hidden.

He checked the room a final time, being extra careful, and then went back to the old woman's bedroom. She was snoring now.

He sat on the edge of the bed and shook her awake. He thought she would scream in horror at a stranger in her room. Her eyes stared at him, muddled, then widened in fear. 'Who . . . Get away from me.'

'I won't hurt you. I'm a friend of Nic's.'

'Friend of Nic's.' She spat at him, made her face a scowl.

'I am. He gave me a job.'

She stared at him. 'Get out of my house.'

He pointed to the healing wound on his neck. 'The people who killed your son did that to me. I want to make them pay.' He tried to smile. What did you say in a situation like this? 'I am his friend, I promise you.'

'His friends got him killed. And now the police, they say all these lies about my Nic. That he did terrible things.'

'Mrs ten Boom, please, let me help you.' He got up and jetted water into a clean glass and brought it to her. She drank it down and then she glanced at the vodka bottle. Uncertain, he poured a tiny bit into the glass. She took a tiny sip, as though embarrassed, and then looked at him with sullen eyes.

'I'll leave you alone,' Jack said, 'but I know of a way to get back at the people who hurt Nic.' Like avenging Nic was his motive. Lying to a grieving mother. Gosh, he was so proud of himself these days. A slow throb of headache began to pulse in his temples. He looked at the vodka glass instead of her, which was fine as she was looking at the vodka as well.

'How?'

'Nic was researching the bad people who led him astray. He learned their secrets. I helped him a bit, but I don't know where he would have hidden the information.'

'He kept everything on computers. I don't even know how to work one. I don't like them.' She flapped her hands, as if computers were gnats floating near her face. Her voice turned a bit petulant.

'It's a notebook. With printouts in it from the computer. Where would he keep it?'

Her gaze went sly. 'How do I know you're not a cop, or one of the people who hurt Nic?'

'If I was a cop, I'd arrest you and take you down to the station,' Jack said. 'If I was your enemy, I would not pour you vodka.'

'You waited a long time to come.'

'The people who shot me killed Nic,' he said. 'I just got out of the hospital. You see the news last night?'

'Yes.' She blinked at him and then sipped the vodka as though it would sharpen her recollections rather than dull them. And maybe, Jack thought, they would. 'Yes. I remember you. Nic's friend. At the coffee shop. The smart boy from Hong Kong.'

'Yes, ma'am.'

'Yes. All right. Give me some more.'

He dribbled more vodka into the glass, feeling guilty with each chug of the clear liquid. No vodka like morning vodka, he thought. She drank it down, wiped her mouth with an age-spotted hand. 'I can't help you. The police came. They took all the computers. They said there were dirty pictures on them, and they said Nicky had hacked into the police's own computers.' She threw up her hands. 'He's dead. No one cares about his reputation any more except me.'

'Well, I do. Do you remember him having a notebook, maybe one that he would have hidden?'

She blinked, considered, drank more of the vodka. These seemed new questions to her, Jack thought, ones the police hadn't asked.

He poured another few fingers of vodka into the glass. 'This notebook will protect you and it will protect me. Think.'

'But you know him and his computers. He did everything on them.' She blinked again, slurped more of her poison. 'But he asked me to go to the store, just this once, and buy a red notebook and tape, something he needed for writing and photos. We didn't have any photo albums. Not after Nic's father left. I don't like them.'

A few photos still dotted Nic's room but Jack noticed he hadn't seen any in this room, or the outer room. A lot of painful history in this apartment, he thought. That he understood. 'So Nic asked you to buy a notebook for him.'

'Yes, a big one, and it was red.'

'Can you tell me where it is?'

'No.'

Jack thought his patience would explode and scatter his brains around the bedroom. He took a calming breath. She was old, drunk, grieving, and she was his only hope.

'Did the police search the entire apartment?'

'Yes.'

'Did they give you a list of what they took?'

She considered this. 'Yes. They did.'

'Where is it?'

'I don't know', and then a rare neuron fired. 'I signed it on the kitchen table.'

Jack got up and shuffled among the debris on the table. Found it: a list from the Amsterdam Police Department, offering an inventory of what they had seized. Four laptops, two desktop computers, financial files, cell phones. Jack wondered if any record there would lead back to him. It made him feel as though time were moving faster. He felt feverish. But there was no mention of a notebook. The police hadn't taken it.

'I have to know where that notebook is.' He tried to keep the panic out of his voice.

She had followed him out of the bedroom. 'I don't know.'

'You don't have any money, do you? Or income, now that Nic is dead.' It was a brutal truth.

She didn't look at him. 'Nic made so much I didn't have to work.'

Because corporate espionage, spamming and porn paid so well. Jack pitied her. If he sold the notebook, he would have to make sure she got some of the money. 'Think. Where would Nic have hidden the thing that mattered to him most? Did he have a storage unit? Another apartment? Anywhere?'

'No, no.'

'They said he did videos.' Jack had to tear the words out of his mouth. 'Um, illegal ones. Did he have a place where he might have filmed them?'

She bit her lip and he could see that if she'd known about her son's horrible activities she'd chosen to ignore them. She sat down.

'Mrs ten Boom. Please.'

'He told me ... he had stopped doing that.' Her lips tightened into a line. 'He promised me.'

'Where?'

'He had an apartment ... he paid cash for it. I think under a different name.'

'Do you know where it is?'

'Well, he never took me there,' she said with some indignation. 'But once ... long ago, I followed him. He told me he'd quit, I wanted to be sure. It was like an addiction, you see.'

The irony seemed lost on her. 'So I followed him and I saw another man bring three teenage girls to his door ...' She blinked. 'I came home and I had a drink and ...' She left the sentence unfinished. But he could guess that painful moment would have been when her drinking started in earnest.

He said nothing for a long minute. He'd thought this woman a stupid old drunk and now he had an idea of what the knowledge of her son's crimes had done to her.

'He was my baby. Every person who does wrong in this world, they were once someone's baby. Full of hope and promise. He was so smart. Where did I go wrong? Where did I bend him the wrong way?'

'Nothing he did is your fault,' Jack said. 'Trust me on this one.'

She heaved a deep sigh and it seemed to take an effort to tear the words out of her chest. 'I can take you there.' She got up and went to the kitchen drawer. She pulled it free and turned it over. Under it was a key, taped into place. 'This is it,' she said. 'This is the only one we've got.'

Jack was afraid to take the bus or the train with his face in the day's papers so he'd borrowed Ricki's little car.

'He was such a smart boy. Like his father. Nic was always good at math, I was terrible at numbers. He got fired from his computer jobs, though. He was smarter than his bosses, they didn't like him.'

Jack didn't respond to this hollow praise. He turned into a parking lot down from a series of apartment complexes. The neighborhood was bad, and graffiti in a half-dozen languages marred the walls. Jack felt sick. Nic traded filth. Jack didn't want to be here. If he'd known this about Nic he never would have worked with him. But what was done was done, and so now he had to see this through.

The address was an apartment in a section of De Pijp that retained the original gritty feel of the neighborhood, untouched by the gentrification that had pervaded this part of Amsterdam in recent years. The halls were clean, but they smelled of cigarette smoke and a heavy, delicious scent of Turkish food cooking. Jack and Mrs ten Boom walked up the stairs and found the door. Jack slid the key in and unlocked it and stepped inside, Mrs ten Boom following him, a slight humming noise coming from her throat.

She was afraid of what they might see here.

Jack did a quick survey of the small, cluttered apartment. In the kitchen were bottles of whisky. And cans of soda and bags of candy. Lures? Or bribes? The apartment made his skin itch with distaste.

He poured Mrs ten Boom a generous shot of whisky and turned on the TV to distract her. It was hooked up to a DVD player, and a children's show was already loaded, bright colored dancing flowers and music. Jack thought he would vomit. He quickly switched the television to a news network.

'Here, Mrs ten Boom, have a seat.' Best if he searched alone, he thought.

Jack began a methodical search of the apartment. He started in the bedroom, going through every lining of clothing, every container in the closet, every box under the bed. Nic had weapons hidden in this place: a 9mm Glock, a Beretta pistol, a hunting knife with a wicked looking edge. Jack put those in a separate box.

He tore apart the mattress, dismantled the bed, pulled the headboard free. In the bedroom closet was a set of expensive camera gear. He searched through the equipment bags. Nothing. He tore up the carpet. Nothing.

A bubble of panic rose in his chest.

He finished in the bedroom. He went into the bathroom, searched every inch. He found a thousand euros hidden in a large plastic aspirin bottle. He went and pushed the cash into Mrs ten Boom's hands; she stared at it in surprise, then put it in her pocket.

He went into the kitchen. There wasn't much food inside the refrigerator: bottles of beer, sandwich meat, cheese furred with mold, jar of mustard. He closed the door on the rising smell. Then he pulled the refrigerator out from the wall. A layer of dust and grit lay on the floor. He began to search the cabinets and the drawers, removing dish towels, boxes of sugary cereal, bottles of hard liquor. Nothing. He pulled up the tatty lining paper to see if anything was hidden underneath. Zero luck. When the cabinets were empty he inspected them, tapping on them.

The top cabinet sounded different.

He tapped again. Then he stepped down and found a knife and worked it against the corner of the wood.

It gave slightly. He stuck the knife in and the wood folded back; there was a hidden hinge.

Wedged in the space was a red book, large, with a moleskin cover and an elastic band to keep it closed.

He pulled the red notebook free. He sat down on the kitchen floor and flipped through the pages. In the den he could hear Mrs ten Boom dribbling more whisky into her glass, moaning, a soft keening of grief.

The first few pages were numbers. Just numbers, in two columns. Maybe a code? Or maybe passwords? Or maybe account numbers. They were written in a neat, spare hand, as though they had been carefully copied.

He flipped to where the columns of numbers stopped.

Next page was a photo. A lean whippet of a man he'd never seen before, older, Caucasian, in a gray suit, walking with another man and a woman. The woman was Asian, striking, in her twenties. The other man was tall, heavy-set, black, also in a fine looking suit, scowling. Behind them was a rather grand house, with a huge porch and columns, with a curving driveway in its front.

He had no idea who these people were. Were these three of the Nine Suns? He realized he didn't know if Nine Suns referred to nine specific people, or if it were simply a dumb code name. Written below the picture, in the same precise handwriting, *First Day at The Nursery, 2001.*

The Nursery. But there were no children in the picture.

He flipped through the rest of the book. It seemed that Nic had printed out an image from the computer screen capture and just taped it into the book. The red notebook was fat with paper. He studied. Photos of people: sometimes what appeared to be family photos, or people in meetings, talking together, in a range of settings: street plazas, sidewalks, office buildings. He did not recognize any of the faces.

Next were printouts of what appeared to be emails and transcriptions of phone conversations: ones where secret, illegal deals were struck between competitive companies, where bribes were subtly offered, where threats were made. The email addresses included government offices in the US, across Europe, and in Japan and Brazil, across Africa. And some of the world's most powerful corporations. It was like a jigsaw of high-powered, white-collar crime: many pieces, and Jack couldn't see how they all fit together.

Then a series of photos that looked like passport pictures, a dozen people, and in the top left of each photo a small notation: eliminated, and a date.

People that Novem Soles had killed? He flipped through the photos: he didn't know who any of the people were. There were no identifiers.

Spreadsheets, partial, with items bought and prices paid: *office rental in London, purchase of C-4 for London bomb, bribes to police inspector in Oslo.* Jack's stomach churned.

This is what his hidden programs had plucked for Nic: financial information that could gut or elevate markets, corporate secrets, a money trail of death, leverage for blackmail. If this was how Novem Soles was going to control people in key positions, and these were the people they used as levers, then one could deduce what their intentions and their targets were, and what their next major plot would be.

He read through the mass of stolen gems but no pattern formed. Maybe this was simply a way to control people in powerful positions who had troublesome secrets and could be manipulated. Other pages were filled with code, with more numbers that meant nothing to him.

But here was his shield; here was his sword. If he could not make full sense of it then he knew who could.

He found a landline phone in the apartment. He picked it up

and was relieved to hear a dial tone. It hadn't yet been disconnected. He unplugged the phone and plugged its cord into the MacBook Pro that Ricki had loaned him. He activated a cheap, throwaway dial-up account. Getting through to the CIA would not be easy. He would have to write a vivid note that would seize their attention, past all the cranks and weirdos who saw a conspiracy in every shadow and emailed their theories to the Agency. He needed to jump to the front of the line of incoming emails. On the CIA's website he found a standard email form for people to share information or comments with the Agency.

He typed in the message page:

I have critical information for a CIA officer named August who was in Amsterdam several weeks ago. I offer serious, actionable dirt on the group called Novem Soles. This offer is only good for three days.

He entered in a prepaid cell phone number he'd bought after leaving Ricki's apartment. He did not sign his name.

He reread the message. If he got too specific August might figure out who he was. This was tantalizing enough, he decided. He would talk to August and only August. August had kept him from being hurt worse; August had argued to leave him in the van, safe from danger.

He pressed Send. He stood, closed the laptop.

'Mrs ten Boom, we should go.'

'No. Nic will be here soon, won't he?' She was drunk again, a crooked smile back on her face. She'd refilled from one of the whisky bottles. 'Nic will be here soon.'

Oh, God, Jack thought, he couldn't leave her. But now that he'd contacted the CIA, he had to move quickly. He couldn't be anchored with the old drunk woman. But he couldn't leave her here either, in the horrible place of her son's worst crimes.

'Let's go back to your place, Mrs ten Boom.'

She hit on the whisky bottle again and she lay down on the couch. 'I want to stay here. Please.'

He stood watching her, and then he said, 'Goodbye. Thanks for your help.'

She was asleep, holding onto the last shred of her son.

Jack Ming stumbled down the darkened stairs, clutching the most important book in the world to his chest.

10

NoLita, Manhattan

August Holdwine took the subway to NoLita, the neighborhood North of Little Italy. He walked under the bright morning sky. The safe house sat above a clothing boutique off Mott Street. He went inside and in the kitchen he found his trackers waiting for him. The guy who Sam had manhandled sat at the wooden table, sourly drinking a caffe latte, ignoring Cuban pastries they'd picked up from August's favorite neighborhood café. Instead of eating he pecked on a laptop keyboard.

'Writing up a report on how you got played last night?' August asked.

'A complaint against you for not taking Sam Capra into custody after he attacked me.'

'Be smarter next time,' August said. 'Email that to me and my supervisor, if you must, but why don't you think about it some more?'

'You should have grabbed him,' the tracker said. 'We got you breakfast, by the way.'

'Did you spit in it?'

'Thought about it. Thought you'd make him come back here and talk.'

'Detention hasn't much worked with him in the past,' August said.

'So, finding this Mila woman, what do we do now?' the woman tracker asked.

August considered. That thought had kept him awake much of the night. He was charged with finding Mila; but what if, despite Sam's protestations, this Mila was helping Sam find his son? Was he going to interfere with that? Duty and friendship were often uneasy partners. But duty had to come first.

Didn't it?

His phone rang. He answered and listened and hung up, then he went upstairs to a makeshift office and locked the doors. Then he called the CIA headquarters back.

We have a phone-in, Langley had told him on his secured phone. *Asking specifically for you, to call him at this number. It's an Amsterdam exchange. Prepaid phone, no record of owner.* That only meant the phone had been purchased in Amsterdam; the caller could be anywhere.

It rang. Nine times. Nine. Novem. Did that mean something? Then a male voice came onto the phone. 'Hello?'

The tracking would begin immediately, August thought. The phone was connected to a laptop, showing on its screen a map of the world. Numbers began to flash across the top as the software traced the caller's location. 'Yes. My name is August. I understand you've been trying to reach me.'

'Yes. I have.' Male, American. No discernible regional accent. 'About a subject of mutual interest.'

'Oh, my God, you sound like a bad movie,' the voice said.

Young, August thought, *younger than me.* 'Novem Soles. You're one of the guys looking for them, aren't you?' A slight shaking in the voice.

'Yes.'

'Well. I can give Novem Soles to you.'

'How?'

'I have information for sale.'

'Information for sale,' August repeated. He would be repeating much of what the caller said. It was a standard ploy to extend the call, simplify the trace.

'The price is ten million dollars.'

'I can't pay that amount.'

The laptop screen's map trimmed down where the call was originating from. Europe. Then western Europe.

'They've got their fingers and reach into governments around the world. I think I am giving you a bargain.'

'Let's say I agree to the price. What are your terms?'

'I will deliver the information to you and you will place the funds in a numbered account in the Caymans. I want immunity from prosecution for any crimes I may have committed. Then the CIA gives me a new identity. I want sanctuary where they can never find me, in an English-speaking country.'

August listened carefully. Did he know this voice? Its tone tugged on the frail strings of memory in his mind. 'I can't commit that kind of money without seeing what the proof is.'

'I have the proof.'

'What is it? Names? Locations? Operations?'

'It's a notebook.'

'A notebook.'

'Full of details on the people in government and business that Novem Soles owns.'

76

'Scan the pages and email it to me.'

The call searcher narrowed. The Netherlands/Belgium/ Luxembourg glowed bright green on the map.

'And once I've done that, then you have the proof, August, and I'm left out in the cold without money or immunity.'

'What's in the notebook?'

'Everything you need to decapitate Novem Soles. They're not just a criminal ring. They're worse, a lot worse. It'll be the best ten million you ever spent.'

'How did you know my name?'

'I have the information and I can either sell it to you or I can sell it to any other number of interested buyers.' Not an answer to the question.

'Well, I'd have to see the notebook, you understand that.'

'I am willing to meet.'

'Where? When?'

'I'll call you back. Give me a number.'

'I'd prefer to call you again.'

'Oh, no. Not how I play, August. Give me a number or I vanish.'

August fed him his cell phone number. 'I can't get you any funds, or any promises, until I know what evidence you have. Until I see it. Tell me your name.'

'Now knowing my name would be dangerous for you, and since we're just getting to know each other, and you're going to get me my beautiful ten million, I don't want you getting yourself killed. We're going to enjoy doing business together, August, you're going to make your career and I'm going to buy my safety and my future. I'll meet you in New York in two days.'

'Where and when exactly in New York?'

'I'll let you know.' The line went dead.

August sat and studied the laptop readout. The call had come from Amsterdam. The city where Sam had wrecked the Novem Soles plot.

Novem Soles. In English, the Nine Suns. The name for the criminal syndicate that had been behind the London bombing that had branded Sam Capra a traitor. Their reach was unknown but they had co-opted at least one high government official in the United States and had attempted to deliver a shattering blow to American society. Their ambitions, Sam had claimed, were limitless.

A criminal organization, not terrorist in its ideology, but one that had tried to destroy a CIA office and wreak political havoc in the United States.

What kind of criminals were these?

He had no answer. The entire Novem Soles cell in Amsterdam had been killed. The only survivor was Lucy Capra, caught in that comatose netherworld between life and death. Lucy knew some of the secrets of the group. But she was beyond helping him.

August replayed his recording of the conversation.

Who was this guy? he wondered. *He kept using my name. Like it was a point of pride that he knew it. He said I was a nice guy. Have I met him before? I thought I knew the voice.* But now he wasn't sure.

Sam Capra might be paranoid about how deeply the criminal network's claws reached into the government, but August Holdwine was not.

He dialed his boss's number. He had to report the offer. But he knew what the bureaucratic response would be. Why pay off an informant when you could fold him under your wing and keep him shuttered up until he was ready to talk for free?

11

Fourteen minutes and thirty-seven seconds after August Holdwine said the phrase *Novem Soles* into his phone a text message appeared on another smart phone's screen. Outside of intra-Company communications, there had been no mention of the phrase in the government's phone and email monitoring database for weeks, since Sam Capra made his one and only statement for the CIA. The public did not know the phrase.

A large percentage of the world's communications were vacuumed into the data tanks of the National Security Agency, to be studied and filtered. In the never-ending torrent of words, Novem Soles was a distinct outlier. Novem Soles were two words so unusual, so unmistakable, that the small bit of software hidden on the servers was able to find, within a few hours, any mention of the phrase and identify the sender and the recipient and provide a text transcript of the conversation during which the magic words were uttered. This transcript was sent to one man's cell phone; he knew then, any time, when anyone in the United States was discussing Novem Soles.

It was, as the Watcher put it to his peers, an eye that never blinks.

The Watcher stepped out from the thrum of a restaurant on South Beach, a place that supposedly provided the best gourmet breakfast in Miami but the Watcher was unimpressed. He knew he could have done a better job in running it and he'd thought of buying it; how nice it would be to run a restaurant and have a simpler job. It was a cloudy, rainy day and in the morning haze of patio he studied the readout: it was the transcript of the entire call from the Langley office to August Holdwine. Someone had information on Novem Soles to sell, someone who had called from an Amsterdam number, and had called the Central Intelligence Agency with an offer.

He felt a jolt of nervous energy ride along his bones.

The Watcher closed the phone. He thought: Sam Capra, now. As soon as he had it rang again. He studied the phone log and answered.

'*Bonjour*,' a woman's voice said. 'We have a problem.'

12

Greenwich Village, New York

Braun didn't return from Langley to New York until mid-afternoon. The study in the Special Projects office smelled of fine cigars and exquisite coffee. August felt he should decline the coffee; he felt jittery enough. But you did not often say no to a legend, and Ricardo Braun was a legend. So August sat down in a heavy leather armchair, a fragrant Brazilian brew steaming from his cup. He had only been to the study once before; Ricardo Braun was an early retiree from CIA who'd come back into the fold a few weeks earlier when Special Projects needed mature, steady guidance after the disasters of the past few months. He made August feel like an ox; Braun was a spare, sleek man, bald, with a strong runner's build, in his late fifties, with gray eyes and an air of unfailing confidence. He wore black slacks and a crisp white shirt. He had what appeared to August to be the world's most elaborate coffee machine and he turned from it now, holding a thick mug of a brew that smelled amazingly rich, a curl of steam snaking from the porcelain.

'What do you want me to do?' August asked.

'Well, write the informant a check, of course,' Braun said. 'Am I supposed to do all the thinking?'

August realized it was a joke so he ventured a smile. 'Above my pay grade. But not yours.'

Ricardo Braun said, 'We're not paying this guy ten million dollars. Not someone who isn't willing to come in. Not someone who wants to hand us off what might be worthless information and vanish before we can confirm it.' He sipped at his coffee.

'He can't vanish, he said he wanted protection from us.'

'Exactly what I'd say if I planned to vanish.' Braun arched an eyebrow.

'He can't think he can hide from us.'

'Novem Soles certainly has hidden themselves well. What do we truly know about them? Nothing. Dead ends and nowheres.' Braun looked at the bourbon in his glass but didn't taste it.

'Do I open a case file?' Special Projects operated by a unique set of rules, free from CIA bureaucracy. But records still had to be maintained, for the branch's own reference. Special Projects could access and use Company databases, but it was not a two-way street. The branch had its own computer network, its own protocols for accessing information from police and corporate databases; some were illegal. It was this willingness to bend the rules that put Special Projects apart from the regular operations of the CIA.

'Yes. Do. But we don't report anything yet to the Company.' He got up and walked to the reinforced glass in the study. 'We know this group penetrated the Company once already, more than once, through bribery. Well, not on my watch. I didn't give up daily rounds of golf and marlin fishing to come back and fail.' He turned back with a stern stare at August. 'We are not alerting any other traitors who are looking for a mention of Novem Soles in an email or a report or a conversation. I want this off the books, for now. Find this informant, bring him in, and we'll see what he's got.' Braun paused. 'Did you get anywhere with Capra?'

'He spotted our shadows, took out one who got too close, and then bought me a martini at a bar he now owns, over by Bryant Park. Called The Last Minute.'

Braun smiled. 'A bar. If I wasn't so irritated with him I think I might get to like him.'

'He won't give any information on this Mila woman and he claims not to know anything more about Novem Soles. I get the sense he's moved on with his life, well past us. He's a business-man now, he's wanting out of the game.'

'And his kid?'

'No news. So he says.'

'I don't believe he's sitting around doing nothing,' Braun said. 'You don't twiddle your thumbs if there's a chance of finding your kid.' Now he picked up his mug and tasted the rich brew within. The best coffee ever. It was so rich and per-fectly roasted his tongue nearly went into shock. Braun gave him a smile.

This is a guy, August thought, who appreciates caring for every detail.

August knew Braun had read Sam's file. 'He may have run into the same walls we have.'

'Could your informant know anything about the Capra baby?'

'I have no idea. I did not ask.' Guilt surged up through his chest. 'The conversation didn't lend itself to detailed ques-tioning.'

'That child could be used as leverage.'

'Only to a point. Sam wouldn't act against us if ordered. He would tell us of any demand made against him for his child's safety.'

Braun raised an eyebrow. 'Does your father love you, August?'

'Yes, sir.'

'Would he kill to save you, if push came to shove?'

August said, 'If I'm being honest, yes, my dad would.'

'Sam might cut your throat to save his kid. Get the meeting. But be very careful.' Braun fixed him with a look. 'Langley says this informant asked for you. That means he must know you're running the task force. This could be a meeting just to kill you, or grab you to see what you know.'

'You've made me eager to get back to work.' August stood. 'Can I ask you something? It came up in talking with Sam.'

'Yes?'

'This Mila woman.' He slid the picture over to Braun. 'She was with Sam again last night. We lost her.'

Braun studied the picture. 'I told you before, I don't recognize her. I was out of the field for several years, though.'

'We picked up some chatter. There is, and has been for the past three years, a million-dollar bounty on her head.'

'I've never heard of a bounty that high funded by a crime ring. How on earth has she survived three years?'

'Very good or very lucky.'

'Maybe no one's gotten close to finding her.' Braun studied the photo again. 'She looks like an elf. Seriously, put pointed ears on her and she'd be the perfect Santa Claus line monitor at Christmas. This big a bounty, and no one even knows who she is? Incredible. Where was this chatter?'

'It's come up on a few discussion forums – usually of extrem-ists looking for funding.'

'Who posted the bounty?'

'It leads to a Gmail account that's never been accessed. Or, I should say, has only been accessed by a non-traceable computer.'

'Are the details in your report?'

'Yes, I'll write it up for you tonight.'

Braun handed him back the photo. 'Make it happen, August. Get us this informant. Get us this woman.'

Or, August thought sourly, get another job.

The internet café was near the NYU campus. He walked there an hour after August left; he did not wish to use a CIA-owned computer. He also wanted to finish the exquisite pot of coffee he'd made. Ricardo Braun went inside and ordered a decaf with little hope that it would match his palate's demands and sat at an internet terminal situated far from any other patrons. He opened an email account he had established six years before and that he only checked very infrequently. It was a hidey hole for him on the web, and he remembered a message he'd seen two years ago. There were only a couple of dozen messages in the account, all old, but kept squirreled away for when they could be useful. Requests for information. Offers of payment. CIA pensions were not what they should be, and, although he'd had family money, Braun felt that more cash was never to be turned down. As long as his small, creative side jobs did not hurt the country he loved, he saw nothing wrong with it. He was simply careful to clean it through investments; the CIA did watch the incomes of its former agents.

The message had held a picture of the woman called Mila. He'd seen her face then for the first time. That fine, elfin face.

He checked the photo stashed in the email address. It might well be the same woman. The cut of her hair was different but the bones were the same in her cheeks, the turn of the mouth, the sharp, haunted eyes. Mila. The photo of her was one with a gun in her hand, wearing a leather jacket and leather pants, glancing about a room. The sort of photo that looked like it had been lifted from a private security camera.

He reread the message. *Text to 45899 to get details on job. High dollar.* He wondered if the job was still open. He texted, on a phone that the CIA did not know that he owned.

He got an autoresponse, directing him to a private website, providing him with a password.

Braun jumped to the site. Its URL was a wild mix of numbers and letters, not the kind of site that someone would ever accidentally stumble upon. He entered the password.

The site opened. It showed more pictures of Mila, shot from the same camera. And the text, in five different languages: $1 MILLION US FOR THIS BITCH. I WANT HER ALIVE. Braun stared. This was the gold standard of hit contracts. A million dollars was usually a sum reserved for leaders of state, heads of organizations. Braun himself had spent CIA dollars to kill a Rwandan warlord for Special Projects for a hundred thousand. A drug kingpin in Ecuador for twice that amount. Braun had his own address book he could call upon when regular CIA personnel were not an option.

Who was this woman and who had the deep pockets to off her? He glanced at the last update: a month ago, a single message. *Contract is still open.* An email address, another blind one.

He sent an email: *Is contract still open? I have a lead on an associate of hers but I need to know I'm dealing with someone who can guarantee payment.*

He closed the email account, the website. He erased the browser history. He left the internet café and went and ate lunch, standing up in a narrow student-geared pizza joint, chewing on a thick slice, drinking a Coke.

A million dollars. The terms of the reward preferred that she be alive. That complicated things.

Braun ate his lonely pizza, then walked home and sat in his leather chair, and thought about Novem Soles, and Mila, and how he could collect that million dollars.

13

Las Vegas

It's not everyday that you a) inspect a new business you own, and b) make plans to meet a kidnapper there. Happy partiers filled The Canyon Bar, escaping the tourist-swollen casino hotspots, searching for revelry and the next place you wanted to be seen.

I was planning how to capture a woman who'd stolen my child.

The Canyon was not a tourist trap bar like so much of the Vegas nightlife scene. I'd noticed in the first hour there this evening that the servers and bartenders were extremely capable; attentive, engaging, focused. Of course, when I'd come around and introduced myself to the staff they might all have switched to best behavior, but you can't hide sloppiness in the running of a first-class drinking establishment.

I'd seen one server gently talk an indecisive customer out of ordering a chocolate martini and into a handcrafted Old-Fashioned: a real drink for a real person. The décor was high-dollar: carefully sculpted beams of wood undulated along the curving walls, the tables were of polished granite, the chairs covered with faux rare animal hides. The Canyon was a destination bar for those too cool for the Strip or who wanted a break from the casino nights and the nerve-numbing rattle of slots, dice, and chips. The crowd was youngish, a mix of more daring visitors and well-heeled locals. There was a dance floor, small, and the DJ was mashing classic Massive Attack with the latest hip-hop star's word play and drum beat.

I watched all this from the security cameras mounted in my office on the second floor of the bar.

I scanned the crowd. I knew Anna's face, from the security photo and the passport photo we'd acquired: tall, dark hair, a beauty mark near the curve of her mouth. But those were elements easily changed. I didn't see anyone who fit her description in the crowded club.

But I did see a face I knew, apparently a recent arrival. There she was, Mila, sitting at a back table, her hair dyed auburn now (or wearing a good wig), flirting with some thick-shouldered guy who wore a well-tailored gray pinstripe suit. His face was familiar, and that worried me until I recognized him – a guy who once played tight end for the New York Giants. Dude probably thought he was about to get Vegas-lucky. Mila wowed him a champagne-fueled smile, although the wine in her flute appeared to be untouched. His was empty. He refilled and guzzled his twice while I watched. I guessed she was conducting her own surveillance, observing every face that came and left the bar. She had to be careful, now that the Company had resumed its interest in me.

I went downstairs to a corner booth that I'd reserved for myself. I wore my hosting clothes: a pinstripe suit, a white shirt, a gray-silver tie. In your own bar, you have to look better than a lawyer. Sharper. And the jacket hid my Browning pistol and my slacks hid my knife, strapped to my calf.

Mila got up, whispering something that was (I am sure) most promising to her male camouflage, but came over and sat at my table.

'I understand I am to be your wife. Every time I play this role, there is trouble.'

She'd taken a later flight than me – best if we didn't travel together. She flew under an assumed name. But no one tailed me at the Vegas airport; I made sure.

'I like the auburn,' I said.

'Thank you.'

I could see the Giants ex glaring at me, waiting for her return. 'Why did you sit with him?'

'I generally ignore your American football. I thought maybe he was a bodyguard for Anna. I have talked to all the large, muscular men here.' She surveyed the crowd. 'Thin pickings. She might send a woman.'

'You don't have to work the crowd for long. We just need to get Anna up in the office, then we force her to tell us where my son is.'

'Simple,' Mila said.

'I see no reason for this to be complicated.'

'You are always such an optimist,' Mila crossed her legs, inspected her fingernails. 'This woman, Anna Tremaine, she tells you the name of the couple who bought your baby. Great. What do you do with her then? Lock her upstairs for a few days while we go collect your son?'

I raised an eyebrow.

'You will have to kill her, Sam.'

'Your bloodthirstiness is really not appealing.'

'Truth is often very ugly, like the orange dress of that woman at the bar,' Mila said. 'An upstairs office is not built to keep a hostage for the long term. And you can't let her go. She will warn whoever bought Daniel so they can run.'

'You have Mr Bell stashed away back in New York.'

'No. Mr Bell's very small brain has been plucked. He is back with his family, and now he is in our pocket when we need him. He is a puppet on the string for me.'

'He knows we killed two men.'

'Yes, so he wants to stay on my good side.'

I let the sounds of the party rise and fall around us. 'I have a plan.'

'I am eager to hear this brilliant strategy.'

'I'll hand Anna over to the CIA. She can tell them all about her employers.' It was certainly better than handing Mila over to them.

Mila seemed to sense the direction of my thoughts.

'What would you do to get your son back?'

'Anything.'

'Anything covers so much.' She glanced across the bar at her neglected conquest. 'Oh, your American football player, I left him uncomfortable with anticipation. He does have a nice thick neck, though. I like a thick neck. Nice to hang onto.'

'That neck is not supporting a large brain.'

'Ha, brains.' Mila gave me a sideways glance. 'Brains do not matter so much as heart, Sam.' She pounded her chest with her little fist.

'Look. We get Anna Tremaine upstairs to finalize our purchase. After she talks, I load her up with an anesthetic and we leave her locked up in the apartment. We find where Daniel is and I go get him and you keep an eye on her.'

'And then what?'

'We give her to August Holdwine and Special Projects and she can tell all she knows about Novem Soles.'

'I have missed the exciting announcement where you have rejoined the Central Idiot Agency,' Mila said. 'I thought you worked for me.'

'And what does the Round Table do with her, Mila? You just told me I'd have to murder her. Am I supposed to think you won't?'

'I'm hurt.'

'The CIA won't.'

'Ah, yes. She will be their prisoner who goes on trial? No. They will make a deal with her. Protect her to talk. To tell what she knows. This is the way the world works. She sells your baby, she gets a plea bargain. A new life tucked away on the other side of the planet, in Sydney. I sometimes think half of Sydney must be people hiding from the rest of the world.' She picked up my bottle of Pellegrino water, took a sip.

'There's a price on your head,' I said.

She stopped mid-swig. She set down the bottle of mineral water. Her gaze met mine.

'Is Mila short for a million? Because that's the price tag. Huge for a hit on someone who says she's a nobody.'

'It's gone up,' she said. 'The power of compound interest.' Then she laughed. 'Or compound hatred.'

'Mila, who wants you dead?'

'Besides you?'

'Don't joke. Don't joke at all about this.'

She took another long drink from the Pellegrino bottle. 'It doesn't matter, Sam.'

'I believe it has the slightest of bearings on working with you.'

She rolled her eyes.

'I want to know who wants you dead.'

'What? So you can help me kill my tormentor? I'm not going to kill him.'

'Him.'

'Someone beyond my reach,' she said. 'It's an uncomfortable fact of life. Like the most beautiful shoes hurt your feet the most.' She shrugged, as though my words, my concern, were nothing more than mist in the air.

'If we're working together, I deserve to know who's hunting you.'

'Just because there is a price on my head doesn't mean there are takers.'

'Have you killed everyone who's come after you?'

'You make me sound so bad.'

'I know you perhaps were unfamiliar with capitalism growing up in Moldova' – she answered my comment with a roll of her eyes – 'but let me tell you, a million dollars on your head is going to lead to an endless supply of candidates stepping forward.'

'They must find me. Then they must kill me.' She shrugged. 'It's like the words at the end of a commercial for a contest: "Many will enter, few will win." The many have failed. No winners so far.'

'People have already been trying to kill you?' I felt a creep of shock along my skin. I'd been worried about the CIA finding her. But they just wanted to talk to her. August didn't want her dead.

She didn't shrug again, because I think she read me and she knew pretend indifference would only make me mad. 'Look. There is a man who is very angry at me. I humiliated him. It was worse than killing him.'

'Who?'

'Not anyone who you should care to know, Sam.'

'Who, Mila?'

'We get Daniel back first, then we will worry about my problems.' She smiled. 'I know how Daniel dominates your every thought. I am flattered you are concerned about me.'

I felt a sick mix of rage and annoyance and fear for her. Mila is not exactly my friend. She's not exactly my boss. I don't know what exactly she is but I could hardly let her be targeted and killed. If I wasn't going to give her up to August I sure as hell wasn't going to give her up to some hired killer.

'And once you have Daniel, you will want a calmer, quieter life, Sam. This is only natural.'

'There is no way that I am abandoning you.'

'Life is a series of abandonings.' She finished the Pellegrino. 'Now. How did you know that my head had a price tag attached to it?'

'August told me when I talked with him at The Last Minute.'

'It's flattering to be on his radar screen. I must have a file at the CIA now. How exciting. What percentage of the world has a file there? Minuscule. I feel special.' She inspected her nails again. 'Should I friend August on Facebook?'

'He wants me to hand you over to them so you can tell them what you know about Novem Soles and who you work for. They are intensely interested in you.'

'I am interested in August. In what he can find out. In how good he is. And in who will try and kill him when he finds out more about Novem Soles.'

'You still think there are people working for Novem Soles inside the CIA.'

'It's a given.' She watched the football player; he'd made

friends with two blondes who looked like they'd missed the turn to the Playboy mansion. 'If August is good at his job, likely he will die. If he is bad, he will retire and get a nice gold watch because he was never a threat to anyone.'

'Do you know if there's a mole?'

'Of course not. And I am hurt you think I would keep such juicy gossip quiet. Plus, if I knew, I would sell his name to the CIA. I adore free markets.'

'You told me when we met that you'd seen the tapes of when the Company interrogated me,' I said. 'You have your own mole inside.'

Again the sideways glance. 'Well, I didn't find the tapes on YouTube, Sam. If you must know I stole them off the server.'

'You stole data off a CIA server.' I didn't want to know more.

'I am making you nervous,' Mila said. 'I'll go upstairs and wait for our friend to arrive. I'll keep an eye on the cameras.' I watched her go up the stairs at the back of the bar.

Anna Tremaine was coming.

The crowd had filled out, the bartenders moving in a constant blur of service. The music pulsed. I scanned the crowd, looking for anyone suspicious who might be here backing Anna. But maybe she didn't need or want security. Maybe this would be easy. She didn't know she was coming onto my turf. For me, the bar was both public and private. So many potential witnesses around would tie her hands but I could get her upstairs and then I'd have the truth.

But I felt haunted by the person who'd been watching me do the parkour run. Maybe the driver had just been curious. Maybe it was nothing more. Maybe I hadn't made a mistake.

What would you do to get your son back?

It was the simplest question in the world, with the simplest answer. But if I made the wrong move, I could easily end up dead, or in prison, or with Daniel no safer than he was now.

Right now, somewhere, a husband and a wife were holding my child, calling him their own. Did they even know he was stolen? Did they care? Did they love him as much as I did, though I'd never even held him?

Here she came.

Anna Tremaine. I recognized her from the video in the French clinic. She was a tall woman, with wide shoulders and the bearing of an athlete. Graceful. Men noticed her as she walked through the crowd; you could see gazes flickering to her as she moved. She was dressed in black fitted jeans and a colorful shirt and an aquamarine and silver choker covered her ivory throat. She was coming, though not from the front door but from the back, where the restrooms were. Maybe she'd slipped in a back entrance. She looked about thirty, raven-dark hair, a hard, cold face that was beautiful in technical proportions, but not because of warmth or kindness.

I stayed perfectly still as she sat down across from me. I didn't stand.

This was the woman who'd stolen my child. All I wanted to do was to fling the table aside and close my hands around that bejeweled throat and force her to tell me where Daniel was. That time would come. Now I had to prime the trap.

'Mr Derwatt?'

'Yes, hello. Ms Tremaine?'

'Yes.'

'Your drink.' I gestured at the martini she'd asked to have ready as a sign. It sat, a bit warm, three olives. She could choke on them as soon as I made her tell me where Daniel was.

'That was only for an identifier. A bottle of Amstel Light, and please tell the waiter to open it at the table.'

Very cautious. She didn't want to risk a drug being slipped into her drink. I waved over a waiter, repeated the order. I kept my voice steady. This was a business meeting and she was treating it like a potential trap. Which it was, of course.

'Your wife isn't here?' Her voice was soft. I suppose you think a woman who steals and peddles babies would sound like the creaking crone from a fairy tale. She sounded educated. A French accent, but very slight, as though she spent most of her time conversing in English.

'My wife is considerably nervous about this arrangement. She's upstairs. She wants to continue to pursue conventional adoption but . . . ' I shrugged. I felt sweat trickle down my spine, dampen my armpits. I didn't get this nervous in a fight. Then my mind shut clear and I knew what I would have to do. This was worse than crossing a minefield. But she was here in my bar, my home ground, and she wasn't leaving without telling me where my son was.

The waiter returned with her bottle of Amstel. He opened it for her at the table, she thanked him, he left, and then she took a long sip. 'Your wife isn't upstairs. Your wife, technically your ex-wife, is in a CIA-run hospital in Bethesda, Maryland, in a coma from which she is unlikely ever to recover. She's your ex not because you are an asshole who divorced a critically ill wife but because she's a traitor who saved your life and then tried to kill you when you came after her. She picked the wrong side and she paid the price.'

I kept my gaze locked on hers. Well. Anna Tremaine was no fool.

'Your name isn't Frank Derwatt, it's Sam Capra.' She took a

dainty sip of beer. 'You enjoy playing monkey in empty buildings when you're not creating trouble for us.'

Fine. Who needs masks? 'Where's my son, Anna?'

'See, I know more about you than you do about me. Anna's not my real name.'

'Where's my son?' I leaned forward. I could produce the Browning under my jacket in one second. I didn't care if I set off a panic in The Canyon. She was going to tell me.

'An hour ago, a friend of mine left a half-pound of C-4 explosive in the ladies' room.' Her smile went coy. She uttered her threat in the same tone as you might say *I love what you've done with the place.* 'The trigger is under my control. You raise a hand against me and this bar burns, with everyone in it.' She glanced at the partiers, the light pulsing in time to the music, laughing, drinking, oblivious. 'I can't say they'd be a real loss. These people are nothing, they serve no purpose.'

'Unlike selling children.' I battled the rage rising in my chest. The rage was like a strange heat. I had killed before, for the first time a few weeks earlier, and in normal circumstances it wasn't ever anything you wanted to do again. But her. I could kill her.

She smiled, the cat's smile at the mouse wriggling under its paw. 'I sell happiness, Mr Capra. I give desperate parents exactly what they want.'

'Where is my son?'

'You keep asking like I'm actually going to tell you.' She took another swig of her beer, scooted a bit closer in her chair like she had a cute story or a joke to tell me as we sat enjoying our evening in the primo bar. 'I won't tell you where your son is. I will tell you how you can get him back.'

'How?'

'I want you to kill a man for me.' She enunciated each word carefully, as though I were impaired.

When I didn't respond, she said, 'It's not like you haven't killed before.'

'Not in cold blood.'

'Will it make it easier to swallow if I assure you he deserves it?'

'Who?'

'My employer has a traitor. We want him dead.' She smiled. 'We have your son, so I think what we want is what you want.'

'Kill him yourself.'

'He's not under our control at the moment. I think you are particularly placed to be able to find him and reach him. You kill him for us and we'll give you back your son, alive and unharmed.'

'And I should believe you *why?*'

'Why? If we wanted you and your son dead, you would both be dead.' She smiled, tasted her beer again. 'Because you have no choice, Sam. That seems to me to be common sense. You must do as we say. We own you.' She leaned back a little. 'Your child is cute. He favors you in the eyes, he has his mother's mouth.'

'You sold him.'

'So you were told. But we didn't. We kept Daniel close, in case he was useful to us. I think it was a smart move.'

'You want me to kill a man.' My mind felt clouded. There must be something very special about this man. He must be hard to kill, or hard to reach, or hard to find.

'And failure, as they say, is not an option. If you don't kill him maybe we won't kill Daniel – you will never know – but we won't sell him to a sweet and kind family. There are all sorts of unappealing people . . . who will buy a baby.'

I wanted to fling the heavy table into her face. But I bottled the rage. Stuffed it down. Not the time. But I was going to make those words taste like ash in her mouth.

'Uh, uh,' Anna said. 'Anger is destructive. Here is what happens now. Nod if you understand me – I've grown tired of your voice.'

Slowly I nodded.

'Your target will be in New York tomorrow. You'll have a partner in your hunt; a woman who's a wizard at finding people who don't want to be found, she's gifted. And motivated, just like you.' Anna gave a smug laugh, she sounded like a bird chirping. 'So. Get to New York, find him and kill him.'

'I need a guarantee that you will give me Daniel.'

She pulled a photo from her jacket and slid it across the table to me.

I knew it was Daniel. I knew it just like a soldier long separated from his child, by distance and normality, gets a picture and can see both himself and his wife in the baby's face. He was wrapped in a blue blanket, green eyes looking up at the camera, not a smile on his face but he wasn't crying, intrigued with the contraption above his head that was taking his picture. One arm reaching up, his mouth a toothless curl, cheeks full and fat. He looked good. He looked loved. Thin, blond hair crowned his head, like mine when I was a baby before it darkened, like his mother's.

I gritted my teeth.

'Now. When you've killed the target, and Daniel is returned to you, we are done. You don't keep coming after us. You don't help the CIA or the FBI or anyone else in pursuing us. You retire from the grand game. Go be a good daddy.'

'I want the protocol for the exchange.'

'When the target is dead, you will phone a number that I give you. When we have confirmed that you've completed your side of the bargain, then the child will be left, with a note with your contact information, at a church. A DNA test will confirm that the child is yours. Simple.'

'No. You're asking me to trust you far too much.'

'You do not have a choice, Sam.'

'If I can't kill or find the target?'

She made a slow little wave with her hand. 'Then I guess you'll have that picture of him as your only memory. Would you like to keep it? Put it under your pillow?'

'If you hurt or sell my son, I'll kill you.'

'Shut up. Do you really think you should threaten me right now? He could get by with nine toes as easily as ten.'

My mind went blank, in the way not of shock but of the way of calculation. I didn't believe in a truce, not now. They were not going to threaten my child and go unpunished. But I didn't let the decision show on my face.

'So. Who is this target you want dead?'

She slid another photo from her jacket to me. 'Him. His name is Jin Ming. At least that's the name he used. I think it's an assumed name.'

I studied the face. I recognized him, although I'd only seen him for a few moments. 'I think you've made a serious mistake.'

PART TWO

THE RED NOTEBOOK

14

Las Vegas

'You want me to kill a dead man.' I shook my head.

'I hope you're better at killing someone than finding a pulse. He's not dead.'

I hadn't had but a moment to look at him, he'd been sadly caught in the crossfire between Piet and his thugs and August's CIA team and he looked dead enough to me. But I was running from the CIA then, and desperate to get Piet, the one surviving smuggler out of harm's way, where I could put him to use – Piet had been my sole link to Edward, the kidnapper of my wife and my son. So I'd made a mistake. 'Who exactly is this Jin Ming?'

'A graduate student from Hong Kong attending the Delft University of Technology, focusing on computer sciences.'

'And he's a threat to you. He's just a geek, a kid.'

'His age is irrelevant. You're going to find him and kill him before he surrenders to the CIA. You have two days.'

Jin Ming had walked in with August and the rest of the CIA team. If he wanted to turn against Novem Soles, would he turn to August? Perhaps this was why Anna was eager to use me. I could get close to August, and therefore close to Jin Ming.

'Why hasn't he surrendered to them already?' I asked.

'I don't know. He set up a meeting with the CIA in two days. In New York. So get there and kill him.'

'He has the goods on you. Poor, poor you.'

'And we have the goods on you, Sam. Your child.'

I shut up.

'Kill him before that meeting so it never happens and he never passes on whatever information he has. You do that, you get your son back. You don't, your son is gone forever.' She slid an iPhone to me. 'This is yours. You do not tell anyone what you are doing. Anyone.'

Between her threat of a bomb in the club and my son, she had me pinned. I hate being pinned. Really, really hate it.

'I'm going to leave now.' She held up the remote control, another iPhone, with a call number selected. 'You do not follow me. If you do, I call the cell phone attached to the C-4 and we have bits and pieces of drunken dancers landing in the parking lot. The signal has a five-mile range.' She kept her thumb right above the number. One tap and we were all done.

'Goodbye, Anna,' I said. 'I'll see you very soon.'

'No, you will never see me again. Do your job, earn your son, and then go on your way.' She stood. 'Don't test that I'm bluffing.' She moved toward the front door and a drunken guy bumped into her and for one moment I thought her thumb would hit the screen. She recovered and she pushed roughly by the drunk. I saw her go past the bouncer and out into the desert-cool night.

I ran toward the back of the club as Mila zoomed down the stairs. 'Evacuate,' I called to her. 'Right now.' Anna didn't want me dead, but I couldn't risk that there was a bomb here in a bar full of innocent people. Mila sprinted toward the DJ's stand and before I reached the ladies' room the lights were up and her voice boomed out over the loudspeakers, the music silenced.

'People, hello, attention please. Please move to the exits in an orderly fashion. We need to clear the building immediately.

There is no danger, no fire, but please move outside and across the street.'

I heard groans of dismay, but the staff moved quickly through the crowd, herding them.

I busted into the ladies' room. Three women at the mirror, fixing make-up.

'Hey, get the hell out of here!' one turned and screamed at me, fueled by Cosmopolitans.

'Evacuating the building, out now.' There were six women total in the room and I hustled them out fast.

Where would she have put it?

The ladies' room boasted a mirror edged with a fake lasso to continue the canyon theme. Stars to duplicate the night sky glittered on the tiled ceiling. I looked in each stall. Nothing. The air vents? It would have taken her minutes to unfasten the grates and put the bomb in; she would have been noticed, with a steady stream of customers.

I looked under the sink; nothing. Then I turned, my face level with the paper towel dispenser, and, beneath it, the metal disposal bin. You needed a key to open it, to access and pull out of the trash can. I peered down into the piles of dirty paper towels. Jammed my arm down as far as I could reach.

At the bottom I ran into a package. Rectangular. I felt a flick of wire along its edge.

Slowly, bracing myself against the wall, I pulled my arm up. The distant hum of people evacuating was growing quieter.

I pulled the package free from the pile.

C-4. It was wrapped in gift paper that read BABY'S FIRST BIRTHDAY. Four wires led off a cell phone, a cheap prepaid model, to curl into the packaging. I had no idea which wire to cut, no idea if the bomb was functioning.

I ran out the back door. Several patrons had gone out this way and I saw people getting into cars, leaving The Canyon now that the party had ended. I ran, holding the package, trying to find a deserted spot where I wouldn't put anyone at risk. A small shopping center stood to my left and I arrowed behind it. Every store was in darkness.

Gingerly I unwrapped the package, careful not to disturb the wires. It was simple. Three of the wires were fakes, going nowhere taped under the paper, a blue one fed from deep in the explosive to the cell phone. I pulled out my pocket knife and I cut it.

I leaned against the building and then twenty seconds later the bomb's phone rang.

When my heart settled back into my chest I answered. 'You bitch.'

'I don't like being called names,' Anna said. 'You can tell how serious we are. You don't deviate from the plan. You don't cross us.'

'You're an idiot to give me a job and then risk blowing me up a minute later.'

'There was no risk. You did exactly what we knew you would do. Just keep doing what we tell you.' Anna hung up.

My hands wanted to shake and I wouldn't let them, I fought the fear down. I walked back to the club.

Lots of the patrons had left but a good sized crowd remained in the parking lot, curious or optimistic. I took it as a compliment to The Canyon that they hung around. I was sure many had walked their tabs. It didn't matter.

Mila met me at the front door. 'Is everything okay?'

'Yes.'

'What happened?'

'She knew who I was. The trap was on me, not Anna.'

'Ah, Sam. I am sorry. What did she say?'

I took a deep breath. 'Rough night. Let's talk tomorrow. You have a place to stay?'

Her gaze burned like fire. 'What are you not telling me, *Samuil*?' Tension broke her voice; she only used the Slavic form of my name when she was upset.

'There's nothing you can do, Mila. Thank you for coming. This is my problem and mine alone now.'

'If she knew who you are, then she had a reason to come meet you.' Realization dawned in her eyes. 'Daniel. She wants to make a deal for Daniel.'

'This is now my problem,' I said again. 'Thank you for your concern.'

'Do not do this alone. What is the ransom? God, let me help you.'

'I can't tell you. She'll kill him.' I kept my voice from breaking. Just barely.

'Sam.' So much in that one syllable. Pain for me, desperation to help, a simmering fury.

'I play by their rules, and that means no you hanging around. Go, Mila. I'm sorry.' The approaching whine of police sirens sliced through the night. Now, empty, the bar was quiet. The air weighed like steel between us. 'I have to go. I have to be on a flight in two hours. If you want to help me, deal with the cops. Oh, and there's a pound of C-4 explosive behind a Dumpster in the shopping center. Get rid of it. I'm not really inclined to leave it lying around.'

'Sam.' Her mouth worked. 'What do they want you to do?'

'It has nothing to do with you,' I said, my voice rising. Her face was stone. This was the woman who had helped ensure the

CIA didn't find me while I hunted for my wife's kidnappers, the one who had given me every support in my new life. She deserved better than my silence. 'They want me to kill a man.'

'Who?'

'Someone who is a threat to them.'

'You commit one murder for them to save your son, they can ask for a thousand more. They can tell you a thousand lies, make a thousand promises, give you a thousand orders, and you will be their slave to save that child.'

I couldn't breathe. 'I don't need you debating me. I do what I have to do.'

'Then go. Go before the cops want to talk to you.' Mila didn't wait for me to answer. She bolted past me and out the door toward the arriving police cars.

I stood in the mess of knocked-over chairs, and half-full drinks, and the eerie serenity of a bar that has been emptied of people in a matter of minutes. The light machine kept playing and gleaming dots danced along my face, my skin.

Get to the airport. Get to New York. Find and kill this Jin Ming. Save my boy.

15

Henderson, Nevada

Leonie opened her eyes, then blinked. She'd fallen asleep at the desk and her cheek felt mashed and drool-stained. Charming, she thought, wiping at her face with her fingers. The computer kept playing music from *Rent*, turned low, set on repeat. She preferred songs with a story these days. She'd filled her iTunes library with musicals and movie soundtracks. She hit the space bar and the rising voices, imploring her to live for today, went silent. She blinked again in the sudden quiet, forcing herself to stay awake.

My God, what happened to me? Fourth or fifth time she'd fallen asleep while working this week. It was getting to be a bad habit. She'd had an early morning.

She glanced at the clock. She'd fallen asleep after putting the baby down. It was close to 10 p.m. Exhaustion had caught up with her. She was still in T-shirt and jeans and got up from the desk in the corner of her bedroom, shucked her clothes, put on thin cotton pajamas. She brushed her teeth, wiped the sleep from her eyes. Now she'd probably have trouble going back to sleep, and the baby would sleep straight through the night. Oh well, she could get some work done. Leonie had decided early on that they called it single motherhood because you had to make every single second work to your advantage.

'Honey,' her well-meaning octogenarian neighbor, Mrs Craft, would say, 'why don't you hire a nanny? I'm sure you can afford it.' And Mrs Craft would look around at the granite countertops, the vaulted ceilings, the plush Persian rug over the immaculate hardwoods.

'I don't like having strangers in the house,' Leonie said.

'A nanny, once you get to know her, she's no stranger.'

And Leonie had just shrugged instead of saying what was in her heart: *I can't take the security risk. I can't have a nanny finding out what I do.* The load of long, solitary working hours and taking care of Taylor was endurable. Taylor was worth every sleepless night.

Leonie brewed a pot of hazelnut decaf and switched to the

Chicago soundtrack on her iPod, connected to a small set of speakers. The saucy strains filtered out quietly over the bedroom. She opened her laptop and checked her emails; she kept several anonymous accounts to stay in touch with clients.

Nothing from Gunnar. She heaved a sigh of relief. As clients went, Gunnar was being rather difficult. Kept changing his mind on what he wanted. First he wanted to relocate to New Orleans; no, he decided it was too close to Atlanta, he would see someone he knew, in the bars of the French Quarter. Too likely he'd be found. Then he wanted Canada. No, he realized actual winters, with actual snow, took place in Montreal. Now he wanted Panama but had started making noises about there being nothing to do in Panama, as though the entire country lacked nightclubs or movie theaters, beaches or bookstores. She couldn't start creating his fake life without him choosing where to hide.

She wanted to say: when you leave your old life behind, you leave it behind, and not soon enough for me, and you have to decide. But you had to avoid getting too snotty with Gunnar, or any desperate client. She knew that too well. Handle him with care, get him set up where he could never bother her, and his life would start again. Panama. She would tell him that was the solution to keep him safe. She was the expert, after all; he would simply have to listen to her. He couldn't continue to waffle.

Once a person had made the conscious decision to vanish, and contacted her for help, then indecision was a nightmare. It made exposure much more likely. A slip of the tongue, time spent on a traceable computer researching locales and such: any of those mistakes could return to haunt you. If you had ever looked in your browser at Seattle or Vancouver or Paris, then you needed to cut them from your vanish list. Fine. Decision made.

She would create him bank accounts in Panama, find him a suitable house in Managua, in a good neighborhood where he would not attract interest. Get him a private Spanish tutor, one who could be trusted. Make him a New Zealander. She could get the right kind of paper for that passport, and the watermarks, within two days. She would rely on her network to cobble together a new name, and a new world for him. Best to get started now.

She got her coffee, ignored the thirst for a cigarette (six months now no smoking), and then she heard the traffic noise outside, a car rushing past, a rise of night breeze. And then a flap of curtain.

The sound seemed much louder than it should. She paused *Chicago*'s singing murderers in the middle of the cell block tango. Listened again. She heard a hard gust of wind.

There was a window open somewhere.

A cold itch wriggled between her shoulder blades. She got up from the computer and went down the hall. She stopped at the nursery door, eased it open. The door faced the window, which looked out onto the backyard. The window stood open, the Pooh Bear drapes dancing in the gust.

Her heart shuddered to stone.

She hurried forward in the dark. The moonlight gleam showed her the crib was empty. Her baby was gone. She screamed, short and sharp, picking up the wadded-up yellow blanket as if Taylor might have shrunken and fallen into its maze of folds. Her scream turned molten in her throat.

She stumbled through the house. Be here, be here, be here, she said to herself.

But the rest of the house was empty, and the fear and the shock juddered through her like a hammer hitting bone.

The phone. Stunned, she stumbled to it. Picked it up. Pressed the 9, then the 1. Then she stopped.

What was she going to tell them? My child is gone. Questions would be asked. Who are you, ma'am? Who is the father? How long have you lived here, who might take your baby from you? What if their questions pierced the truth, that she lived here under a false name, that she wasn't who she said she was.

She hung up the phone. She had to think before she called the police. She had been so careful. She had hidden so well. No one knew where to find her. Except . . .

The phone rang in her hand and she nearly dropped it as though the sound could turn to heat, scald her skin. She stared at the screen. The number, blocked.

'Hello?'

'Hello, Leonie. How are you?' A woman's voice, gentle, and known to her. Anna Tremaine.

'Where? Where?' she sobbed into the phone.

'Oh, are you missing someone? Young mothers can be so forgetful.'

'Where is my baby?' she screamed. Now the fear was gone. Snap, vanish. Just a fury in its place.

Anna's voice was calm. 'Let me assure you your child is safe.'

A ragged moan escaped Leonie's throat.

'Are you listening, Leonie?' Anna said. 'It will be tiresome if I have to repeat myself.'

'Why have you done this? Why?'

'Because, Leonie, you are going to do something very important for me, and you're going to do it right away, no argument.'

Leonie forced herself toward calm. 'What do you want?'

'You're so good at hiding people for us, darling, but can you do it in reverse? Can you find someone who's hiding?'

'Yes,' Leonie said. It was inconceivable to give any other answer. She'd do anything for Taylor.

'All right. If you have another client right now, get rid of him.'

She thought of Gunnar. He needed to be hidden. Okay, whatever, he couldn't decide what he was doing or where he wanted to go, screw him for eternity. He would have to wait. 'Okay. Please don't hurt Taylor. Please. Please.'

'Get a hold of yourself. I need you to be calm.'

'You could have just asked! You could have just asked me for help! You know I would, I already . . .'

The woman's voice was a slow purr. 'I needed an assurance you would act.'

'I'll do whatever you want.'

'You're going to work with a gentleman. He, like you, is very motivated to do a good job for us.'

'I don't work with other people.'

'You will now, Leonie. Unless you're willing to pull the trigger on a gun yourself and kill a man in cold blood. Your job is easy. All you have to do is find a target. This man will then kill the target. And then you get Taylor back. Easy.'

Panic churned her guts. She sank down onto the couch. Okay, she thought, this is the reality of the moment. Deep breath and deal. 'Um, who is this man I'm supposed to find and who is it I'm working with?'

'I love the smell of cooperation in the morning,' Anna Tremaine said. 'You're very good at making last-minute travel arrangements, darling. I'll let you meet him at the airport. His name is Sam Capra. He can tell you the details.'

'Anna, is Taylor all right?'

'Perfectly fine. Asleep on a blanket.'

Leonie felt fear like ice pierce her skin. She forced herself to

113

listen intently. Anna, or one of her people, must have taken the baby in the past couple of hours, while she was absorbed in her work, or dozing at her desk. Which meant that Anna might still be in Las Vegas, or was in a car. She tried to hear the hiss of tire against road on Anna's side of the phone. She heard nothing. If Anna was pulled over, then there might be traffic as the background noise. A clue that would tell her where Anna was. The rumble of an eighteen-wheeler, a whine of engine passing Anna's car. She heard nothing. She cursed herself for not listening sooner. But shock had frozen her. She tried to manipulate her memory: force herself into replaying every word of the conversation again. Every nuance. Because if she did what was asked, and her child wasn't returned, the person she would be finding and killing was Anna Tremaine.

'You know not a hair on the head will be hurt,' Anna said in a babyish sing-song. 'Haven't I always been nice to you? Check the email address we used in the past. Details will be there, and final instructions. Pack a bag for a few days. Be at your smartest. Be brave. Do a good job, Leonie. For your child's sake.' Then the phone went dead in her hand.

Final instructions? Leonie got up and ran toward the laptop.

16

Las Vegas

I hurried toward the ticket counter at McCarran when a woman stopped me. She was slightly built, auburn-haired, with a full mouth and purple-smudged eyes. She wore jeans and a green blouse and carried a small briefcase and a travel bag. She was pretty but she looked like she'd had a night as rough as mine.

'Sam Capra?' Her voice shook slightly.

I nodded.

'I have your ticket. For the flight to New York. I just bought it for you.'

'Okay,' I said. This was the woman who would find Jin Ming. My motivated partner, as Anna had said.

She gave me the ticket. Her hand trembled. Then she looked at me, studied me as if my face were an interesting map, then she turned away from me and went and sat down. The security lines were long but moving.

I followed her. We were being forced together and I did not want anyone else knowing my business; especially when my business involved killing a man. 'Who are you?'

'Leonie. I'm supposed to come with you.' She wiped her nose with a tissue.

'Why?'

'To help you find the target.'

'I don't need help.'

'Well, I'm helping you because they have my kid. So you don't get a vote.' She said this staring straight ahead, not looking at me.

I sat down next to her. 'Anna took your child?'

'Yes. My daughter, Taylor.' Leonie didn't look at me. 'We should go through security, we don't want to be late for the flight.'

'You could go to the police.'

'Not an option.' She looked past me, at the crowds. People seemed oddly happy and energetic in the Las Vegas airport. Happy to leave because they'd had a great time, or happy that

115

they'd just arrived, flush with money and with promise and ready to spin the wheel.

'Why not?'

'Our lives are not each other's business.'

'I'm supposed to go on a job with you. I want to know what the hell I'm signing up for.'

'You're signing up to do what Anna tells you. She has your kid, too, right?'

I said nothing.

'I'm sorry. I'm supposed to help you find this guy Jin Ming. We needn't talk unless we're discussing him.' One stray tear of upset tracked her cheek and she wiped it away with quick resolve.

'How are you going to find him?'

'There is no place on earth he can hide from me.' She stood. 'We should probably go through security. I could use a drink. I really hate flying.'

We had thirty minutes before they would be calling our flight. I followed Leonie to a private lounge where we were admitted by our first class tickets. Inside was a scattering of business types and lushed-up couples, a few keeping the Vegas party going. One guy, lubricated with gin and tonic, complained with his megaphone voice about having lost ten thousand dollars. I would have traded problems with him.

We sat down in a far corner. A sleek hostess – truly sleek, her hair was gelled back in a severe cut, her dress was silver, she looked like her day job was testing wind tunnels – brought Leonie a large glass of pinot noir and me a whisky, neat.

'When did your kid vanish?' I asked.

She took a fortifying sip of the wine. 'Earlier tonight. Anna, or her people, took her from her crib while I was working in my bedroom. I fell asleep at my computer. I never even heard them in my house.' The moment her voice started to quake she caught herself.

'Listen to me.'

She looked at me.

'Unlike most parents of missing kids, we know exactly what we have to do to get our kids back and we know who has them. We can't waste mental energy on blame. We have a job to do. Our kids need us.'

She nodded; took another sip of the wine. 'Wow, do you double as a life coach on weekends?'

'No. Where's your husband?'

'I'm a single mother.' She watched, past my shoulder, the drunk complainer order another round. 'Where's your wife?'

'Ex. In a coma.'

'Coma.'

'Yes. One of Anna's buddies shot her in the head a few weeks ago.'

She let five seconds pass. 'That sucks.'

Really, what else do you say? Then she said: 'I mean, I'm really sorry. I'm not quite myself this evening.'

Of course she wasn't – she had to be in deep shock. 'What's your connection to Anna?'

'None of your business. I don't know you, Sam. All I want is my child back. That's all.' She rubbed at her jawline, glanced at the clock. She did not want to seem to look at me. Her daughter had been kidnapped only hours earlier. Her self-control was extraordinary. I reached out and touched her hand with my fingertips. Just a reflex. She flinched.

'We're on the same side. I'm in your shoes. They have my son, too.'

'So Anna told me.' She studied her wine. 'Do we have to talk beyond finding Jin Ming? Seriously?'

It occurred to me that maybe she was a plant; someone Anna sent along to make sure I killed Jin Ming and didn't try to use him back as leverage against Novem Soles. I didn't know if she really had a kid or really had suffered a kidnapping tonight. She could simply be a convincing actress. She could be lying through her teeth. But I couldn't get anywhere with her if she knew I harbored suspicions. She was supposed to be a panicked mom, I was a desperate father. Let us, I thought, play true to our parts.

'Yes, we do have to talk. I know you are upset. I know what you're feeling because I'm feeling it, too. If we can't trust each other, we won't get far in finding Jin Ming.'

She gave me a doubting look. 'I tell you where he will be. You kill him. That's all we have to discuss.' She took another hit of the pinot.

'Leonie—'

'Listen. This is the single worst day of my life. You are a dude who kills people. So I don't want to know you. I don't want to be your friend or join your support group for parents of kidnapped kids. I just want my Taylor home.' She picked up the wine glass. She stared past my shoulder toward the loud group in the back corner. 'If those assholes are on our flight, I may end up punching someone.'

A dude who kills people. That was so not what I was. But now wasn't the time to reassure her I wasn't some slavering ax-wielder. Winning her trust would be a slow process. 'This target. What can you tell me about him? What does he know about Novem Soles?'

'I don't know.' She didn't flinch at the name of the group; she'd heard it before.

'You must. That knowledge would be key to tracking him, predicting where he will run, who he will ask for help.'

'All you need to do is kill him.' She set the wine glass down hard. 'You're the bullet, I'm the brains. I just tell you where to shoot. The bullet doesn't need any details except a location.'

Well. 'Did Anna threaten your daughter if you tell me something you're not supposed to?'

'I would say kidnapping in itself would be threat enough. I . . . know Anna. Children are simply a commodity to her. Products that other people make for her and from which she profits. She'll kill or sell our kids and we'll never find them if we give her anything other than complete obedience.'

Was she trying to provoke me? See how I'd react? I studied her again. Fierce intelligence in the eyes. I leaned forward.

'Has it occurred to you that neither of us is getting our kid back? We have zero guarantees she'll honor her side of the bargain. We need to find a way to protect ourselves, to make sure she hands the kids back. We could trade her Ming, alive, for the kids.'

'You listen to me.' Leonie pointed a finger at my face. 'You hear every word I'm saying. Don't you dare think of going against Anna. If we deviate from the plan, Anna will kill the children.' She lowered her voice to the barest whisper. 'We are doing exactly what she tells us to do. If you try to fight back . . . well, you won't.'

'You'll kill me?'

'I'll do anything for my child. Anything.' Stare down between us.

'We are on the same side,' I repeated.

'This is crazy. Please, Sam. Let's just try to get along out of necessity.'

I'd mishandled this. But where was the primer for this

situation? I got up and fixed us two sleek plates of appetizers, laid on the sleek buffet by the sleek hostesses. Leonie watched me. I brought back her food, set the silvery plate in front of her.

'Thank you.' She nibbled at a meatball, then at a carrot stick, out of politeness.

'You hold yourself together remarkably well for someone whose child was just taken,' I said. 'I have the advantage. My child was taken weeks ago. I have had time to . . . adjust.'

'That's a white lie,' she said. 'I don't think you're adjusted at all. It's all stifled just inside.'

I ate a slider, sipped at the whisky.

She looked at me. 'Inside I'm a wreck.'

'When my kid and my wife were taken – I couldn't eat or sleep for days.' I was also framed as a traitor, undergoing inter-rogation in a CIA-run prison in Poland, but that was an avalanche of detail right now for Leonie.

'Your wife was taken. I thought you said . . . '

'Anna's people grabbed my wife when she was seven months pregnant. I've never seen my son face to face.'

She just stared at me for a long moment. 'How awful. I am sorry.'

'Let me guess why you can't go to the police. Anna provided you with your baby girl.'

She ate some more of the carrot. She did not seem the type for an impulsive admission. 'Why would you say that?'

'You said you work on hiding people which suggests to me you are breaking a few laws, committing forgery for new papers, maybe credit fraud. You know her. She got you your kid. What Anna giveth, Anna taketh away.'

She was good at concealing her emotions – after all, me dissing her was nothing compared to the agonies she must be feeling for her kid – and the only sign of betrayal on her face was the momentary quiver of her lip. 'No. Taylor is mine. But I've done work for Anna. Sometimes the children she places with parents' – note she didn't say the unthinkable word of *sells* – 'need birth certificates. I forge them for her. And I've helped hide people she sent to me.'

'Did you do a birth certificate for Julien Daniel Besson?' My breath couldn't move in my lungs. I leaned in close and she leaned back. I grabbed her hands again. 'That was the name my son was given at birth. He was born in France. Julien Daniel Besson.'

'I didn't. But if Anna's using your child as leverage against you then she hasn't placed him. She'll only place him now if she doesn't need him any more.'

Her words were a knife across my throat. She saw it.

'I'm sorry, Sam. I really am.'

'You help her, forging certificates.'

I thought I could hear the soft burr of her grinding her teeth. 'It's not a choice.'

I stared at her. 'They have more dirt on you.' I didn't know yet if I could trust her. Cornering her about her secrets wasn't going to win her over to my side.

'I am not up for Twenty Questions.' She stood. 'Don't talk about defying Anna. We do what she says, and nothing else. I'm not putting Taylor's life at risk. And you shouldn't be endangering your own child's life, either.' She spat the last word like I was the scum of parenting.

There was no point in saying, you're wanting us to entrust babies to killers and murderers. 'Okay, Leonie. Okay. Calm down.'

'I don't need to know you, you don't need to know me.' She downed the pinot noir in two hard gulps, picked up her bag. 'Let's go get on our plane.'

17

Flight 903, Las Vegas to New York

We sat together in first class. Most of the cabin, weary from partying in the desert and not looking forward to a work day tomorrow in New York, slept. I watched an old movie, *Aliens*, on my personal viewer in the chair back and thought, now there's a movie about how you save a kid. I had seen the film a dozen times before and I could watch it without thinking, without having to follow the story. Leonie's eyes were closed. She had spoken so few words to me on the flight I felt sure no one believed we were traveling together. I got up to splash cold water on my face in the lavatory. Most of the other passengers were locked in their own digital cocoons, watching movies on their personal movie screens or hooked into their iPods or iPads. Technology has made it easy for us to be totally alone in a crowded room. I envied those who slept. I needed sleep, badly, but I couldn't settle my mind. I've never been good at sleeping on planes.

I sat back down and Leonie opened her eyes. She stared at me, blinking, as though unsure where she was wakening. I was surprised she'd managed to doze off. The adrenaline shock from her daughter's kidnapping was fading, the inevitable exhaustion settling into her. She looked guilty at having done anything as weak and self-indulgent as sleep, when I knew it was the body's natural response to cope with crippling stress.

'You okay? You want something to drink?' It's the bar owner in me. I always want to offer a drink. The flight attendants should just let me man the beverage cart. They could go watch the movie.

She shook her head. The silence hung, like smoke ruining the air.

I started to put my earphones into place. No point in talking with her.

She put a hand on my arm. 'Your son, he was given that name. If you got to name him, what would it be?'

'Daniel. My ex did get to name him. For my late brother.'

Her mouth pursed, like she was tasting the name. 'When did Daniel . . . vanish?'

'Right after he was born. I've only seen a picture that Anna gave me.'

'And you're sure she gave you a photo of your kid.'

'I am.'

'Show him to me.'

I showed her the picture of Daniel that Anna had given me. She studied it, then looked at my face. 'He's a handsome boy.'

'He's never been held by either of his parents,' I said. 'But there he's smiling. How does that affect a kid – to not have been held except by people who want to use you?' The words spilled, unexpected. I didn't talk about Daniel. Who was I going to talk about him with? My crazy Moldovan boss with the million-dollar price on her head? My old friends in the CIA who weren't my friends any more? My customers at the bar? No. Every flick of pain I felt about Daniel coalesced in my chest. I shut my mouth. I didn't want to talk about him.

'When you get him back, then don't ever let him go.' She handed me the photo. 'How did you and your wife ever cross Anna's path?'

'My wife got bought by Novem Soles. She was a CIA officer. She was a traitor.' It was a strange thing to say in the hush of a first class cabin. I glanced up from the photo. The flight attendants congregated in the galley ahead of us, people either slept or sat earplugged into oblivion. Yes, let me talk about my wife. The love of my life, the woman I gave my life to, the woman who betrayed both me and country and then tried to save me. Let me talk about the most incomprehensible person I ever knew and how machines keep her breathing and digesting and living like a ghost bound in flesh.

'I'm sorry, that sucks.' I was figuring Leonie was a master of understatement now.

'It does.'

Leonie pulled a photo from her purse. It was worn, dog-eared from too much handling, as though it had lived a hard life inside her wallet. 'This is Taylor.' She was a bigger baby than Daniel, a few months older, rounder-cheeked, with darker hair and soft, sweet, brown eyes.

'She's a cute girl.'

'Yes. Very.'

'So never a husband?'

'We're not involved any more. I prefer to deal only with actual human beings these days.'

'Not an amicable parting.'

She took Taylor's photo from me and carefully fitted it into a back slot in her wallet, away from the credit cards. I could see a smear of ink drawn on the back as she worked the photo into the slot. She dumped the wallet in her purse. 'No.'

'How will you explain to him that Taylor's gone?'

'He is utterly indifferent to her. He couldn't care less. He's seen her once and made it clear he didn't care to see her again.'

'How old is Taylor now?'

'Almost a year.' She took a heavy, restoring breath. 'So, Taylor is my life, Sam. Everything.'

'We'll get her back. We'll get them both back.'

'Anna must get both kids to New York.' Her voice was just a whisper. 'If she sticks by the agreement. I'm wondering how she's doing that so quickly with mine.'

'Because they're lying to us,' I said quietly.

Her gaze snapped to mine.

'They might give us our kids back, but they're not going to want us anywhere close by after we ... deal with the target,' I said. 'This phone call, this church pickup – it has to be a lie, Leonie. They don't want us getting caught. You don't linger in the area after a job. You create distance.'

She was silent. She tensed when I said the word 'job', as though the drowsing businesspeople and hung-over Vegas escapees around us would translate 'job' into 'hit'.

'You're not used to violence,' I said.

She didn't look at me. 'No.' She rubbed at her face. She leaned close to me. I could smell breath mints on her mouth. 'Don't take this the wrong way, but you don't look like much of a killer.'

I had killed. Never before my wife had been taken. But I had killed, multiple times, to save myself or save others since my life had been derailed by Novem Soles. I would like to say it weighed on me heavily, this human cost, but that would be a lie. They'd taken my wife, my child. They'd gotten in the way of me getting them back. They'd tried to kill me. Why should I feel guilty? The deaths were nothing I savored, and I never wanted to kill again. I dreamed about it sometimes, and I didn't want to think that the experiences were rewiring my brain, like a soldier who sees the worst horrors in battle.

But this kid, this Jin Ming. He'd been grabbed by the CIA,

clearly, in Amsterdam, forced to give them access to the machinists' shop where the gunfight erupted. And now he was turning against Novem Soles. I ought to be applauding him, protecting him, picking his brain. Putting him into my own witness protection plan so he could tell me what lovely, dirty secrets he knew and then I could start slicing the core out of the so-called Nine Suns.

He and I could have talks. The Best. Talks. Ever.

Instead, I was going to kill him. I closed my eyes. He was, what, twenty-two, twenty-three? At the beginning of his years. The thought that someone barely out of his teens could be a mortal threat to an international criminal syndicate (that was my theory as to what Novem Soles was, fancy-ass Latin name aside – maybe one of them had read a branding book and wanted to sound more gothic, ancient or mysterious) interested me.

I didn't need to think about him. Just kill him. Be a weapon. I could do that and I'd worry about the mental cost later. Or, maybe, not worry about it at all. But if I did that, what sort of father would I be for my son?

'I'm not much of a killer,' I said to Leonie. 'But I will be.'

18

Flight 902, Las Vegas to New York

In first class we got a decent dinner: shrimp salad and steak medallions, a potato galette and a wannabe crème brûlée.

'So. It's up to you to find our guy. Where do you start, beyond knowing he's in New York City?'

'If you don't mind, I'll keep some secrets to myself.'

'I think we need to discuss our options if they betray us.'

'If I lose Taylor, it's over for me anyway. I'm not continuing to breathe, Sam. I'm not existing then.'

There was nothing more to say; the flight attendant stopped and asked us if we wanted coffee. We both declined. Leonie announced she would sleep the rest of the flight. I closed my eyes and thought about a plan of action.

One thing I did do: I surreptitiously snapped a picture of Leonie while she dozed. I thought, for some reason, that it might be valuable to have a photo of her. She was a woman with a lot of secrets, and I might need to know more about who she was.

We landed at LaGuardia late, delayed by dodging a goliath of an early summer storm raging over Kentucky and Ohio. We rented a car – no way I was trusting cabs and the subway during a manhunt – and drove to a midtown Manhattan hotel, the Claiborne, where Leonie had already booked us rooms across the hall from each other. The rest of the hotel seemed ready to rouse, the city stirring awake, but I was already dead on my feet. My energy was gone because we had no clue where Jin Ming was.

'Go sleep,' Leonie said at our doors.

'I can't.'

'I can't have you hovering over me.'

'How are you going to find him?'

She patted the laptop, raised the cell phone. 'It's what I do, bullet.' She tried a smile but it was an awful, desperate thing and she knew it. 'Sorry. Just trying to stay sane.'

'Jin Ming vanished from Holland, no trace.'

'There is always a trace,' she said. 'Always.'

19

New York City

Jack had a window seat on the flight from Brussels; no way he was going to fly from Amsterdam – Novem Soles would be watching, he thought, the train stations and the airports. Ricki drove him to Brussels and left him at the airport. He went into a bathroom stall and shut the door. Then he oiled and combed down his hair to look like his new passport picture. He stuck a thin, bulbous piece of plastic in each cheek, to subtly change the shape of his face. He put in the false teeth; they slid over his own teeth. This meant he could not eat during the flight but he didn't care. He put on a pair of slightly tinted glasses. They were not to change his eye color but Ricki said that every bit that made him look less like himself, or hid him, helped. She'd almost cried as she slipped the glasses on his face.

He exited the stall and gave himself a short, quick glance in the mirror. He couldn't stand and preen or adjust the implants. He still looked like Jack Ming but not exactly, and with any of the biometric scans at customs in the United States, if he was on a watch list, perhaps this would give him a cushion. He wore a white shirt and jeans and sneakers and looked anonymous.

He had no trouble in the Brussels airport. He tried not to watch everyone, for fear of looking paranoid, but he kept scanning faces, looking for another face looking back at him. He took his seat. An older lady sat next to him, immediately produced a thick novel with a swordsman and a dragon on the cover and opened it at the first page, almost defying him to try and make conversation with her. He sighed in relief. He cocooned himself with his iPod and wrapped himself in Beatles music. He closed his eyes then woke up with a start, one of the cheek implants almost half out of his mouth. *I could have swallowed this.* Not awesome if he choked on his own disguise in the middle of a transatlantic flight. He tongued the implant back into place and glanced at his traveling companion. She was lost in her own world, paying him no heed.

New York, shrouded in cloud, opened up beneath him and he stared down. Home. Never thought he'd see it again. Never thought he'd come back. But what choice did he have?

He walked through customs, the new burgundy passport identifying him as Philippe Lin, a Belgian national, remembered to breathe while the customs agent inspected it, scanned it, asked him his business in the country. He was here to visit family. She asked for the address where he would be staying; he gave her one provided by Ricki's friend. She asked if he was traveling anywhere else other than New York. He said he was only visiting New York because no other city could compare. She looked hard at him, as though his affable tone were an affront to the seriousness of the moment. He thought: *what the hell are you doing, trying to make a joke?* His stomach twisted, dropped. She was a big-built, older lady who did not seem at all bored by her work. She glanced at her computer screen, glanced at him. He willed himself toward calm.

In Amsterdam, Ricki sat with her hands on the keyboard. She had pierced the main database for Belgian passport information, kept in the Federal Public Service Foreign Affairs department in Brussels. The database was accessed if there was a question about any Belgian passport from a friendly nation. The imprinted number could be scanned via a watermark or entered into the host country's passport inquiry database. The confirmation was sent, a returning ping of approval coming back to the country's host system.

She had made a few phone calls past midnight, and found a hacker in Antwerp who was willing to help her.

'All I need,' she said, 'is for you to trick the system into approving every Belgian passport in a time window.'

'I can do thirty minutes. I don't want to leave an open feed into the system longer than that, and I don't want to leave code behind,' the hacker said.

'Thirty minutes.' And if it took Jin Ming longer than thirty minutes to get through customs . . .

'Now,' she said into the phone.

The hacker pressed the button.

According to the airline's website, the flight from Brussels had landed. Don't be in the back of the line, she thought.

Ricki heard a knock on her door. She stood up. Then she leaned down, typed a code into the program. The system logged out, encrypting itself to await further instructions.

Ricki put her eye up to the keyhole to see who was there, and the door smashed inward.

The customs agent glanced back toward her terminal screen.

Oh dear God, Jack thought. I'm sunk. The irony that he was an American trying to get into America under a false name and flag hit him hard. My face. How much is my face like what might be in their database? What if Ricki's scheme hadn't worked? And if he was arrested, what deal could he cut? I'm here to give the CIA proof that they need to bust a crime ring. Yes, you're welcome, let me go now.

Then the customs agent stamped the passport, slid it back to him. 'Thank you, Mr Lin, enjoy your visit in the United States.'

He nodded and he walked on, the agent's eyes already turning toward the next arrival in line.

He kept the implants in place. The customs agents searched his bag and waved him through. He kept his head down as much as he could, navigating through the rest of the terminal, sure that he was being photographed on security cameras, just as everyone else had been. Novem Soles had already shown that they could pluck data from police and government, and he knew from the printouts in the notebook that they owned people inside several governments; maybe they were looking for him even here. He took the AirTrain to the Howard Street station and boarded the subway to take him into Manhattan. No one glanced at him, no one paid him any attention. As the subway chugged toward Manhattan, he ducked his head down and spat the teeth and the implants into his palm. Then he slid them into his bag.

He needed to be Jack Ming again, just for ten minutes. Just long enough to say goodbye.

Thank you, Ricki, he thought. You got me here, you're the best.

20

Amsterdam

'You know, a friend is a good thing to have.' The Watcher sat down across from Ricki; she perched on the edge of the couch, shivering. He had forced his way in, the gun steady on her.

'You don't need to be afraid.' He smiled. 'All I want is information and then I'll leave.' And to prove it he put the gun down.

'We have a mutual friend. Pierre in Brussels, who just rushed creating documentation for a friend of yours. A Chinese boy.'

She said nothing.

'Pierre found out that we were looking for your friend after he overnighted you the false IDs.'

'Pierre doesn't work for you.'

'He doesn't have to work for me. He's just afraid of me.' As soon as the Watcher had received the tip that someone using an Amsterdam exchange dial-up had contacted the CIA with crucial information on Novem Soles, he had known it must be the Chinese boy, the one their hireling had failed to kill. He was the only remaining loose end from the spring offensive. And now he was a real danger.

'I don't know anything about Ming's business.'

The Watcher smiled at her. She was lovely. He'd spent a lot of time in Nigeria, in Italy, where many of the women in his former line of work were African. He had not taken one in a long time. So much for past pleasures.

He studied her wall of bootlegging machines. 'You knew my friend Nic, too?'

'Yes. Slightly.'

'Of course. You worked in film ... and he worked in film. I guess content is really what computers are all about now. Remember when they used to be about solving problems? Thinking more creatively?'

Ricki stared at him.

The Watcher put on his warmest smile. It was a very cold flexing of the mouth but he was unaware of this; he thought it looked like a real smile. He smoothed a hand along his thin mohawk. 'So you steal and copy movies and he made nasty ones.'

'I didn't know about that. I just knew him because he sold me software to crack the copyright codes.'

'Nic was generous. And now you are generous to his friend Ming.'

Ricki ran her palms along her jeans. 'Ming wanted to get out of the country. All I did was give him some names of people who could help him.' She raised her gaze to his, her eyes defiant.

Oh, a bit of spark. He used to know how to stomp out that flicker of individual flame. 'I want to know where Jin Ming is, and what evidence he has about the people Nic worked with.'

'I don't know the answer to either of those questions.'

'He is eventually going to New York. I have someone trying to crack the flight reservations database to find out if he's flying from here or another city. But I'm guessing you can just tell me and save me the money and effort.' His steely gray eyes looked at her, then at the gun, then at her again.

She didn't speak.

'It's really best that you help me.' He stood up. 'How much is this equipment worth to you?' He pulled a weight from his pocket. A magnet, a large one, the kind you'd find in a factory. Pierre in Brussels had told him what kind of work Ricki did and so he'd decided to take it away from her. He began to run the magnet along the shelf.

'Stop it, you'll ruin them!' She stood up, horror on her face.

'Yes. I'll erase' – and he laughed at the idea of it – 'about forty thousand euros' worth of business in about five minutes if you don't answer my question.'

He thought he saw one more flash of anger in her dark eyes. Then she gave in. 'He flew to Dublin,' she said quietly. 'Then a direct flight to Boston. Then a train to New York. He was trying not to be obvious.'

'Thank you. He is meeting the CIA there.'

'I don't know. He didn't tell me.'

He believed her.

'He has some evidence against me. What is it?'

Now her fear – and he knew it was there, under the surface of her false confidence – showed itself. 'I really don't know. He didn't show me any evidence. He wouldn't tell me, and I didn't ask. Better I don't know.'

'Better, of course. Did he have a computer?'

'Not when he got here. I gave him a spare laptop.'

'What about a disc? Or a flash drive?'

'I didn't see one, but he could have hidden it.'

'How can I reach him on the phone?'

'He didn't take a phone with him. I don't have a way to call him. He didn't want to implicate me if he got caught.'

Once again he believed her. 'He has evidence I want. You know it.' He slid the barrel of his gun along her jaw. 'You have such a good bone structure, Frédérique.'

She paused. 'He … He … '

'What?'

She trembled. 'He left today. Before he left, he got dressed … and when he was putting on his shirt I saw he had an envelope taped to his back. He lied and said it was a bandage but I could see it wasn't.'

'How big?'

She made a rectangle with her hands. Maybe a bit smaller than a sheet of paper.

'What was inside the envelope?'

She bit her lip. It made her look gentle, pretty. Oh, he thought. The hunger, it never went away. Ever.

'Ricki. I'll make sure your business is safe if you tell me. I'll give you the equipment to grow it, young lady. Or I'll destroy it. Your choice.' He could tell by her hesitation that she knew. She knew. Maybe she'd looked at it when Jin Ming was in the shower, or while he slept.

'It was a notebook,' she said. 'Like a journal. A red moleskin cover.'

'And what was in this notebook?'

'Photos. Emails. Screen captures. Spreadsheets. Printed out and pasted in. But I didn't understand any of it, I didn't. He said it was stuff Nic had stolen from people you were blackmailing.'

The Watcher's mouth twitched. 'Did he digitize the notebook?'

'Not here. It would have taken a while.'

Her equipment would have to be taken or kept, analysed, checked to see what actions had been performed. Jin Ming might have left a trace to follow. The Watcher decided he had to get to New York, now.

'Excuse me, please, Ricki.' He opened up his phone, ordered the person who answered to come around to Ricki's address. He said, 'Hold on one moment', cupped his hand over the receiver, and said, 'Here's what I can offer you, Ricki, and I'm sorry it's not a better deal for you. My group is taking over your business. You will continue to run it, but we will take fifty per cent of your profits. Do well and we'll help you take over other operations in Brussels, Antwerp, and you can run them. I'm going to have some people in here soon to go through your computers to make sure you're telling me the truth. Then we'll leave you alone.'

'You can't,' she said, shock in her tone.

'I certainly can. Now, if you decline or you betray us, what we'll do is I'll have one of my employees load you up with heroin, hand you over to a dealer in whores who will rape you and sell you, probably to a brothel in Nigeria or Morocco or South East Asia. You might have an easier time of it in Asia; a girl from Senegal would be considered more exotic, and would be treated better.'

She stared at him, speechless, jaw quivering.

He gestured to the phone. 'I'm waiting.'

'Get the hell out of here.'

He stood up and he slapped her, hard. She fell across a stack of counterfeit SpongeBob DVDs, scattering them to the floor.

'Hostile takeover or heroin and whoring, bitch, decide. I don't have all day.'

She looked up at him, her mouth trembling. 'Hostile takeover.'

'That's the right decision. You'll see I treat my employees very well. Unless you betray me. If that happens you'll be dreaming up chances of suicide, because you'll see death as the least of all evils.'

He opened his phone, made another call.

'Bring someone who knows computers. I want to know what photos have been scanned here, what emails sent, even if they've deleted the photos or the emails. Keep Ricki off the systems.' He listened. 'No, man, you don't get to rape her when you're done. Behave, all right?' He winked at Ricki. 'She's one of us now.'

He clicked off the phone. 'I think Jin Ming will know when we find him that you must have squealed on him. Let him think you cared about him, until then. He calls you, you say nothing. You warn him, our deal changes.' He patted the top of her head; she flinched.

He headed for Schipol airport to catch the next flight to New York.

A notebook. Of all the things to be afraid of. Of all the things that could destroy him.

21

Claiborne Hotel, Manhattan

I awoke with a start. I'd fallen asleep with my clothes on, on the bed, exhaustion piercing past the feverish high I'd had running for hours. I hate sleeping in my clothes; it always feels like the sleep has seeped into the fabric. I heard the knock on the door again, insistent. I'd put out the Do Not Disturb sign. I reached for my gun and then remembered I didn't have one. There was so much paperwork involved in transporting a gun; I'd get one from my bar, The Last Minute, later.

'Sam. It's me.' Leonie.

I glanced at the clock. Ten in the morning. I got to my feet and opened the door.

'I want you to order coffee and breakfast for us, to your room. I don't want the maid to see my room right now.'

'Why not?'

Leonie rolled her eyes. 'Do what I tell you. Coffee, two pots, French roast. Breakfast, make it big, I don't know when we'll eat again. Come get me when the food is here.' She turned and went back into her room.

I obeyed her, ordering us a spread and two pots of coffee. I showered like a man running late, pulled on jeans and a fresh shirt that I could wear untucked. I checked my personal phone, where Mila would call me. There was no message. Maybe she'd keep her distance. There was no message on the phone Anna had given me.

The food arrived: two omelets, bacon, bagels, hash browns, juice, coffee. A New York room service breakfast only costs a fraction of the national debt. I signed the check and then knocked on her door.

'Bring it here, it's going to be a working meal,' she said.

She held the door for me while I carried in the big trays.

The walls were covered with white sheets of paper, big ones, as though torn from a presentation pad, and scarred with heavy marker. The laptop lay open and it looked like she was in a chat room. An ashtray, full, sat next to it.

'I didn't know you smoked,' I said.

'I'd quit. When Taylor was born. Now I've started again and I hate it.'

Leonie sat down and began to shovel the cheese and mushroom omelet into her mouth. 'I hate cold food,' she said. She ate with concentration for a long minute while I drank a cup of coffee, which I needed like oxygen. 'Okay. First things first. Jin Ming did not exist before he arrived at Delft.'

'False identity.' I raised an eyebrow, reached for my own plate of food.

'His student transcripts are almost perfect.'

'You broke into the university's server?'

She shrugged. 'Universities are easy to hack; they have to maintain large networks with lots of unsophisticated users – even at a technical university. Think of a college as one giant coffee shop, everyone with a laptop. It's not hard.' She ate some more, so fast I thought she wasn't tasting the food. 'All his documentation points to him being from Hong Kong. Makes it easy then to explain his excellent English. But I dug deeper. There is a Jin

Ming from Hong Kong who shares his birthday on the university records; he died at the age of five, drowned in Repulse Bay.'

'Our target hijacked an identity.'

'Yes. And filled in the back details. He supposedly attended Hong Kong International School there, falsified transcripts. The actual prep school has no record of him.'

'Did you break into their computer database?'

'Oh, no. I called, pretending to be from New York University.'

I sat down. 'Why would Jin Ming pretend to be from China so he could go to grad school? I mean, people fake IDs so they can clean money, so they can cross borders. Who the hell steals an identity so that he can go to graduate school in Holland? And pretends to be Chinese? What if he got deported? He'd totally be screwed.'

Leonie smiled. 'So if you see someone with a Chinese passport, you don't entertain the notion that he's *not* Chinese. He can't be who you're looking for.'

'Brilliant,' I said slowly.

'Jin Ming means "golden name". A legitimate name, yes, but I think there's even a sense of purpose behind his selection. A golden name, one perfect for him to hide behind.'

I rubbed my forehead. 'This is not an ordinary kid, is he?' Dumb people are easy to hunt; smart people are a challenge.

'I think he's a fugitive.' Leonie crossed her arms. 'Someone who is hiding but badly wants to continue his education, and especially at a prestigious technical university. And not very many people would think to falsify Chinese documents because they're afraid of being deported to China and then not getting out. It's actually very smart. Right now when I see a Belgian or a Costa Rican passport I straight away start to think it's been faked; they're the most popular nationalities for people who want to disappear. I think he picked Hong Kong because he'd been there before, maybe he could pass as a native. But my guess is he's American or Canadian or English or Australian.'

'Surrendering to the CIA in New York? He must be American.'

She shrugged. 'Don't make assumptions. For all their faults, the CIA is still the most powerful intelligence agency in the world, and our mysterious Mr Jin may just want to deal with the biggest.'

'For all their faults?' I said. 'You sound like a veteran.'

A blush spread across her cheeks, up to her auburn hair. 'Don't. I'm not. I don't have anything to do with the CIA.'

'So what now? You look for criminal computer science students of Chinese descent who have gone missing?'

'Yes, actually, I do,' she said. 'But here's the other thing, Sam. New York. If Jin Ming wants to surrender to the CIA, why isn't he doing it in Amsterdam? There are agents there. They could easily pick him up. Why does he need to run?'

'You ask like you know the answer.'

'I do. Right now he's wanted in Amsterdam.' She pulled up a web page of the Amsterdam English language paper. 'He left a hospital where he was a patient. A man was found dead there, beaten to death with a metal pole. The dead man has a criminal history as hired muscle.'

'They tried to kill him once before.'

'Yes. And the supposedly helpless hacker killed the thug.' Leonie sounded almost proud of him. 'The police seem to think Jin's in danger, and running, and are trying to get him to surrender.'

'But he could still surrender to the CIA there. In fact, he has even more reason to because he's being hunted. But he's not turning himself in to the closest CIA office. What's here? What's in New York?' I said. I hadn't thought of this. The kid had to have a compelling reason to take the risk to come to New York.

'Two reasons,' I said. 'He knows a CIA contact here.' August had dealt with him in Amsterdam; maybe while in their care he'd heard something that tied August to New York, and wanted to meet him specifically. I didn't know the whole story of what had gone on between them when August grabbed Jin Ming from the coffee shop.

Leonie waited.

'Or he's from here, and he's running home.'

'Why run home?' she asked. 'He's been very smart as to how he hid himself. Very. If he's a fugitive from here, it implies he's wanted here. Huge risk to return.'

'Maybe he has family he wants to collect and protect. Maybe he needs to say goodbye to them if he's going to vanish.'

'I assume that if he was living in Holland under a false name he's already vanished once before.' Exhaustion crept into her voice. We couldn't let the toxic mix of lack of sleep and emotional turmoil derail us. 'If he was already hiding, then why does he come home? That seems to be a bigger risk than he needs to take.'

I shrugged. 'I've heard of people in witness protection coming home. They just get tired of living a lie.'

'My clients don't do that. Once I hide them they stay hidden.'

I don't know what possessed me. 'Nice. I mean, you shelter people fleeing murder raps. Scum that Novem Soles needs protected. Nice.'

'You don't know a single thing about what I do or who I help.'

'As if you'd tell.' She knew more about me than I knew about her. Whose fault was that?

141

She raised an eyebrow at me, took a long drink of coffee to let the tension melt in the room. I felt mad at myself for provoking her. I needed her right now; moral judgments had to be saved for later. 'If he's from New York, then that narrows down the possibilities considerably.'

I leaned forward and looked into her computer screen, studying the chat room, with nested columns of comments to show threads of conversation. 'What is this site?'

'DarkHand. A hacker community.' She started to type. 'That's how I found out about Jin Ming. I found hackers who had existing back doors into the systems I needed to access. By the way, you're paying them for their time.'

'How much?'

'You'll launder some money for them. Both are Chinese, they want to clean about fifty thousand bucks into US accounts. You'll make that happen.'

'How, exactly?'

'Through your bar in Las Vegas.'

She knew about The Canyon Bar. Not just that it was where I'd met Anna but that I owned it. 'Your hacker friends are not washing their dirty money through my bar.' God only knew what the money might be. Hackers might have cracked open ATMs for cash, might have committed extortion not to bring company websites down. She was involving me in new crimes. She seemed almost amused at my outrage.

'You can't refuse. The deal is done. It's for the children.'

She was, of course, absolutely right. 'For the children': the three most powerful words in the language. Fine, I thought. I'd deal with that problem later. 'Don't make any more promises you can't keep.'

'Do you want to find this guy or not?' She stood up, rage bright in her eyes. 'You'll do what I say. No argument.'

142

'Calm down,' I said. 'I have every right to know if you're dragging me and my business into criminal activity.'

'And I have every right not to care.'

I let five beats pass in peace. 'So. Let's operate under the proposition he has a personal tie back to New York.'

She nodded. 'We find the tie, we find him.' She turned back to the laptop. 'Let me get back to work. Thanks for breakfast.'

'And, what? I wait? No.'

'Do you have any idea on how to be useful?' Her voice had taken on a hard edge to it. 'I find him, you kill him, bullet. You have the easier job.'

'I don't get to ask my crooked friends for help,' I said. Which was a lie. I had resources, through the Round Table, that I had no intention of sharing with her. I gave her my cell phone number. She didn't write it down but she repeated it back to me.

'Where are you going?' she asked as I headed for the door.

I didn't answer her. She didn't need to know. Her way was going to take too long.

22

Chelsea, New York City

Most code names in the Company are not jokes, but his was: Fagin. Charles Dickens's master of thieves from *Oliver Twist*, who pulled in the wayward children of London to shape them into pickpockets. The Fagin I knew put his own modern take on the identity.

I took the subway south to Chelsea. It was mid-morning now, and shoppers walked the streets, eyeing the art in the many gallery windows. I walked down to the last address I knew for Fagin. I hoped he hadn't moved. I went up to the top floor of his building, knocked, listened. I picked the lock and went inside.

It was a large apartment (I didn't even want to think about how much it cost) and still his place. A picture of Fagin and his wife hung on the wall, smiling, tropical forest behind them. He was thin and wore a reddish beard and had very dark brown eyes, the color of coffee. Dirty breakfast dishes stood stacked in the sink; a coffee mug half full. I lived in spare apartments/offices above bars; I was starting to forget what it was like to live in an actual home. Lucy and I had owned a beautiful place in London, not far from the British Museum. A home that was a comfort to return to in the evening, full of touches of the life we were building together. Best not to dwell on that right now. You might guess that a person named for the Fagin in *Oliver Twist* would not respond to a sentimental plea to help me save my poor child.

It was a four-bedroom apartment. One bedroom had an IKEA bed, a scattering of men's and women's clothes on the furniture and the floor. Fagin was a bit of a slob. The second bedroom had six computers in it, all along a table, a bean bag chair, a TV with an elaborate game station attached. Fagin – still up to his old tricks.

Two young Oliver Twists – maybe sixteen or so – sat at the computers, plugged into their iPods. In their envelope of music they hadn't noticed me. So I went back to the kitchen, got an apple from Fagin's fridge, and washed it. I took a knife from a drawer because I didn't know these sixteen-year-olds and I went back to the computer room.

I bit into my apple and came up behind the first Oliver Twist. He was a thin kid, brown, curly hair, a scattering of pimples on his cheeks. He was intent on what he was doing on the computer screen, fingers hammering on the keyboard.

I glanced at the screen over his shoulder. Computer code, but with comments written in Russian. I scanned them. Interesting mischief the Oliver Twists were conjuring.

I popped out an earplug and said, 'Hi, whatcha doing?'

He jumped out of his chair. His eyes widened at the knife in my hand.

'Uh . . . uh.'

The other kid – African American, a bit older, wearing a New Orleans Saints T-shirt, jeans and the ugliest yellow sneakers I'd ever seen – bolted out of his chair. I showed him the knife and he stopped.

'What. Are. You. Doing?' I asked again.

Neither answered. 'Hacking into China or Russia today, boys?' I pretended like I hadn't read over their shoulders and took another bite of the apple. 'Or perhaps another country? Fagin loves putting the screws on Egypt and Pakistan.'

Again, neither answered. They glanced at each other.

'Silence bores me,' I said. 'It makes me want to play knife games.' Aren't I nice, threatening teenagers?

'Russia,' the Saints fan said after a moment. 'We're laying data bombs into their power grid.'

'Sounds very patriotic,' I said. 'Is Fagin due here soon?'

The Saints fan nodded. 'Yes. He went to go get snacks.'

'You poor, deprived things didn't run out of Red Bull, did you?'

'Um, actually, we ran out of Pepsi,' the thin kid said.

'Well, far be it from me to interfere,' I said. 'Fagin's an old friend. I'm just going to wait for him.'

Slowly they sat back down and put their hands on their computer keyboards and resumed their work, typing at a much slower level. But neither slipped their earbuds back into place.

I ate my apple and watched them and waited.

Fagin showed up ten minutes later, opening his door, holding a paper bag of groceries. He dropped the bag when he saw me. An orange tumbled from the depths and rolled to my foot.

'What the hell. Sam Capra.'

'Hi, Fagin.'

His mouth shut tight. I picked up the orange and tossed it to him. He caught it.

'Are you going to run or shut the door?' I asked.

He shut the door. He set the small bag of groceries down on the counter. He went to the door and made sure the two Oliver Twists were fine.

'Please,' I said. 'I wouldn't hurt your kids.'

'He stole an apple,' said the Saints fan.

'Really? Did he interfere with your work?'

'No,' they both said.

'Back to it.'

Almost as one, the Oliver Twists put their earbuds back in place. Fagin set a can of cold soda by each of them. The typing speed on the keyboards increased.

Fagin crossed his arms and said, 'Whatever you want, the answer is no.'

'That's a harsh hello,' I said.

I had met Fagin back in my days working on the CIA's task force on global crime aka Special Projects aka The Dirty Down Jobs We Gotta Do But No One Is Supposed To Know. Our

146

purview covered everything from human trafficking to arms dealing to corporate espionage, in the aspect of when it threatened national security. Crime at this level, hand in hand with terrorism, is a threat to the stability of the West. It reaches inside and poisons government, it undermines the basic social contract down to the bone of civilization. Twenty per cent of the economy is now illicit. The criminals are becoming more mainstream.

But in stopping this crime we sometimes committed crimes ourselves. Fagin was an example. Remember reading in the news, when Russia and its much smaller neighbor, Georgia, got into that brief war a while back? The Russians launched not only bullets and missiles at Georgia, they took down all of Georgia's internet access. With a massive cyber attack against critical servers, the Russians managed to cut off an entire nation of four million people from the internet. If you were inside Georgia, and you tried to access CNN or the BBC web pages, you got served Russian propaganda. If you tried to withdraw money from Georgian banks, your funds stayed put. If you tried to email people in other parts of the country, you sat and stared at your unsent message still warming your mailbox. The cyber attack, the Russians claimed, was not done by government hackers, but rather by patriotic, good-hearted, milk-drinking Russians acting independently who wanted to help fight the enemy. After the war, NATO and the highly irritated Georgians determined that some of the hackers who launched the internet attack were tied to some of the most notorious criminal rings inside Russia. If this vigilante hacker corps wasn't an official part of the government, they were at least protected by the government, and their presence gave the Russian leadership necessary and plausible deniability.

The best hackers are not always on government payrolls. Sometimes you need your hackers to not be connected to you, when you spend days breaking laws and flouting treaties.

Fagin was our back pocket, our deniable warrior. He and his digital Oliver Twists. When we needed things broken or stolen and there was no way it could be tied to the CIA, ever, then Special Projects and Fagin stepped in to pick the pocket and scurry away.

'You don't work for Special Projects any more, Sam,' he said. 'Get out.'

'I'm a freelance consultant, like you. Not exactly on the formal benefits package.'

'Really? *Really?*' Fagin's favorite word, delivered with a sneer. I had once counted how many times Fagin uttered *Really?* in a meeting and stopped at fifty.

'I am here to ask you for a favor.'

'Really? I repeat. Get out.'

'I'm pressed for time. Tell me what I want to know or I'll tell the North Koreans about you and your crew. And the Russians. And the Chinese. And the Iranians.' Fagin and his cadre of hackers spied on and created hassles for a variety of enemies. Maybe even some friends. Let me just say the French, the Brazilians, and the Japanese also all have reason to hate Fagin. They just don't know it.

'You really wouldn't dare.'

'My child's life is really at stake, Fagin, so, yeah, I would. Sit down. We're going to talk.'

He sat. He still looked like the computer teacher he'd once been, in a New York high school. On the back wall was a Teacher of the Year award he'd gotten years before, back when he still taught, smelling of chalk, dry-erase pens and fusty computer labs. Of course. Fagin had been so talented at encouraging young talent and honing minds. Unfortunately he encouraged them to hack into banks and government databases, usually as a prank. Special Projects had recruited him when he and his keyboarding artful dodgers tried to delve (unwittingly) into a front company for the CIA, kept him and his iPodded foundlings from a prison sentence and guided him toward more constructive pursuits. To the outside world he worked as a software design consultant.

'Your child's life? Aren't you being really melodramatic?'

He didn't know anything about my personal life – as far as I knew.

'I'm looking for a young hacker, of Chinese descent, who might have grown up here in New York.'

'Oh, that narrows it down.' He rolled his eyes. 'Really. Do you want the left or the right side of the phone book?'

'Do you know a hacker who's vanished in the past couple of years?'

'No.' I saw his crossed arms tighten for just a moment. I would have to ask very precise questions to get a useful answer. The basic principle of Fagin's psychology is that knowledge and intelligence are the only currencies. Really.

I produced my cell phone. I didn't say anything. I just wanted him to see it. Right now it was more frightening than a loaded gun.

'I think he was from New York and he did something bad enough to hide out under a false name, Jin Ming, at grad school at Delft University of Technology. He has come back to New York, at huge risk, when he has every reason to dig a tunnel below a Dutch canal and hide for the next ten years. So I'm thinking it's for a family reason.'

'A lot of Asian kids study computers, but not a lot turn to hacktivism. Cultural mores. More respect for authority in Chinese families.' Fagin studied his fingertips. 'Not to stereotype or generalize, really.'

'So how many do you know?'

'Well, several, still. A few came through my, um, camp. I've kept tabs on them.'

'Because you don't want them talking about their work with you or because you'll need them again?'

'Both. If I show you their faces, will you leave?'

'I need a name, Fagin.'

'And then what?'

'You don't say anything to Special Projects that I was here, and I don't give your home address and real name to your many enemies overseas.'

'I'm really hurt. I don't think you'd do that, Sam.'

'My child. The rules are off.'

He stood. I followed him to one of the computers. I leaned close. I wanted to be sure he didn't send an email to August or anyone else in Special Projects. Hackers are trickier and more subtle than pickpockets. He could hit a keystroke and reformat the entire network for all I knew. Watching Fagin at a keyboard was like watching the cobra slowly rise and undulate from the reed basket.

'I keep a dossier on all the Oliver Twists,' he said. He entered in a passcode too fast for me to register it, then another one, then another. He had a file labeled TWISTS and he opened it up. Dozens of names. He clicked on a few and their files opened. Complete with pictures. I doubt Fagin had made them stand still for a picture; these looked stolen from passport and driver's license pictures. Or even school pictures: some of the kids looked to be barely thirteen or fourteen. Your government at work, ladies and gentlemen.

He began to click through the photos while I watched. 'No. No. No,' I said.

It would have been too much to hope that Jin Ming had worked for him; if so, then if he wanted to surrender to someone he could have run straight back to Fagin. 'None of these are Jin Ming.'

'Jin Ming. Jin Ming. I remember a Jack Ming.'

'Jack Ming. That name's too close to Jin Ming for it to be a good alias.'

'Don't be stupid. Jin would be the surname, not Ming. He'd be called Ming by his friends, not Jin. And a good alias is one you can remember.' He sat down, searched on Jack Ming on a Google search. News reports came up. A picture.

'Oh, yeah,' Fagin said. 'Him.'

It was the young Chinese hacker. 'That's him. What did he do?'

'I only knew him by reputation. Supposedly he hacked Bruce Springsteen's laptop once. Stole recordings of an album in development.'

'That is such heresy. And that's why he's a fugitive.'

Fagin fidgeted. 'Um, no, he was really good at hacking copiers.'

'Copiers?' I raised an eyebrow.

'Yes. Office copiers. Most of them have microchips now, and they have internet capability. They can connect to the web if they have a repair that needs to be made. They can either self-download a fix if it's a software problem or tell the repairman exactly what parts to bring.'

'And Jack Ming would hack ... copiers?'

'Yes. He would rewrite the software in the copier.' Fagin tented his cheek with his tongue.

'To do what?'

'Well, you could rewrite software on the chip to overheat the copier, damage it or destroy it. He set a copier on fire at a firm where his mother worked as a consultant. The sprinklers came out, caused several thousand dollars' worth of damage.'

'Big deal. Is his mommy ignoring him?'

'Or,' and Fagin gave his throat a polite clearing, 'you could program the copier to save an image of everything it scanned and email it to you.'

'Wow.' Okay, that was huge. Consider what a compromised copier could give you: business proposals, legal filings before they were given over to the court, product plans, confidential memos. Even with email now, paper copies of critical documents were still used. You could learn a lot about a company, a project, sifting through every image that came across the copier. 'Corporate espionage, Fagin?'

'Maybe, just a touch.'

'Is that why Jack Ming had to leave New York?'

Fagin gave a slow nod. 'He stole secrets from companies, and he must have tried to sell them. Or somehow they backtracked the hacking to him. I think if he could make copiers spy for him, he could write other software to do the same.'

I considered. Maybe he had, maybe this was how he'd stolen Novem Soles's secrets.

Fagin shrugged. 'Um, I don't think he'd come back here to see family.'

'Why?'

Fagin cracked his first smile. 'Well, the rumor was, he caused his dad's death.'

23

Midtown Manhattan, New York City

His mother's apartment was several blocks north of the United Nations Plaza, on East 59th Street. It was convenient, and his mother had always treasured a smooth road in life. She was not a woman who cared for bumps along the ride.

Jack Ming didn't recognize the doorman, and he didn't have a key, so he sat in a small, elegant tea shop across the street, sipping a strong cup of Earl Grey, staving off jet lag, waiting for her to come home. The sky rumbled, louder than the traffic. The clouds began to smother the hard, bright morning light. A warm, gusty rain began to fall fitfully. He watched an umbrella salesman suddenly appear on the street corner; it was almost as if the rain had conjured the man out of thin air. It was unusually warm in New York after the unseasonable chill of Amsterdam.

He thought he would never be back here. He had expected a tidal wave of emotion; but instead, worse, he felt a slow, rising flood of remorse and sorrow. The kind that drowned you by inches.

He tasted the risk, like wet steel on his tongue. Novem Soles might send a hired troll, like the one he'd killed in Amsterdam, to watch his mother and kill him if he turned up. Or maybe the CIA had figured out who he was after he made his offer. Of all the moves he'd made since being shot, coming home felt like the most dangerous one. He glanced around. If her apartment was being watched then the watchers should have grabbed him the moment he appeared across the street. He tucked an earphone bud into place but he kept the iPod silenced. He had called the house using a prepaid phone he had bought when he arrived in Manhattan. As he got his mother's answering machine, he had hung up and decided simply to go to her apartment. His father had been wealthy and the Mings had invested carefully from their days in Hong Kong and she still worked as a consultant from her home when she pleased.

Mom, come home, he thought. He tried her home phone again. No answer. She could be traveling for work, which could mean she was anywhere from South America to Hong Kong to Canada. She could be screening her calls. He could try and hack into her laptop; she wasn't very security conscious. But that felt like rifling through her clothing drawers, or love letters from her teenage years. You didn't hack your mom.

He waited, watching the warm, intermittent rain streak the glass, his heart pounding. She might spit in his face. She might scream for the police. She might call him his father's murderer again and he wasn't sure he could take that pain.

24

Fagin's Nest, Chelsea, New York City

Fagin poured himself coffee. He didn't offer me any.

'Sandra Ming is former State Department. Now she consults. Very well connected in both business and government. She sits on boards of directors for two Fortune 1000 companies. American-born but related to a prominent Hong Kong family. The husband's name was Russell Ming. Real-estate developer, he died about the time that Jack vanished. Owned properties around New York and New Jersey. Heart attack about the time Jack lit out.'

For a moment Fagin's eyes went merry.

'Heart attack over his son's crimes?' I asked.

'The rumor mill suggested,' Fagin said.

'That's a hard cross for a kid to bear,' I said.

Fagin made a noise. He'd seen as many damaged kids as a social worker. 'Life is full of hard crosses. If I could have recruited him I could have shielded him. The Oliver Twists have never, ever been caught.'

'Connected to government and business,' I said, repeating Fagin's own words. Could his mother shield him, or help him reach the CIA without me finding him? I had one choice: I had to go to the mother's house. I glanced up at Fagin.

'Would Jack contact hackers here in town? Did he know any of your Twists?'

'Not if he wants to keep his head low. If there's a price on him, I might be tempted to collect it.'

'At least you're consistent, Fagin.'

'And what a joy that makes me.'

'But you, you're not likely to turn him into the police. You don't like talking to the police, Fagin.'

'In my defense, they don't much like talking to me, either.'

'Where does Mrs Ming live?'

Fagin consulted a computer database. I looked at the photo of his mother we'd loaded into a browser: it showed an elegant woman touching her chin in that weird author-photo pose. She was pretty, but in a cold, cubic way.

He gave me Mrs Ming's address.

'Thank you.'

'That's it? Thank you?'

'You're not going to tell anyone that I'm here, Fagin.'

'Wouldn't dream of it.'

'Because I will tell the people who are looking for Jack Ming that you might know where he is. And if I do that, they will order me to force information from you, and then to kill you.'

'You should find a better class of person for your associates,' Fagin said. 'And, really, you needn't turn into a bully.'

'Tell me, hacker man,' I said. 'Have you ever heard of a hacker in Las Vegas named Leonie?'

'Leonie, growl, I like kitty-kat-style names,' Fagin said.

'Just answer.'

'No. But you know, online, we don't use our real names.' He widened his eyes. 'Shocking, I know.'

'She's a relocator for people who want to vanish. She deals with hackers around the world to get information or to help her create new identities.'

'She's not a hacker, then, she's an information broker. Hires hackers to do a bit of a job for her, then uses someone else. That way you never know exactly what it is she's working on or who it is she's working for.'

'You know anything about her?' I showed him the picture of her I'd taken on my phone when she slept.

'You bored her into a sense of complacency to get this picture, right?'

'Have you seen her before?'

'No. But isn't she the pretty one?'

'You ever hear of a woman named Anna Tremaine?'

He considered, and shook his head.

'How about Novem Soles?'

'Sounds like a Catholic retreat.'

'It means Nine Suns in Latin. You ever hear of a group with that name?'

'No.'

I got up. 'Thanks for what you could give me, Fagin.'

'I can give you one more thing. Good luck, Sam, on finding your kid.'

I must have let my surprise show.

'What, I can't wish you luck?'

'Just keep your mouth shut, Fagin, about me being here.'

'I don't stand between kids and their parents, man. By the time the kids come to me the parents have already shoved them away.'

Fagin watched Sam leave. Then he reached for a phone. Sam Capra could make all the threats he wanted, but he did not pay the bills.

Fagin reported the discussion, and then he hung up to go see if the Oliver Twists were done laying their electronic mousetraps inside Moscow's power grid.

25

Midtown Manhattan, New York City

An hour later Jack saw her.

His mother came along the sidewalk, walking in her stiff, formal way, wearing a light blue raincoat. Her hair was impeccably styled and more gray streaked it than he remembered. She held bags from a local artisan grocery, and the plastic bulged with her purchases. He crossed the street, cutting toward her.

Please don't turn away, he thought. Please don't.

He stood and he waited for her to come to him. 'Hi, Mom.'

She stopped and glanced up from the sheltering curve of the umbrella and seemed to study him as though he were a picture she'd found in a drawer, and couldn't place when and where it had been taken. Every moment of her silence was an agony. He wanted the concrete beneath his feet to open like a chasm and swallow him. Drops of rain curtained off her tilted umbrella. 'Jack. Hello.' She just didn't seem ... surprised.

He reached for the bag of groceries. 'Those look heavy.' He could see in the bag rice and chicken, but also Oreos, apples, jalapeño potato chips. Weird, she still bought his favorites.

She allowed him to take them. 'Yes, they are. Thank you.'

'Could we talk for a minute?'

'For just a minute?' she asked and now he heard the slight edge of pain in her voice.

'Not for long. I know you're busy, Mom.' It had been the litany of his youth: not now, Jack, I'm busy. Yes, darling, I'll look at your painting in a minute, Mama's busy. I can help you with your math later, Jack, right now I'm busy. And finally: what do the police want to talk to you about, I've got a meeting with the Ambassador. He remembered announcing once, when he was nine, that he was Ambassador of Kidonia, the nation of kids, and she'd laughed and hugged him and not realized he was begging for her attention. He was proud of himself for keeping the bitterness out of his voice.

'Actually, I'm not, and I'm very pleased to see you.' She reached over and gave him an awkward hug. The last hug he'd gotten from her was when he graduated early from NYU, two years ago. Before the FBI showed up at the doorstep, looking for him. He resisted the urge to embrace her, to seize her hard in a hug from which she couldn't easily escape.

She put a hand on the side of his face. He tried not to close his eyes in relief. 'What happened to you? Your neck, that's a surgical scar.'

'I was in an accident.' They shot me Mom, I got shot. Your son got shot. But he couldn't say this, even the thought of the words rising in his throat made him sick.

'What accident?'

'It doesn't matter.'

'Of course it matters, Jack. Why didn't you call me? Where have you been?'

'It doesn't matter.' The nakedness of the lie nearly made him gasp but instead he just held on tight to his mother. After a moment her hands touched his back, pressed into his flesh, cautiously.

'Jack, are you all right? Perhaps we should go inside.' A bit of panic edged her voice.

He pulled back from her and he felt, mixed with the wet air, tears on his face. He felt mortified. She said nothing as he wiped them away with the back of his hand. Her own face was dry, as it always was.

'Have you come back to turn yourself in to the police?'

She was a diplomat, so he gave the diplomatic answer. 'Yes. I'm tired of running, I'm tired of hiding. I wanted to see you first. Before I go to the police.' No, Mom, I came to say goodbye, he wanted to say. Goodbye forever. I shouldn't have come. It's too hard.

'Well come inside, we'll have some coffee and we'll call the lawyers.'

She was still briskly efficient, he thought. 'I just want us to talk first. You and me. Before lawyers, okay?'

His mother hurried him past the doorman and they rode in silence in the elevator, up to the apartment. He wanted to look at her face but instead he watched the umbrella weep leftover rain onto the floor. Jack stepped inside and despite the muggy warmness of the spring day he felt chilled. The apartment was as he remembered: magazine-perfect, accented with her collection of Chinese art on the red walls, along with photos of his mother with presidents, business leaders, diplomats, and other notables. Art from her various postings in the State Department: Hong Kong, Vietnam, South Korea, Peru, Luxembourg. It was as though she'd played magpie around the world, plucking beauty wherever she stopped, decorating a nest where no other birds wished to live. There was a family picture of himself and his father, off in a corner. On the periphery of his mother's life, the edge of the circle.

'Would you like some decaf?' she asked.

'Do you have any regular coffee? I'm zonked.'

'Um, no. I now find too much caffeine disruptive.'

Only a food could be disruptive to you, Mom, he thought. Jack felt torn by need and resentment, two ends of the same rope, tugging straight through him. 'Decaf is great.'

'Are you hungry?'

'No.' He followed her into the kitchen, watched her putter with the coffee maker. 'How are you, Mom?' I shouldn't have come here. The sudden temptation to tell her everything, lay out an epic confession of the danger he faced, to ask her for help was overwhelming. *Say your goodbyes, and go, and don't look back, ever. No good will come of anything else.*

'I'm all right.'

'You still consulting?'

'Yes, here and there. Thinking of writing another book.'

'I'm glad.'

She poured water into the coffee maker. 'Jack, where have you been hiding?'

'The Netherlands.'

'I suppose I should have considered that as a possibility. So many young people from around the world, crowding around the canals. You went there for the drugs, I suppose.'

'No, Mom, I went to grad school. I tried pot but frankly I would rather read a good book or see a movie.'

She blinked. A smile wavered near her mouth. 'Grad school. On the run from the police, you go back to school.'

'Well, under an assumed name.'

'How did you get a new identity? Transcripts? How did you pay for tuition?' Then she raised her hand, as if warding off a flash of fire. 'Never mind. Best I don't know what additional crimes you've committed. You can tell the attorney. My God, now the Dutch will be bringing up charges against you.'

Including manslaughter, he thought, maybe. Best not to go there.

'I would like to see Dad's grave.'

'There is no grave. I had him cremated. He's in the study.'

'He's here?'

Now she turned back toward the coffee maker. 'Of course, did you think I threw him out?'

'They call it spreading the ashes, Mom.'

'Well, he's still here.'

He wandered back into the den. An urn sat atop a large bookshelf, next to a row of volumes on art history. It was very pretty. He felt tears hot inside his face, aching for release. He glanced at the desk, at the carpet, the grief a well in him, deep and dark, and every awful memory rushed back in an unbidden surge.

'How could you be so thoughtless?' His father's voice rising in shock and shame. 'The police want to arrest you. What you've done is a felony.'

'I know.'

'A felony! What the hell did your mother and I ever do to you to deserve this? You've destroyed your life, do you understand that? Over what? Pranks? Proving that you're smarter than everyone else? Because all you've done, Jack, is prove that you're stupid beyond compare.'

'Yes. I'm sorry. I'm so sorry.'

'Sorry you did it or that you were caught?'

'I don't know. I just did it.'

'You're not innocent? It's not a mistake?'

'No, sir. I did it all.'

'Why? Why? Did you sell the information you stole?'

'No. I don't know why I did it.'

'You expect me . . . ' his father caught his breath, 'you expect me to believe that a boy as smart as you is incapable of knowing his own motives?'

'I just did it, it's done.' Jack's voice broke. 'I love you, Dad, I'm sorry. I love you.'

'You love me? Then why do you flush your future down the toilet?'

'That's all you care about, my future?'

'Are you trying to suggest you did this for our attention, Jack? Oh, please. That's such a shallow reason. Babyish, almost.'

'I don't know why. I just don't.'

The agony in his father's eyes had cut Jack more deftly than any ax. Then his father had sat down at his desk, pulled a yellow legal pad toward him, picked up a pencil. He began scribbling thoughts on the paper. 'We have to start considering your options. Your mother . . . and I . . .'

And then his father, bunching up the cloth of his shirt over his chest with a surprised fist, saying 'That's not right . . .' and then collapsing to the carpet.

His mother, hurrying in, screaming his father's name. Jack grabbing the phone, calling 9-1-1, pleading for the ambulance to hurry.

He'd set the phone down and then his mother, very calmly, said: 'Get out.'

'The ambulance is coming, Mom.'

'Get out.'

'I can't, I won't leave him.'

'You did this. Your selfish stupidity did this to him and I want you gone.' She knelt by her husband; she didn't look at her son. 'You have to go or the police will arrest you.'

'Mom, I can't leave Dad.'

'You know, in jail, there will be no computers. I don't quite know what you will do.' Odd, her calm.

'I don't care.'

'He's dead.' His mother looked at him with a fierce, burning glare that frightened him, because it was hatred. 'You've taken him away from me. Go. Get out of my sight right now, Jack. I don't ever want to see you again.'

He had turned and ran and when he went out of the building the ambulance was at the curb, lights flashing, too late.

*

163

His mother stood in the doorway, watching him stare at the urn. 'I think, from a legalistic standpoint, Jack, you should surrender to an attorney immediately.'

'I wanted a night here, Mom. At home first. Please.'

'Of course.' But the tension was tight in those two words. As if she was the one who was going to be in trouble. She walked back into the kitchen; he followed her.

'I'll stay out of sight. I know what you said before – but if you didn't want to see me you wouldn't have let me come up here. Don't you want to spend time with me?' She didn't answer; she upended the precisely measured water into the brewer. The maker began to chug.

'Of course,' she said again. She was turning over his crimes in her head; he knew the pinched look on her face. What he had done here was nothing compared to his misdeeds in Amsterdam. *Well, I hacked for some bad guys. I didn't know how bad they were but now they want me dead and I have a notebook that they want so badly they will kill me for it because it will blow them open and I don't even understand what I know means and I'm going to sell it to the CIA and you'll never see me again, Mom. But you were already resigned to never seeing me again.*

'I think tomorrow we should call a defense lawyer.'

'You're right, Mom. Tomorrow, okay?'

His mother turned to him, an uncertain smile on her face. 'I'm right? Um, you've never said that before. I don't know what to say.'

'I wouldn't say I told you so. Maybe just enjoy being right. For once.'

She surprised him with a laugh. 'All right, I'll bask in the glow. I am happy to see you, Jack, I really am.'

'Mom . . .'

The awkward silence felt like a curtain. Neither seemed to know what to say, how to lay the first plank in the bridge.

'I wish I hadn't gone to Amsterdam, Mom.' He wanted to grab the words hanging in the air. What had possessed him to confess this? It was pointless. He'd only come to say goodbye before he vanished to Australia or Fiji or Thailand or wherever he went with the CIA money. What was he hoping for? She didn't know what he was here for. She was just someone to whom he needed to say goodbye. 'Jail would have been better. At some point I'd have been free. Now I never will be.'

She said nothing and the coffee maker gurgled in the quiet. 'What kind of new trouble are you in, Jack?'

The back of his eyes felt warm. He blinked. 'I'm not in any trouble, Mom. Any new trouble.' He forced his emotions down, but the heat kept rising into his throat.

'Don't you lie to me, Jack. I know . . . I didn't help you very much before.' She twisted the dishrag in her hands. 'Let me help you now.'

'I can't.'

'You can.'

'I . . . I got involved with some bad people . . . Some really bad people, Mom, I didn't know how bad . . . '

She took a step forward. 'Tell me.'

'They . . . nearly got me killed. I got shot. Hurt bad. Then in the hospital, they sent a guy to kill me.'

He saw her go pale with shock. 'Oh, my God, Jack.'

'I killed the guy. I killed him and I got away and I think they will try and kill me again.'

His mother knotted the dishrag. She didn't take a step toward him and he could see her playing out the possibilities of what they should do next in her mind. 'It was self-defense,' he said.

'Tell me what happened.'

He did.

'Did you see the gun before you hit him?'

The question felt like a shove. 'He shot at me. Mom, for God's sakes, don't you believe me?'

'Yes. Of course. And then you fled.'

'Yes.'

'And then what?'

He did not want to tell her about the notebook. Right now it lay taped to the small of his back. 'Then a friend helped me get out of the Netherlands. On a Belgian passport.' He said this in the tone that he might once have used to admit he cut school.

'You entered the United States under false pretenses, with the Dutch police looking for you?'

'I had to.'

'Jack, you always *have* to do the exact opposite of what you should do.' She put the dishrag on the counter. 'Perhaps something strong with our coffee.'

'Mom. I'm sorry.'

Then she surprised him: 'Don't apologize, Jack. Not for surviving. Not for staying alive.'

'I said more than I meant to.'

She had been walking toward the counter and his words stopped her in her tracks. 'More than you meant to? You weren't going to be honest with me?'

'I was going to be honest with the lawyer,' he lied. 'I didn't want to burden you.'

'Oh, Jack. You think I'm the delicate widow?'

It was two jabs in one. 'You're not delicate, Mom. I don't need to be reminded you're a widow. You're still a mother.' The words spilled out like quicksilver, faster than he could stop them.

'You're right. You're right. The way I spoke to you when your father died . . . well, it's done now. You cannot blame me for you running away and getting into deeper trouble.'

He blinked. 'I don't blame you at all, Mom.'

'Of course you do. You blame me for being a bad mother. You think I'm a bad mother.'

'No. I don't.' He couldn't look at her face.

She mercifully changed the subject. 'Why exactly are these people after you?'

'It's a long story.'

'I'm going to cancel my appointments this afternoon,' she said. 'We'll plan out a strategy. Just you and me. They want you dead because you know something?'

'Yes, ma'am.'

'What?'

'Well, I don't know anything. But they think I do.' Telling her the truth was only putting her in danger. He couldn't do that. He'd lost his father to his mistakes; he was not going to lose his mother.

'All right. But you have information you can give the police. We need to be able to make a deal, Jack. That's what I'm asking. What's your leverage?'

Always the diplomat, always the deal maker. He wanted to turn around and leave. Just walk out the door. Would she call the police on him before he reached the elevator? Or would she let her only son simply vanish again, because in the end it would be less trouble for her?

'I can give them some names. Guys in Amsterdam and New York.'

'Well, then. That's a start. But surely if they want you dead, you know more than that.'

167

'Not really.'

'Why don't . . . I know you're exhausted. Why don't you go get showered? Your clothes – they should still fit, I kept them all.'

'Mom.'

'I knew you'd come home.'

You have more faith than I did, Jack thought. Suddenly the idea of his old room felt like heaven. A cocoon to transform himself, where he could be the old harmless Jack Ming again, not be the kid being chased by the bad guys, not be the guy sneaking into his own country under a false name, not be the disappointing son coming and confessing his sins to his mother. 'I don't want to talk to the lawyer until tomorrow, though, Mom. Okay? We'll call him in the morning.' He would get what he needed here, for the meeting with the CIA, and then he would vanish. This was the goodbye to his mother, every moment of it.

She poured him a cup of coffee and he drank it down in silence. It was delicious. His mother always made good coffee, and he thought it funny that this was the comfort food he remembered of her: not peanut butter sandwiches or handmade ice cream or wonton noodles, but coffee. She'd let him start drinking it too young. Never objecting when he'd dump a dollop from the coffee pot into his milk. Just to see what she would do.

'Are you hungry?' she asked him. Now she sounded like a mom.

'Yes.'

'Well, why don't you go shower and get into some fresh clothes, and I'll make us lunch. Then we can talk.'

'All right.'

She went to the refrigerator and opened it, peering inside, clearly hopeful that appropriate ingredients would be present. He went into his room. It seemed to be an echo of his old life: the framed certificate of achievements from his school in math, the worn paperbacks he'd plowed through as a kid, a neat stack of video games of which he'd explored every detail of every level. A row of CDs he'd forgotten he'd owned, bands that screeched about suburban angst. He thought he'd known then what feeling trapped was like, and, oh, was he wrong.

He turned on the shower, waited, flicked fingers beneath the water. Cold. He wanted it as hot as possible, to rinse the dirt of Amsterdam off himself. He hated to stand by a shower to wait for it to warm. He could go get what he needed while the shower heated; his mother was busy in the kitchen.

He ducked out of his room, padded down the hallway to his father's study. Weird to think of Mom living here in an apartment that seemed more dedicated to men who had left her than to her own life. He ducked into the office. He stepped quickly around the desk – his dad's heart had stuttered and failed, standing in front of that desk, and he didn't like to let his gaze linger on the spot; it creeped him out: he could still hear the thud of the body striking the floor.

He opened the desk drawer. The keys to all seven buildings his father owned in the New York area remained in their places. Mother hadn't sold them, thank God, and he knew better than to ask. He sat at the computer and brought up the Ming Properties website. The Williamsburg, Brooklyn, property was still empty. His father had not been willing to make the investment to renovate it alone and he'd died before he found a partner. Mom hadn't done anything about it, either, and thank God. He took the one set of keys and tucked them into his pocket. She wouldn't think to miss them, not with his surrender – his disappearance – on her mind.

Next to the keys: his father's gun. He'd gotten it when he used to own buildings in neighborhoods that weren't quite gentrified yet. Jack lifted the gun and studied it. He inspected the clip: three shots in it. He double-checked on the safety and he stuck it into his pocket. It felt awkward. He would put it in his knapsack.

He went back toward the shower – it should be nice and steamy now – and it was then that he heard the quiet of her voice. She must have thought he was still in the shower.

She stood, her back to him, speaking softly, over the hiss of boiling water. 'Yes. He's here. Where do you want me to bring him?'

He stood back from the door, the notebook itching in the small of his back.

'No. I won't do that. But I want to make a deal for him.'

Shock reached inside him and wrenched his stomach. She had lied. Who the hell was she calling? A lawyer.

'So where do you want me to bring him?'

Bring him. You promised, Mom. He listened to his mother, sewing up his betrayal.

'Send a car for us. He might . . . resist.' She dumped noodles into the pot. She stirred in chopped vegetables. He took a step backward. 'Not sure I can get him out of the apartment without help.'

Resist? A chill flicked along his spine.

'No. No one else saw him. He wants to hunker down here today.' Silence. 'I am so glad you called me about him. Thank you.'

Jack Ming stepped slowly back from the kitchen. He tiptoed back to his room, back to the hissing steam of the shower. He grabbed his backpack. He left the shower jetting against the

170

porcelain, the steam curling from the bathroom like fingers raised in farewell. He spared his childhood room a final, bitter glance. And then he hurried toward the door.

'Jack?' his mother's voice sliced across the room.

He glanced back at her.

'Goodbye, Mom,' he said.

'You lied to me!' she said. And he knew she meant the shower, that she was the one outraged that he had not done what he said.

'Goodbye. Forever. I still love you.'

'Jack, wait! *Wait!* They can make all the charges go away. They called me, all right, they called me first . . .'

She knew I was coming? Panic flushed through him. He ran, not wanting to wait for the elevator, feet hammering down the stairs.

He bolted into the lobby and out onto the street. He ran the whole way to the 59th Street subway station. He got onto the first train that arrived. He sat huddled on the cold plastic bench, holding the backpack close to him.

Send someone. He might resist. Who the hell had she been talking to? Who would call her before he arrived?

This can't be. Not my mom.

He rode down to Union Square and then he changed trains and rode the L train into Brooklyn, getting off at Bedford Avenue station in Williamsburg. Trust no one, he thought. So much for help and shelter from his mother.

He exited onto Driggs Avenue and crossed the street and watched the faces of those who'd left the train with him. Could his mother have called someone? Could he have been followed? Her betrayal cut him to the point he could not breathe.

They can make all the charges go away. Then who the hell were they?

He was going to have to be very careful. A plan began to form in his mind.

26

Manhattan

On my walk to the subway I texted Leonie, told her that Jin Ming was really a guy named Jack Ming and to drive our rental car and meet me at the East 59th Street address. We were so close now.

If I didn't find Daniel – well, that was an option I couldn't face. Anna's grim words *I won't sell him to nice people* shivered in my blood, like a plucked wire. Daniel, with my eyes and his mother's mouth, handed over to someone who would abuse him, use him, eventually kill him when his usefulness reached its end. Or, if he lived, would the horror he survived shape him into a person bent, wrong, broken. I had never held Daniel, never seen him with my own eyes, but I could never abandon him to such a fate. Never.

It was strange to ride the subway, knowing I was heading to kill someone. A guy who smelled of mints stood too close to me, a girl with purplish, lanky hair stared at my shoes and through her earphones, just once, I could hear distant strains of Mozart, wandering into the train like a lost tourist. Two people across from me chatted in Portuguese and I eavesdropped on their gossip. You spend your childhood traveling the world, you pick up a little of a lot of languages. They were talking about a boyfriend, his pros and cons, his smile, his cheapness in picking restaurants, normal everyday talk, and I was sitting there thinking about how to kill a young man in cold blood.

Across from Sandra Ming's apartment tower stood a sushi bar. It was decorated in a spare, minimalist style and in the background regrettable Japanese pop played, but at least at a whisper. The chef seemed very angry; he scowled as he chopped at the ahi, the sea urchin, the inoffensive salmon. He muttered in Japanese and I nearly told him in his own language that he might consider anger management classes. I could tell from his face that he liked chopping flesh apart. It was good that a man like him had a creative outlet.

I got my lunch and sat watching in the window. The fish, the rice, the wasabi, all had no flavor to me. Rain, heavier in the morning, had lightened. Now the day was gray, the wind carrying the scent of the unfallen storm. I had not seen any sign of Mrs Ming or her son arriving at or leaving the building. I didn't want to think of him as a Jack. Jack Ming sounded like the name of some kid I could have known in any of the American or Anglican schools I'd attended in fourteen different countries in my misspent youth, hauled around the globe by my parents, who worked for a relief agency. They were good people, but more concerned with fixing the world than paying more than five minutes' attention to their own children. I loved them and they appeared to love me, and not much more else to say on that front. I'm sure the armchair psychologists would have a field day dissecting my youth and how it related to my stolen child. But it's not like I could let any child be taken this way. My son or not. There are standards. You have to fight back.

Leonie slid onto the stool next to me. 'You found him.'

'I did.'

'Without a database.' She made it sound like I had somehow cheated.

'Yes.'

She opened up her laptop. 'And now what? We sit here and wait for him to show up and' – she lowered her voice – 'you shoot him dead in the street?'

'No.' I swallowed the last bit of sushi on my plate. It offered only sustenance, not pleasure. Waiting to kill someone makes you feel dead inside.

'We're only supposed to do what Anna told us,' she said and I wondered what she would do if I picked up the chopstick, oiled with soy sauce and wasabi, and shoved it into her ear.

'I have done both my job and a key part of your job so far,' I said. 'You are rapidly losing your right to a vote in this.'

'Sam. Okay. You had resources I didn't. But I found out about Jack Ming, something you didn't know.'

'What?'

'I don't think he will come to see his mother.'

'Why not?'

'She blames him for his father's death.'

I glanced at her. 'How would you know?'

'I built a network of names around Jack Ming,' she said. 'Yes, he went to NYU, so I did searches on people that were in his Facebook account before he canceled it. I wanted to expand our search, see how many links I could find, people where he might hide.'

I didn't ask how she'd gotten this information; she'd worked her stealthy, smoky fingers into the right database or paid off the people who could. 'And?'

'And one of his friends wrote a blog post about Jack's situation. Apparently his father died of a heart attack when he found out that Jack was wanted by the FBI for questioning for hacking copiers and stealing proprietary information from a number of law firms and software companies. He died ... here. At Jack's feet.'

'His friend wrote about this?' Honestly. People will say things on the internet now that they might once not have told their parents. A little secrecy is not a bad thing. I will confess I don't get the whole need to Twitter and Facebook and share my every reaction to a TV show or to bad service at lunch or to post every news article I find remotely interesting. I'd spent five minutes looking at Twitter once and felt I'd wandered into a poker game where everyone immediately displayed their hands against the cool green of the felt. I suppose an ex-spy cannot get over his or her innate quiet, the need to keep thoughts and secrets close. But Jack Ming was a kid, and he'd left electronic breadcrumbs at the feet of his friends.

There is always a trace, she'd said, and now she'd found it.

'His friend wrote about Jack's mother.' She opened the laptop, turned it toward me so I could read:

I understand grief, I think, because my grandparents died when I was young, and my dog died last year. Death is part of life. But what I do not understand is blame. My friend Jack's father died because he got a shock over something Jack is accused of doing, not anything proven. And even if Jack did do this, to blame him for killing his father? What kind of mother says that to her son?

I am thankful for my mom right now.

Good Lord, I thought. What did we do before blogs? Would anyone have written this up and sent it into the newspaper's letters' section or stood on a tottery soapbox at the corner of the park and brayed out their thoughts about a private family matter while still somehow making it all about themselves? Jack must've confided in the friend after his father's death.

I turned my gaze back onto Mrs Ming's building doorway. The doorman stood there, watching the rain. 'So our Jack and Mama Ming are not close.'

'But he's desperate. Truly desperate. And . . .'

'And what?'

'If he's turning himself into the CIA, then he's planning to vanish. Maybe he wants his mother to go with him. Or maybe he's coming here to say goodbye to her. A final goodbye.'

'I don't know.' I didn't want to know this about Jack Ming. I didn't want to know him as, you know, a *person*. I wanted to know where he stood at a certain moment and where I could kill him without getting caught. I closed my eyes. Novem Soles was going to form me into a monster, sure as Dr Frankenstein stitching together the quilt of corpses' castoffs and blasting wasted vein and muscle with electricity. I didn't know what I would be when I arose from the laboratory table, except I hoped I'd be a father with his child back.

But I didn't want to know about Jack Ming's . . . problems. His problems were all going to go away very soon.

Jack Ming's dad dying at his feet. It made me think of Danny. My brother, not my son.

My brother. He'd died in an awful, humiliating way, gone to Afghanistan as part of a relief team. He'd pushed past the boundaries of common sense in his drive to help people, ventured with a college friend into the scrubby hills beyond Kandahar, gotten grabbed. No one heard from him for three weeks and then the video flickered into monstrous life, viraled by YouTube: Danny

176

my brother kneeling on a dried mud floor, surrounded by bala-claved thugs who made him spout nonsense in a voice so quavering it was hardly his own, then spoke their own sacrificial junk, then cut off his head while the camera ticked off every final second. Then they cut his friend's throat.

You think murder splinters a family or brings it closer together? I don't know; depends on how thick the glue has already been laid. But execution is a different kind of murder. When your brother is decapitated with an arm-sized knife because he went to help people, and anyone in the free world can see his final moments courtesy of the unthinking, unblinking internet, then it is your family's worst nightmare made public, made entertainment, made eternal. You can never block the memory of it; the horror is just a few clicks away.

Would you believe people emailed me the link to the video? They did. I don't know why they would, what kink of cruelty drove them, but they did.

'Do you think he could turn to one of these old friends?' I asked.

'He's still wanted for questioning by the FBI. So, he might not get a warm reception from a friend who doesn't want to be made an accessory.'

'Those charges will go away if he gets his meet with the CIA,' I said. 'It'll be part of the surrender deal, guaranteed.'

'But surely his own mother would be the least likely person to turn him in.'

'True. She's a career diplomat. She has a lot to lose if he resurfaces; he could be an embarrassment.'

'So what? We sit here and wait and scarf California rolls all day like private eyes on surveillance? He could have already been here and gone.' The desperation painted her voice.

'No,' I said. 'We go in and, if he's there, well, that's done, and if he's not, we find out where he is.'

A limo slid up to the curb. A uniformed man with a strong build got out, spoke to the doorman.

A few moments later, Sandra Ming stepped outside.

'Where's the rental car?' I said.

'Around the corner, in a garage.'

'I want you to follow that limo, I want to know where she's going.'

Leonie slammed the laptop shut. Mrs Ming spoke with the driver; he appeared to be showing her some sort of ID. The doorman had taken a careful step back toward his usual perch. 'It'll be gone before I can catch up,' Leonie said.

'Just go, wheel around, she'll still be here. I'll make sure.'

'I don't know how to tail a car.'

'Follow where it goes and don't get caught. It's for the children.'

'Thanks.' Leonie sprinted out of the sushi bar, the angry chef glaring at her like she was dodging the bill. I threw ample dollars at the wasabi bowl.

As I came out onto 59th, into the humid curtain of the day, the limo driver closed the rear passenger door behind Mrs Ming and ducked back behind the wheel. I had to time this as carefully as a shot. Get across the street without being hit by either a cab or a bicycle or another car; time it so I got a word with that driver.

I pulled my phone from my pocket, placed it before my eyes, the modern electronic blinder. My thumbs scrabbled on the touchscreen like I was writing the most urgent message in the history of humanity. I kept my gaze down, hung back from the car, trying to move fast enough and also not veer out of the driver's blind spot. I risked a glance. A taxi barreled toward me, but I still had room. He was clearly expecting me to jog, pick up the pace. New York cabbies are reincarnated kamikaze pilots and they subscribe to the inarguable theory that it's best that you get out of their way. It's the food chain at work.

The limo yanked out from the curb, and I stepped right in its way. The right front fender clipped my leg, a nice hard tap that would register not only in my pain centers but inside the limo itself. I yelped and fell, sprawling back into the street, diving like a soccer player hoping for a red card against the opposition, and the cab stopped about a foot from my head; I could see the reflection of my face, carnival-house bent, in the gleam of its newly washed fender.

The driver and the cabbie both burst from their cars, the limo driver saying nothing, which made him very unusual. You might expect protestations of innocence, or of concern. The limo driver just looked at me with eyes carved from the same indifferent chrome as the cabbie's fender. The cabbie practically brayed at me in English, accented with a sharp Hebrew.

The doorman, though, he was golden. He bolted forward, knelt by me. 'Sir? You okay?'

'Ohhhh,' I moaned. 'My leg.'

'You stepped out in front of me,' the limo driver said. 'It's your fault. Watch where you're walking.' He spoke with a mild eastern European accent.

Sandra Ming, I saw, remained in the limo.

'You're right,' I said. Shakily, the doorman helped me to my feet. 'I . . . I think I'm okay.'

The limo driver, the doorman, they exchanged a glance. Pure unease. The doorman's said *I don't think this is the kind of guy who's gonna sue if we help him.* The driver's said *I don't care.* He looked like he'd just as soon run over me as he would a speed bump.

The cabbie hovered, uncertain. 'Good *you* were paying attention,' I said to the cabbie. 'Unlike some others.'

There: I threw down the gauntlet. The limo driver slid his steely stare back onto me as the doorman forced me toward the curb. Traffic began to back up behind the cabbie, horns jeering in the infinitely patient way of New Yorkers. The cabbie saw I was now the doorman's problem. He started to slide back into his taxi.

And, four cars behind him, I could see Leonie, in a silver Prius. She wore an expression on her face that mixed nervousness with the determination only a parent can have.

I staggered to the curb, waving off help. 'I'm all right,' I said. Normally a person might ask the driver for his license, or his phone number, in case there was a further injury. And I thought about it, but I weighed that it might send his suspicions soaring. I didn't like the vibe from him at all; he was watching me in the way that the interviewers did years ago when I applied at Special Projects. Measuring me, solely as an enemy. I didn't know who he was and I decided it was best to play nice now that Leonie was in position. I raised a hand. 'It was my fault, you're right, I wasn't watching what I was doing. Sorry.' I put my phone down at my side and powered it off.

The driver inspected me with a studied glance.

'What? What the hell now?' I said, earning an Oscar nomination for my role as Irritated New Yorker.

The limo driver got back into the car without another word and he inched away from the curb. Other cars caught in the jam had filtered past him, but, when he merged into the stop and start traffic, Leonie in the rented Prius was two cars behind him.

She looked like she intended to cement herself to his bumper. I noticed she'd put on large, heavy sunglasses big and dark enough that she could have done welding wearing them, and her lush auburn hair was pulled back and covered with a Mets baseball cap. Something about her look was vaguely familiar.

I was nervous for her. She wasn't trained to shadow someone, she'd been up most of the night and was running on excitement and fear. The driver looked like a tough customer. She was clearly smart, book-smart, and if she was used to dealing with criminals she must have developed her own toughness. She had to follow him.

'You sure you're all right?' the doorman said.

'My leg's hurting and I think my phone's broken. I just need to sit down for a minute.' I was careful not to ask him to let me inside the building. Let it be his idea.

'Sir, come here, why don't you sit inside for a minute. Or at least wash the grit off your hands. Is there someone I can call for you?'

The air inside felt nice after the humid squeeze of the afternoon. The doorman pointed to a bathroom where I could rinse my bloodied knuckles and I thanked him.

'I'm sure I'm okay, I don't want to be any trouble. I'll just wash up and let myself back out.' I limped extra hard as I walked to the men's room. Another resident, a heavy-set man pushing an older woman in a wheelchair, exited the elevator and the doorman moved to open the door for them. The heavy man was busy convincing the wheelchair lady that going for an outing, even with the chance of rain, was a good idea, his words running over the protestations of the woman like water gushing in a stream.

I washed my hands, quickly. Then I glanced out the bathroom door. The doorman was busy hailing the pair a cab. I had gotten very few lucky breaks since my pregnant wife vanished but this was one of them. I ducked into the elevator.

Sandra Ming was on the fourth floor.

The doorman would likely look for me, or he might assume I slipped out when he was hailing cabs or providing directions to confused tourists. So I didn't have much time.

No answer to the knock at the Mings' door. I dropped to my knees and brought out the lock picks. Thirty seconds later the door was open.

I shut it behind me and listened to the hush. No one was here. I didn't have a gun with me and I moved through the rooms. Den, decorated with objet d'art from China, from Africa, from South America. A Mayan mask frowned at me from the wall. A kitchen. The coffee maker was on, the scent of dark French roast a caress in the air. A length of hallway, and a master bedroom. Immaculate. A woman's room – it held a woman's scent, a subtle mix of irises and Dior perfume. My wife had worn the same scent and for a moment grief overwhelmed my caution. Nothing like a memory of your wife's skin to bring down the avalanche. I pushed it away.

Back down the hallway. Past a study, where I glanced into the doorway. A large desk, one with a masculine weight that didn't quite match the feel of the rest of the apartment.

I stepped into a bedroom, frozen in post-collegiate amber. Jack Ming's room. A framed diploma from NYU. A collection of books, but not textbooks: these were books he liked to read. A well-worn history of Hong Kong – had he been happy there? Biographies about computer pioneers like Charles Babbage, Ada Lovelace and Steve Jobs. George R. R. Martin's epic fantasies. A bound collection of graphic novels, of Iron Man, Spider-Man, the Avengers.

From the wall Jack Ming's face looked out at me from a scattering of party pictures, the kind taken by a pro photographer at college events. His smile looked pained, as though the party wasn't quite his deal. His hair was longer and his face was fuller. His friends often had buzzed smiles and protective arms around Jack's slender shoulders. He had a shy but sincere grin.

He was just a kid, goddamn it, just a kid I was supposed to kill.

The apartment was cool, but a finger of humidity slid down my spine as I walked into the bathroom. I checked the tub. Droplets still beaded the surface. The bathroom was connected to his room. No reason for anyone else to shower in here.

Jack Ming had been here. Recently. Within the past hour. I might only have missed him, arriving at my perch at the sushi bar, by minutes.

Daniel could die because I'd missed him.

Dust, a light coating, touched his bedroom desk. It didn't look like he'd set anything down in here. I could see the barest indentation on the bed where he had sat.

He'd come here, he'd left. Without his mother. Had he said his goodbyes? Was she not helping him? Your wanted son reappears, on the run, and within an hour the reunion is done and he's fled and Mom's in a limo with a driver who looks like he used to train boxers for the Russian Olympic team.

What had Jack Ming needed here? Something more than saying farewell to his mother?

I went back to her bedroom and made a fast but thorough search. I found nothing of interest: Sandra Ming had stripped her life down to the barest essentials. There was a small, elegant phone by the bedside. I picked it up and hit star-69. The phone rang.

On the fourth ring, someone picked up. But there was only silence.

I waited. The other side waited. I could hear a soft, soft breathing.

I took a jump: 'Yes, I'm calling on behalf of Mrs Ming.'

The other side hung up.

Who would she call when her son arrives, out of the mists for a presumably unexpected reunion? Was that who had dispatched the limo driver?

I went into the study. Jack Ming's father, Russell, had gotten his start in the madhouse of Hong Kong real estate and then set up a property development company here. Framed on the walls were photos of him with other famous developers, New York celebrities, smiling politicians. Several pictures of him and Jack, his arm around his son. People sure liked to put their arms on Jack's shoulders. Maybe he was one of those people who inspired a need to protect, to shelter. I tried not to dwell on those pictures. He couldn't be someone's son, not like Daniel was. He just had to stay a target, faceless, inhuman. I hadn't wanted to know about his life, just how to end it.

There were no pictures of Mr and Mrs Ming together. The absence of a picture is also worth a thousand words. A thin sheen of dust on the desk had been disturbed. It didn't seem to be used by Mrs Ming; there were no papers or files on its surface. A screen saver danced across the monitor. I looked at the keyboard. Dust on some keys, not on others. Someone had used this keyboard for the first time in a long while. Jack.

I moved the mouse and the computer woke up. It wasn't passworded. The screen background was a picture of Jack and his father. A click gave me the most recently used applications: Word, Firefox, Excel. I started them, went to the histories of each, opened the most recent files. The Excel spreadsheets were over a year old, and had been created by Russell Ming as part of his business. The Word documents were also all Russell Ming's — mostly related to his business but one that was a letter to his son Jack.

Reading this felt like peering into a grave. I didn't want to see it but you couldn't help it, it was like a diary falling open to a page.

Dear Jack: First of all, you know this, but it bears saying. I love you. There is nothing you can do, or could ever do, that will lessen my love for you. I want you to tell me what it is that is troubling you so. And I want the truth, as much as it could hurt, I want to know what you think you've done. I want you to tell me. Not your mother. Let's have this be between us. Because I don't think that she will

And there the letter stopped, as though he'd decided not to continue with an unspoken, unspooled thought. What had he not wanted to say about his lovely diplomat wife? Did the heart attack take before he'd finished the sentence? I checked the date on the document. The day that he'd died. These might have been Russell Ming's final writings. Or maybe this was when Jack came into the room, and it was better to talk to his son than to write him a letter. Daniel, if I find you, I promise my last word to you will not be an unfinished sentence.

I checked the browser history. The last website visited had been about a property in Brooklyn, in Williamsburg. It was on Ming's company website. Seven commercial properties were listed and this one was empty, unrented. The browser showed the previous six entries were all for other Ming properties. Jack had checked all his father's holdings, found one that wasn't in use.

Maybe a good place for him to hide? I memorized the address.

It was the only vacant property belonging to the management company.

I started to search the desk. Very little here: Russell Ming's expired passport, pens and pencils, a legal pad with a faded pencil sketch that said *Jack's options. 1. Surrender to the police 2. Let Jack ...* and then nothing else written, as though the thought had been interrupted, like the Word document. In one drawer was a nest of keys, with tags on them, addresses marked in a careful blue pen. I searched through them. The keys for the Brooklyn property were gone.

An empty building, where he controlled access. The perfect place for him to surrender to the CIA and make his deal with August. He'd come home for the keys.

I looked through the rest of Russell Ming's computer quickly. Jack Ming was a hacker, the kind of kid whose fingertips felt lonely without a keyboard. He had evidence against Novem Soles, and maybe he'd backed it up here. But in the machine's history there was no sign of new files, or of downloaded or uploaded files on this system, no emails sent. He hadn't even bothered to clean out the browser history. Maybe Leonie could make sense of it. I unhooked the laptop from the external keyboard and monitor.

Maybe – a thought rumbled in my ear. Maybe what he's got on Novem Soles isn't on a computer. Maybe it's physical. Something he's carrying. Maybe a hacker who knows just how vulnerable most computers are won't trust this information to a machine.

I had to find him. Now.

He'd taken the keys to the Brooklyn building. Maybe that's where he intended to hide, maybe where he would go right this moment.

27

Morris County, New Jersey

If there was something worse than feeling helpless, it was feeling useless.

Leonie gripped the steering wheel as she followed the limo. Sam had found Jin Ming, or, rather, Jack Ming, and she had done, *what?* Frittered her time away trying to delve into databases, bribing hackers to unlock the secrets of the man who had snuck into the country. Sat typing while these murderous freaks had her child, and ... Now what? She didn't know how to tail anyone. She kept expecting the limo to pull over to the side, the driver to watch her glide past with a knowing sneer, that he knew she was there and that he could lose her at any time. Or worse. Maybe he would kill her to protect Mrs Ming.

Was he CIA? Was he Nine Suns? If he was, why didn't he just hand Mrs Ming over to her and Sam?

The limo headed west, into suburban New Jersey along Highway 80, finally turning north on 206 toward Lake Hopatcong. The rain parted like a curtain; the sky showed elusive patches of gray-blue, weak sunlight fell in rays among the breaks like a handful of sand sifting through fingers. She kept two cars between her and the limo, and every time another car tried to edge in she would grit her teeth and stand her ground and think, God, don't let me lose them. She nearly wrecked twice driving through Parsippany, cars trying to get across lanes and her not yielding an inch. Her hands trembled on the wheel.

The limo turned off the highway into a stretch of parkland. She hung back; it was more dangerous to get too close to the limo. She craved a cigarette.

The limo whipped around a turn, shaded by oaks. Signs indicated this was private property and warned against trespassing in the strictest terms. She drove past and if the limo driver was watching her, was suspicious of her, he would think he was wrong.

She hoped.

She pulled the car off to the side of the road, nosing it into a thick grove of oaks. She could wait for Sam. That would be best.

And if the driver's job was to eliminate Mrs Ming? Or to question her about Jack's whereabouts? Then all was lost. She and Sam had to find him first, had to eliminate him before he could betray Novem Soles. She shivered.

She tried calling Sam. The call rolled to voicemail. She told him where she was and that she was going to follow the road the limo had taken on foot. She kept the tremble out of her voice.

If you stay in the car your baby could die. Don't be afraid. You can do this. It's up to you.

And a strength flooded her. She could do this.

She got out of the car and she started to walk through the dense woods. She could see the thin line of paved road the limo had taken. She reached a fence, eight feet tall. Another big NO TRESPASSING sign. She clambered over the fence, using the sign for leverage. She dropped down into high grass.

She ran parallel to the road, staying in the heavy growth of trees. Mud sucked at her shoes; the air felt stitched with the damp. Rain, lingering on leaves, fell onto her shoulders and her head.

The road turned again. She climbed over some rain-slick rocks, feeling breathless. She would see what the driver and Mrs Ming were doing. If she could she would get the woman away. Because if Mrs Ming was the key to knowing what Jack was doing next, then she must belong to her and Sam alone.

Nature, she thought. The air smelled heavy with moss and an underlying scent of heat-hurried decay. It wasn't so bad out here. Maybe she should get away from the computer more. She imagined going for a long hike – although she hadn't gone hiking since long childhood walks – with Taylor secure on her back, the sun warm on their faces. Not in Vegas. Too hot. She could take Taylor to Lake Tahoe for a long weekend, soon, when all this was over. Stroll in the shade of the trees, point out the flowers, imprint good memories. Do the things she'd said she'd do if she ever had a child ... if she ever had another chance.

Grief prickled her face.

You can do this.

In the distance Leonie heard a woman scream, short and sharp. It was as though the wind carried the noise, dropped it into her lap like a gift.

For a moment she froze. Then she bolted, dodging through the trees. She slipped and skidded down a muddy incline. She'd slid down to the road, which curved hard and fed directly into an old house ahead of her. She saw the limo parked there, and no other car. The house needed paint, it needed a carpenter: odd impressions that flickered across her mind. Between her and the house there was a big square of clear lawn she would have to cross.

No sign of the driver, or of Sandra Ming.

She ran across the lawn. She went onto the porch, trying to be quiet. The boards creaked slightly, and every moan of the wood felt like a knife in the skin. She kept waiting for the driver to explode out of the front door. But the door stayed shut. She pressed an ear to a window. Listened. Heard nothing but the rasp of her own breathing.

Sam, please, where are you? Please get here. For a moment she thought: maybe whoever this is, CIA or whoever, maybe they got Sam. They left someone behind at the Mings to wait for Jack and they've killed Sam.

Maybe it's just me left to save my kid. Me alone. You've gotten through worse, she told herself.

Curtains, thick, streaked with age, blocked her view through the window. The porch felt exposed. It offered little cover.

Weird, she thought, I'm thinking like a soldier.

She crept around the corner, staying on the porch, toward the detached garage. She stayed low and moved quickly and she was so proud of herself that for a moment she didn't feel when the Taser needles hit her, but the charge made her dance off the porch, tumbling into the neglected rose bushes, the thorns pricking her face, the bolt surging pain into her bones like water flooding a pipe.

She turned, saw the limo driver thumbing the controls for another hit.

The last thing she smelled was the rose petals crushed under her body, like a grandmother smell, her mouth twisting, trying to scream for Sam to help her.

28

East 59th Street, Manhattan

I ran back down to the lobby. The doorman stood by the glass entrance and when he saw me exit off the elevator – carrying a laptop – he stormed back through the door. Well, stormed rather politely.

'Sir, I know you needed to recuperate, but this is a private building and—'

I punched him, hard, one smart blow in the tender spot between the edge of the jaw and the lip. He staggered back and I hammered a fist into his gut and then into the vulnerable joining of neck and nerve.

'Sorry,' I said. 'Really, mister.' He folded. I knelt, went through his pockets and found a passkey. I stood and hurried down the hallway. Saw a door marked Security. I keyed the door with the passkey. A rented cop stood before a set of monitors. He charged at me, going for his holster. I knocked him down and I took the gun from him. I told him to sit down. He obeyed.

'Turn around. And, no, I'm not going to kill you.' I slammed the gun into the back of his head, three times, and he went down. I went to the security recording. Rewound. I saw myself enter, I saw Mrs Ming exit. I saw people come and go, as fast and as energetically as if they had espresso in their blood. Then him.

Jack Ming, leaving, alone, practically running out of the building. At the exit he turned left.

A bit more rewinding and I saw him enter the building with his mother. This I played slowly.

On another monitor a woman got off the elevator and screamed when she saw the fallen doorman. Okay, I was officially out of time, thank you for playing.

Footage of Jack Ming, walking inside the building with his mother. The body language was clear. The kid was anxious. He was holding two grocery bags and he kept swinging them over his feet. A small knapsack sat on his back that he'd left with as well. He kept glancing about, not even looking at his mother, while they waited for the elevator.

And Mrs Ming. You could tell this was not a happy reunion.

She was not touching her child. She was not looking at her long-departed, wanted-by-the-police kid. She was looking at the tile floor, and her watch. Did she have an appointment to keep? She looked as though she wanted to wriggle free of her own skin and slither away. She kept shaking the rain from her umbrella. It was a constructive action, something to do other than watch her kid.

I stopped the digital recording. I erased it, from Jack's appearance to now, and then I powered down the cameras. There was no point in me being remembered either.

I hurried out the door, past the woman crouching by the unconscious doorman. She had a cell phone pressed to her ear. She called to me to help her but I ignored her.

I let the traffic carry me along. I wanted out of this neighborhood now. I went down to the 59th Street subway station, rode the train to Grand Central, got off. I found a store in the terminal and put the laptop in a knapsack I'd bought.

I tried Leonie on the cell phone; there was no answer. I didn't like that at all. Maybe she didn't like to talk on the phone while she drove but I figured that for me she'd make an exception.

For a moment I felt torn. I had the address of an empty building where my target would be, and if you're planning to kill someone an empty building in New York City is convenient. But having Leonie tag after the limo driver felt like a mistake now. Jack had left his mother behind, and maybe she knew where he was, but maybe she didn't. I had an address, an actual, throbbing clue, and Leonie could be off with our car on a fool's errand. I stepped back out onto the street, trying to decide what to do.

The wind broke the rain clouds into jagged curls of gray; the sun flooded the sky, weak as tea.

The iPhone rang inside my pocket. The phone that Anna had given me.

'Yes?'

'Sam?' Leonie. Her voice tight and stiff, rattled by fear. There is a certain pronunciation made when the lips are bruised; you don't quite form your words right.

'Yes?'

'Oh, God, I messed up, I messed up, please . . .'

And then the limo driver's voice. 'You. You sent this woman to follow me. Who are you?'

'Don't hurt her.'

'If you don't want her hurt, then you come get her.'

No. Not now. I had the address where Jack most likely had run. I had Jack Ming in my grasp.

What would you do to save your child? she'd asked me.

A choice. What would I do to save my child? Would I sacrifice this woman who was basically a stranger? A little, awful voice inside me said, *you don't need her. You found Jack, not her. What good is she, what has she done to help save your kid?* It was from a dark corner deep in the well of my soul, but when you are in a battle for your child's life darkness stands close to you, whispers in your ear. Nine Suns wasn't going to give me Daniel, or give Leonie her daughter, if Jack Ming breathed long enough to turn himself into the CIA.

'I strongly suggest that you listen to me, mister. Retrieve your bitch. Or I'll cut her throat.'

In the background I could hear Leonie, gasping, saying, 'Don't, don't!'

I couldn't tell if she was talking to me or to the driver. Then a piercing scream.

'Where are you?' I managed to say.

He gave me an address and directions to Morris County, in northern New Jersey.

I clicked off the phone. If I made the wrong choice I could be abandoning either a woman I barely knew, who seemed to hold me in contempt, to death, or my own child.

If the situation was reversed, what would I want her to do? Leave me to die? Absolutely. Go save the kids, lady, what happens to me is nothing. Go.

We hadn't anticipated an enemy beyond Special Projects, who would not have grabbed one of us and threatened us with death. Caught up in the mad rush to find Jack Ming, I had not planned for this contingency. It was on me.

I went outside, stood on the sidewalk in the warming humidity, and I started to shudder. It felt like every nerve in my body was wired to open current. I gave myself thirty seconds of weakness and I stopped shivering then I put the decision aside. Leonie was in the greatest danger right now. I could no more leave her to die than I could anyone else.

I started to walk. I needed a car.

A couple of turns later I saw a parking garage, four suited men coming down the ramp to merge into the river of pedestrians. I maneuvered carefully, bumping directly into the one who'd had his hand in his right front pocket as he had turned from the ramp onto the sidewalk.

'Jesus, watch where you're going, jerkwad,' he snapped at me.

'My bad, I'm very sorry,' I said. I turned into the parking ramp and hurried up the stairs. I didn't even glance to see which keys I'd pickpocketed off him until I was on the second level. A Mercedes logo on the keychain. I ran along the parked cars, testing the automatic unlock, until headlights on an SE flashed at me.

One minute later I was heading toward the Lincoln Tunnel.

If you save her and Jack Ming gets away . . .

I had to get a grip. Focus. I wanted to make good time. The

limo driver apparently had and I thought, please, don't let there be bad traffic or an accident. Don't let the guy whose car I'm stealing realize his keys are gone. Let the doorman and the guard be okay after I punched them. Forgive me everything I do to save my son.

Don't let me fail.

29

Along Highway 206, New Jersey

The Garden State. You tend to forget that New Jersey deserves that name when you're stuck driving through an endless unfurling of suburbia. I drove at top speed and the rain that had hurried in from the Atlantic passed through here. The rain was like a hand cleaning a slate. The air smelled wet and fresh and new.

I drove. I didn't use the car's GPS – if it had been reported stolen by now, I didn't want the system tracking where I was. I kept it switched off.

Okay. Now: who had Leonie and Mrs Ming? Jack's mom had called someone. And then the limo driver had collected Mrs Ming. Now, I would not put it past Special Projects if they figured out like I had that Jack Ming was their new best buddy – Fagin might have tattled – to scoop up Mrs Ming for her own protection against Novem Soles. And they might even, to lure me in close, pretend-threaten Leonie's life. If August was at this house, fine, we'd talk, and maybe he'd let me take some photos of Jack Ming looking dead, if his people had already nabbed Jack.

But. *But.* If August was involved in this operation, the limo driver wouldn't have been on the phone. It would have been August. Right?

I was not optimistic that Special Projects had Leonie. It had to be the dreaded 'Someone Else'. An enemy I didn't know.

The phone Anna gave me rang again as I turned into the address. 'Yes?' I said, sounding impatient.

'Hello, Sam.' Anna Tremaine.

'What?'

'I would like to know your status.'

'I'll call you when the job's done.'

'Has Leonie found the informant?'

'I'll call you when the job is done.' I made the words short, clipped.

'You know,' she said, 'I don't think you've heard your baby cry. He's been rather fussy today. Well, both these babies are unhappy. I wonder, do you think they can sense their . . . precariousness?'

I don't know how to describe the dark surge over my heart. I don't have the words for it. It was a blackness. I hadn't felt it in my worst moments, when I saw my brother die on a scratchy video, when my wife was kidnapped in a street of fire, when I was tortured and accused of being a traitor, choking to death when I couldn't give the Company answers I didn't know. I've had more than my share of really bad moments. This was even darker. This was reaching into me and smearing something foul on my soul. It took all my will to keep my breath steady. 'I am doing what you asked. You don't hurt him. You do not hurt either of them.'

'But the job's not done yet and you won't tell me what's happening.' She sighed. 'I'm playing with his little fingers right now, Sam. They're more delicate than bone china.'

I told her briefly what I knew, and what I was doing. For several moments she was silent.

196

Then she said, 'Listen, Sam. Listen to your son. I'm going to put the phone right by him.' And I could hear the phone, a hiss of breath, a gurgle. My son. I had never heard him. A soft ahh-hhhh, all baby breath, all happy, toothless mumble.

Then choked, frustrated gurgling; he wasn't happy. Bored or annoyed at the phone resting next to his face.

'Daniel. Daniel, this is Daddy.' Like he could understand. Like my voice would mean anything to him; my soft baritone was as alien to him as any other sound he'd never heard. My words, my voice, could give him no comfort. I'd never thought about what I'd say to him: he was a baby, what would he understand? I'd never been around babies. I was the youngest in my family. 'Daniel. It's Daddy. I'm coming to get you.'

He fussed, he squawked, he cried. Maybe he wanted Anna to pick him up again. He wanted Anna. The idea made me want to vomit. He wanted a woman who would hurt him. That was true innocence.

'I'm going to be there soon, son, we'll be together. Okay? This is Daddy. I love you, Daniel. I love you.' I did love him. I loved him, sight unseen. 'I love you. I love . . .'

'Sam,' Anna's voice was back. 'Listen to me.'

30

Morris County, New Jersey

Leonie looked up from staring at the floor. The driver hadn't planned on two victims, she supposed; he only had the one set of handcuffs and he'd chained Mrs Ming to another wooden chair. He'd bound Leonie with rope from a closet in the house. The living room was small, the wallpaper old and twenty years out of fashion, musty with grime. The house carried the feel of a way station, a place used infrequently. Leonie sat, her knees folded beneath her, watching the driver pace the floor.

The driver had moved into the front rooms, to watch the windows for Sam.

'Help me,' Mrs Ming whispered to her.

Leonie glanced at her. 'I'm curious as to what you expect me to do.'

It wasn't the answer Mrs Ming was looking for. 'He's not from the CIA. He's not. They said they would send someone.'

'The CIA?'

'Yes!' Mrs Ming said.

Leonie inched closer to her. 'The CIA is looking for your son.'

'A man who said he was from the CIA called me this morning. They said Jack might be coming home. To call them if he did. I . . . I didn't know to believe him, but I went to the grocery, in case. I got Jack's favorite things to eat.' Her voice sounded lost.

Leonie looked at her. 'Where is your son?'

'I don't know . . . '

'Tell me.'

'He left, I don't . . . '

Leonie leaned back and head-butted the woman. 'Tell me where he is!'

Mrs Ming howled in anger and pain.

'Hey! Hey!' the limo driver said, hurrying into the room, kicking Leonie onto her back. 'Stop it!' He murmured again into his open phone, too low to hear, and then clicked it off.

'You're not from the CIA!' Mrs Ming said, blood oozing from the corner of her mouth, her forehead vivid with the imprint of

Leonie's head. 'You cannot keep me here. You cannot. They will look for me.'

'You,' he said to Leonie. 'You're with Sam Capra.'

She said nothing and he responded, in his accented English, 'Bitch, I am short on patience', and he began to kick her. Hard. The first blow sent her across the room.

Then he asked her a question, received hazily through the pain, that made no sense to her at all. 'Where is the woman called Mila?'

31

Morris County, New Jersey

I saw the rental Prius, nosed into a grove of trees. I turned in and climbed a wall and headed down a long, paved road. A sign read PRIVATE DRIVE. NO TRESPASSING. Ahead was a long, curving driveway and a house that looked like it might once have been a grand home or summer retreat from the start of the twentieth century. She'd tried to sneak in, but I was expected. Zero point in anything except walking straight into the house.

My phone rang again. 'Come to the front door. Nothing funny or the redhead dies and you get to watch.' Short and sweet.

I made my way to the front door, across a grand porch. I opened the door and stepped into a large foyer.

'Here,' a voice called.

I headed back from the front of the house and went to my left and entered what might once have been a library or study. The limo driver must have been a Boy Scout. He was extremely well prepared. He aimed a gun at me, and held another pressed against Leonie's temple. He had a Taser tucked into the side of his pants. Leonie's face was bruised along the jawline.

'Hi,' he said. 'You heal fast, bumper boy.'

'Vitamins and milk.'

'But those are not brain food,' he said. He tapped Leonie's head with the gun for emphasis. 'I'm thinking you know the drill.'

'I'm not armed,' I said.

'Liar. If I check you and you have a gun, I'm going to shoot off this bitch's thumbs.'

I produced the security guard's gun from the back of my pants and dropped it on the floor.

'Kick it over,' he said.

I did as he said.

'Who are you with?' he asked me.

'Me, myself and I,' I said.

He switched the gun over to Mrs Ming's head and she began to wail. 'I don't believe you. I'm not sure who you're more interested in – your partner here or your target.'

'I don't want anyone hurt.'

'Then who are you with?'

'I'm with nobody,' I said. 'We're looking for Mrs Ming's son.'

'And you thought I was bringing her to him?'

'I did. Not now.'

He gave a twisted little laugh. Now that I was unarmed he put a gun up against each of their heads. Toying with me.

'I'm not sure which one you want alive the most,' he said.

'Both of them.' Ten feet separated us, plenty of time for him to shoot me if I made a move.

I knew at least that with Mrs Ming he was bluffing. He'd

brought her here to hold her or to question her, on someone's orders.

'Are you with Novem Soles? Because we're on the same side, then, and this is a misunderstanding.' The thought that Anna could have opened up a bounty on Jack Ming occurred to me. They just wanted him dead; they wouldn't care if it was by my hand.

'Novem *what*?'

'Nine Suns.'

'Sounds like a slant restaurant.' He seemed to be taking my measure with his gaze. Mrs Ming stared at him with hate in her eyes. 'You're the one answering questions, not me, who's your friend?'

'Her name is Leonie.'

'And where would I find Mila? I gave your friend a roughing up and she didn't know.'

Not a question I was expecting at all. What the hell just happened? 'I have no idea.'

He eased the gun over toward Leonie's eye. 'I want you to tell me how to find Mila.'

'Mila contacts me when it suits her,' I said.

'You're going to tell me how I can find Mila, or I'm going to kill one of them.' He shoved the guns hard against their skulls; Mrs Ming let out a twisted moan; Leonie bit her lip and her gaze locked with mine. 'Not sure which. Guess we'll know when I pull the trigger. On five. One. Two. Three.'

'She sometimes meets me at a bar,' I said in a rush. 'She calls, she picks the bar.'

'And define sometimes.'

'Once a week, when I'm in New York,' I lied. 'But it's on her schedule, not mine.'

He studied my face. 'Sit down on the floor. Keep your hands behind your back.'

I obeyed. He took the gun off Sandra Ming and holstered it, and then he produced a cell phone from his pocket. He tapped buttons. And in Russian he said: 'Yes, sir. I have him now. He says the woman will meet him at a bar every week, but she calls him.' He listened for thirty seconds. 'Yes. All right.' He closed the phone.

It's hard to keep three prisoners when one is unsecured. Right now he wanted me talking. But he hadn't secured me; he'd used the women as hostages, but he was keeping his distance from me. The women were my bonds.

But his bonds were that he wasn't master of his own fate. He had to call someone. Someone he called *sir*. He had to take orders from someone, and, speaking Russian into the phone, he hadn't wanted me to know that. He hadn't wanted me to know he was, well, not the top of the totem pole.

But he didn't draw the second gun again. He felt very much in control. I watched him. He watched me. A minute ticked by. Then another. He didn't shoot any of us or ask any questions or say what was going to happen next.

'I find silences awkward,' I said.

He clearly didn't.

'Let me guess. Your boss said not to ask us any questions.'

He looked at me.

'I'm sure he doesn't want you to know what the information we have is worth. You might cut a slice for yourself.'

'Shut up,' he said. 'You bore me. You didn't even try to fight. Coward.'

'Did he tell you how much the bounty on Mila is?'

'Shut up,' he said again, but after a pause.

202

'I presume once he gets here, all you do is dig the graves,' I said. 'I bet he doesn't even give you one per cent of the cut on Mila. What are you, paid by the hour? I'm sure that was why you came to the land of opportunity, to dust grave dirt off your hands while your boss collects an insane amount of money he wouldn't get without your help.'

He stared at me. His mouth opened and I could see a little strand of spit bridge his lips.

'He told you to sit on us, he'd be out here soon. Or she.' I was quiet for a minute. 'He didn't tell you how much Mrs Ming's son is worth, either?'

He stared at me, but he swallowed at the same time.

I had a noose around his neck now, so to speak, so I gave it a hard tug. 'Mila presently has the highest price on her head in the world, for someone who isn't a head of state or terrorist. And I know how to get her, and you're just going to hand over that information to your bosses and let them score the profit. But that's okay, I guess you get to wash the limo at the end of the day.'

'I would like to know who the hell Mila is,' Leonie said.

'Shut up,' the driver said to her. He looked back at me and laughed. 'Why would you want me to profit more than my boss? It makes no difference as to whether you live or die.'

'I've been screwed over by a boss before,' I said. 'Very badly. I don't much like bosses because I always did the hard, dangerous work and they got all the credit. Mila's my boss and I'm not about to die for her.' Then I played the trump. 'A million. That's what the bounty is. And I know some people who will pay at least a million, probably double, for Mrs Ming's son. He stole something from them, they want it back. Your boss will be taking that money to the bank as well.' Watch me tap dance, I love to improvise.

He said nothing, he just stared.

His cell phone rang again. He opened it and said, in Russian, 'Yes?' He listened. 'Yes, I can stay longer. Of course. Is . . . is there anything you want me to find out from them?' Silence. 'Yes, sir.' He clicked off.

'Let me guess. He doesn't want you talking to us,' I said. 'I love being right.'

'He's been delayed.'

'And he doesn't want you knowing what we know. You might decide that you could profit.'

'I don't want this man mad at me,' he said.

'Of course not,' I said. 'He has all the power. What do you have? He's going to have three million dollars. A million for Mila, a million for the kid, a million for what the kid stole.'

His mouth worked.

'What the hell are you doing?' Leonie said. 'Shut up.' She stared at me, the barrel of the driver's gun still indenting her hair.

'You and I could cut a deal,' I said. 'You let these two go, and you and I collect the bounties. Together.'

He laughed. 'And I trust you *why?*'

'Because I've told you the truth, and you suspect I'm right, and your boss hasn't told you squat except spit out a bunch of orders and let you take all the risk.' I put a heaviness on those final words. 'You're the errand boy. You're not a player. I guess you're not ready.'

'Shut up,' Leonie said.

'You be quiet,' the driver said. 'I let them go, they go to the police.'

It's always delicious when a not-bright person begins studying the angles.

'No. The people paying the bounties have their kids,' I said.

'They've got control over them. They will go home and cry for their kids.'

Sometimes the unexpected happens. Sometimes a word is a bomb. Leonie's eyes went wide with shock, her jaw trembled. She turned her head and the driver's gun lay square in her forehead. She stared up past the gun at him, coiled. He glanced at her. Then he made his mistake. He looked up at me. 'How do I know that any of what you said is true?'

Lying is not hard. I don't know why the psychologists pronounce it as difficult. Lying is the easiest thing in the world. Truths are far more difficult. 'Call your boss and tell him what I've told you,' I said. 'Tell him you know where Mila is, right now, and you know she's worth a million. See how he reacts. See what he tells you to do.'

'What if I kill the two of them and you and I work out a deal?' he said. Testing me.

'Sam, stop it,' Leonie said, her voice a razor wire.

I shrugged. He smiled.

There are two kinds of killers. Those that don't kill unless they believe they absolutely must, and those who kill with a greater ease. The driver was the second type. He liked the power. He liked the control. He was a small man on the inside, and killing made him feel big. I had made him feel small, seen the truth of who he was. It's not complicated. The reaction tells you whether or not you can kill them without hesitation. I believe in do unto others, you know.

'You throw her away easily,' he said to me. He looked down at Leonie, as though considering what a waste that would be. She stared right back up into his eyes, the gun pressed now against her forehead, and ten feet away I could feel the fury radiating off her, the fire of inchoate anger and frustration.

'Same as your boss is doing to you. Throwing you away.'

Later, replaying it in my head, I think that phrase did it. An accidental tripwire inside Leonie's head. The idea of someone being thrown away. I didn't know until much later how much of a nerve I struck with her, and at the time I thought she was thinking of Daniel and her daughter. I didn't intend for her to fight the battle.

I just wanted him consumed with doubt, with greed, and if I got him close to me, to talk, then I could take him. That was when Leonie attacked. She timed it right. She did her best. Now, a person bound to a chair, it's not really much of an attack – more of a low-aiming shove. She took advantage of the fact that he was standing right next to her and she slammed her weight, chair and all, into him, fueled by an incoherent rage.

Because he was going to interfere, and he would cause her child to die, to be thrown away.

Leonie knocked into the driver like a knee-hugging tackle, her feet kept propelling into him, and he staggered to the side, crashing into Sandra Ming, who obligingly screamed.

I ran forward.

Time didn't slow. It always slows in the movies but in this dirty, abandoned old house it seemed to speed up, to accelerate beyond my control. The driver's gun spoke, twice spitting, and I heard a scream, close as my ear as I dived toward them. The driver threw Leonie off him – picked her up, chair and ropes, and threw her at me – he was counting on me being kind and catching her. I didn't. I ducked and the legs of the chair brushed my back. She slammed into the wall behind me, high up, falling to the gritty wooden floor. But throwing her off him meant he was off-balance, both hands employed in tossing her, and I charged at him. I pile-drove him hard into the wall, jamming forearm against windpipe, looking to crush it. But I hit him a fraction too high and I caught more jawline than throat.

We snapped back into the wall and he hooked a leg behind me. I fell and then I saw the gun, firm in his hand, and his wrist pivoted toward me. I caught the gun's barrel and pushed it away. He lay atop me, in the stronger position, and I kept the gun at bay with my right hand. My left hand I used to make short, hard chops in every vulnerable spot: throat, solar plexus, testicles. Three fast brutal ones. He hissed out bad breath in sharp pain and I got a better grip and broke his wrist. The crack was loud. I slammed elbow into throat and he coughed and spat blood.

Money versus child. You tell me who fights harder.

Leonie landed on us. Her chair splintering had unbound her from the ropes. She pulled the gun away from him. He tried to lever an elbow back in her face and he missed.

She got the gun. But instead of shooting him she ran, simply trying to get the weapon out of his reach. She fired a round into Mrs Ming's handcuff, anchored to the top rung of the chair, and pulled the older woman out of the room. Leaving me to fight the driver.

He slammed a roundhouse into my face with his good hand and I fell back against Mrs Ming's damaged wooden chair. It was ladder-backed, no arms, worn with age. A weapon at hand. I grabbed the chair with one hand and swung its weight into him. Then again. Then again, each time dodging the blows he tried to connect against me. He screamed, in pain and frustration.

I had a good grip now and I swung for all I was worth. One of the legs cracked, separated from its weak nails and I flung it aside. He rolled and I smashed the chair into the floor, missing him, and the seat, torn from the chair, skittered across the floor. I was conscious of blood masking his face and coating my hands.

He snarled; he was coming apart, same as the chair. He knew I was going to beat him to death.

He scrambled backward now, fleeing me, retreating back toward a window.

'Tell me who your boss is and I'll let you live,' I said.

He made a noise and then he went backward, through the window, arms up to protect his battered body, flinging himself out onto the grassy hillside. It was only about a five-foot drop but he fell and rolled like he'd plunged from a great height.

The last big fragment of the chair still in my hand was a length of the ladder-back, with bits of wood dangling off it. I stripped them free; now all that was left of the chair in my grip was a two-foot length of tough oak, its top splintered into a sharp spear.

I jumped out the window after him.

He staggered through the trees, survival instinct fueling his run. But I'd broken him – maybe ribs along with the wrist – and his speed wasn't top. Today had spun out of his control and he was bent by the reversal of fortune. He dodged me through the shade of the oaks and as we ran downhill he stumbled over a white outcrop of rock and he took a cruel fall.

I landed on top of him, knees digging in, the sharp wood raised above my head. 'Talk,' I said.

He spat at me.

'Who do you work for?'

'You are so fucked. You don't even know who you've pissed off.'

'Tell me.'

He smiled through a bloody gash across his mouth. 'No.'

I showed him the makeshift spear and said, 'I will run this between your ribs and then stir.'

'I was told to come get the Ming woman and her son if he was here. Bring them here. See what evidence the Ming kid has.'

'And to hold us.'

'Yes. For questioning.'

'But you know about Mila.'

'My boss does. He knew you were connected to her. I never heard of her until tonight.'

'Who do you work for?'

'I can't tell you because I don't know.'

'You're lying. He has to have a name.'

'Do you think he's ever told me his real name?'

'How does he give you work?'

'I get a phone call. I do what he asks, and a lot of money appears for me in a Caymans account.'

'You're ex-what?'

'I used to be Latvian intelligence,' he said.

Very small spy agency. 'Didn't it pay well?'

'No. Money is better doing freelance work. I drive limo here, I do what my boss asks me. He knew my background before he ever called me. Please.' He could see that if I hammered the spear into him it would slide deep into his windpipe. 'Let me go,' the driver said. 'Please.'

I knew he would not have shown any mercy to me or Leonie.

'Get up,' I said. 'Give me your wallet, your car keys.'

He obeyed. He wheezed; I'd broken ribs with the chair. His face was a bloodied wreck and his shirt and pants were torn. He wouldn't look at my eyes. 'You can't leave me behind here, he'll kill me. I know he'll kill me.'

The wooden, pseudo-spear felt heavy in my hand. But I couldn't kill him in cold blood. 'Start walking. You can stop when you cross into Pennsylvania. If I see you again I'll kill you without hesitation.'

He nodded. He stumbled, fell to the ground.

'Get up,' I said.

He nodded again, agreeing with me that getting up was a capital idea, and I leaned down to yank him to his feet.

The rock crashed into the side of my head and I went down to my knees, eyes thrumming with pain. He scrabbled across me, trying to seize the improvised spear and shoving my arm into the mud. Then he raised the rock again, slammed it into my face. I twisted my head so he missed my nose but hit my shuttered right eye. It hurt like hell.

I felt the butt of the spear grind into the mud and so I pushed him up. His feet scrabbled in the muck, obliging me, and then I drove the spear into him. It hurt him, he howled, but it didn't pierce his side. He writhed away and then I was on top of him and I drove it, point down, hard into his belly.

I walked back up to the house, bleary with pain and my mouth tasting of puke. My eye was swollen nearly shut. It hurt but it wasn't anything more than a black eye, I thought, not a broken socket. I stumbled and kept my feet moving.

Leonie stood in the door, shivering. With my good eye I could see her clutching at her elbows.

'Mrs Ming . . . ' she said. 'Hurry, in here. Where's the driver?'

'Dead.' I didn't add it hadn't been a good death to see.

'You killed him?'

'That's usually what dead means. Thanks for the help. Thanks for shooting him once you got the gun and everything. Really appreciate it.'

'I had to try and help Mrs Ming . . . ' she moaned, and then I ran into the house.

*

The driver's stray bullet had punctured her chest. Her skin was pale and gray as a clouded sky, blood easing from her mouth, her nose. Leonie had tried to staunch the bleeding. I knelt by her.

'Mrs Ming.'

Her eyes fluttered open.

'Mrs Ming. Where has Jack gone?'

Her bloodied lip thinned. 'Won't tell you . . . You people want to kill him.'

'Is he going to go to his father's building in Brooklyn? He took the keys from your house, I think.'

'Tell you nothing . . . You want to hurt my son.'

'I can help protect your son,' I said.

'Liar.'

Oh, God, please, I thought, please help her talk to me. 'Mrs Ming. I worked for the CIA. I don't *want* to hurt your son. Look at me.' Her face focused on my bruises. 'I just killed the man who kidnapped you. I'm trying to help you. I lied to that man. So I'm Jack's only hope. The CIA is looking for him.'

'The CIA called me . . .' she said. 'Liars. All liars.' Her eyelids fluttered.

Her words hit me hard as a punch. 'Who in the CIA called you? Who?'

Her lips moved, and her breath gave what sounded like a final hush. 'They wanted a deal . . . protect Jack, protect me . . . if you came I was to keep you at the house until they got there . . .'

'Who in the CIA did you talk to, Mrs Ming?'

But she didn't want to talk about that, not with fewer breaths than fingers left. Mrs Ming said, 'My son . . . help my son, please.'

What was I supposed to promise her? I was supposed to kill

211

her son to save mine. I took her hand. 'Jack will be all right,' I said. 'I promise you. I promise you.'

'I loved him,' she said. 'Forgave him . . .' And the words, the breath, faltered and with a bubble of blood at her lips she was gone.

'Oh, my God,' Leonie said.

'Are you all right?'

She nodded. She stared at the dead woman. She pressed fingers against her throat, so as to be sure there was nothing to be done. 'What do we do? His boss is coming . . .'

'I know. These are our choices. I know where Jack Ming is hiding. He might be there if we go there now. Or we can wait and see if the driver's boss shows up, learn who we're up against. We can't do both.'

'Jack Ming,' she said. 'No question.'

32

Manhattan

Leonie drove, I sat hunched in the seat. She smoked a cigarette, blowing out the cracked window. I told her she wasn't supposed to smoke in the rental car and she'd given me an incredulous stare and then laughed and kept smoking.

The phone call came as we were driving silently back into Manhattan. I answered.

'Yes?' I said.

Anna. 'We have a confirmation that Jack Ming is going to meet his CIA contact tomorrow.'

'Tomorrow. What time?'

'He has told the contact he'll call him at noon with instructions.'

So Anna had someone inside the CIA.

'I know where Jack wants to meet them. So your worries are nearly at an end, Anna.'

'Tell me.'

'No.'

'I said tell me.'

'We ran into a problem. I think you might have a leak on your side.'

'Impossible.'

'Jack Ming's mother is kidnapped and now dead, and so is her kidnapper. If you don't have a leak, then a third party is interfering in our work.'

A chastised silence. 'Don't lie to me.'

'I'll talk to you after Jack Ming is dead.'

She hung up.

'You can't cross her,' Leonie said. 'She holds all the cards.'

'No,' I said. 'She only thinks she does.'

'So who's trying to screw us? Is it the CIA?'

'Anyone could say that they're CIA,' I said. 'I don't know. But as long as we find Jack Ming first, it won't matter.'

'Who is this Mila?'

How do you explain Mila? 'A friend.'

'Who has a price on her head.' Her voice was steady.

'An interesting friend.'

'You were just trying to panic the driver.'

'I wasn't going to sell out anyone, thanks for the vote of confidence.'

'Thank *you*. You got us out of that alive.'

'We're in this together.'

'Yes,' she said, but now we believed it in a way we hadn't before. She fell silent. I thought about how Special Projects might have identified their informant as Jack Ming in the past few hours. I thought about Fagin. I thought about him talking to his bosses at Special Projects and whether anyone there would hire an ex-Latvian spy and current limo driver to do their dirty work.

We drove to Williamsburg, Brooklyn, to the address of Russell Ming's property, the one for which Jack had presumably taken the keys. All the windows were darkened. It was a squat, four-story building – it wore the look of having once been a small factory. It had not been redone into shops or studios or apartments for the throngs of young, hip professionals and former Manhattanites crowding into Williamsburg. The windows were boarded. A sign on the side read MING PROPERTIES.

'Do we break in?' she asked. Her voice was strained.

'Yes. He could be inside right now.'

I picked the locks and we went inside.

An alarm sounded.

'Hell,' I said. We bolted back to the car. From a side street we watched. First a private security car responded. The guard went inside, stayed inside, turned off the alarm.

'I don't think Jack Ming is there,' Leonie said.

After a few minutes the guard came back out, locked the door, did a final walkthrough around the building, and then left.

'No Jack,' she said.

But he'd taken these keys for some reason. If he wasn't here now, he soon would be. I refused to consider the possibility that I was utterly wrong.

'Do we wait here? Wait here for him to come?' she said.

The pain in my head throbbed. My eye was nearly swollen

shut; I was going to have a shiner and I didn't want a shiner. Black eyes are memorable. I needed to be invisible.

'We need a vantage point,' I said. 'We need to be able to watch the building, know how often the private security comes and goes.'

We drove past the building again and our headlights danced on the sign. Security by Proxima Systems. She looked them up on her iPhone. Then she pulled Mrs Ming's phone from her pocket, listened to her voicemail and dialed the number.

'Proxima New York.'

'Yes, this is Sandra Ming of Ming Properties. I own a building in Williamsburg for which you provide security.' Leonie made her voice brisk, slightly deeper.

'Yes, ma'am, and may I have your account passcode.'

She hesitated about five seconds. 'Jack.'

We could hear typing and then 'Thank you, ma'am, how can I help you?'

I stared at her. How had she known?

'I need to confirm the security check schedule for that building. I've heard from other property owners that there might be a crime increase going on in the neighborhood and I just got a phone call that there had been a breach.'

'Yes, ma'am.' Typing noises. 'The guard comes by at 11 p.m., 1 a.m., 4 a.m., 6 a.m., then again at noon, with up to a ten-minute variant. If he will be later than that we contact you. Do you want to increase your patrol profile?'

'Not now. Thank you,' Leonie said. She hung up.

'You should have canceled the service,' I said dryly.

'Generally that requires a face-to-face meeting, or a separate confirmation password,' Leonie said. 'I didn't want to arouse attention. We know our time windows now.'

'How did you know the password?'

'Because I'm a mom. Moms use their kids' or pets' names, or a variant as passwords, like eighty per cent of the time. It was worth a try.'

'So we know when the guard comes. Yes, and there's a long gap when Jack and August can meet.' I considered. 'And I don't think Jack is going to camp out inside the building. He risks being caught by a security guard as well, or being noticed. But we need to find a place to watch from, to be sure.' I scanned the buildings. 'There. Two away. That's a hotel.'

33

Hotel Esper, Williamsburg/The Last Minute Bar, Manhattan

Leonie got the room at the Williamsburg hotel, a trendy, high-end spot with the meaningless name of Hotel Esper (was it short for *esperanza*, hope? Or did it imply you could read minds while a guest there? I wondered); just one room, with a window facing the Ming building. We were going to be awake in shifts and if anyone else – say a rogue element in the CIA – was looking for us, they'd be looking maybe for a man and a woman checking in together but in separate rooms. I drove back to our Manhattan hotel and washed my face clean of dirt and blood. I looked okay except for the black eye. It wasn't so bad. I gathered all Leonie's notes and papers and stuffed them into her small suitcase. I put on fresh, untorn clothes and collected our bags and checked out for us both.

Then I took the rental and swung by my bar, The Last Minute. I looked like a wreck going in and Bertrand raised an eyebrow at me. I went straight upstairs. There was an apartment up there but I didn't dare bring Leonie to it. She already knew I owned The Canyon in Las Vegas but she didn't need to know more of my business. And I didn't need Mila knowing what I was doing.

But when I opened the door, there Mila was. Sitting at the computer, a neat Glenfiddich at her elbow.

She was typing something. She looked up at me and wiped her hand back across her eyes.

Seeing Mila cry? Never in my lifetime, I thought. But I actually hadn't *seen* a tear.

'You look like hell,' she said.

'I know. Are you okay?'

'Fine. What's going on?'

'I need some gear.'

'What are you doing, Sam?'

'I am getting my son back. I need you not to ask questions, okay.'

She stared at me. It was weird to have Mila stare at me. She knew so much about me, and I knew so little about her.

'But you asked me a question. I get to ask back,' she said.

'What?'

'You wanted to know why there is such a high price on my head. I am writing you my detailed answer.'

'You're not exactly the essayist type.' Mila was a woman of few words.

'Please know I won awards for my essays in school.' She put her fingers back on the keyboard but kept her stare locked on me.

'So, in Moldova, a school prize is probably a goat?'

'Not always. Once I won a copy of *A Wrinkle in Time*. The message of the book stayed with me. Never give up against darkness.'

'And love conquers all.'

'Yes, *Samuil*. Love conquers all. Or at least it tries.' Now she looked back at the screen.

'And when do I get to read your true confessions?'

'I am sure publishers will fight to the death, gladiator-style, for my story. But you can read it first. And when you tell me what you're doing and how I can help you.'

'Help me by staying out of this.' I went into the storage closet. I put two pairs of binoculars, a pair of small flashlights and a Glock in my bag. I selected a Beretta for Leonie, for her protection. Picked out rounds of ammunition. I packed a Burberry Prosrum suit I'd liked, shirt, tie and shoes to go with it. I might have to play a part to lure Jack close.

Mila stood in the doorway. 'You don't have to fight your war alone.'

'I'm not alone.'

'Why reject my help?'

'Because you are in danger. Stay out of this. Get out of New York, Mila, now.'

'I do not worry about muggers.'

'I'm serious. I killed a man tonight who specifically wanted to find you, wanted me to give you to him, and he has a boss who wants you. Someone in the CIA.'

She made a dismissive wave. 'They want me for questioning.'

'I don't think that's it at all. I think someone's after the bounty on you.'

'Then for my own safety,' she coughed, 'I should stick with you. Help you. We will take the fight to them together.'

'No.'

'Why?'

'Because you want this informant alive. The guy who could give you Novem Soles.'

'Of course he could give us Novem Soles. And maybe he in turn could give me the guy who posted the bounty,' she said.

I let her words settle. 'Novem Soles has posted the reward for you.'

She nodded. 'One of them is behind it, yes. If I can kill the man who wants me dead, no one will fund his revenge. They won't care. This is his private vendetta.'

'Then why hasn't this guy in Novem Soles asked me for you in exchange for my son?'

'They don't know we know each other,' she said. 'No one who could tell them that is still alive.' She paused. 'Except August, and whoever he has told inside the CIA.'

'Why didn't you tell me?'

'Because you have to kill the informant. For your son.'

'The informant may know nothing about how to find the man who wants you dead.'

She shrugged. 'You pick up a thread, unwind it, it can pull apart the entire blanket. My aunt always says so and she is right.'

'Who wants you dead?'

'He is a man called Zviman. He hides from me like I hide from him. There is a price on his head as well. We shall see who gets bought first.'

'Zviman?'

'Yes.'

'Why does he want you dead?'

'It will be easier for you to read than for me to tell you. I have told my story only to one other person. I don't normally talk about it.' Mila's voice went quiet.

'Don't joke.'

'I hurt his pride.' Mila smiled. 'Where are you going?'

'Let me do this. If I can find where Zviman is from Jack, I will.'

'That's a sweet lie, Sam.' She held the whisky glass. 'Do you want me to tend to your eye?'

'No.'

'Good luck then.' And then Mila did something she had never done before. She embraced me. I was holding the clothes bag and a backpack with the guns. Not really in hugging mode. Her hands ran down my back, then she patted the front of my shirt. 'Be careful. I hope you get your son back.'

'Thank you.' I smiled. 'Why are you in New York?'

'Shoes,' she said.

'Ah. Don't get killed, Mila. I would miss you.'

'Do not get killed, Sam. I would miss *you*.'

I left without another word. My insides felt knotted. I went out into the cloud-smeared, starless night.

I was going to get my son back, and nobody, nobody, was going to kill Mila.

High expectations.

I patted my shirt pocket. She'd slid in a small chip, thin as paper, when she gave me my hug. I held it up to the streetlight. Tracker, like a modified phone SIM card. She wished me well but she wanted to know where I was going. To help me or to fight her own battle? I didn't know. I tried not to care.

Two customers were leaving the bar and I thoughtfully hailed them a cab. A bit bleary from The Last Minute's excellent martinis, they thanked me and as I opened the door for them I flicked Mila's tracker onto the cab floor.

Let it take her where it would, out of the battle, into safety, perhaps.

I headed back to Leonie, and the long night of waiting.

34

Morris County, New Jersey

It is a very small world, and getting smaller, he thought.

Ricardo Braun stood above the speared body of the limo driver. He muttered a curse under his breath. He took his gun and with care shot off the man's face. He had to do this by flashlight, with the moonless sky, and he was careful to avoid getting any blood or tissue on his shoes or his jeans. He reloaded and then blasted off the ten fingertips. This would buy him at most a few days if the body was found, but even a narrow margin of time had saved him in the past. Then he removed the limo's plates and stripped out the forged registration and insurance papers. Its vehicle identification number had long ago been filed off. He dumped the corpse in the trunk, then put in Sandra Ming's body.

There was a large pond on the property. He found a rock and put it on the accelerator and watched as the water settled over the limo. It took surprisingly little time for the car to sink. He waited until the water was still, the last ripple smooth.

Then he got into his Mercedes and he drove back to his apartment in Greenwich Village. It was very late now and he sat and drank coffee and watched the stars and wondered how much in danger he was. If anyone knew what he was doing, and why.

Sam Capra. He could have stopped him, if he had not had to meet with the assholes from Langley who'd insisted on a quick report. Special Projects was a beehive; and only he and August knew about the Jack Ming affair. Well, and now Fagin, but Fagin would never speak. Eliminating Fagin would create far too many questions; he was golden, untouchable. But a healthy deposit in Fagin's account would ensure silence, and, hell, most of the Company had no idea Sam Capra had saved the CIA inconceivable humiliation in the Yankee Stadium incident. Most of them, if they knew who he was at all, thought he was still a suspect character, untrustworthy.

He felt a slight rage that he had allowed this to spin out of control. Right now he sat at his laptop and accessed a private website, within the Special Projects computer network, and clicked on an icon that read BANISH. That was the code word August had set up for the Jack Ming case. The only two people who could access this folder were August and Braun.

He read: *heard from target via phone call, he will call me again at 12 ET tomorrow with instructions for meet*

Tomorrow, then, this would all be settled. If Ming wasn't dead before tomorrow's meeting, then he would take custody of Jack Ming, tell him that his mother was already secure in a Special Projects safe house, seize whatever evidence he had, and he would make Jack disappear forever. The only way to be safe, the only way to be sure.

August might be a problem but a quick reassignment to another division would solve that dilemma. He was a good soldier; he'd take his orders. In a few months Braun would go out and visit him, treat him to a steak dinner, and tell him Novem Soles had been wrapped up, neat as a napkin.

And no one would ever know.

Ricardo Braun considered the one hint that he had for his other agenda: Mila. Sam had told the driver, who had relayed it to him, that she sometimes met Sam Capra at a bar. Not exactly actionable information to find Mila.

Unless Sam Capra wanted to be followed, wanted to see who it flushed out into the open.

It wouldn't matter, though, would it, if Sam Capra was dead by tomorrow?

The whole incident was a shame. He had studied the Capra file. The world still did not know that the bombing of a London office was an attack against a Special Projects team; did not know that a CIA officer, pregnant by another officer, committed a grievous treason; did not know that more than one traitor, bought not by ideology or disaffection but by cold cash, had been flushed out of the Company. Did not know that a man scorned by the Company as a traitor had been its savior. Capra had done his duty.

Duty. It was the red in Braun's blood, the oxygen that he breathed. Duty was all. Duty was what forced you to push boundaries, take chances, give your life to something and still have the bravery to reap the rewards from it.

Once Braun had written essays and poems on duty in his journal, to try to understand his own feelings about it, but finally he had burned them all.

If Capra had come back to Special Projects when the job was offered – if he had stuck to his duty – then this would not have to happen. It was a shame. He didn't want Capra dead. At the least he wouldn't be an enemy, but a sacrifice. That was somehow nobler, Braun thought.

With Andris the limo driver dead and floating in eternal

223

company with Mrs Ming, he was going to need someone else to handle Capra and Jack Ming. The best thing about Special Projects was that, since it was supposed to be separate and deniable from the Company, he was allowed, when needed, to use non-Company personnel. And keep them out of the record. Like Andris and his limo company, funded by Company dollars that had been washed by Special Projects.

Or the sisters. Yes, the sisters would be a good choice for tomorrow. They always brightened his day.

35

Brooklyn

Jack Ming sat in a movie theater. He was on his fourth feature film of the day. The theaters were nice, dark and quiet and he could think. Right now a romantic comedy, indifferently written and acted, played in front of him. He didn't really want to see or hear anything violent or twisted. He didn't like movies with gunfire, not since Rotterdam. Right now the movie's hero thought his girlfriend's mom had the hots for him, which wasn't true, but, you know, was just hilarious. Not. His dinner had been a hot dog and a soda he bought at the theater and he rattled the ice in a jumbo cup.

His mother's betrayal had stopped itching at him. He could not be surprised. She would never let him do as he wanted; the only freedom he'd had in his life was when he had run away and worn another name, in another country.

The notebook sat in a square, taped to his back. Earlier, in a

Starbucks, he'd sat down in a lonely corner and paged through its mysteries again. Account numbers, pictures, email addresses. He studied the photo of the three people that had the words *The Nursery* written underneath. The word *Nursery* was suggestive: a place where something was born, or something was protected and grown. Just a photo of three people. But clearly three people who, by virtue of being together, revealed a secret about themselves. If Nine Suns meant nine people, then this was a third of them, and if you could take down a third, perhaps you could find out who the other six were. Perhaps you could cripple them.

He thought about trying to contact any of the people being blackmailed, but he decided against it. If he frightened them, they might vanish, and what would make the notebook valuable was if the people corrupted were still in place. If they took off running or hiding, then they would not be useful. On one page he'd found a single phone number. He was so tempted to call it, and fear and curiosity played over his heart.

More than ever, the notebook was his ticket.

But. He wondered why, if his mother had called the CIA, they weren't already there when he arrived. Why not snatch him up at home? Had they just figured out it was him? If they waited for him to show up, and lounge around at home, they could take him with less fuss, perhaps.

He didn't know what to believe.

He needed a place to sleep. Hostels were out of the question; he didn't know who his mother would have looking for him, much less Novem Soles. If homeless people could sleep on the streets, he could as well. Just for one night.

He left the movie theater and ducked into another coffee shop. Lots of people his age, on laptops, chatting, pretending to write the next great American novel while they idled away their creative time on social networking sites. He got a decaf and sat in the corner and opened up the notebook, staring at the one phone number on the last page.

36

The Last Minute Bar, Manhattan

Mila ordered another Glenfiddich from Bertrand and a bacon sandwich from The Last Minute's small kitchen. She put aside her confessions for Sam; the story of herself that she had only told one person before – and she opened up the tracking software on the laptop, which would tell her where Sam was going.

She studied the route. From The Last Minute to a hotel in Greenwich Village to a nightclub to another hotel. She didn't believe he was nightclubbing. And she didn't believe whoever he was tracking was out nightclubbing either. He'd found the tracker she'd planted on him and put it in a cab. She smiled. Sam was no fool. And now he knew she'd tricked him. For a moment she considered deleting the confession; she was mad at him, unreasonably, she knew, but mad all the same. She was alive and she felt sure his baby was probably dead or lost forever to him, no matter what promises Anna made. Novem Soles had no honor, no sense of justice, no kindness. They would never give him his child back and she knew it and she wished he could know it as well. She could not make him understand; she could not force him to abandon hope.

She could not do to him what had been done to her.

She took a long sip of the whisky and put her fingertips back to the keyboard, the letters on the electronic screen hanging like small, curved ghosts before her eyes.

37

JFK Airport

The Watcher stepped off the plane. His mouth tasted sour from his in-flight doze. His suit wasn't as clean as he'd like for it to be. He waited for the press of folks off first class to pass (to his great annoyance he couldn't get a first class seat) and then he obediently followed the rest of the coach passengers off the jet. The flight attendants gave him robotic nods and thanks.

He waited in the queue at Customs for non-US citizens and finally presented his Dutch passport. It passed muster without a hesitation, and he even managed a smile for the customs clerk who wished him a pleasant stay in the United States.

He stepped out into the city – one of the greatest dining cities in the world, he dreamed of a vacation where he did nothing but eat and talk with chefs here, but he could not think of food now. Novem Soles had found the record of Jack's alias taking a flight out of Brussels; Ricki had lied to him. She would pay when he had time to focus on her. Jack Ming was in this city now, with his book of secrets. Sam Capra and Leonie Jones were going to kill Jack Ming and then they would die. It would close a book on the CIA's own investigation of Novem Soles, once a former CIA agent had been identified as Jack Ming's murderer. And then the circle would be closed, and the circle would be safe.

His phone rang. 'Yes?'

Silence on the other end.

'Yes?' the Watcher said impatiently.

'Yes, hello,' a voice said, and it was one he'd listened to in the recording of the CIA conversation before, a voice he knew by heart. Jack Ming.

'Hello,' Jack Ming said into the sudden silence.

The Watcher froze. 'Who is this?'

'You don't know me,' Jack Ming said, 'but your phone number is in a book I found. May I ask who this is?'

'Well, no, because I don't know who you are,' the Watcher said.

'I think you are being blackmailed,' Jack said. 'Are you? Because if you are, maybe I can help stop the people who are hurting you.'

'You . . . you.' The Watcher said. 'Who are you?'

'Since you didn't say no, I'll assume you're being blackmailed.'

The Watcher's mind spun. What exactly was in this notebook? A cold chill inched up his spine. 'Listen. Okay. I don't know who you are, this could be a trick to get me to say something I shouldn't.' Play the victim, draw him close. 'Tell me exactly how you got my number.'

'A friend gave me a book. It has numbers – bank account numbers – and emails and photos in it. I think it's a book used to extort people all over the world, people in positions of business and government.' Silence. 'Do you fit those criteria?'

'I might. Oh, my God,' the Watcher said. The fear in his voice wasn't exactly false. He cursed. He was standing out near a taxi pickup line at JFK. He had no equipment with which to trace the call; no way to alert any of the technical resources of Novem Soles. He would have to draw Jack in himself. *And, honestly, if you can't do that with a grad student you don't deserve your job.* 'Look, if this is a test, I've done what you said. I have. Everything. Please. *Please*.'

'It's not a test, I'm trying to help you. If you can tell me who you are and what they have you doing . . . '

'I'm not confessing anything. Oh my God, oh my God. You tell me who you are, where you are. Give me a reason to trust you.' The Watcher made his voice a slice of panic.

'I am going to give this information to the authorities,' Jack said. 'The whole book. Now. If you want these people broken and off your back, I can make that happen. I can tear off your phone number from the book before I give it to the authorities. That way, you are never exposed.'

You devious little bastard, the Watcher thought. I want to kill you all myself.

'And then you're never in trouble. I'll do that for you, I'll pull this page from the book, if you'll tell me what they have you doing.'

'I have to think for a minute,' the Watcher said. Delaying.

'Well, one minute is what you have,' Jack Ming said, trying to sound tough.

'Don't threaten me, I'll hang up.'

'And then when the police show up at your work, or at your door, wanting to know why you cooperated with a criminal ring . . . '

'I'm not going to talk to you on the phone,' the Watcher said. 'Could we meet face to face?'

'This is a Paris number and I'm not in Paris.'

'I'm not either, I'm in New York.'

It was a gamble to admit this, that he was in the same city as Jack Ming. Jack was silent.

'I'm here for them, they've made me come here.' The Watcher said this as though tearing the words out of his own chest.

'Your minute is about up,' Jack said.

So the Watcher decided: 'I work for a major financial services firm. I give them data from my company. I deliver it once a month. Financial particulars, insider information, plans for investment. Confidential knowledge that they can use to profit on the stock markets in France, the US, Hong Kong.'

'What did they have on you?'

The Watcher thought. He had to sell this. 'I engaged in some insider trading. They found out about it. They said they would expose me if I didn't help them. I don't trade any more, I just feed them the information. If I disobey them they'll expose me and if I talk about them, they'll kill my entire family. So please don't tell any one. Please.'

'Why are you in New York for them?'

'They wanted me to get some information on a stock deal.'

'Whose deal?'

'I won't say. If it leaks then they'll know I leaked it.'

'I'm sorry,' Jack said. 'Thank you. I'll tear your number from the book.'

'You can't give that book to anyone,' the Watcher said. He had to try. 'You can't. You'll destroy dozens of lives.'

Silence. 'How did you know they're blackmailing dozens of people?'

'Stands to reason if it's enough to fill a book.'

The ten longest seconds – at least since he'd encountered Mila – of the Watcher's life ticked past.

'You're not being blackmailed at all,' Jack Ming said. 'You're one of them, aren't you?'

'No.'

'I think a person being blackmailed would probably disconnect the phone immediately and not say a word. How do you know I'm not the police?'

'The police would show up. They can't trick a confession from you, not this way.'

'They could if they had a bug on your phone,' Jack said.

'You cannot give them that book. Please.'

'Your number won't be in it now, so why worry? So concerned for your fellow victims?'

'I just don't want innocent people hurt.' The night breeze, the smell of jet fuel in the airport wind, blew over him. He had to stop this little lunatic, somehow.

'Very considerate of you. This has been so illuminating,' Jack Ming said. 'Thank you . . .'

Time for Plan B. 'They know who you are, Jack,' the Watcher said. 'Which means they know who Ricki is, and who your mother is. They will find everyone you've ever cared about and they will burn them and everything you love to the ground. Oh, yes. You know why I'm really here? I'm going to destroy you financially, your family, everything you hold dear. Your mother will be selling herself in alleyways after I'm done.'

Stunned silence on the other end. 'What?' Jack said finally.

'There is another option for you. I'll buy the notebook. I'll buy your silence.'

'I don't believe you.'

'Ten million. It's a nice round number and you can easily live off that for the rest of your life.'

'Unworkable,' Jack said. 'Ask the dead dude in the Amsterdam hospital if you think I'm going to meet you face to face.'

'That was done without my approval, in panic, by a fool. Let's deal like adults. I'll put half the money in an account for you. You mail me the notebook and I'll pay you the other half.'

'And when I show up at your bank or move the money, you find me and kill me. No thank you. Plus, you can't trust I haven't copied the notebook.'

'Let me propose this. A cash drop. We agree on a place for you to leave the notebook. And a place for me to leave you cash.'

'Ten million in small bills is not exactly transportable by one guy in a hurry,' Jack said. 'I don't trust you.'

'I can give you a better deal than the CIA can. Twice the money.'

'And dead twice as fast.'

'Jack. Play nice, or I will burn you down.'

'You're just trying to lure me in. No. You know who I am. I know what you are. And when I'm done with you, you son of a bitch, there is no hiding place for you.'

This little nobody, threatening *him*. The Watcher heard the snap in his own voice. 'You are nothing but a contemptible punk. When you die, and you will, I'll throw a party. I'll have people over for drinks and we'll watch you being slowly tortured to death. I'll have it catered. It won't happen in some dark warehouse or basement. It will happen, with people standing around having drinks, laughing while they watch your skin pulled off, your eyes gouged, your ears burned to a crisp.'

'Someone's going to burn,' Jack said, 'but it's not me.' Then he hung up.

The Watcher stood there, the red rage slowly building in his eyes. He closed the phone and walked forward slowly to join the line of travelers awaiting a taxi.

38

Hotel Esper, Williamsburg

'I want to know who owns that property in New Jersey,' I said. We were in the hotel room; Leonie sitting at the table, me standing at the window, looking down toward the Ming building's boarded windows.

She opened her laptop. 'It would help if we had an address. It's out in the middle of nowhere.'

'It was marked as River Run Road. See you if you can find a county property map. Or find it on Google Maps.'

She tapped, and hummed under her breath. Leonie on a computer reminded me of my wife Lucy. My ex-wife. Lucy was very clever with computers, too. I stared out at the night and let her work. She tapped, found maps, compared them with the route we'd driven.

'The property is owned by Associated Languages School.'

'A language school?' No wonder it was derelict. Didn't most people learn foreign languages these days through software programs? And it was out in the boonies. 'Maybe it's supposed to be an immersion program?'

I watched her fingers fly across the keyboard; she nibbled her lip in thought. 'They have a very basic website.'

'Where are they headquartered?'

'New York. They have immersion programs in rural New York, Florida and Oregon that they offer. But it says their next three sessions are full.'

'Maybe the driver knew that the house was unoccupied.'

'Yes. Maybe he drove students out there before and knew it was shuttered now.'

But it didn't quite ring true. 'Would it be shuttered if business was booming?'

I picked up my phone, sat down on the bed and called them. 'You have reached the offices of Associated Languages School. We offer instruction and translation services in' – and then the recording went into a tiresome listing of every major language spoken on four continents. I considered hanging up the phone. Maybe that's what they wanted me to do. Finally, I was invited to leave a message. I hung up.

'Front company,' I said. 'Nobody makes it that hard to do business.'

'A front for Novem Soles?'

'Maybe. Can we find out anything else on them?'

'Yes, but is that going to help us find out anything about Jack Ming? Let's not lose focus here, Sam. If we do this right we have our kids tomorrow. We vanish, and we don't ever worry about Novem Soles again.'

I got up and stared out the window. She tapped away at her computer while I watched the night.

'I got into Proxima Security,' she said. 'Via Sandra Ming's account. I've got access to a monitor log. It will tell us if anyone enters the building and punches in a code.'

'We know the guard has the code.'

'And we can assume Jack does. We know the guard's schedule. If someone comes at a different time, I think we'll know it's Jack.'

'Could you disable the alarm?'

She shook her head. 'Separate system.'

'Well, at least we'll know when people come and go.'

'I'll put an alarm on my laptop to chime if there's an update to the log,' she said. 'Can I give you some advice?'

'No.'

'Give up on fighting Novem Soles when this is done,' she said. 'Revenge is the most worthless motive in the world. Your wife made her choice, yes? You get your son back, then you have all that matters. All right? Don't try to keep fighting them. Go live a safe, good life.'

'Move on and put out of my mind that I'm going to kill a young man who could bring them down.'

'To save your son? Yes. Put Jack Ming as a human being out of your mind. People put ugliness out of their heads all the time. Jack Ming made his choice, same as your wife.'

'And now he's trying to unmake it,' I said. 'Does that count for nothing?'

She was silent.

'He's trying to be the good guy. If he'd turned on Novem Soles seven months ago he might be surrendering to me, and I'd be getting ready to take a bullet for him if that's what it took to save him.'

Leonie got up and sat at the window. She stared down at the building. 'Some choices can't be unmade. So we should watch for him?'

'If you want. But I seriously doubt he's going to come around to be discovered by the security guard. We have to trust Anna's source.'

'You're sure?'

'I think so. He's not a trained operative. Daylight is easier. He can see what he's facing. I'm thinking he's camped somewhere else tonight. He needs his sleep, too.'

'But why not go to the CIA already?'

'He must have a reason. He's in control of the meeting. We know he wanted to spend time with his mom, but she kicked him out onto the curb and he lost his hiding place. So he might be seeing another friend, he might be studying the evidence he's got against Novem Soles and – I don't know – building his case. He could be making this up as he goes along. Don't hackers improvise?'

We didn't have an unobstructed view of the Ming building. We could see the back alley approaches to it, but not the entrance itself. The angle was impossible. I kept watching the black, boarded windows, for any seep of light, but there was none.

I left her at the window and lay down on the bed. My head ached. My eye hurt. Sleep. Just for an hour or two, I thought. 'When you got Mrs Ming away during the fight ...'

'I wasn't trying to abandon you. But only she could tell us where Jack was. So I thought.'

'Your focus is admirable,' I said.

'So is yours,' Leonie said softly. 'You killed that man.'

'Yes.' I kept my eyes closed.

'Is it upsetting?'

'You should hope not. I have to do it again tomorrow.'

We listened to the distant hum of traffic, the breathing of New York. 'If only we'd caught Jack at his mother's house.'

'I got to see his room. He's just a kid, in many ways.'

'Not in any ways that matter. Don't you start to feel sorry for him.'

'I'll feel what I like, thank you,' I said. I thought I should have kept my mouth shut. All I did by showing sympathy to our target was increase Leonie's distrust of me.

'I knew a man who killed. It never, ever bothered him.'

I opened an eye. 'Did you help him disappear, too? Give him a new identity?'

'No. I gave myself one, to get away from him.' She sat huddled by the window, knees drawn up to her chin. 'I left him because he didn't want kids. Too much of a hassle with his ... work.'

'Leonie.' I wondered if it was her real name. It didn't matter. I wouldn't ever see her again when this was done.

'I mean, you know, I could have had a killer as the father of my kids. There's a wise choice. What a laugh he would have been at careers day.'

'Leonie, it's okay.' I had killed and I was a father. What she was talking about wasn't the same. Or was it? Yeah, I was going to be a cold-blooded killer by tomorrow. All so I could be a father. What a screwed-up world.

She moved a lock of her auburn hair out of her face. She came to the bed. She put her fingertips on the side of my face and inspected the bruising. 'You have little cuts here from the rock.'

'They'll heal.'

She didn't take her hands from my face.

'You have to kill Jack, Sam. You can't feel sorry for him. You can't feel emotion for him. You just have to kill him. It will be ... easy.'

Easy because she didn't have to claim a human life. I closed my eyes. Jack, in the pictures of him in his room. Arms around his thin shoulders, his protective college buddies looking out for the likable geek. The books he'd loved, the gap-toothed child smiling from the photos.

I needed him to be a faceless stranger but his mother had died holding my hand.

'I'm full of crap,' Leonie said. 'It's never easy, is it?'

She moved her hand from my cheek to my forehead, caught her fingers in my hair.

What? I thought. I'm just so clever.

'You must have really loved your wife.'

It was a strange observation to make. I opened my eyes. 'I don't want to talk about her.'

'Anna told me that you tried to find your wife . . . her way of saying you were a decent man. Anna didn't want me to be scared of working with you.'

Scared? I was supposed to be the good guy. Raised by globe-trotting Christian relief agency do-gooders, the nice boy who went to Harvard and stayed on track, the smart brother who didn't go to Afghanistan and get himself and his best friend killed, the boy who became a man in the CIA, fueled by revenge but tempered (I hoped) by fairness. And now what was I? Someone who'd been accused of being a traitor because I'd married the wrong woman (an actual, *technical* traitor) and had dodged the CIA and now was in an awful limbo of untrustworthiness as far as that fine agency was concerned.

Death is a weird thing. The death for the driver was egregiously bad: being impaled is never anyone's exit of choice. And for Mrs Ming, she had died with an awful uncertainty clouding her mind and corroding her last moments. Leonie and I had nearly died tonight. Death makes us thirst for life and all its basics: a comforting meal, the breeze of our own breath in our lungs, the warm press of human flesh.

Leonie leaned down and she kissed my bruised lips.

No woman had kissed me since Lucy. I froze for a moment. This was crossing a line I'd seen from the corner of my eye, this was knowing Lucy was gone and was never, ever coming back and even if she did come back that I wouldn't want her back. I felt myself . . . unfreeze.

My whole face hurt but I pressed my lips to hers in response.

The kiss didn't accelerate, it grew slower. More thoughtful. She nibbled at my lower lip.

'Sam,' she said very quietly.

'Yes.'

'Afterwards, will we be cool?'

'Yes.' I didn't exactly know what cool meant but I wasn't going to say no.

She started to kiss me again. With heat. It didn't matter that my face ached. I wanted her with a sudden, fierce certainty. I had not been with many women before Lucy. The idea that every spy is a womanizer is a patent falsehood. You are usually keeping people at arm's length. I never had time and I didn't now but that did not seem to matter. Her kisses were quick and darting and urgent. Her tongue, her fingertips were everywhere. I'm not even sure we got all our clothes off and then I joined to her, Leonie groaning against me, a low, throaty growl, her face close to mine.

After a delicious while, she shuddered, her breath warm against my bruised eye, looking deep into my face as though surveying curious terrain. Then she laid her face on my chest. I gasped in release a minute or two later, her urging me on with cooing sounds. Her body felt lush and warm and smooth.

It was good but it was more comfort than passion. We stripped off the rest of our clothes and clutched at each other. Neither of us wanted to talk. We just wanted to be.

'Promise me,' she said, lying curled next to me. 'Promise me we'll get our kids back.'

'I promise,' I said. What else could I say?

I just had to make it true. That promise bound us together. That promise would change everything.

39

Hotel Esper, Williamsburg

We slept late, longer than we should have. Normally I can't sleep late in New York because the rising noise of the traffic is an automatic alarm clock. When I woke up Leonie was showered and dressed and tapping at her laptop. 'No intrusions at the building other than those at the security guard's regularly appointed rounds.' She looked up at me and gave me a wan smile.

What did I do? Kiss her, nuzzle her, pretend last night didn't happen? My marriage with Lucy – full of deception and lies and my own blindness – convinced me that I suck at relationships and it wasn't like we were going to have a long-term one. We would get our kids and part ways and never see each other again, except in our memories about the worst few days of our lives.

The newspaper websites in New York and New Jersey carried no mention of two bodies discovered at the abandoned Associated Languages School in Morris County.

'I'll go get us some breakfast,' I said. Leonie made the noise one makes when one is absorbed in a computer screen. Again, like Lucy.

'What are you doing?'

'I thought about what you said last night,' she said. 'I'm going to find out who that driver was.'

'He doesn't matter any more.'

'You're not working alone,' she said. 'Why presume that he is? We don't know how much of a head start we have on finding Jack. We may have none. And I'm not going to sit here and fret and wait and do nothing while waiting for Jack to show up.'

I walked to a diner on the corner and got breakfast for us to go: mushroom and spinach omelets, hash browns, fruit, bacon, coffee, orange juice. You eat when you can because you never know when you might get your next meal on days like today.

When I came back we ate. I tried to make conversation.

'Where are you from?' I asked.

She seemed to measure her answer by staring into her Styrofoam coffee cup.

'I know your real name isn't Leonie, that you live under a false name.'

'Trust me, it's better you not know much about me. I am infinitely boring.'

'I know that's not true,' I said with a smile.

She smiled back, just for a moment. 'You, where are you from?'

'All over. My parents worked for a relief agency. My mom's a pediatric surgeon, my dad's an administrator. I lived in over twenty different countries before I was eighteen.' I finished my coffee. 'If I don't make it, and you get my son back from Anna, you can take him to my parents. They live in New Orleans. Alexander and Simone Capra. They're in the phone book.'

'Are you close to them?'

'No. Not at all.'

'Why?'

'My brother died and it ruined their hearts. They either want to take over my life entirely or shut me out completely. Him dying made them a little crazy.'

'How did he die?'

'He went to Afghanistan, to do relief work like they'd done for years, and he and his best friend from college, they got captured by the Taliban. Their throats were cut in a propaganda video.'

'Oh, my God,' Leonie said. 'I'm so sorry.' It was about the

best thing she could say. Really, it's so horrible, it shocks people. You cannot imagine what it is like to see your brother die, help-lessly. To see his friend die. Then to see them discussed on every news channel, as though they are just names to learn, *Danny Capra, Zalmay Qureshi,* not people, just distant unfortunates, just names. 'That was when I joined the CIA.'

'But you're not with them any more.'

'When your wife betrays the CIA, it kind of destroys your career path.'

'I would think.'

'A constant cloud of suspicion.' I stood up and shoved my Styrofoam food holder in the trash. 'So we parted ways.'

'And she had this baby while you were apart?'

'Yes.'

'What was she like? Your wife?'

'Why do you care?'

'I'm just curious. You seem too smart a guy to be easily fooled.'

'We all have our blind spots. She was one as large as the Sahara to me.'

'Sometimes we don't pick wisely.'

'No. And the price we pay is very heavy.'

Leonie turned back to her computer.

'Any luck with tracing the driver?'

'No,' she said. Not looking at me.

'Really? No track on his driver's license or his limo plates?' She had memorized the plates during the long haul out of Manhattan and New Jersey, following him.

'Stolen, I guess,' she said. Still not looking at me.

I stood up and watched the Ming building with my binocu-lars. Two o'clock couldn't come soon enough for me. I needed inside that building now, in between the last pass of the security guard and Jack's (presumed) meeting with August.

And then I thought of a way.

40

Hotel Esper, Williamsburg

I left Leonie in her room and went down to the lobby. I called Russell Ming's property company, now owned by his wife.

'Ming Properties,' the woman answering the phone said.

'Hi, may I speak to,' and I looked again at the name I'd jotted down, the one under the number on the Ming Properties sign, 'Beth Marley?'

'This is she.' She sounded bright and enthusiastic, like talking to me was the highlight of her day. I'm sure it was.

'My name is Sam Capra, and I'm interested in the building in Williamsburg.'

'Oh, great.'

'I own the The Last Minute Bar, over by Bryant Park.'

'I know that bar!' she said.

'Oh, that's great. I'm interested in leasing some property in Brooklyn that you own, in Williamsburg. Would it be possible to see it today?'

'Today might be difficult, sir. What about tomorrow?'

'I'm just in town for the day. In fact, I might be interested in leasing the whole building. I just happened to see it and think it's perfect for what I need.'

'Well. Okay, let me do a little juggling.' I could hear her

flipping papers. 'Sure. I could do eleven o'clock, would that work?'

'You're so kind. That will be great. I'll just meet you there, okay?'

'Thanks, Mr Capra.'

I hung up and went back to the hotel room. 'Well, that was easy. I have an appointment.'

Leonie, crouching over her computer, didn't answer.

41

Special Projects headquarters, Manhattan

Ricardo Braun was not concerned with legalities as much as expediency: after he had discovered the limo driver's body, he had Fagin and the Oliver Twists setting up electronic surveillance on every person in New York connected to Jack Ming, with careful instructions to report only to Braun, not to August Holdwine or anyone else in Special Projects. Braun preferred that Jack Ming's identity not be known to anyone else.

So Fagin and the Twists watched Jack Ming's friends on his abandoned Facebook account (which were few, mostly friends from his NYU years), a few family friends, his father's property company. The initial surveillance centered on monitoring Facebook pages and personal email accounts. The only phones to be tapped via a hack were the phone of his father's company and the cell phones of his two closest college friends.

The silence on Jack was deafening. There was no mention of him at all.

Until a mid-morning phone call struck Braun's interest, not because it was about Jack Ming. No. It was about Sam Capra.

Braun called the sisters. He hoped they could contain their crazy long enough to do the job the exact way he wanted it done. He got Lizzie on the phone. He would have preferred Meggie. She was the more reasonable one. But you didn't put off Lizzie. She held grudges.

Lizzie listened to his instructions. 'The two men, Ming and Capra. Can we play with them for a while?' The sisters had a cabin in upstate New York where they entertained special guests when the need took Lizzie, or when Braun needed someone interrogated, with guaranteed results.

'If you needn't kill them straight out, they're yours. I would like to know what they both know. Get that out of them and report back to me.'

'What about anyone else with them?'

He thought of August, with regret. 'You can kill anyone else if need be. If there is a woman named Mila with him, I want proof of her death.' The sisters needn't know about the bounty. He would collect it himself, throw them a little bonus.

Lizzie laughed. 'Thanks for the work.'

She hung up and looked at her sister. 'Go get dressed. We have a lead on the job.'

'All right, but you promised to make those phone calls about the cruise.' Her sister Meggie stood up from the couch. She had been reading a Special Projects file on Sam Capra that Braun had just emailed her. Know thy enemy.

'Yes, yes,' Lizzie said. 'I'll get to it.'

'Don't put it off,' Meggie said. 'They book up like a year in advance.'

'Cruises are for old people,' Lizzie said.

'That is completely untrue.'

'They keep a morgue on those boats because so many old people die during cruises. I saw that on TV,' Lizzie said.

The sisters considered this interesting tidbit.

'You are not going to have fun on a cruise. I mean, that kind of fun,' Meggie said. 'Parameters for today?'

'Capture if we can, kill if we must. Capra's sort of a pretty boy, don't you think?'

'Not really.'

'His file says he runs parkour. That daredevil running where you jump from building to building.' Lizzie's smile sparkled. 'Do you think I'll get to chase him? I better use a weapon that helps me *catch* him.'

'No.' Meggie rolled her eyes. 'He won't get a chance to run. Let's focus, Lizzie.'

'Your standards are far too high,' Lizzie said. 'Not every apple has to be perfect, you got to give it a big bite to see how sweet it tastes.' She glanced over at her sister's laptop screen, at Sam Capra's photo looking out at her. Brownish-blond hair, green eyes, high cheekbones, a full mouth. 'I like his face. It would take a lot of time and careful thought to ruin it, truly. Those cheekbones, probably you'd need a touch of acid for them. And that runner's body, lovely and spare. Braun had said I could play with them if we aren't forced to kill them outright.'

Meggie didn't care much for the fixated tone in her sister's voice. This was always the way with Lizzie: an idea elbowed its way to the front of her mind and bit down in Lizzie's brain with deep teeth, and wouldn't let go until it was appeased. Her sister's hungers were dark ones.

'Guns?'

'Naturally, but if we want to keep them for a while I don't want to deal with gunshot wounds. Bandages are such a pain. I'm in kind of a Japanese mood today.'

'Fine, but I don't want you playing all week, you said you would research a cruise and book it.'

'Fine, whatever. I'll pack along the brochures.'

42

Ming Properties office, Lower Manhattan

My lucky day, Beth Marley thought. She'd already dodged a bullet: the other two employees in the office were out today, downed with food poisoning brought on by a highly questionable chicken curry they'd eaten while lingering at an unforgivably long lunch yesterday, one that Beth hadn't gone on because, you know, she was too busy doing all three of their jobs.

And now this. Beth Marley tapped the stack of papers straight on her desk and thought: well, I can't wait to tell Sandra that I might lease an entire building. Then Empress Ming'd have to get her ladder and climb down off my ass.

Beth canceled her lunch with her best friend via her BlackBerry, apologizing profusely, and saying that she might pay her back with drinks later in celebration of a big deal. And this would show Sandra Ming she could seriously handle the work: Mrs Ming always looked at her as though she weren't quite sure Beth could tie her shoes much less manage properties around the city.

She sat down at her computer, summoned up the web

browser, Googled Sam Capra. She got a number of hits relating to some poor guy getting killed in Afghanistan, with a brother who had granted a couple of interviews as the family spokesman; probably not related to this client. Not a lot on him. Hmmm. She Googled The Last Minute and found the bar's website. She'd met girlfriends there for drinks a couple of times. Well, if he was thinking of a bar in the building, it would probably be high-dollar. The Last Minute was a well done space, clearly money had been dropped on it. She picked up the phone to call Sandra, and then decided to wait until she actually had good news. If she told Sandra she had a fish on the line but then didn't reel it in, she'd never hear the end of it.

She was gathering her purse and her phone to leave when the office door opened. Which was weird, because there was an electronic passkey and you couldn't just open the door. Oh, she thought, as two women stepped inside. I must not have shut it all the way. They were both stunning. One was blonde, hair pulled up into a bun, tall, with cool green eyes and cheekbones that Beth instantly coveted. The other was a brunette, with lovely chocolate eyes, her hair trimmed into a stylish short cut. Beth instantly wanted to ask: where do you get your hair done? Both women were, oddly though, dressed identically, in form-fitting gray pinstripe suits, and silky black dress shirts.

Beth couldn't think of women who voluntarily dressed alike. She thought: missionaries?

'Hi, may I help you?' she said.

One of the women shut the door behind her. The other stood in front of Beth's desk and smiled. 'Yes. Are you Ms Marley?'

'Yes.'

'Super.' She gave a bright smile in return. 'This is what we're going to need from you. Your cell phone, your car keys and the keys to the building in Williamsburg. Also, the alarm access code. Is there a closet where we can lock you up?'

Beth gave a nervous, uncertain laugh. 'Is this a joke?'

'No. We're keeping your appointment at the building. So. Cell phone, please, and the closet would be where?'

'Get the fuck out of here!' Beth reached for the desk phone. Security was one press of the button away.

The brunette slammed a fist into Beth's face. Hard. Beth had never been hit in the face in her life and the pain astonished her. Another blow to her throat cut off her scream, a third busted her nose. Faster than she would have thought, the brunette was over the desk and one hand was on her mouth, the other on her throat. Crushing against her windpipe.

'Listen to me. I don't wish to kill you. We have a phone tap on you, so we know you're meeting Sam Capra. It would be really pointless for you to die over a cell phone and an appointment. Yes?'

Beth nodded, too dazed to cry, her nose bleeding, her mouth covered by the woman's hand. The pressure on her windpipe eased very slightly.

'In fact, you won't die. Instead my sister will go kill your seven-year-old daughter in Ridgewood, and I will go kill your father in Queens. I often find people care about the lives of loved ones more than their own.' She gave a little shrug. 'Aren't people funny?'

Terror flooded Beth.

'Will you play nice nice?'

Beth nodded. Very eagerly.

'Now don't you get blood on my suit, I will be most unhappy,' the brunette said, as though Beth could stop the blood oozing from her nose.

They shoved her into the small kitchen that doubled as an office supplies storage area. They handcuffed her to the sink pipe.

'Now. The access code. If you lie to me your family's dead. But we'll come back here first and shoot off bits and pieces.'

Beth did not lie. She gave them the code. The pain in her face was now agony. She tried to fight back the tears.

'Very good.' The brunette pulled Beth's cell phone from her purse. 'Where are the property keys?'

'My desk drawer. Tagged as Williamsburg.' Her voice trembled.

The blonde vanished, returned in a moment, the keys dangling.

'Please don't hurt my family, please . . . '

'Beth, chillax, we're all cool. You're just going to tell whoever finds you that you were mugged. By two big Chinese guys. Just provide a couple of pointless yet specific details. They wore red shirts. They had body odor. Two details, no other. You'll be very convincing. You never saw us. You will never speak of us. If you deviate from that story, your daughter and your father will die, guaranteed, no matter how long it takes. Because the threat against your family stands as long as you live. It doesn't have an expiration date. But if you talk, then your family has an expiration date. They will die and the white lilies at their funerals will be from me and my sister. Are we clear?'

Beth nodded, tears brimming her eyes. They stuffed a washcloth from the kitchen drawer in her mouth, bound her lips with tape.

'Have a nice day,' the brunette said, and they left her.

43

Hotel Esper, Williamsburg

I decided to suit up for the meeting. I wanted to look like a legitimate business owner for the property management company, and I thought, given that I had a black eye, I needed every ounce of respectability I could muster. And I didn't want Jack Ming, if he was hiding in the building, to see me as a soldier. I wanted to look like the other side of my life, the owner of a really nice bar. When I worked undercover for Special Projects I quickly learned that most high-level criminal groups adopt a stylish look. I would prefer myself to always be in T-shirt and jeans but life demands more. So I figured out, like a personal shopper to an assassin would, what suits worked for my build as well as what I could wear if I had to fight while dressed to the nines.

Also, even though I didn't pay much attention to The Last Minute as I launched my search for Daniel, I was conscious of when I looked rattier than Bertrand (who always looks annoyingly dapper) and the staff. So, I'd grabbed from my office above The Last Minute the dark navy Burberry Prosrum suit, sleek-fitting. I put on a light gray shirt, a soft silver tie. To the back of the tie I attached a small, thin fighting knife; it stayed in place thanks to a customized loop I'd sewn in. The blade's handle was extremely slender, and the weight of the knife kept the tie tucked against the shirt. I buttoned the jacket; you'd have to look hard to see the blade. I attached a holster to the small of my back; my Glock went there. Another thin blade was bound to an ankle; I put on a pair of Allen Edmonds shoes, with a slightly thick heel. I am man enough to kick when there is a need to.

I left Leonie tapping at her keyboard. 'He's probably not there, but if he is, and I get him, we'll have to run quickly.'

You don't rush in if you can help it. We had to be prepared for a couple of eventualities: that Jack Ming might somehow already be here, and have turned the building into his own fortress, and that the CIA might be here as well. Anna could be wrong about the rendezvous being set for tomorrow. Her source inside could be wrong, and, with our children's lives on the line, neither Leonie nor I had any intention of walking into a trap. If we were caught, our children were lost to us.

Would Jack Ming hide where he planned to meet? Possibly. But if I were him, I would try to stay on the move as much as I could. Hunkering down in a place tied to his father could be dangerous, an unacceptable risk.

Of course, he was a twenty-two-year-old grad student, not a trained operative. He might not think the same way I would. But he'd run home, the most dangerous thing he could do if his false ID in the Netherlands had been cracked, and so he might commit a whole chain of mistakes. If he didn't realize that his mother was gone, he might feel perfectly safe coming to this building that he knew to be empty.

He, after all, had to have taken the key for a good reason.

The building was enemy territory. It could be a kill zone. I had only seen it in the dark late last night and now it looked like a difficult place to defend. It was neat red brick, windows covered to keep damage and neglect at bay. An outdoor market was in full swing two streets over; pedestrians passed on their way to and from the stalls.

I walked down to the building a few minutes late. If Jack was inside I didn't want him to spot me until the very last minute. I had no idea if he had seen me in the Rotterdam shootout, or if he would register my face from those horrible few minutes.

As I walked up to the door, a Volvo sedan with New Jersey plates pulled up. Two women got out. Great, I thought: if Jack Ming is holed up inside and gets violent then I've got two people to protect. They both wore practically identical pinstriped suits. Maybe Mrs Ming enforced a dress code. They were both in their late twenties, I would guess. One was dark-haired, dark-eyed, with a lovely face and a kind smile. The other was blonde, steel-eyed, a bit taller, but something in her face registered wrong. Like the smile was just for practice.

'Mr Capra?' This was the brunette.

'Yes.'

'Beth Marley.' We shook hands. 'This is my associate, Lizzie.'

She offered her hand, I shook it, and she held onto it a little longer than necessary. 'Oh, what happened to your face?' Odd tone to her question – she almost sounded disappointed. I thought for a moment she was going to reach out and touch my black eye.

'Surely not a bar fight?' Beth said.

'Yes,' I said. 'And that dude won't walk a check again.'

'Oh, rough stuff,' Lizzie said. Her smile didn't waver. I felt sure commercial leasing agents have seen nearly everything.

'May I see your ID?' Beth said.

I understand leasing agents have to be careful, going into buildings with strange men. I gave her both my New York driver's license and my Last Minute business card, which looked even sharper than I did. She inspected them and handed them back to me.

Beth gestured to the building. 'Shall we?'

I nodded.

Beth unlocked the door with a key with a small tag on it. She stepped inside and punched in the code for the building. She didn't hide her tapping finger and I saw the code was 49678. She seemed to hesitate for just one moment, as if expecting the alarm to sound, but it stopped its warning chime and the indicator light turned green. But I stepped away from her before she could register that I'd been watching and turned my gaze critically to the ceiling, as though I expected to see a pox of water leaks. Lizzie stayed close to me. A little too close. I didn't like her, all of a sudden.

On the first floor was some unfinished plasterboard, a wall left undone.

'Did someone start to remodel and forget to finish?'

'Apparently so. Of course, if you lease the whole space we'll remove any left-behind renovations that were incomplete.'

Beth started to tell me about all the building's wonderful features, of which there were three. She embellished in the way that best sales people do. I let her lead me but I stepped first through every door. I didn't think Jack Ming, if he'd hidden himself inside here, seemed like the type to just start shooting; I didn't even know if he had a gun. But I wasn't going to risk the leasing agents getting hurt.

We walked through the building. The first two floors were configured for offices. Beth was giving me a very generic patter. On the top floor we could see the roofs of the adjoining building, which only went to three floors. This floor was mostly cleared concrete space.

'So you're thinking a bar on the ground floor?'

'Yes. And private party rooms on the second and third floors,' I said. 'Office space on four.'

254

'Oh, party space, I hope you'll invite us,' Lizzie said. 'You won't make us wait in line, will you? Can we jump the rope?'

I gave her a smile, but I didn't much care for the smile she gave me back. She kept standing a little too close to me, clutching her oversized purse. 'I'll make sure you're on the special guest list.'

'Next door it's being renovated into restaurant space,' Beth said. 'I believe the top floor is going to be a sushi bar. They're opening next week, I think. You could have a synergy, depending on their clientele.'

'I'm all about the synergy,' I said. I never know how the hell to use that word in a sentence.

The fourth floor was mostly open space. Russell Ming was using it for storage. Boxes of all shapes and sizes, Chinese paintings, a set of rounded tables in a row, lightly covered with dust. Windows faced out onto the neighboring roof; below was a skylight that looked new. The sushi bar, celebrating natural light, I guess.

In the back corner there was a door.

I walked straight over to it and tried the doorknob. Locked.

'What's in here?' I asked. My voice sounded a little louder than I'd intended.

'Storage, I believe. Don't know why it would be locked.' She stepped forward. She opened the door with another key. I tensed in case Jack Ming had set up camp inside the room. He hadn't. It was empty. I tried not to breathe a sigh of relief. He wasn't in the building. I knew the access code now and I could pick the locks. I didn't need Beth and Lizzie so best to get them out of the way, come back and wait for Jack Ming.

'You seem to be … expecting to see something here,' Lizzie said when I finished twisting the knob as I stepped away from the door. She leaned against one of the square tables.

'Just counting the footage in my mind,' I said.

'I like math,' Lizzie said. 'I like to add things up.'

'So,' Beth said smoothly. 'How would this property work for you, Mr Capra?'

'I think it might work well indeed. How firm is the leasing price?'

'Pretty firm, I would think. The original owner died a couple of years ago; his wife has it now, and she would rather hold out than lease too cheap.'

I had my back to them, surveying the adjoining roof. Could he enter the building this way? No, I thought not. 'Well, I think I've seen enough,' I said.

'Enough to know Jack Ming's not here,' Lizzie said.

I turned. Beth had a Glock 9mm aimed at me. Lizzie was pulling from her oversized purse a metal chain, an iron weight at one end, a steel spike at the other, firm in her grip. *Surujin*. A weapon I'd seen before in Japan, mostly used these days for individual martial arts practice. The weight dangled like a pendulum; she started it on a gentle sway, just above her feet.

'Hands still, where I can see them, please, Sam,' Beth said.

'Are you kidding me?' I nodded at Lizzie's toy.

'You're supposed to be a graceful runner. I brought it to leash you in case you ran. Don't make me chase you.' Lizzie's smile didn't quite just look socially awkward; now she looked coolly cruel.

'I wouldn't dream of it,' I said.

'We just want to talk,' Beth – well, I knew now that wasn't her name, but her name didn't matter – said. Her aim steadied on my chest.

'Gun on the ground, please,' Beth ordered.

I obeyed. Dropped it to the hardwood floor, kicked it over to her. I kept my hands slightly raised, in front of me, where she could see them.

'Hands on head. Lizzie, search him.'

She did with gusto, fingers dancing over me, exploring more than she should have, while Beth kept the gun leveled at my head. She probed my arms, my groin, my backside. She ran her hands along my ribs and my legs. Lizzie found the thin blade at my ankle. She ran her fingernails along the skin of my leg. She was so busy toying with me that her search was incomplete. She'd not thought to pat down my tie.

'Boys and their toys,' Lizzie said. She flicked the knife at my face. I didn't flinch; she stopped a good inch away from my cheek.

It seemed to displease her I hadn't given the reaction she wanted. 'I *can* make you flinch,' she said. 'I *will.*'

'Lizzie, step back,' Beth said. Lizzie obeyed.

'The preference is not to shoot you,' Lizzie said. 'It makes a mess.' She stepped back, tucked my knife in her belt. She picked up the *surujin* and began its slow swing again. There is a whole subclass of punk-ass killers who have seen a Hong Kong or Tokyo gangster movie and decided to flash up their act a bit. One supposes they think it makes them look more dangerous. Most of them are older than me and honestly should know better. I'd dealt with one back in Amsterdam with a Japanese sword fetish and now he was dead.

Lizzie just kept smiling at me. Like she wanted to encourage me to ask her on a date.

'Are you kidding me?' I said again. 'Put that down.'

She didn't. She laughed. The little weight kept spinning, slicing the air; it sounded like a knife. 'See, with this, I don't kill you, I knock you around a bit, bad bruises, yes, cuts, yes, but those can heal without too much care. I can play with you a lot more. A gunshot takes forever to heal, trust me, it's so annoying. And smelly.'

The other one – Beth – looked embarrassed, for just the barest moment. 'Where is Jack Ming?'

'I don't know. I thought he might be here.' Truth. 'That's why I was eager to look in that locked room.'

'And why you tried to shield me in case he was there with a gun. Oh, how sweet,' Beth said.

'I won't shield you again.'

Lizzie started swinging the *surujin*, harder, higher; it made a steel halo around her head.

'Why are you looking for him?' Beth said.

Well, I wasn't expecting that question. But I like the cards on the table in moments like this. 'Why are you?'

Lizzie threw the *surujin*. The weight slammed into my shoulder with the force of a savage punch. With a flick of the chain she'd drawn it back to her, whirling the weight in front of her. She actually knew how to use the thing. Where do you go to *surujin* school?

'She can break your nose, shatter your teeth, shred your ears with it,' Beth said. 'I really suggest you tell us what we want to know.'

'Talk, talk,' Lizzie hissed.

'Because the people who have my child want him dead.'

'That's very moving.' Lizzie walked to one side of me, the weight orbiting her head. The sound it made was an awful whirring hiss. She was at both her weakest and her strongest when she threw it, if I could keep it from coming back to her. The spike was to stab someone tangled or stunned by the weight and the chain. It was like a Swiss Army knife of weapons.

'And these people, they just want Jack dead?' Beth asked.

'Yes. Kill him and I get my kid back.'

'That is *so* sweet,' Lizzie said. 'You'll be the bestest daddy ever.'

Beth said, 'Jack Ming is going to die. You can see it happen, if you like. But we do the job. Not you.'

Something inside me broke. They had a gun on me, fair enough, and the one playing at samurai was crazy as hell. But this was over.

'You'll forgive me if I don't trust you to do what needs doing.'

'We're taking the responsibility off you, man,' Lizzie said.

'And then what?'

'Then we talk.'

'No. Then I go get my son if Jack Ming's dead.'

'No, that's not going to happen, I'm sorry,' Lizzie said. I wasn't sure what she enjoyed more, the stab or the twist.

Beth said, 'I would like to know where we can find your friend Mila.'

'I don't know,' I said.

'I think you're lying,' Lizzie said. 'This – whatever you're doing, on the side – it ends now.'

'On the side?'

'Working for someone other than Special Projects,' Lizzie said. 'We're on the same side, babe.' She made the last word sound like a plop of poison. 'You just have to stand aside and let us clean up this mess.'

Oh. These two were going to kill Jack Ming, all right, but they were going to kill August, too, and whoever came with him, and they going to kill me after I'd told them where Mila was.

Someone inside Special Projects was protecting Novem Soles and knew about the bounty on Mila, and had decided to kill the proverbial two birds with one stone. And that someone did not care one whit whether I lived or my child lived. August knew. Who else?

'Okay,' I said. 'You kill Jack Ming, then I get my kid back and walk away.'

'You walk away if you give us Mila,' Lizzie said.

I didn't nod for twenty seconds, and let the agony play out on my face. Then I nodded, once.

'Where is she?' Beth asked.

'She's coming here. In an hour. To help me dispose of Jack Ming's body. She got a confirmation he was going to be here. A phone call to a friend.'

'She's hunting Ming?'

'Yes.'

'Why isn't she here with you now?'

'Because killing him is my job. Not hers.'

The *surujin*, wound in an increasing arc while I talked, lashed out at me.

It caught me in the side of the throat as I tried to dodge and felt like a baseball bat had swung into my flesh. I staggered back, choking.

'He's lying,' Lizzie said. 'I know a liar and he's lying. He's not giving Mila to us.'

She flicked it again at me and this time I whipped out my hand and caught the weight. It hurt – like a hammer pounding into my palm – but I yanked on the chain and Lizzie flew toward me.

I slammed a fist into her face but she kept her grip on the chain. So I threw her into Beth, who was holding fire to keep from shooting her partner.

The two women hit the floor. Where was my gun? Beth had kicked it somewhere. I didn't see it.

First things first. Don't get shot. Lizzie clambered to her feet. I whirled and powered a kick into her chest, knocking her back into Beth. The gun fired into the hardwoods; shards and splinters kicked up by Lizzie's foot and she screamed. I couldn't tell if it was rage or pain.

Right now the biggest threat was the gun. Lizzie threw three brutal sharp jabs, *muay thai*-style, connecting with my jaw, my nose, my mouth, and then kicked me in the chest. Strong as hell. I staggered back and she whipped the weighted end of the *surujin* downward, anchoring my hands, binding my wrists together. But now she didn't try to drag me back; I was caught, she had the other end of the chain. The spike gleamed in her hand.

She rushed me, stabbing at my shoulder, just as Beth charged at me, gun in hand, doing what I would do to subdue a prisoner with useless hands: put the gun to my head, order me to stand down. So, no. I dodged two stabs of Lizzie's, and since I was bound to her, she was bound to me. Beth lunged at me and I drove an elbow into her nose. It broke and she staggered back, for just a moment.

That was my advantage: they wanted me uninjured enough to talk, to give them Mila. I wanted them out of the way between me and my son and that could mean hurt or dead. It made no difference to me, at that moment in time.

I seized, with my bound hands, Lizzie's arm with the spike, levered it up. I had to get free of her; Beth ignored the blood streaming from her nose, raising for her shot. There was a connection between them – they were partners, not just two people assigned to kill Jack Ming together. She would not risk a shot to Lizzie's head. I hoped.

I swung Lizzie hard, and her arms plowed right into Beth's head. Beth went down, and I yanked again, pulling Lizzie along with me. We trampled over Beth, then I yanked her back again, stumbling and stepping hard on Beth a second time. My foot hit the gun and I kicked, scuttling it into the mass of Russell Ming's junk.

'Goddamn it!' Lizzie screamed. Easily frustrated, not calm.

I got my hand on the dangling weight since Lizzie still had her death grip on the spike. She jabbed the spike straight at the center of my chest, hitting my tie. It hit the metal of my knife, instead of soft flesh.

I clubbed the weight into the side of her head. She fell, hard.

I pulled free from the *surujin*, kicked back from her, just in time for Beth to nearly open my throat.

She had my blade, the one Lizzie had handed her from my ankle. I ducked as she slashed at me; she was only missing by a centimeter.

I threw myself back in a herky-jerky dance as she advanced, chasing me. The blade scored along the front of my jacket, slicing the lapel. She overextended on her thrust and I caught her and threw her to the side. I groped at my tie for my blade.

My tie was gone. She'd sliced the whole thing off, severing the silk, leaving a faint score on the shirt. Where the hell was it?

Beth stumbled, back on her feet, her hand bleeding from where the blade had turned on her. Lizzie, untangling her deadly Japanese not-really-a-toy. My severed tie lay on the floor between them.

I ran, grabbed the cloth, felt the reassuring weight of the knife under the silk. I skidded under the row of tables bordering the boxes where Russell Ming stored his junk. I worked the knife free from the silk, closed fingers around the handle.

The top of the table exploded into splinters, punctured by the weight of the *surujin.*

My shield – the table I was under – flew up, the two of them throwing it off me.

Which meant they each had one hand otherwise occupied.

I slashed with the knife, at knee-level. I caught Lizzie but not Beth. Lizzie howled but hammered the weight into the small of my back. Pain exploded along my spine. My knife clanged against Beth's, slash, parry, slash. She cut at my suit sleeve. I sliced across her knuckles.

I backed away. She stayed level, knife out. She knew what she was doing. Next to her, Lizzie raised and started whirling the *surujin.* Then I saw the weight in her hand.

She whirled the end with the spike.

Lizzie exploded it toward me and it missed me by inches, drilling into one of the crates. She yanked at it with a gasp but it caught in the hole she'd pierced in the wood. Beth crouched before me, defending her partner. All that mattered was that for one moment the field was equal.

'It doesn't have to end this way, bitch,' Beth told me. 'We are going to win. We are going to wear you down.' The fact that she was even negotiating was telling me I'd fought harder, hurt them more than they figured I would.

'You're between me and my kid. So you either walk away and don't look back or you're dead,' I said.

'When I get you in the playpen . . . ' Lizzie hollered. 'You will not ever make another threat to us again.'

'We could see. Trade the notebook for my son.' I yelled.

For the barest moment Beth paused. 'What notebook?'

'The one Jack Ming filled with dirty secrets.' Our knives clanged as she pressed the attack. Behind her Lizzie yanked the spike free from the crate. She started whirling the damned *suru-jin* again, running toward us.

'We're sort of kind of on the same side,' Beth said.

'Who's your boss,' I answered.

Lizzie whipped the spike toward me, arcing hard. I parried it with the blade and it slammed, sideways, back into Beth's head. Her temple, the soft part. The impact was squelchy and thudding and Beth fell, timbering, boneless, her head a sudden brutal mess on the side.

For a moment neither of us moved. The blade was broken by the blunt weight of the spike. I held it because I had no other weapon.

And then Lizzie began to scream, incoherent rage, the kind of fury that rises like a storm in the soul. She screamed: 'Meggie!' She yanked back the spike by seizing onto the chain, whipping it into a cloud of frenzy.

I dropped the broken knife, grabbed the one still clutched in Beth's hand. I stood and the weight of Lizzie's *surujin* began to spiral around my neck. Instinct to save my throat kicked in and I raised my arm. The weight and the chain caught it, pressing it against my face, the blade now above my head, wedged and useless. Lizzie yanked me toward her, the spike raised. The whirring had cleaned a fair amount of Beth's brain and blood off of it.

No playpen for me. No keeping me alive now. Now there was just the vast, awful, empty rage in her eyes.

So I flowed with the tug on the chain and I threw myself into her.

We crashed to the floor. She hit me in the head with the spike and the weight at the same time, cymballing my head. I couldn't shrug free from the chain to release my arm and she whirled me

264

loose and snapped a brutal kick into my face. I fell back and then she looped the chain in a savage noose and began to squeeze, her knees in my back.

Colors swam before my eyes, broke apart, descended into grays. I gritted my teeth. The blade was beyond my reach. I pulled away from her, like a plow horse dragging an impossible weight. Grasping for the knife. She howled and shoved her foot hard against my spine.

Daniel. The thought of him fueled me. My hand closed around the knife.

She leapt over me clawing for it. And this is how a person dies.

The pressure on the chains eased.

We both grabbed for the knife.

I could hardly breathe. When she tried to pull it away, I let her do the work and I just steered it. With a thrust that surprised us both the blade pierced her chest.

She gasped, a very quiet sound for such a loud, bragging fool. I lay beside her. There was not a lot of blood because it had slid into the heart with a pure straightness.

She didn't die as fast as Beth but then she was gone. I pushed her off me.

Special Projects was basically a rogue group. What happened when you had a rogue inside the rogue? *They know about Mila, and they know about my son. I'll do what they want and they'll just ask for Mila next. It won't ever end. Ever.*

I staggered to my feet. I pulled the chain free from my throat like a man just spared from the gallows. I got to the window and I spat blood.

Think. I dug in my pocket, I found my cell phone. I just hoped I still had my voice.

44

Special Projects headquarters, Manhattan

The phone buzzed early, at 11 a.m., and August had changed the ring tone to match an appropriate song: Aretha Franklin's classic cover of 'Until You Come Back to Me'.

'Hello,' the informant said.

'Hello,' August said.

'So, we're doing this. An hour early. Forgive the change of plans.'

It didn't surprise August; the informant was trying to keep him slightly off-kilter. He supposed it gave the informant a sense of control. 'Yes.'

'I want you and you alone showing up.'

'Why?'

'Those people I pissed off are threatening to kill me and say they can do it as soon as I surrender to you. That they've got people inside your team ready to bring my head on a platter.'

'That is what is known as a scare tactic, my friend.'

'You're not my friend.'

'I'm trying to save your life.'

'Yeah, whatever.'

'I can assure you of your safety.'

'I am so reassured, August.'

'You haven't told me how you know my name.'

'I'll tell you when you've made me safe.'

August was silent.

'You don't tell anyone where you're going. You come alone. Understood?'

'And when I've seen the evidence we get you to a safe house and we get you your money.'

'It'll be worth it, August, I promise. They are insane that I have this. Insane.'

'Understood.'

'Don't lie to me. I have had a shitty week. I want this to go smoothly and to be a day you talk about when they hand you the gold watch.'

'I'm all for that,' August said.

'Go to the United Nations Plaza. Be there in thirty minutes. Alone, like you promised. I'll call you then.' He hung up.

August folded the phone. He headed out the door. He told no one where he was going. But two men on the street followed him.

A visitor might expect the United Nations plaza would be a riotous color of international garb, but it seemed most people wore the same dark suits nowadays. And everyone seemed to be speaking English. August stood at the plaza's edge for four minutes before his phone rang.

'You came alone.'

'As promised. Where are you?'

'Not here. Go to FAO Schwarz on Fifth. I'll call you there. Stay alone. I'm watching.'

How? August thought. He pocketed the phone in annoyance. He understood the informant's precautions but this seemed almost theatrical. Was the informant watching him now? He glanced around, smoothing out his pale hair with his hand. He walked and doubled-back. He did not spot a tail.

The two men tracking him fell off, to be replaced by two new ones, one staying ahead of August, one behind, frowning.

*

At FAO Schwarz, tourist children danced on keyboards and August thought: they still make those? Kids swarmed the aisles and standing there alone, childless, August thought: I don't want to draw attention. One mother, with four-year-old twin boys orbiting her, gave him the greasy eyeball of doubt. He told himself he was a visiting businessman buying a gift for his own child and that's how he would act.

The phone rang as he surveyed an astonishing display of action figures. I'd like my own action figure, August was thinking. New York Spy Skulking Guy. He answered the phone.

'You're supposed to be alone, August,' the informant said. 'I spy, with my little eye, two goobers who picked you up at UN and are still with you.'

August kept his poker face in place. How did he know he had agents following him, tasked to help him scoop up the informant?

'Now. Those guys could be your buddies, backing you up, or Novem Soles, following you to get us both into a corner and to kill me dead. Lose them.'

August was silent. Shocked.

'Do you know what they look like?'

'No,' August lied.

'One is black, wearing a blue suit and dark rectangular glasses. The other has brown, slightly longish hair, wearing jeans and a maroon shirt. Lose them. When you have lost them I'll call you back.' He hung up.

August lingered for a moment in the aisle, shaken, and doing his best not to show it. When he walked out of the store he brushed his hand twice through his thick, blond hair. It was a signal: the meeting was off. The trackers would retreat back to the Special Projects office. He had not anticipated his shadows

268

being spotted, not by a kid. He stood outside the store, hailed a cab and got inside.

The phone rang before he had the door shut.

'Go to Brooklyn. The flea market in Williamsburg. Don't be followed.'

August figured it out en route to Brooklyn. The clever little punk had hacked his way into the traffic camera system. And into the private security cameras at the toy store. Any place he sent August had an active, multiple-camera presence – all were very public spaces. That's how he was watching August. He would have an entrance into the flea market's camera system as well.

He called the Special Projects office.

'He's tracking us via traffic and store security cameras. See if you can trace him off the FAO Schwartz or Williamsburg Brooklyn Flea Market camera feeds, he's hacking into them right now. Get a team to Brooklyn now, we need to scoop him up immediately when he gives me a final destination.'

'Will do.'

August leaned back in the cab. The phone rang.

'Yes.'

'I changed my mind. Here's where I want you to go.'

45

Ming building, Brooklyn

Leonie stared down at Beth and Lizzie. Her mouth trembled.

'I know them,' she said, in a hushed tone.

I sat on the floor, inspecting my injuries. I was sore and exhausted but I didn't have time to hurt. Nothing was broken, as far as I could tell. I unknotted my slashed tie, threw it on the floor. 'How do you know them?'

Her mouth worked. 'I made new identities for them.'

'As Lizzie and' – I remembered the name Lizzie had screamed – 'Meggie?'

'No. Those were their real names. Lizzie and Meggie Pearson. They were from Oregon. Their father . . . he killed their mother in front of them and then told everyone his wife and kids had left him, but he kept the sisters in a cage in his basement for three years when they were little. The father finally got too close to the cage and the girls strangled him against the bars. They were maybe ten and nine. Didn't you hear about that? One of those stories where they were all the news for five minutes then the world forgot about them.'

'I grew up overseas, no, I never heard of them.'

'They got put into foster care but . . . I don't think they ever recovered. No family would keep them for long. Meggie was cold and calculating, Lizzie was crazy and vicious. They were in trouble with the law a lot; there was talk that they had killed a college student who knew Lizzie slightly, nothing was proven, but he was found dead in a cage in an abandoned cabin.'

Cage. Playpen.

'They had to vanish.' Leonie's voice broke. 'Oh God, oh God, we have to get out of here.'

'Why?'

Leonie stepped away from Lizzie's body. Shuddering. 'Because . . . someone I knew once wanted them to come work for him, and he needed them to have new identities. Not be the

270

least bit notorious. New names. New histories. So they could work for him . . . unimpeded.'

'As hired killers.'

'Yes, and as interrogators. Lizzie is supposed to be good at getting information out of people.'

'And you hid them.'

'Yes. That's what I did, for three years, hid people for him. Before I hid myself.'

'Who?'

'The man I'm hiding from, Sam.'

'Who, Leonie?'

'His name is Ray Brewster. He must be behind all this. He must be.'

'Who is he?'

She stared out the window, through the slats. Her fist pressed against her mouth. 'They're here.'

46

Ming building, Brooklyn

I stepped next to Leonie and I watched through the slats. August Holdwine approached the building from the sidewalk, via the back entrance along the alleyway. Alone. He was in jeans, a dark, untucked shirt, a summer-weight jacket, probably to conceal his weapon.

So if August was here, where was Jack Ming?

August moved along the alleyway, hand tucked under blazer, being careful. Maybe if I stood and waved he'd wave back. Could invite him up to hang out with Leonie and me and the dead sisters. After all, we're all looking for the same guy.

'Stay here,' I said to Leonie. She'd heard my shocked intake of breath, come closer to the window.

'What is it? Is it Ming?'

'No. Someone else has shown up here.'

'Who the hell is that?'

'The CIA.'

She sucked in breath. 'Has he tracked him here?'

'Either that or he's meeting him, which means Anna's source is dead-on right.' Anna had someone inside Special Projects. Was it this Ray Brewster? I wasn't sure if that theory made sense.

I had thought I could grab and deal with Ming before the meeting, before August or anyone else showed up. Now I was literally out of time. Where was Ming? He had to be close, probably watching August to ensure that he showed, and perhaps that he showed alone. Conditions for the meeting would have been set.

'Stay here. Don't let him see you. Let me handle this,' I said. 'If this goes wrong and we get separated or I'm captured, go to a bar called The Last Minute. It's right by Bryant Park in Manhattan. Ask for Bertrand, tell him you're a friend of mine. He'll protect you.'

She nodded. 'You know this man,' she said, pointing down toward August.

'Yes.'

Leonie clutched my arm. 'You are not negotiating with this man, Sam. You have to kill Jack Ming. End of story. You must.'

'I—'

'Will your friend there walk away without a fight?'

'His name is August. No. I know him too well. No.'

'Then are you going to kill August? Who matters more, your friend or your kid?'

No, never, I thought. *How far would you go to save your son?* Leonie's words ricocheted around my brain.

'Quit being so bloodthirsty. It's not your friend and your finger on the trigger. It's not your conscience.'

She flinched. 'I'm not bloodthirsty. I just want my child back. Don't you?' Then, before I could answer, she made her voice a knife. 'Maybe not. It's not like you've seen him. It's not like you could really love him.'

I yanked my arm from her hand.

The shock on my face must have been reflected on her own. 'Oh, my God, Sam, I am so sorry – I don't know why I said that . . . Please . . . '

'Listen to me,' I said. 'Right now, call my cell phone. I'll listen on the earbud. I'm going to keep August downstairs and talk to him. But I want to know if Ming comes into sight. I want to know immediately if you see him.'

She nodded.

'Don't hang up and don't panic.'

47

Ming building, Brooklyn

I hurried down the stairs to the second floor. Were the doors unlocked? I waited at the top of the stairs that led down to the ground floor.

August opened the door. He came through with gun drawn,

arm extended, classic stance to sweep the room. He froze when he saw me. I kept my hands raised, empty of a weapon.

'Hi.' I didn't know what else to say.

My best friend stared up at me in shock. For one moment he wavered. Five long seconds ticked by. But he kept his gun leveled at me. 'You look like you've been beaten to hell, man.'

'Yes,' I nodded.

'What are you doing here, Sam?'

'I have a favor to ask you. Biggest one ever.'

'Come down here.'

I stayed put. 'This is what I need you to do. Turn around and leave. You hear from Jack Ming again, you ignore it. Let him go.'

'Jack Ming. Is that my new friend's name? Why would you want me to give him the cold shoulder?'

'Shut the hell up and just go.'

'No. Why are you here, Sam?' Now August's voice rose.

I started to walk down the steps. My gun was holstered in the small of my back. My hands were in the air.

I knew there was a spy inside Special Projects. Another traitor who'd likely been bought. Maybe this Ray Brewster. And if I told August the truth the traitor could learn it, no matter how careful August was. It could be his team-mate, his boss. And they would never give me back Daniel if I exposed their man.

So I lied: 'This is a trap. Novem Soles wants to capture you. Pick your brain.'

'What are you doing here?' And I heard what I didn't want to hear in his voice. Suspicion. 'How did you even know I'm here?'

He thinks I'm one of them now.

'Oh, my God, Jack Ming is here,' I heard Leonie's voice in my earbud. 'He just ran to the door from the building across the alleyway, he's coming in *now . . .*'

No time. No time to react.

The door slammed open and caught August with its edge. He staggered back. I saw Jack Ming power up a gun, aimed at August's head.

'Drop your gun,' the young man screamed.

And August did and the young man looked up at me. I'd pulled my weapon and he still had his gun leveled at August.

'Drop it!' he screamed. 'Drop it now!'

Shoot him, I thought. Just shoot him and this is over. But the gun, his gun, so close to August's head. I couldn't. I dropped the gun.

'*You*,' he said and I wasn't sure if he was speaking to me or to August. But he aimed his glare at me.

I was the surprise. Not August.

'The Chinese hacker from Amsterdam.' August paled. 'You were shot.'

'You were dead,' I said. 'We thought.' He didn't need to know I was hunting him. I wanted him to think I was just as surprised as August at his identity. Notice my clever use of *we*.

If he was surrendering to the CIA then let him think I was part of the CIA. Even if it bought me ten seconds of confusion.

I would have to kill him in front of August. That was that. Then run, like a coward, in the slim hope that Novem Soles would give me my child back.

August said, 'The past is the past and I'm guessing since you're coming to me that all is forgiven.' I remembered the CIA team roughed up Jack a bit.

Jack gave a little shrug.

'We had a deal. I'm ready to carry forward that deal. Lower your weapon. Let's talk about Novem Soles,' August said.

The young man's gaze slid to me. I remained very still. If I moved for my gun he could blow August's brains onto the wall.

But then he swung the gun toward me. 'Not yet. Why is *he* here? He's one of *them*.'

'No. I'm not.' This had all gone south. I couldn't draw on him and risk August's life. But for Daniel to live he had to die.

'I saw you in Amsterdam,' he said to me. 'You were working with Nic.'

'No. I was working with *him*.' I nodded toward August. August, thank God, kept his mouth shut at this lie.

'No. The CIA was hunting you. You'd run from them. They talked about you in front of me when they thought I didn't understand.' Jack Ming's mouth narrowed. 'What the hell is this? Why is he here, August?'

After a long, long moment, August said: 'Answer the man, Sam.'

I said nothing.

August said, 'Listen to me. Sam used to be CIA, he has fought against Novem Soles, and he's okay. I can assure you of that.' He stared up at me.

Jack's hand with the gun was shaking, ever so slightly. The hacker had claws and didn't know what to do. A weird back corner of me wanted to say *your mother is dead, I'm sorry. I'm sorry it's come to this kind of awful. I'm sorry I have to kill you.*

I couldn't use August to help me.

'I said only you to come,' Jack said to August.

'I didn't invite him,' August said.

Oh, no.

I played my hand. 'Listen to me. There are two dead women upstairs. They were here waiting for you, Jack. Novem Soles is hunting you. I became . . . aware of this fact.'

'And aware that this was where we were meeting? How could you know?'

'Because I figured out who you were. Really were. Not a Chinese student from Hong Kong. Jack Ming, New Yorker and runaway hacker.' I needed three seconds to shoot him. I needed him not to be aiming at August's head. 'I know because I was smart enough to find you.'

'Who are these women, Sam? Did you kill them?' August asked.

'Kill Jack, what are you waiting for,' Leonie hissed in my ear. '*What are you waiting for?*'

I was waiting because, if I didn't kill him, I wanted to find a way to burn Novem Soles to the ground and still get my kid back. The thought had been in the back of my mind, a constant trickle I wouldn't hear.

But consider the sisters. They tried to take me without killing me, and it didn't work out. I couldn't end up like them.

Ming swung the gun away from August and aimed it at the center of my chest. He clutched it with the other hand and for an amateur it telegraphed he meant to fire. August threw himself into Ming and the bullet cracked, two inches from my head. I jumped down from the stairs and pulled them apart. I wrenched the gun from Ming's hand and knocked him to the floor. His gun dropped to the concrete. Jack's foot hit it as we struggled and it skittered into shadows beyond the dim gleam of the entry light.

August stood, raising his own gun. Oh. Did not want that.

'Thank you,' I said, and slammed my fist into the side of my friend's head. He staggered and I hit him again, hard, across his wrist. The gun fell from his nerveless fingers.

'What the hell!' he yelled and he parried my next blow. 'What are you doing?'

Leonie, who had been silent, started screaming in my ear, wanting to know what was happening. I couldn't shoot August. I wouldn't shoot him. I just needed him sidelined so that I could kill Jack Ming. I would explain later, if he let me. If he didn't shoot me on sight.

I hit August, a hard right cross, catching him off balance, and he fell. But as he hit the concrete, he kicked out at my legs. I hit the floor, mad. We'd entered Special Projects together, trained together, sparred together. August was bigger than me, heavy with Minnesota farm and college football muscle that he maintained. And now he was mad at me for screwing up what had to be a career highlight. He delivered a kick toward my chest and I caught his foot.

Corner of my eye, I saw Jack Ming scrambling for his gun.

He might shoot both of us. I would if I were him.

I pulled on the foot, going into a roll, knocking August off balance. He was bigger than me but I was more wiry and faster. I couldn't think of him as a friend, I couldn't. Not now.

He wrenched free from my grip – despite his bulk, I underestimated how strong he was – and kicked me, catching me in the face. Heel hit jaw, hurt like hell where I'd already been battered by the sisters. I felt blood on my lips. August circled me, a look mixing disgust and confusion on his face, and hammered three hard, fast punches into my chest. I fell back against the wall; I felt the raised thumbs of the light switches stab my spine. He started to scream at Ming and I, stumbling back, twisted to see Ming running. Gun in hand, but running. From both of us, throwing himself out into the alley.

'Grab him!' August screamed and I didn't know if he was

talking to me or to a partner who was listening in, same as Leonie.

I yelled 'Ming's heading out!' But I already heard footsteps pounding on the stairs. Leonie dashed past me and August. He made a grab at her but she dodged him, mostly because I round-house-kicked him as hard as I could in the chest.

He fell but as I turned to pursue Ming I stumbled over his backpack. He'd left it behind in his panic. I fell. August, huffing, closed hands around my throat and threw me into the adjoining, unfinished wall I'd complained about to Meggie when she was pretending to be Beth Marley.

The drywall gave way and we tumbled through it together. Coughing, I fought to free his grip from my throat. He wouldn't let go and those damn sausage-thick fingers started to squeeze the life out of me. He didn't want me dead, he wanted me out of the way. So I sagged, like I was passing out. He let go and levered back a fist to slam it into my face.

I clawed my hands around his fist and held it still.

'Why?' he yelled.

'They're gonna kill my kid if I don't,' I said, before I could think.

'Evacuate the informant if you have him,' he yelled. Oh crap. He was talking to someone. He was wired. A team was here.

I shoved him off me and I seized a splintered support from the broken wall. I wrenched it free and I skimmed it right across the back of the skull. He collapsed.

For one horrifying second I thought I had killed him. I checked him. He was breathing.

I ran, stumbling into the alley, after Leonie and Jack, into whatever awaited.

48

The Streets of Williamsburg

Jack Ming bolted from the building into the cool of the alleyway. The red notebook, wedged in the back of his pants, hidden under a jacket, rubbed his skin at the top of his butt. He could hardly breathe.

This had been a trap. Either August had set him up or August had been set up himself. There would be no surrendering to him today. That Capra guy was after him. He stumbled. He had to get out of the neighborhood. Neither of those guys might be here alone.

He heard the *chook* of the discharge from a small gun, nearly soft in the humid air. He felt the heat of a bullet whizz close to his ear.

Someone was shooting at him. He stumbled, turned, and saw a woman racing after him. She was petite, red-haired, with mouth gritted. She wore jeans and sneakers and a blue T-shirt and she looked like a young suburban mother. She stopped and she stared at him as he stared back at her, backing away in shock, and for a second he screamed, 'Get out of here, someone's shooting . . . '

But she raised a gun. It shook in her hand.

'Forgive me,' she said. 'You have to die. I'm sorry.'

And she fired as he turned and ran toward the end of the alley. A black Lincoln Navigator slammed to a stop thirty feet ahead of him, blasting toward him.

He had nowhere to go.

49

I heard the distant pell-mell of shots. The space between them told me they weren't fired with confidence. I hit the door and ran into the alleyway and headed toward the gunfire.

It was the battle of the hackers who couldn't shoot straight. Leonie stood, discharging the weapon at the running Ming. She hadn't hit him as far as I could see.

Two men in suits spilled out of a Lincoln Navigator, braked in the alley. I know Special Projects when I see it and these two were August's men.

I hurtled past Leonie, told her to run, take cover.

Jack stopped, tottered, caught between the twin threats. One of the men seized him from behind as he turned back to Leonie – just as I ran past her – and levered him toward the Navigator. The other man – stocky, short, with a neck thick with muscle – raced toward us, aimed his weapon at me.

'Don't shoot!' I yelled. 'Holdwine is in trouble!'

And he paused. He knew me; we'd worked briefly in New York before Lucy and I moved to London. His name was Griffith. And that moment of recognition, tethered to doubt, bought me three seconds I wouldn't have had otherwise.

'He's been shot by that kid!' I yelled.

'He's lying!' Ming screamed.

'Stop,' Griffith yelled. But too late: I slammed into him with a jump; if I'd stopped to throw a punch it would have telegraphed my half-truth of being on August's side.

I knocked the wind out of his chest, tumbled to the pavement, rolled against a Dumpster. The other agent – who I didn't know – strong-armed Jack toward the Navigator and aimed his pistol back across the hood at me. Jack fought him, and he had to turn his attention to Jack, to force him into the car, and I ran toward them both.

The agent shoved Jack into the driver's side, then followed him into the Navigator.

He wheeled hard, rocketing out of the alley, backing into traffic with a blaring of horns. He had to wait several seconds to execute a U-turn. He was leaving Griffith and August behind. Which meant they were under orders that Jack Ming had to be protected at all costs.

I ran at full throttle. I hoped the adrenaline rush would make up for any lack of gracefulness like I showed in my sloppy running back in Las Vegas. I didn't dodge into traffic behind them. I read the road, the direction they'd gone, with a glance – the level of traffic, the obstacles, the shifting pattern of the cars. You have to read the terrain in a parkour run and that's why normally you only run where you've walked and explored, thoroughly. I was breaking a basic rule.

He was out in traffic, I couldn't catch him. But. One chance. Insane but I did it.

Running at full power, I jumped onto the trunk and roof of a parked car next to the alleyway and launched myself, timing it to land on the side of a moving NY Metro bus barreling past, closing in on them. I gripped a side ad of the bus and clambered – past the astonished stares of the riders – onto the roof.

Everything hurt. Fingers, arms, chest, legs. Brain.

The bus driver, trying to figure out what that sound of an impact was against his bus, slowed. No doubt the passengers were telling him a crazy man was on board. I ran the length of the bus as it slowed, launching myself onto the roof of the Navigator.

Just one perfect shot and my son would be safe.

Training dictated that I eliminate the bigger threat: the other Special Projects agent. He could kill me before I got to Jack. And although I was willing to kill Jack I wasn't eager to kill an innocent man.

The Navigator skidded into a parked car, on the passenger side.

I slid off the roof onto the trunk, on my knees, gun drawn. I emptied the clip into the windshield. The reinforced glass pocked but didn't surrender to the bullets. I placed my shots hard and neat where Jack Ming sat and I swear above the roar of traffic and horns and the gun blasts I could hear Jack Ming screaming.

But the glass held. Through the blizzard of fractures in the windshield I could see Jack scrambling toward the back of the Navigator, squeezing between the driver and passenger seats. Wriggling toward the rear exit. Panicking.

The agent was brave. He was going to cover Jack Ming's escape. Good guy, doing his job. My throat thickened at the thought of what I would have to do. He jacked down his window and he snaked an arm around the windshield to fire at me.

I dropped off the trunk, heard the first bullet kiss the paint. I was trapped in a narrow wedge between the parked car and the Navigator. The pavement was warm. The tire slanted toward me and I barely had room to curve and wriggle between the cars to get under the Navigator.

I started snaking toward the back. The car's heat radiated against me.

To my left the driver's door opened and I saw a foot hit the ground.

I shot the agent in the fleshy part of the calf. He howled and the leg withdrew into the car.

Ahead of me I saw red Converse sneakers hit the asphalt. Running. I writhed out from under the car, dodging through stalled and slowing traffic. The sidewalks had cleared at the first sound of the shots. Thank you, considerate, frightened pedestrians. But I had to dodge cars and Jack, fresh and unbeaten, bolted at full speed on the fast emptying sidewalks.

He rounded a corner and vanished.

I chased him. He glanced back, fear on his face. An ache tore through my ribs, in my chest, where August had dealt me a beating. Where I'd thrown myself against the bus. Trying to sneak up on them had hurt me.

A cheap street market loomed up ahead, one of those full of stuff like prepaid cell phones and knockoff purses and anything from lingerie to DVD players still in original packing, but not sold at original prices. People thronged between the booths, along the edges. Old folks, kids, babies in strollers, scatterings of families.

I couldn't risk a shot at him. Not there. Too many people.

Jack dodged between the tables and the booths. Loud Chinese pop and a competing undercurrent of reggae thrummed the air. I risked a backward glance and saw Leonie, a few blocks back, weaving toward us. She'd had the presence of mind to hide the gun. I didn't see either August or his men. But they would either be coming, very soon, or calling in reinforcements.

I tailed Jack Ming into the marketplace. He glanced back every ten seconds to see if I was following. We were blocks from where we'd started and this crowd was calm, and he wasn't eager to panic them. He wanted them between me and him. He wasn't screaming for help. Or for the police. He was determined to run. And he was determined to stay in a crowd.

The fear in his face tore at me. I didn't *want* to kill this man.

50

August opened his eyes. His face hurt. Everything hurt. Blood on the back of his head, sticky. He got to his feet.

He heard the whine of the metal door opening, footsteps pounding the concrete floor. He groped for his gun. Gone. His head felt broken and dreamy and misty. Concussion, probably.

A woman. Petite, red hair pulled back into a ponytail, wearing jeans and a T-shirt. She stared at him and raised the gun in her hand.

'Stay there,' she said. 'Stay right there.'

He stayed right there.

He saw her gaze dart about the room. She ran to Jack Ming's knapsack, lifted it almost gently. Before she picked it up he could see in its unzipped opening a small laptop. She grabbed the knapsack, put it over her shoulder. She kept the gun leveled at August.

'Just stay there,' she ordered him.

'Who are you?' he said.

Of course she didn't answer. She kept her gaze on him, tightened her grip on the gun.

She vanished back out into the alley.

August staggered to the door. Who the hell was she? Was she in league with Ming or with Sam?

He came out into the alley and she shot at him. Not close enough to hit but, you know, a bullet in your general direction is enough to make you retreat.

'I told you to stay!' she screamed at him.

One of the backups, Griffith, was lying in the alley, groaning, pawing at his ribs. No sign of the Navigator. He counted to twenty and risked coming out the door again. The redhead was gone.

He keyed his earphone. 'Two, this is One, report?'

'I'm getting the informant away, we're being pursued, an armed male, he knew your name, he said you were shot—'

And then chaos. The distant thrum of metal against metal crashing, the drum-drum-drum of gunshots hitting bulletproof glass. Grimes cussing, screaming at someone to get down and stay down, Jack Ming's voice answering *I am getting the fuck out of here.*

'The hostile is trying to kill the kid,' Grimes said and then more shots. Grimes howled and cussed again. August ran now. 'Where are you?'

The hostile. Sam Capra. His best friend – who should have wanted nothing more than an informant from Novem Soles coming forward – was trying to kill their best hope of unveiling the ring's every secret.

August ran.

51

I ran.

Ahead of me, Jack Ming dodged a booth full of DVDs from Bollywood and Hong Kong, leaping over the stacked tables, scattering packaging and earning a scream of annoyance and rage from the elderly vendor. The man hollered at him in a quilted howl of obscene English and Mandarin. Ming stumbled and his

T-shirt hiked up his back. He reached for something in the small of his back and I thought it was a gun and I couldn't let him shoot the old man but it was a swath of red leather. Like a book or a journal, firmly lodged in the back of his pants. He yanked his shirt back over it.

He was making sure it was still there.

The notebook. The secrets of Novem Soles.

I hollered in Mandarin: 'He stole my wallet!' There are decided advantages to having parents who give you a nomadic, worldwide existence as a kid. I can produce a large selection of random utterances in two dozen languages. I knew that phrase because I'd had it yelled at me, more than once, in Beijing when I was fifteen. I got bored easily.

The vendor grabbed at Jack, who screamed: 'He's lying, he's trying to kill me!'

Which story is more likely to be believed in New York?

The vendor closed his hold on Jack, who kicked away from him, landing an awkward punch on the man's face. The old man fell back onto a stack of Bollywood epics that now spread on the asphalt like a fallen house of cards.

I was jumping over the table when Jack proved himself.

Next vendor over was a stir-fry stand and Jack seized the searing hot pot and flung it at me.

I twisted and ducked and the scalding grease and shreds of meat landed against my jacket, in my hair. Real, honest pain. I dusted the meaty napalm free from my head and shoulders and singed my palms and fingers in the process. Glops of grease bubbled the plastic cases of the DVDs. The vendor caught a small splatter of it on his arm and cried out in pain.

I gritted my teeth, finally free of the searing mess, and ran out the booth.

Jack was gone.

Fifteen seconds is a lifetime in an urban chase; that was about what I had lost. Run. Catch him. How hard could it be to kill a computer geek?

I saw him skid into a cross-street and grab a cab. He piled in the back and the cab roared forward. I reached the intersection, hurrying to its middle, trying to see the cab name and a number. A guy in a Ducati motorcycle nearly ran over me, yelling at me in furious Spanish as he barreled past. He called out unkind words about my mother.

I ran after him. The Ducati slowed for braking traffic; the cab was several cars ahead. I stayed three steps behind Mr Ducati, just past the corner of his eye, and as he came to a stop I introduced an elbow to his throat, between the shielding of the helmet he wore and his jacket.

When I hit, I don't tickle. I hit hard. It's a lot harder blow than I look like I can deliver. The guy was blocky and squat and he perched on the Ducati like it was a mobile throne. He'd mouthed off at me, the fool in the intersection, and then forgotten about me, his eyes looking ahead for the next obstacle.

I slammed him off the bike. He didn't yell, he just went over and he made a choking noise. I knew he'd recover; I'd pulled the punch.

'Manners,' I said in Spanish. And I roared onto the sidewalk.

People screamed and parted out of my way. I could see the cab, four or five cars ahead of me, to the right. I was surrounded by witnesses but he was here. He was here and I had to make this work. The gun felt heavy at the back of my ruined suit jacket. I left it there.

I veered the Ducati hard, past a parked truck between me and his cab.

And saw the cab's back door open, swinging as the cab braked. Jack had jumped somewhere along the street. He'd seen me pursuing him.

I scanned the crowd. Alleyways, streets, doors.

Then I saw him. Stumbling, running in the distance.

I powered the Ducati, cutting across the traffic.

He ran up the stairs in front of a hipsterish, modern-architecture brownstone that was all glass and cube. And I saw him pull a small gun awkwardly from his pocket.

The door opened and a young woman exited. Jack waved the gun in her face and she screamed and crouched, obeying his order. Then Jack vanished inside. The cowering woman kept the door propped open, frozen in fear.

I roared the bike up the stairs after him, through the open door. I wanted him scared. I wanted him panicked. I wanted him not stopping to aim at me.

He ran up the apartments' stairs as I vroomed across the tile floor of the lobby. Eyes forward, intent on fleeing. Only glancing at me.

I braked with a foot, wheeled the Ducati in a circle with a deafening screech, and powered the bike up the sleek steel stairs, the motorcycle jittered and roared, not built for this punishment, but I rocketed it. The roar of the bike made him run and he was about to run out of road, so to speak. I spun on the landing, zoomed up the next flight. My spine felt like it was about to separate from my body.

He ran up the final flight. I followed, the engine huffing its protestations. He glanced back at me once, but because I hunkered down on the bike, when he shot, the bullet zoomed well past me. He was unnerved.

I needed him to stay that way if this was going to work.

I reached the landing and Jack ran hard down the hallway, in the direction of the street, toward a window-covered dead end.

Fear is a weird mistress. She can stop you dead and cripple you, or she can harden your heart with courage.

Jack Ming's heart hardened in those last few seconds.

52

He spun and he fired, the blasts from the gun bright and heat-dizzying in the dim of the hallway.

I fell back off the bike and it roared forward the remaining few feet, straight toward him. He threw himself out of the way. The bike rocketed past him, smashing through the glass wall. It tipped out into the sudden glare of the day, and I distantly heard it crash three stories down onto the pavement.

For a second, lying on my side, time froze. Jack leveled the gun at me, face wrenched with shock and horror – I had nearly run him down with the motorcycle, and the gust of wind from the window ruffled his hair.

Now I could see every detail of his face. He was barely past being a kid. He fumbled at a door lock, the door marked with a red Exit sign. The knob wouldn't move.

I groped at my back, my fingers searching, my ragged voice saying, 'I'm sorry.'

But my gun was gone from my holster.

He stared at me as he worked the knob.

Oh, God, I must have lost it, either in the jump to the car or along the hallway when I skidded.

Then he fired the gun. But not at me. He shifted its aim, sent a bullet into the lock of the door marked STAIRS. The lock broke. He shoved the door open and he ran.

I lurched to my feet as he bolted through the door.

I followed. He hurried up a short stairway and then through a rooftop door he opened and then slammed shut.

On a rooftop I could be king, and Jack Ming had no chance.

I grabbed the doorknob as he tried to shut it. The door froze in our tug of war. Then the little gun appeared in the gap, close by my head.

I ducked. He fired. I let go.

The door slammed shut.

I counted to ten. Fifteen. The moment I opened the door he could shoot me in the head.

Twenty. I yanked open the door, just a bit.

I could hear, in the open air, the approaching whine of a police siren. This building would soon be swarming with New York's finest and, if they caught me before I could reach Jack Ming, my son was dead.

I eased out onto the roof. I didn't see him. Lots of places for him to hide: water tanks; AC units; vents. All he had to do was wait until the police showed. Maybe he'd surrender to them and they'd ferry him to August or Special Projects. Compared with the option of dying at my hands, he'd prefer the police.

The roof was quiet. The neighboring roofs were both a half-story higher; but I didn't think he'd have had time to clamber up them. Then I saw him. Running. He had scrambled onto the roof next door, hunkered down for a moment, but I could see the top of his head, ducking back down. He'd risked a look. It was a bad risk.

I ran toward him and scrambled onto the neighboring building – there was no alley dividing the two – and Jack sprinted full out, dodging between the obstacles on the roof and jumping across a narrow gap to the next building.

Most people hesitate at a jump. He didn't. Brave. Or desperate.

His arms caught the wall. He screamed in terror, that sort of blind terror that makes your bones hurt, then he pulled himself over to safety.

My turn. I shoved my mind into the old parkour groove. See the obstacles, find the fastest and most effective way over them, under them, through them. I timed the jump and launched myself. I cleared the edge of the building and landed in a roll. My muscles howled – they had missed this particular form of exercise. I spotted Ming, running full out. Looking back at me once, terror bright in his gaze. Then he fired a shot at me and kept going.

Just chase him off the roof, I thought. If he falls he's still dead at this height. And Daniel is safe.

I ran. I had to catch him. Daniel, the son I'd never held, crowded out every other thought but run, jump, catch. My blood fevered, my mind went primeval. Simple. He had a head start of fifty yards on me, and I had to catch him.

Forty yards. He pulled himself up a REMODELING NOW CONDOS AVAILABLE SOON! banner, using the edge of it like a rope, onto the roof of a neighboring building. I arrowed straight toward him. He stumbled again. I glanced behind me. The roof we'd exited onto was empty but it wouldn't be for long. The police would be swarming. What with the cycle crashing and shots fired, it would be more than a single patrol car responding.

The thoughts went scattershot through my brain in seconds. I focused on running. Jack was running very, very hard. Survival instinct kicked into full. But I was trained in this, and I was faster.

'Police!' I heard a voice boom across the rooftops. 'Stop! Lay down your weapons!'

I glanced back. Two officers, scrambling out the door where Jack nearly shot me in the head.

I put my gaze back to where Jack was running.

Gone.

I scanned the roof I was approaching. Ming had been running across it, stupidly, in a straight line, and he'd vanished onto a lower roof when I'd glanced back at the sound of the pursuing officer. Now I'd lost him. No.

'Halt!' the police yelled as I topped the roof's edge and dropped onto the next building. He'd run out of space. Chimneys, vents, a brick shack for the doorway to the stairs into the building. There was equipment up here, the bright blue blisters of building wrap, scaffolding climbing above the farthest edge of the roof. Renovations were underway. Maybe he'd ducked under the wrap, which was everywhere. Maybe he'd gone through the door. If he dropped down into a building's stairwell I could run right past him. Panic frosted my heart. I headed for the door. I had to choose, now; the police would be broadcasting my location and other units responding would be directed to intercept me.

I rounded the corner to the stairwell entrance and Jack swung a heavy flowerpot at me. I caught it on my arm and the bone screamed. I fell back and he raised the gun; it clicked, empty. He moaned.

I slammed my foot into his stomach. He grunted, breathlessly, and staggered back.

'Police! Down on the ground! Down!' They were drawing closer. Maybe forty yards away. Two of them climbing up onto the roof. I guess the other cops didn't want to make the same leap Jack and I had made.

I jumped to my feet.

'Don't kill me, please, God, don't kill me.' His voice pleading. A voice ragged with tears. He yanked on the door; it was locked from inside.

I grabbed him with my good arm.

I'd had thoughts of trying to use him against Novem Soles, build an insurance policy to get my son back, fragments of a crazy plan that wouldn't have worked.

But there was no time. No time for him or for me or for Daniel. My arm didn't feel right where he'd clipped it with the heavy pot. I could break his neck if I had a minute. But the police were closing in on us, just thirty feet away. I didn't have the time.

I shoved him hard toward the edge of the building. Pushing him toward the edge, keeping him off-balance, in an unyielding grip.

'Sorry.' I said it so soft I didn't think he heard me.

'Get away from there! Get on the ground!' one of the cops bellowed at us.

Jack fought me, screaming, begging. If I just wrap arms around him and shove, we both go over, and the cops can't beat gravity, I thought. Ten more feet.

'No, no!' Jack screamed.

'They'll kill my kid if I don't. I'm sorry,' I yelled.

If we both went over ... maybe they would give Daniel to Leonie when they give her back her daughter. She would make sure he's okay. I knew her well enough to know her basic decency.

He'll be dead, it'll be in the paper, my job would be done. My son, free.

'No! No!' Jack Ming screamed. My grip on his forearm closed like an iron cuff. *This is the only way.*

I threw us both off the gravel roof.

53

And my foot landed on . . . scaffolding. This side of the building was under remodeling. Jack, arm pinwheeling, screaming, grabbed at an upright bar but I yanked him away from life, from safety. I saw his fingertips brush the metal pole and miss. The balls of my feet hit the edge of the scaffolding and I pushed beyond, my hands gripping his arm.

Into air. Gravity slipped its fatal embrace around us. Jack Ming's scream rose and rushed hard into my ears.

Three stories. It's not far to fall but it's enough. The images of the alleyway below burst through my mind, a memory that would only imprint for a moment before death.

I can't see the asphalt of the alleyway.

Parked in the space between the buildings are big dump trucks.

Blue canopies. More scaffolding on the sides, now behind us.

The renovation gear crowded the alleyway. We plummeted toward blue canopy, a surprising pond. Jack wrenched free from my grip. Two more seconds and we hit, ripping the thin plastic sheet, but it slowed our fall, like rain striking a leaf before dripping onto the mud. The canopy tore, yawned like a sleepy mouth. Metal rods snapped loose from under the canopy, cracking like bones. Then the tearing fabric, having cocooned us, spat us both free in a slow, awkward tumble. Just below us was a truck, its load covered in black plastic.

We tore through the plastic and hit sand. A metal rod clanged against the back panel of the truck. Pain gripped me, shook my already hurt arm. A drift of canopy settled on me like a blanket. I realized I was still breathing. Every inch of me recategorized pain, but I still breathed. I kicked the shredded canopy off me. Sand abraded my face.

'What the hell!' a guy exclaimed; he stood on scaffolding, six feet away from me and seven feet above. He hovered over me, inspecting me as though he couldn't believe I'd fallen out of the sky. 'What the holy hell?'

If I'm still alive then so was . . .

I saw Jack, scurrying off the sand at the front of the truck, on the driver's side of the cab. The sand had scraped his face raw, he bled from his ears. He fared better in the fall than I did. He dropped out of sight but moments later the truck gave a little shift, like a door had opened and slammed closed.

'Stop,' I said but there was hardly any breath in me. My arm – the same one Jack had nailed with the heavy ceramic pot – didn't feel right. 'Stop him.'

The engine started and the truck jerked forward. Jack bulldozed the truck through the detritus of construction: the canisters of paint, the stacked drywall, the wooden barriers erected to keep out the curious and the sticky-fingered. He blared the horn, skidded the truck out into the Brooklyn traffic.

I gripped the edge of the truck with my good arm. Holding on for the ride.

The sand truck smashed along the cars parked on the side of the street. Metal crunched, glass shattered. I tried to get to my knees on the sand.

And then the back of the truck's bed fell open. I didn't know if Jack got clever and resourceful – he was already that, he'd thought of stealing the truck before I did – or if he just hit the wrong switch, or if the rods that hit the truck when we fell damaged the catch that kept the hinge of the bed in place.

The sand spilled, as though from a broken hourglass, and carried me with it into a slide onto the street. Cars behind the truck braked as the sand exploded out onto them. Which was good because I tumbled out with the sand and I landed on a heap of it, approximately three feet in front of a honking cab. I leapt forward and the sand stopped the cab's bumper, just short of my shoes.

I tried to scramble to my feet.

Jack hammered that sand truck through the traffic, leaving a swath. I saw him barrel through a red light, turn, and he was gone. I pulled myself out of the sand heap. I saw the cab that nearly hit me was empty and so I kicked the sand heap smooth.

Back toward the building where we'd fallen there were multiple police units and officers racing down the sidewalk.

I felt certain someone was going to point at me at any moment. I did not care to have a discussion with the police. So I got into the cab. There was no one in the back seat.

'Hi,' I said to the cabbie. 'Are you for hire?'

He stared at my sandy self, turned around in the seat, gaping. My once-sleek Burberry suit was a ruin; I was bloodied and holding my arm awkwardly, and I still had that black eye.

I glanced at his name on the cab permit. Vasily Antonov.

Russian. So I said to Vasily, in Russian, 'Can you take me where I need to go?'

Speaking Russian must have reassured him. Cars behind him were honking so he inched forward, over and through the sand. The cops stormed past us, toward the intersection where Jack had turned. 'Where do you need to go?' he asked me back in Russian.

We pulled up to the intersection where Jack had turned with the truck. 'Turn right, please.' Still in Russian.

'You want me to follow the sand truck?' he answered.

'That would be great.'

'This man stole your truck?'

'Yes.' Sounded as good a reason as any.

'You look like you put up a good fight for your truck.'

'I tried,' I said.

Six blocks down the truck was pulled over. The door stood open, the cab empty.

Jack Ming was gone. My arm was broken. He knew my face. He knew I was hunting him and intended to kill him. And the police swarmed everywhere. I had to retreat. Daniel, I'm sorry. Dad is so sorry, baby, wherever you are.

'Take me here.' I gave him The Last Minute's address. I had to hope Leonie had made it there as well.

'Nice bar, yes, I've gotten fares there.' He glanced at me. 'So. Where in Russia are you from?' I guess I had no accent he could detect.

'I once lived in Moscow.' It was easier to lie than to explain my globetrotting childhood, salted with a dozen languages before I was even sixteen.

'Ah, I did not know a Russian speaker owned that bar. I will recommend it to the tourists.'

'And you are always welcome to come in for a drink. When off duty.'

'Ah, thank you.'

'Thank you, sir,' I said, and leaned back against the upholstery. The cabbie slid in a tape of Russian pop music to pass the time. Electro-style, sounded like Tatiana Bulanova. So thoughtful. It had a beat and you could dance to it.

I did my best not to pass out.

54

Brooklyn

You have to look normal. Slapping the sand off his clothes and from his hair, Jack ran down to the Marcy Avenue subway station. The luck he'd wheedled from the world shone on him for the last time for a while: a train pulled in just as he reached the track. He didn't care where it was bound; he joined the press of people.

He sank down into one of the hard plastic seats. The shock of what he had survived made him shiver. No one sat next to him and that didn't surprise him. He was filthy from having hit the sand. His wrist hurt where Sam Capra had grabbed it when the lunatic, the absolute fricking crazy-ass lunatic, had thrown them both off the side of the building. He leaned forward, clutched his elbows with his palms. The gun he'd taken from his mother's apartment was gone; dropped on the roof before the fall. The clip was empty anyway. He should have shot the man dead when he had the chance but he didn't know if he could fire a gun into another human being's face at point-blank range and he'd taken the chance to run. But that Sam Capra bastard was crazy.

He had thrown the two of them *off a building*.

The notebook. A cold terror seized him. If he'd lost that he had nothing to bargain with for his life. He felt its cool weight in the back of his pants. The red leather had slipped further down, caught in his boxers, one strip of the tape torn loose, the other still, thank God, in place. He pulled out the notebook, ignoring the momentary stares from the women sitting across from him. Not much in New York rated more than a momentary stare, including producing a notebook out of your underwear. He brushed the gritty sand away from the red leather, hugged the volume close to his chest.

He couldn't go home. His own mother had betrayed him; the CIA had failed him; Novem Soles had sent Sam Capra and that redheaded woman to the rendezvous point to kill him.

Novem Soles had infiltrated August's group. They knew about the meeting.

What do I do now? he thought. *Where do I go?* And for the first time, Jack Ming didn't know an answer, or have an idea. He pulled up his knees and he rode the train under the great beating heart of the city, the only way at the moment he knew how to hide.

What do I do?

The notebook's weight in his hands, like gold. All he had. He'd lost his knapsack, his laptop.

Sam Capra's odd words rattled in Jack's head. *I have to. They'll kill my kid if I don't. I'm sorry.* What did that mean? And the redhead: *I'm sorry. I'm sorry you have to die.*

Why the hell were Novem Soles flunkies apologizing to him? It made no sense.

But he was willing to die to kill you. He apologized for having to kill you. That's not the act of a hired killer. That's not the action of a CIA agent gone bad.

That's the act of a truly desperate man.

They'll kill my kid.

Jack ran his fingers along the edge of the notebook.

Well, I'm sorry for that, Sam Capra, he thought, but I'm not dying for your kid. Sorry.

His first impulse was to run and keep running, maybe until he hit the Pacific Ocean, or the Andes. Sounded like a masterful plan. But you can't run forever. Running is what they expect you to do. You have to stop them or you'll never breathe free. Look where running has gotten you. Nowhere, nearly dead, alone. Fight back, do what they don't expect. Which means using the two weapons you have. Your brain, and this notebook.

Not weapons. Bait. Bait to lure them in at the time and place of his choosing.

He started to think about a plan. And he wondered that if someone would be nice enough to turn on his lost laptop, he could remotely access it and he could set his burgeoning plan into motion.

55

The Last Minute Bar, Manhattan

Sandy and torn-suited and arm-busted, I entered The Last Minute, looking like the sort of guy I myself would throw out. Fortunately I still had the black eye to make me look even more respectable. I saw Leonie sitting alone at a corner table, a barely touched pint of Guinness in front of her. Her eyes widened when she saw me.

The bartender on duty – a guy I didn't know – actually started coming around from the bar to hurry me out. A few patrons stared at me, just to see how long and how noisy the ejection would take.

'Uh, sir, do you need help?' the bartender asked. This was the polite first volley, second volley to be, *now get out.*

'I'm Sam Capra. I own the bar. Is Bertrand here?'

'Uh, no, Mr Capra, he's not on duty today.' At least the bartender recognized my name.

'I've been in an accident.'

'Yes, sir, um, do you want me to take you to the hospital?'

I could feel the heat of Leonie's gaze on me. Wanting to ask: is it done? Is Jack Ming dead?

'No. I want to go to the office upstairs and I want you to call Bertrand and have him get here now. Immediately. Then please bring me two martinis, each with two olives. Made with Plymouth gin.'

'Yes, Mr Capra.'

'That lady in the corner table, drinking the Guinness, she's a friend of mine, comp her tab.'

The bartender nodded. Eyes of customers were still on us. I didn't like that. 'Are you sure you're okay, Mr Capra?'

'Yes. I'll be okay.'

'You're, um, hurt.'

'Yes, I know. Call Bertrand, make the martinis. What's your name?'

'Clark.'

'Thank you, Clark.'

I walked past Leonie, gestured slightly with my head to follow me. She scooped up her backpack and her pint. She waited until we were up the stairs and the door was closed behind me.

'My God, what happened?' she said.

'My arm is fractured. At best.' I emptied my pockets: rental car keys, wallet, phone.

'No, Sam, what happened to Jack Ming?'

I looked at her; the weight of my failure suddenly felt heavier than my bad arm. 'He got away, Leonie. We underestimated him.'

'You were going to kill him.' She said this to me in the same tone as one might say you were going to pick up the milk or you were going to mail the bills. Her mouth trembled. 'Sam. The kids. They will kill our kids ...'

A knock sounded on the door.

I put a finger to her lips. Clark came in, two martinis on the tray. I thanked him. He handed one to me and one to Leonie, who started to shake her head.

'Those are both mine,' I said. My voice sounded thick. Leonie set the martini back on the tray.

'Anything else for you, ma'am?' Clark asked Leonie. Give him credit: he was trying to act like this was an everyday duty. She shook her head, hardly looking at him, fighting for control. He blinked at her, embarrassed, and turned back to me. 'I called Bertrand, Mr Capra, and he'll be here in fifteen minutes. I told him that you were hurt and he said a doctor will be here shortly.' If he thought it unusual that a physician would make an emergency call to a bar, he said nothing. Times are tough and I figured young Clark valued his job. I realized that I might be in shock. I sat down.

'Thank you, Clark.' I took a sip of the martini. It was perfect, like chilled steel. 'If you make all martinis like this one, you will always have a job here if you want it.'

'Thank you, sir.'

'You better get back downstairs.'

'Yes, sir.' He glanced at me and Leonie and shut the door behind him.

'Nice kid,' I said.

Leonie's mouth worked, as if she fished for her words. 'You failed to kill him,' she said, 'and you're going to sit there and drink a martini?'

'Two martinis. I don't have any painkillers.' James Bond drank martinis when he was in a tux and moving in for the kill. I drank them because my arm was broken and I had badly messed up and I had to stop and think about what to do next. I fought the urge to gulp the cocktail down. 'Yesterday I speared a man through the gut and held a woman's hand while she died. Today I fought and killed two crazy mercenaries who came within inches of killing me and I beat up my best friend and I jumped on top of a moving bus and I crashed a motorcycle through a window and I threw myself and another human being who never hurt me off a building.' I raised my eyebrows at her. 'So, yes, Leonie, I'm gonna drink this martini right now.'

Leonie sat down in front of me. 'Tell me what happened.'

I drank the first martini and then I told her.

Leonie folded her hands together, as if in awkward prayer. 'We have to tell Anna that Jack Ming is dead.'

'Lying to her is a death sentence for the kids. But he didn't meet with the CIA, and now he'll be afraid to deal with them. We ruined his trust in them. That's the best news.'

'That's not as good as killing him. That's what you said you would do. You promised.'

'I'm so sorry I've let you down. After all, you were supposed to find him, and I found him, not you, and I kept my mouth shut about your failures.' My words came out like a cruel stab. 'You could have shot him in the alley and you missed. So, don't judge me.'

She opened her mouth, closed it, opened it again.

I reached for her hand. She let me take it. 'I'm sorry. I'm frustrated. Because you're right. I failed.'

I took a long sip of the second martini.

'I'm sorry, Sam, I know you tried. I know. I'm sorry.'

'Don't cry, we're going to get them back. We will.'

She pushed her barely touched pint toward me, like a peace offering. 'You are goddamned crazy.'

'Crazy does not equal efficient. We would have had him if he'd come and August and his men wouldn't have been there.' I gulped the ice-cold martini. It wasn't really killing the pain in my arm. 'Are you okay?'

'I will be.'

'How'd you get away?'

She licked her lips. 'I stole Jack's knapsack and I ran. His laptop was inside; I thought maybe his notebook was in there, too. I don't think I was followed.'

'I saw the notebook. He had it taped to his back. It's red.' I ate the olives and I took a long sip of her Guinness. I know it should have tasted great but I don't recommend drinking one right after two martinis.

'Let's review. Novem Soles blackmails us into finding and killing Ming. But suddenly, we're getting hirelings interfering. The sisters tried to tell me we're on the same side. But that makes no sense for Novem Soles to interfere with us.'

'Maybe they thought we couldn't do the job.'

'I don't think that's it. There's a third party here. And that party is inside the CIA, serving Novem Soles, or with his own agenda. I think it's this Ray Brewster. Tell me about him.'

Leonie massaged her temple. 'He ... he found people who could be useful – let's say people who had a natural talent for killing, or for theft – and instead of them being bound for jail, he got them to work for him.'

'Was he in government?'

'I don't think so. Why would he need me to give them new identities? The government would be better at that than me.'

'Did he find you?'

'Yes. I'd gotten involved with a forgery ring. They were about to get busted. He made a deal with me to shield me if I worked for him.'

I stood, I paced. Ray Brewster might not be CIA but he had a resource in Special Projects. Or he could be part of Special Projects. The question was, why would August believe anything I told him now?

'Do you think Ray Brewster is part of Novem Soles?'

'If he is, then he's operating without Anna's approval. Maybe he's named in the notebook. Maybe Jack Ming has really damaging goods on him. Maybe the goods that he doesn't want anyone, CIA or Novem Soles, to know.'

'So do you know his secrets, Leonie?'

'No.'

'What was he to you?'

She didn't look at me now. 'We were together for a while, then we weren't.'

'And he didn't like that. Since you created a new life for yourself in Vegas.'

'I thought it better to start fresh.'

'Is he Taylor's father?'

'No. He's not. Don't ever suggest that he is.'

I watched her. I needed to know her secrets while keeping my own. No way I could let her know the sisters had an interest in Mila. If she knew there was a bounty on Mila, and that Ray Brewster wanted it, then Leonie had a bargaining chip. One I could not allow her to use.

'You knew that CIA contact. August. He's your friend,' she said.

'We used to work together. We ... we used to be friends.' Were we any more? I didn't know. It might be a friendship too expensive for either of us.

'What exactly did you do in the CIA?'

I took another sip of the martini. 'I worked for a small, secret branch called Special Projects. August and I worked on transnational criminal rings. They often have ties to intelligence groups or to terrorism. Very much a black ops group. I think we're actually hidden in the budget under "vending machine contracts".' I was in a confessional mode. Thank you, martini, and blinding pain radiating up my arm. 'That was a joke, Leonie.'

'August saw me.'

'You?'

'Yes. I stole Ming's knapsack. At gunpoint. Before your friend could get it.'

'So he knows both our faces now.'

Leonie put her face in her hands, and maybe she freaked out or she mourned or worried but she only did it for twenty seconds. Then she stood up. 'Okay. Regroup. We have to figure out where Jack will go next. Is there a place where I can work on his computer without interruption?'

'Yes. In there, there's a bedroom.'

'Then why didn't we just stay here?'

'Because I didn't want you to know my business. That I own this bar.'

'Don't you trust me?' she said. 'Well, I guess I answered my own question.'

'It was need-to-know. The situation has worsened. I have resources here.'

'Resources.'

'Yes.'

'Okay, another secret. Fine.' She stood.

'Hey. Do we tell Anna we have Jack's computer? You know she's going to want all the data in it.'

'Yes,' Leonie said without hesitation. 'Maybe it's enough. Maybe they'll trade us the kids for the laptop. They could know what he knows then.'

'Or the laptop could give us weapons to use against them. Information on who and where they are.'

'No. We give it to them.' Fear creased her voice.

'No. We don't,' I said. 'We use it against them. We have no guarantees they'll give us our kids back, Leonie. We need every ounce of leverage we can get.'

'If they know we have it, and we withheld it, they'll kill the kids. We have to do what they say. Exactly. I won't risk any other action.'

'Then they don't ever know we have it. This is our guarantee, Leonie. That we can get the kids back.'

'They want his notebook.'

'Yes. Maybe the laptop has the same info on it.'

'I don't get why a hacker would keep a paper record of the most important information. It doesn't exactly fit his psychology.'

'I don't care. That's what they want. We can use Jack Ming's laptop to find where he might go next, to see who he could turn to. Go work. Delve. Figure out where he'll go.'

'If my child dies because you failed . . .'

'What, Leonie? You'll kill me?'

'No. I'll just never forgive . . .' But she knew what I would lose as well, and she choked on her words. 'Okay. What's done is done. We have to find him.' She paused at the door. 'This Special Projects group at the CIA will be hunting us now?'

'Oh, definitely.' I thought it best not to mention that August and I had had a drink here at The Last Minute a few days ago, and he knew I owned the bar.

'Well, at least you're not dead.'

'There is that,' I said. The phone I'd been given by the lovely snake Anna rang. Leonie sucked in breath.

'Is he dead?' Anna said by way of hello.

'No.'

'I am very disappointed.'

'He's hurt. He was meeting the CIA. I screwed up the meeting for him. Hopefully he will not trust them enough to make another approach.'

'And where is he?'

'He's running.'

'You failed me.'

'Technically. But I also kept him from surrendering to the CIA and pretty much ruined their relationship.'

'That's not enough.'

'I probably would have killed him by now if you didn't have people interfering.'

'What do you mean?'

'Ray Brewster has sent three people on us.'

309

'Who the hell is Ray Brewster?'

'One of your people inside the CIA.'

'Sam. I know you are not inclined to believe me on any point, but I do not know a Ray Brewster.'

'You have an ally inside the CIA. Reel him in. Or you don't get Jack Ming dead, or his notebook of goodies.'

'Who . . . who are these people?'

I told her what I knew.

'And you dispatched them?'

'They won't be troubling us any more.'

Anna was silent. 'This isn't our doing. At all. It's your problem. Put Leonie on the line.'

I gave the phone to Leonie. 'Anna. Is Taylor all right? Can I listen . . . Listen to . . . ' Her voice broke. I don't know if she listened to her child or to Anna but she said all right and she handed me back the phone.

'Yes?'

'The next time we talk and you tell me that Jack Ming isn't dead, your child will suffer.'

The phone clicked off.

56

Leonie helped me shower in the apartment's small bathroom. The blood and sand rinsed from me. I sported cuts and bruises and a nice slice across my chest, blood caked on my belly. She washed my hair for me in silence, soaping out the grains of sand.

She helped me dry off and I found boxers to put on for the doctor's arrival.

I didn't tell her Anna's threat against Daniel. The idea would unnerve her, and we had to keep our focus. I was horrified enough for the both of us.

She closed the door behind her. My arm was a dull ache. My whole body was a dull ache. But if I was hurt, then so was Ming and he couldn't run as far, or as fast. We might have clipped each other's wings.

I drank the rest of Leonie's Guinness. It felt good to be alive. I wanted to keep the kids alive. The past two days made me very tired of death. I could hear the hustle of Manhattan traffic outside the windows. I closed my eyes and I only opened them again when the door opened.

Bertrand stood there. He wore a tailored, subtly pinstriped suit on his tall frame, gray, with a sky-blue tie. He muttered something in French when he saw me, which I couldn't quite hear. He shook his head as he closed the door. I raised my arm, which screamed in protest.

'The doctor will arrive soon, Sam.'

'We could be in trouble. Where is Mila?'

He shrugged. 'There was a man here. Asking for you.'

'Blond?' I thought it might be August.

'No, dark-haired. He asked how often you came by the bar. I said about once a week, and you had been here yesterday. He wanted to know where you lived. I told him I didn't know that, all I had for you was a phone number. I gave him a fake one. I don't think it occurred to him that you have an apartment here.'

August would send someone, the bar might be under surveillance. Or it might not be. They cared about finding Jack

Ming more than they cared about me. Special Projects did not have an inexhaustible supply of resources. Eight people in the New York office. If they needed more feet on the ground they'd have to call Langley.

I told Bertrand what happened. He took away the martini glasses and the pint glass and brought me ibuprofen. I swallowed four.

'I suspect,' he said, 'you aren't going to find this Jack Ming again.'

'We have his computer. Leonie is going through the files.'

'Alone? You trust her?'

'I have to.'

A knock on the door. The doctor. There are all sorts of medical professionals who are willing to practice on the side to not require you make a trip to an emergency room. Usually they're doctors or nurses who have been bankrupted by a lawsuit or they have a prescription med monkey on their backs. This doctor was a woman, fiftyish, and seemed delightfully sober. She had a backpack on and blue jeans and inside the backpack was an army field medical kit.

'Doctor Smith,' Bertrand said.

'Smith,' I said, 'I hope I can remember.'

'Doctor I'm Not Going to Say Your Real Name doesn't quite trip off the tongue,' Bertrand said.

The doctor said nothing to me except 'tell me what happened' and 'does this hurt? Does this?' She did not blink when I described getting hit in the arm with a flowerpot, or throwing myself off a building, or landing in a sand truck. She ran fingertips along my arm, tested it, watched me wince. 'At worst a simple break.'

'Can't you tell?'

'The kryptonite is interfering with my x-ray vision,' she said dryly. 'I can equip you with a fiberglass cast. You need to rest the arm, though. No more jumping off buildings.'

'Okay,' I said. She set about her work of setting and casting my arm. Bertrand went and turned on a television to a local twenty-four-hour news station. After a weather update, and a political scandal out of Albany involving a state senator and a prostitute, the gun chase through the streets of Brooklyn and us falling off the building were the top stories. But they hadn't caught me, and they hadn't caught Jack Ming.

'I need you to move into fast gear, Doctor, because I got places to be.'

Bertrand said, 'Inspect his head for concussion, please.'

'I don't have a concussion.'

Bertrand brought me black slacks and a black shirt. The doctor assembled a bandage around my arm and put on the cast. I got dressed. She said hardly a word. She left me instructions and a large bottle of illicit painkillers. Bertrand stuck a wad of cash into her hand and she was gone.

'What is it you want me to do?' Bertrand crossed his arms. He looked like he should be in charge, not me.

'Special Projects will be working to find him. But they won't go to the police because they don't want to explain why they're causing gunfire in the streets. Now I just have to figure out where Jack will go.'

'Sam!' Leonie screamed. 'Sam, come here!'

I hurried into the room where Leonie sat. A messaging window was open on the screen. Leonie pointed and I leaned down and read the words **you will never find me losers so fuck you**.

'Jack?'

'Yes. He's got a remote access program. He's got control of the system.'

Damn. He could format the hard drive remotely; he could wipe out all the information on the system.

I leaned down and typed I want to make a deal with you. We have a common enemy in Nine Suns.

The words stood alone until another sentence appeared below them: Is this Sam Capra?

Yes.

'Don't tell him anything. Don't,' Leonie said.

You say you want me dead to save your kid. I know. But you know even if you kill me, your kid is dead.

'He's lying,' Leonie said. 'He's lying just to protect himself. To scare us.'

Give us the notebook and we'll tell them you're dead, I wrote. You can hide or surrender to the CIA or whatever.

I have no reason to trust you, he wrote. You threw me off a building.

I'm sorry. We have a common enemy. You know I'm being forced to work for them. We can both be free.

This is a trap and I'm not stupid.

Why are you even talking to me then? I wrote.

I want you to know you've lost. You will never, ever find me. I'm sorry about your kid.

We could fool them together. Give them a fake notebook. Tell them you're dead, they're not looking for you. We get our kids back. We all win.

No. I won't risk it.

I took a deep breath and typed: I'm sorry, Jack. They killed your mother. I'm sorry to tell you this.

Long silence. Then: You're lying.

No. I'm not. We tried to save her. They took her and they killed her. At a house in Morris County, on River Run Road. Only house on the street.

I expected then that he would cut off the communication. He would reformat the drive, he would steal our hope from us, he would snap the link.

I offered the sparest of olive branches: **I killed the man who killed her. If that's consolation.** The words just felt so empty.

How did they? The letters appeared one at time, typed slowly, as though his hands were shaking.

They shot her. We tried to help her.

Sure you did. Sure you did.

Will you listen to me? I wrote. **Please.**

Silence again.

I wrote: **They will kill you, Jack. Our only hope is to help each other. We fake your death, you're free of them and we get our kids back.**

That requires me to trust you, and that's not going to happen, Sam. They're going to want proof. A body.

I will give them proof that satisfies. I have an idea on how we can do it. They care more about the notebook.

'What the hell are you promising him?' Leonie said. 'Anna won't believe us.'

'We're not delivering a body to them. Just proof. She wants that notebook more than she wants anything else.'

I've read the notebook, so I'm a dead man. So are you if you read it. They'll draw you in to give you back your kid and then they'll kill you. There is no way out of this that works for you. If you let me go I can use the information in the notebook to bring them down. That's the best I can do for you.

No, I wrote.

The CIA is going to find you before you find me, Sam.

Leonie said, 'I feel sick.'

Is there mention of a man named Ray Brewster in the notebook?

A pause. **No.**

That's the name of the man who's after you, we think.

I don't know that name.

I know you don't trust me. I know. All I'm trying to do is save my son.

We waited for Jack's words to appear.

'If they find him first and they tell him that you offered him a deal . . .' Leonie started then stopped.

I waited, fingers poised above the keyboard for him to answer. He didn't. I typed into the void: Please don't let my son die. He's never had a chance at life. He's only a few months old. Please.

They won't let Daniel live. I feel certain. You don't know how bad these people are.

Daniel. He knew my child's name. A cold fear struck me: Is there something in the notebook about my son?

Yes.

Behind me, Leonie sucked in breath. What?

No. I won't tell you.

That was his insurance then, to stay alive at my hands.

All right. But then you know I've told you the truth. This is our only chance, for both of us. Let's meet.

Silence for the thirty longest seconds of my life. What do you propose?

We meet. You give me the notebook. We pose you in some photos to appear dead, which I take. I deliver the notebook and proof of your death. I get my son back. Nine Suns thinks you're dead and they never touch you again.

I have to have money.

That was why he went to the CIA, I realized. He wanted to sell the notebook. I can get you money, I wrote.

How much?

A half-million. And a new name, and a place to hide.

Thirty long seconds. **All right, meet tomorrow at the Statue of Liberty. 3 p.m.**

Then the machine whirred, the hard drive reformatting. He seized remote control of the system and he blanked out all the files. Leonie hit keystroke combinations, but nothing worked. The screen went gray and blue and a reformat progress window appeared. 'I can't stop it,' Leonie said. 'Damn it to hell.'

'It's all right.'

'I can't believe he agreed to meet us.' She sounded stunned.

'Oh, he didn't,' I said. 'It's completely a trap. He's going to tell August that's where we will be. He knows we're after him, and so is August. This ties up both sides as pursuers. Maybe if someone inside Nine Suns tries to warn us it's a trap, Jack will tell August that information will ID who the mole is. Everyone who's chasing him tangles and then Jack's running and gone.'

'But he needs money.'

'The one thing we know about Nine Suns is that it's global. So he didn't sell the information to the Americans. He can sell it to the British, the French, the Chinese. Someone will pay. And then Jack hides, and our kids are gone.' I leaned back. 'The only trump I had was his mother.'

'What do you mean?'

'He might really want justice for his mom. That might make him take a risk.'

'But you said he wasn't close to his mom.'

'She's still his mom. Don't you think one day Taylor would do anything to save you?'

Leonie swallowed. 'I would hope.'

'Mrs Ming died and he's going to feel responsible. He wants

to set a trap for us; we have to set one for him. One where we can grab him and get the notebook and then draw in Anna.'

'Kill him and take the notebook. Why is this so hard?'

'They will not just hand us back our kids, Leonie. That notebook is our leverage. We have to have it to guarantee a safe exchange for the children.'

'I do not like this.'

We were at an impasse.

'I've told you what I'm doing. Either you want to help me or you don't. If you think you can track Jack and kill him, then, please, by all means.'

The silence grew uncomfortable. 'Fine,' she finally said. 'We'll do it your way. Not that you're leaving me much choice.'

'I told you we will get our kids back.'

She nodded. 'I'd like to eat.'

'I'll have food sent up. There's a menu over there. Order whatever you like.'

Leonie got up. She stretched hands above her head. She studied the menu. 'High end bar fare. A calamari panini? Mini caviar sliders? Yuck.'

'Bertrand likes to experiment. I can recommend the Kobe beef burger and the fish and chips.'

She put the menu down. 'I hope they're feeding our babies okay.'

'Leonie, hold it together.'

'I am. I have been.' She steadied her voice. 'I'll go downstairs and order us some food. What would you like?'

'You order for us both, I like everything on the menu. Perks of being the owner.' I tried to give her a reassuring smile. I supposed she might take her revenge on me by bringing back that questionable calamari panini.

She went downstairs. And I wondered what was her limit, would she break under the pressure, would she decide that my way was the wrong way?

What would *she* do to save her child?

57

Special Projects headquarters, Manhattan

Ricardo Braun held three different cell phones; what he was not holding was his temper. 'Go find out who we're dealing with beyond Capra,' he said to August, 'while I do my damnedest to help you keep your job.' His normally cordial, calm voice trembled with barely contained anger.

'I'm sorry, sir.'

'You should be,' he snapped. 'Do as I told you and when you've got some information, come see me. I have to be on the phone with the gods in Langley, explaining how our inability to secure our informant caused a gunfight in the streets of Brooklyn and ended up on the national news.'

August tried to swallow and couldn't. He turned.

'August. There's a shoot-on-sight order on Capra. You should know. No one is expecting you to shoot your friend. But he attacked you and two other officers and nearly killed Ming. We're not chit-chatting with him again. He's going down, dead or alive. Do you understand me?'

'Yes, sir.'

August went back to the conference room next to his office, where the team, restless and angry, waited.

August still commanded the Novem Soles task force. So he put all remaining six agents in the Manhattan Special Projects office on the search for Ming and Capra. Agents headed for the Ming apartment; the Ming Properties building; and one for The Last Minute, where he had an unproductive talk with Bertrand. Another agent monitored all incoming traffic on the emergency rooms in Manhattan, Brooklyn and Queens. Just as Jack Ming tapped the cameras of a toy store and a traffic light, Special Projects had a bird's-eye into the emergency room entrances, feeding off security cameras. Monitoring software scanned flight reservations and train ticket purchases.

The shoot order meant August knew *he* had to find Sam before any of the other agents in Special Projects did.

Okay, first figure out who these women were – the dead and the living. The redhead with the gun who was intent on grabbing Ming's gear. Who was she? Who were the dead pair in the building? Special Projects was not exactly equipped to work a crime scene; they had possession of the building (thanks to Beth Marley, who cancelled the security service after being assured her family would be protected) and the bodies; a forensic team, and backup agents who were willing to overlook the fact that the CIA is not supposed to operate on American soil, were flying from Langley to work the scene.

But he couldn't wait on them. If Sam was the pawn of Novem Soles, so, perhaps, was the redhead. As for the two dead women, if they'd been there to kill Sam, then the women must be an enemy of Novem Soles. Drones for a third player. The thought deeply unsettled him.

August got pizza and a big soda and he sat down in front of a secured workstation at the back of the New York office. His jaw ached from where Sam had hit him but pizza was all that sounded good to his empty stomach. He kept his phone's earbud in place so he could get updates from the field teams scouring the city for Ming and Sam.

The Company owned, along with the National Security Agency, the most advanced photo recognition software available. He used a software program to assemble a face matching that of the woman he'd seen. Reddish hair, hazel eyes, a small nose, high cheekbones, a constellation of freckles. Her ears stuck out slightly; it made her look younger. He closed his eyes repeatedly, pictured her, tried to cement the memory in his head. Her chin was a bit pointed. Throat narrow. He guessed her height at close to 5 feet 5, weight maybe 110 pounds. When he finished the composite he considered: where to look?

He loaded the reconstructed face into a search database for CIA personnel. He got back eighty-nine matches. He scanned through the faces. None were the woman.

He loaded the face into a search database for known British intelligence agents. Sam had spent most of his career working out of London. A dozen matches. None were exact.

He accessed a database of retired CIA personnel. Again, a scattering of matches but not his woman.

Special Projects, whose purview was where criminality intersected with national security, had its own set of databases. He accessed them.

He pulled up a list of known computer hackers. Ming was a hacker and the redhead coming back to grab his knapsack seemed odd. While the number of female hackers was growing, it was still a male-dominated field. If she'd been arrested in the United States or by a Western ally for hacking, her smiling face should be in this database.

It wasn't.

He got up, began to pace the floor. He ate the pizza, chewing on the discs of pepperoni until his jaw hurt, settling the hunger in his stomach. He studied her face. He changed the hair, made it longer. He put glasses on her.

He opened another database of CIA informants. People who had traded information to the Company, people who ranged from foreign dignitaries to common criminals. The list numbered in the thousands. He entered the woman's face into the search parameters.

Three matches.

There she was. Her name on the file was Lindsay Partridge.

Lindsay Partridge had vanished from New York two years ago on 17 April. August rubbed his eyes. 'Hello, there,' he said.

She had provided the Company with information on a forgery ring, creating both counterfeit cash and passports. No charges filed against her, her name never given to the police. She dropped out of the ring and vanished, and the authorities arrested the remaining forgers. He opened her file. No other information. She had not done any other work for the Company. He entered in a special password that would open any encrypted parts of her file, which were for Special Projects eyes only.

The file was locked. That couldn't be. He couldn't be locked out.

He phoned Fagin.

'What?' Fagin sounded tired and stressed.

'Why would I be locked out of an SP file? I have a master access code.'

'I don't know. The stars didn't align. Someone doesn't want you to see it. The operation was mothballed. Or it's embarrassing. Or maybe it's gruesome and your delicate little eyes can't handle it, August.'

'I need that file cracked.'

'Well, get in line, we're really busy.' Fagin could sound as irritable as any corporate IT help desk. 'Fill out a ticket . . . '

'Now, Fagin. This is highest priority.' He gave Fagin the file details. 'I want to know what's inside there. Get your smartest Twist on it. Now or—'

'Or what? Damn, every one is quick with a threat this week. Really.' Fagin hung up.

What did that mean? He'd ask Fagin when he heard back from him.

Via tunnels carved out by Fagin and the Twists, Special Projects could dive into all sorts of databases – even illegally – to provide a path of footprints to follow. August scanned her trail. There were no recorded activities on Lindsay Partridge's charge accounts past that final April date. Her email and social networking accounts had been abandoned. She'd dropped out of the graduate program in design at NYU. A CIA informant and art student, maybe that was a first, or she had design talents to be put to legitimate use. She had not paid her taxes for the past two years and she had not reported any income. Here one day, gone the next. No one seemed to miss her. This didn't feel like foul play. This looked like someone rolling up the loose threads of her life, tying them into a tidy knot. Walking away.

Lindsay Partridge wanted to vanish. Had the CIA looked for her? Just to keep a tab on her?

August opened his phone and started to make calls. He gathered the threads of her vanishing: Lindsay Partridge handed her landlady a check for the rest of the year's rent, said she had to go home to Miami for a while, but never came back. The landlady received a letter that followed two months later, giving notice on the lease. He got a copy of her transcript, faxed over from NYU, and called her academic adviser. She'd told her instructors at NYU she was withdrawing due to a family emergency, returning to Miami.

And now she was just a locked file.

It was like she and Sam were both dirty secrets, ignored and forgotten by the Company.

He entered in the scant information they had on the sisters. He fed the photos of their faces, taken at the Ming building, into the facial recognition system to let it work its magic. One had a New York driver's license in the name of Amy Bolton and a Brooklyn address. The other lacked an ID on her.

He checked the databases: Amy Bolton had a credit history, a mortgage. She worked for a company called Associated Languages School. He checked the company's website. Very bare bones, and pages where there should have been more detail were 'under construction'. But they offered instruction in a wide range of languages and translation services. But no photos of the staff, no outlining of classes or programs, no listing of upcoming schedules.

Business must not be good.

August tapped at his lip, then went to Google and entered the following: foreign language schools Brooklyn. He got back a few results, with locations highlighted on the Google map of the borough.

No Associated Languages School.

Now, he wondered. A modern business, especially a service business, needs to come up on search engines these days to thrive. And here was one that didn't appear in the search results at all. Almost as if it were hiding.

He pulled up the address for Associated Languages School on

Google StreetView. The building was under renovation, being converted into condos.

So much for Associated Languages School. It was a sham.

The computer kept checking its digital rogues' gallery for a facial match on the two women.

He grabbed a soda from the refrigerator and returned to his office. And he activated the camera.

Lucy Capra lay in her bed, the wires and the feeds branching about her. She rested on her side; the nurses must have come in and moved her, regular as clockwork. He could see the savage scar along her skull, the mark where the bullet had left its fragments, her ticket to this long limbo of sleep. It had torn her soul and mind away, if not her body. The monitoring camera was fixed in place. He looked in on her once a day, sometimes more. He wondered why he did. It was a thing he would not have told Sam.

He didn't love Lucy. He had toyed with loving her once, but then she and Sam got involved and he'd taken what he'd felt for her and put it away, like a gift you can't use gets put on a shelf. And in his moments of shame he thought: thank God she didn't pick me. How different his life would have been; he might have been the one caught in this awful limbo instead of Sam.

But he could not understand why she had done what she did, why she had betrayed everything. Sam told him she claimed it was money. Money; it boggled August. She was lost in a shadow world, a nothingness where he suspected not even dreams intruded. But he knew that if she could have risen from the bed in pursuit of her child she would have.

He turned off the camera to see what the facial software kicked back to him, to see what news the field reports held.

And then his phone rang.

58

August stared at the number on the cell. Blocked. 'Hello?' he answered.

'You screwed me,' the informant yelled. 'You screwed up!'

'I'm sorry, Jack.'

A shocked pause. 'And oh, great, screw-up, now you know my name.'

'Yes. We do. All we want to do is help you.'

'All you did was nearly get me killed. Do you know what I've been through?' Jack's voice quavered.

'Come in to us. We can protect you. I'm sorry, I didn't know the surrender had been compromised ...'

'Well, clearly not. You're an idiot. Do you know how he knew?'

'No. But the man that is after you is ex-CIA.'

'Yes, and you're going to stop him from coming after me.'

'What?'

'He's agreed to meet me tomorrow at three at the Statue of Liberty. Be there, grab him, arrest him and this woman who's with him, who, incidentally, also tried to kill me, and then maybe we can talk.'

'You talked to Sam?'

'They took my computer and I erased it long-distance. But first I set up a meeting with him, you're welcome, now take him out. I've done your hard work for you.'

'He's after you because Novem Soles has his infant child as a hostage.'

Silence. In the background August could hear a pulse of

music, a hiss of traffic. 'I'm sorry for that, I am, but it's not my problem. Sam Capra is your problem now. You want Novem Soles, you take this guy down and then maybe I'll think about coming out of hiding.'

'Okay. Part of the info you can turn over to me: does any of it include anything on his kid?'

A long hesitation. 'Why should I tell you anything?' His voice went to a low whisper. 'How do I know you're not the one compromising me, selling me out?'

'Well, you don't. You called me.'

Silence again. 'Sam Capra said my mom's dead.'

August digested this. 'Then it's true. He wouldn't lie about it. I'm sorry, Jack.'

'He said her body could be found at the only house on River Run Road in Morris County. Will you go get my mom's body, please?' Jagged breathing now.

'Yes, of course,' August said. 'You come in, now, though, let us protect you.'

'If he's telling me the truth about my mom, maybe I'll tell him what this notebook says about his kid, once you have him in custody. I'll call you back later.'

Jack Ming hung up.

August checked the address, in rural New Jersey, on a satellite map program. A large house, on acreage, with a good-sized pond. He scoured the database for an owner.

Associated Languages School.

He stood. He should tell Braun, pull Griffith down, get a team together.

You've been compromised.

But someone in this office was a leak. Maybe he wouldn't tell anyone. He sat down, though, and entered in a report on what

327

he had found so far. He passworded it and secured it on the private Special Projects network.

Then he looked up. Braun stood in his doorway. Not holding his collection of cell phones, not pleading Special Projects' case.

'We need to talk. My office. Now.'

59

Special Projects headquarters, Manhattan

'Do you know what they called me in the old days, August?' Ricardo Braun asked.

'No, sir.' August could hardly get the words out.

'Mr Ideas. I was the one with the fresh ideas, I was willing to try what was never tried before inside the Company. Do you know how hard it is to innovate inside a large bureaucracy?'

'It's difficult.' He wondered where this was leading.

'Special Projects was my idea. I tested many ideas for ways for the Company to fulfill its duty, do its work, the most important work in this nation.' Braun paused. 'Not every idea is a success, of course, but you must have a willingness to try, to fail, and to learn from that failure.'

Maybe, August thought, this was a talk about redemption.

'I failed today, sir,' August said.

'You did. And I've been trying to come up with an idea or an innovation that will save you, Mr Holdwine, and I am failing.' Braun cleared his throat. 'I want to be sure I understand the unfolding of events. You came into a rendezvous site to meet possibly the most important informant we could get on Novem

328

Soles and you failed to secure it. You saw a former officer on the site, one who you knew could be under the control of a hostile group, and you did not secure him.'

'He appeared to be unarmed, sir. He had clearly been in a fight.'

'Appeared. He beat you up and then he nearly killed your informant. I've just spent the past hour on the phone to Langley, trying to explain how we failed to capture a computer geek and how that resulted in open warfare on the streets of Brooklyn.' Braun crossed his arms. 'You understand, we're not supposed to be operating on American soil. We are breaking laws here, August, for the common good. We all take that risk that it could come back and bite us. And here your team is, screwing up, and putting our entire branch at risk.'

'Sam Capra killed those two women who apparently wanted to kill Ming. It could be argued he saved Ming's life.'

'Because he wanted to kill him himself.' Braun shook his head.

'These people have his child. They're using Daniel Capra for their own ends. Forcing him to act. He told me himself.'

'I am not unsympathetic to his motivations, August. On the contrary, it breaks my heart. But we can't have him interfering in our work. I cannot have it. Sympathy doesn't play beyond a certain point. Sam could tell them anything about our operations against criminal networks.'

'Our operations have completely retooled since Sam Capra left Special Projects,' August said. 'They're not mining him for information. They're converting him into a weapon.'

'Capra could have come to you, August. He could have said, "they have my kid and they want me to grab their traitor for them". He could have worked with us.'

'If they were holding a gun to my baby's head,' August said quietly, 'I believe I'd do whatever they say.'

'I think I would first remember my duty,' Braun said.

'You certainly enjoy using that word,' August said. Anger rose in him. 'You don't think Sam has a duty to his family?'

'The Company is family, too, August, and you should remember that.'

August was silent. He wished Braun had stayed in his glorious retirement.

'Now. These two women in the building,' Braun said.

'We're working on getting an ID on them. They drove a car registered to a Beth Marley, who works for Ming Properties. We sent someone to the office, they found her handcuffed in her kitchen. She's being questioned by our people, but she doesn't know anything.'

'Interesting,' Braun said. 'Novem Soles has Capra hunting Ming, but who is hunting Capra?'

'Someone else who wants Ming. Who wants what he has.'

Braun turned to him from the window. 'So how do you intend to get both Ming and Capra?'

'I'm not worrying about Sam. I sent a man to his bar, they haven't seen him. He may be more of an absentee owner since he's searching for his son. From what the witnesses said, he's hurt. We'll monitor the emergency rooms, but I'd rather put the people we have on finding Ming, not Sam.'

'Ming can't expose us. Sam can. We are not going to be exposed. Ever. We are not going to be embarrassed.'

'So, I'm chasing him or I'm chasing Jack Ming. Which is it?'

'I'm simply being practical. I'm thinking like the bad guys.' He smiled, tapped his temple, and August thought: *it's not about innovation, it's about your ego*. 'They're playing on Sam's emotional vulnerability as far as his child is concerned. We can't fall into the same trap. I swear to you, we'll take Capra alive if possible and if we find where his son is, we will move heaven and earth to bring that baby home.'

The line was drawn in the imaginary sand on Braun's desk, drawn with those many *ifs*. He was putting catching Sam, for having defied them, ahead of catching Jack Ming.

'If you don't,' August said, 'I'll make sure the whole Company knows that we didn't go after an employee's captive child.'

'Sam Capra is not an employee.'

'He was. Didn't you just say we were all family, Ricardo? Or is that only when you make a point.'

'You wouldn't expose Special Projects work.' Braun's voice went icy.

'I would. How much loyalty would employees give the Company if they knew we hadn't already moved heaven and earth, as you like to say, to get back the Capra baby? If that baby isn't safe, none of our loved ones are, Braun. I'm tired of this bull-shit attitude of ours. We should have fixed this months ago, we should have found and rescued that child. You talk about duty. What about our duty to Sam?'

'I advise you to be careful about what you say next. You messed up today, August, you don't have a great deal of wriggle room with me. Worry about your own duty.'

'Duty. Innovation. They have to be more than buzzwords, Ricardo.' August couldn't keep the disgust out of his voice. 'We've kept everything about the Capras quiet. What Lucy did, what we did to Sam. We control hundreds of intel assets in the world, and none of them knew to look out for leads that could have given us Daniel Capra. We turned our backs on Sam and we helped create this situation. That gets out, there'll

331

be investigations, there'll be cuts in funding, there'll be resignations.'

'The Capras were an anomaly. Not standard operating procedure and Lucy Capra was a confirmed traitor.' Braun nearly spit as he said *traitor*. 'People will not see themselves as the Capras, it won't happen.' He steeled his voice. 'I gave up my retirement to come back here, after more years of service than you'll ever see. Don't you dare to suggest that duty is simply a buzzword to me.'

'I'm sorry,' August said. 'But there is a disconnect between what you say and what you're proposing.'

'I think you have too much emotional involvement, August. You were his friend. You're relieved. I'm not going to keep taking bullets for an ingrate who can't do his job.'

'What does that mean, I'm fired?'

'Of course not. But turn in your gear, your keys, your access codes. Take a week off to think about what you want to do because you'll never be doing field work again. Then crawl back to Langley and you can beg them to keep you. I think you'll be very good at pushing paper and,' Braun put disgust into his voice, 'writing long emails full of bullet points.'

'I am going to write a long email. Mostly about you.' August placed his phone, his gun, his passkeys on the desk, got up and left.

Braun watched him go. Then he let out a long, ragged breath. Worse and worse. Desperate times, extraordinary measures. August walked like a man who had no idea how close he'd come to dying. And he'd no doubt August would identify the sisters, if not the truth about them. And he'd already identified the redhead; every data search August made displayed on Braun's own computer.

God only knew what was in that damned notebook.

And exposure just couldn't happen. It just couldn't happen.

He had to shut this down, now. If Ming and Capra were dead that was the end of it.

Like most jobs, Braun thought, if you wanted it done right you had to do it yourself. He might need to return to a more private retirement, and that million dollars for Mila would be a good cushion for a new life.

He got up and left.

Sam Capra owned a bar, so August had said, and Ricardo Braun felt like a drink.

Twenty minutes later, when a pack of information arrived at Special Projects' network via Langley, a confirmation message echoed back to Langley's computers. Hiding inside that message was another one, and that hitchhiking bit of data dropped off along the way and snaked to its natural home. The tiny bit of computer code that allowed this action was very much like what Jack Ming had written for Nic, to spy on people. A Special Projects computer had been infected weeks ago, via a spreadsheet sent to it by one of the people in the Company later exposed as a Nine Suns operative.

The Watcher's phone beeped with a new text message.

60

The Last Minute Bar, Manhattan

'Hello.' Mila closed the door behind her. 'I haven't heard from you, Sam.' She glanced at the fiberglass cast on my arm. 'I would have sent flowers.'

'Hey, Mila,' I said. I wish Bertrand had given me warning she had arrived but he hadn't. Leonie looked up from her dinner and stared at Mila.

'Who is this?' Leonie said.

'Mila. A friend.'

'And I am also his boss,' Mila said. 'Sam. We need to talk. Alone.'

'We're busy right now,' Leonie said. I could read her expression. Mila was not connected to the search for our kids. Therefore, Mila was a distraction. Leonie didn't know about the Round Table, the private vigilante group – I honestly don't know what else to call them – that hired me to run the bars and gave them to me as cover. First to help me find my son, and with the hope that I would do work for them in the future. To be Their Man in Havana, and a few dozen other cities. To Leonie, Mila-as-boss must mean she was concerned with the running of the bar. Which paled in importance to our kids.

The realization went through my mind in a second. 'Leonie. It's okay. It'll just take a minute.'

'You could go downstairs and get a drink,' Mila said helpfully. 'Perhaps one with an umbrella in it.'

'I don't want a drink,' Leonie said. The ice for the drink she didn't want found its way into her voice.

'A coffee, then. Although you seem anxious. The decaf here is excellent.' Mila smiled.

Leonie didn't get up.

'Is English a second language for her?' Mila asked me. She looked back to Leonie. 'I want to talk to him. Alone. Please go downstairs.'

Now Leonie got up but not with grace. More with fury.

I stepped between them. 'Leonie, please.'

'How is she your boss if you own the bar?'

'Just give us a minute, okay?'

'Actually, I need a shower. I'll take it now and you and your charming friend can talk.' Leonie retrieved her bag and vanished into the bedroom. She slammed the door closed.

'She thinks she is so smart,' Mila said. 'She runs a shower, but she tries to listen. The doors are soundproofed. We added those last year after Bertrand and I beat up a man in the bathroom to get him to tell us . . .'

I didn't need to hear about her past crimes. 'Don't be adversarial.'

'I just enjoy it. Where have you been?'

'Here.'

'And hanging out at this bar is so dangerous you manage to break your arm. I watch the news, Sam.' She went to the small bar in the corner, poured herself a neat Glenfiddich. 'Maybe this man you hunt is a huge threat to Nine Suns. Maybe I could find this man useful to me. Maybe I don't want you to kill him because I might want to have a nice, long, whisky-soaked talk with this man myself and let him tell me all his secrets.'

'You can't have him,' I said. 'No.' Leonie would be ready to kill Mila if she interfered.

'Your child concerns me,' Mila said. Her voice went low. 'Did you think I would ever let you fight this battle alone?'

'Mila, please don't do this.'

'You do not want my help.'

'I have my orders.'

'I am so hurt. I thought only *I* gave you orders.' She took a sip of the Glenfiddich.

'Mila. Let me handle this.'

'And this woman, this Leonie—' she said the name as though

mispronouncing *leprosy*, 'she is, what? Your new assistant? I did not approve a hiring.'

'She has her reasons for assisting me.'

'Who is she?'

'Someone with very good reason to help me.'

'Do you think you can keep a secret from me? That is so cute.' She smiled over the whisky glass.

'Mila, go. Leave.' There. I can slam a door with the best of them.

'I will leave. When you tell me who is this man you kill for your child.'

'No.'

'The bars – which are providing you with meeting places, and staying places, and getting-your-broken-arm-set places – were given to you easily, and they can be taken from you just as easily.'

'Take them, then.' I stood.

'I am not your enemy.' She set down the whisky glass. 'Do you think you're the first person I've recruited to work for the Round Table?'

I said nothing.

She ran a finger along the rim of the glass. 'Often the second job shows more about the new person than the first job. You helped us break up the assassination plot. You worked hard, you made a great impression. Self-starter. Very tough. Resourceful. Slightly crazy in a good way. Now you are settled into the job, into working with me, now suddenly I see your secrets, your bad habits.'

'This is not a job for you. This is my son's life at stake. We are not negotiating.'

'All I want to do is to help you.'

'Sure. And if you get info on Nine Suns, then all the better . . .'

'What is this ransom, Sam? You owe me. You know you owe me.'

I put an elbow down on the table; I rested my head against the heel of my hand. 'They want me to kill an informant who is attempting to surrender to Special Projects. He has information that could gut Novem Soles. I broke up his surrender to the CIA. But someone else is hunting him; I've killed three assassins already who tried to get to him before I could' – now I raised my gaze to meet hers – 'and all three of them asked me about you.'

'Me.' Her expression was unchanged. Poker players should have bowed to it in respect.

'Yes. Someone wants to collect the price on your head.'

This silenced her.

'You and I have a common enemy, Mila.'

'Tell me what you're thinking, Sam.' She said it low, soft, the way you might to a lover lying next to you in the warm bed. The thought of Mila that way jolted me.

'Sam,' Mila said, 'what is it Americans say? Let us kill the two birds with the one stone.'

61

The Last Minute's lights were low when Braun stepped through the antique doors. He scanned the room. A dozen people at the bar, mostly corporate types in suits having a drink at the end of the day. One knot looked like financial types, another like publishing types. The financial suits were stiffer and all the way across the room he heard a woman bray a laughing comment about how to get kids to read. Fifteen tables, half of them occupied. An old lady sat at a piano, playing languid, soft versions of Louis Armstrong standards.

No sign of Sam Capra. Or the woman Mila. He noticed a tall black man in an impeccable suit, behind the bar. Manager on duty, he decided. Or, considering the man's stately authority, a partner in the business.

He could play this two ways. Either march up and announce he was looking for Sam Capra, or sit and wait. But he had no other lead, and he had no one else in New York to send against his enemies. Sam Capra had killed them all.

Braun sat down at the bar, in the dead zone between the two loud groups. He ordered a Harp lager. He took one sip of it, didn't touch it again. He didn't much like alcohol and he didn't often drink. It was a waste; a lowering of necessary defenses.

He could see the range of tables, the front door, if he kept his eyes to the mirror at the bar. He sat and he looked ahead, in his particular quiet. The groups on both sides laughed and talked and for an odd moment his own loneliness made him sad. It was strange to watch people with friends; their laughter, their openness filled him with unease. He had long resigned himself to his own company. He got up from the bar and retreated to a corner table. He watched the laughing women and silently hated them. Anyone you let close might have had a knife ready to slide along your throat.

Lindsay, for instance. She'd tired of him, she'd left him. She'd run away, and after all he'd done for her. Bad, bad girl. Friends were too much trouble.

'Is everything all right, sir?' The tall black man in the suit stood at his table. He had a very slight Haitian lilt to his voice.

Braun brought a polite smile to his face. 'Yes, fine.'

'I just noticed you took one sip of your beer and then left it. Does it taste all right?'

Awfully observant for a bar manager, he thought. 'Yes, it's fine. Thank you. I just got lost in thought.'

'Is there anything else I may get you, sir?'

'Uh, perhaps some food. Is there a menu?'

'Of course, one moment.' The tall man smiled and left him to his beer while he got a menu.

Braun waited. He wasn't hungry but food was good camouflage. He watched the door.

62

'Two birds,' I said.

'Yes. End both threats without jeopardizing your child.'

I waited.

'You and me, we capture the informant. We don't kill him. We take what information he knows. Fake his death, if need be. Use that information to mount a rescue operation of your child. This seems clear to me as a superior solution.'

'Leonie is very reluctant to defy them.'

'That is good to know.' Then she slapped me, hard. I took it.

'You bloodied their noses before. They have no reason to give you back your child.'

'If they kill Daniel I will never ever stop hunting them,' I said. 'I will burn them down. They know this.'

'They're not afraid of you. They respect you. But they don't *fear* you.'

'My problem,' I said. 'We will stay out of each other's way.'

'This is not the Sam Capra I know.' She laughed and it broke something inside me. I could almost hear the snapping of my heart.

'I'm not risking Daniel's life for your agenda, Mila.'

Mila said, 'If you betray us, I'll kill you.'

Her threat made me blink. 'What? How the hell did you get back on that track?'

'You need a guarantee that your child will be delivered to you after you kill the informant. I don't intend to be the sweetener in the deal.'

'I would never betray you.'

Now she stared at the floor, then her gaze met mine. 'Really? Not even to save your son?'

'Mila. Don't even go there. Even if I offered them you, that is still no guarantee I get Daniel back. All I can do is what they've asked me to do.'

'Why use you to eliminate this threat?'

'I don't know. Because I can get close to him.'

'Why? Because you're ex-CIA? Because August will let you get close? Not any more.'

'Because they have my son and they want to put him to good use. I don't know.'

'And what happens next, after you dance to their tune and they still want you to dance. I told you, they will never let you go.'

'I do this, that's it.'

'No. You and I must come up with a way that saves Daniel *and* breaks their hold on you.'

I said nothing for fifteen seconds. I counted them out. It takes about fifteen seconds to weigh up alternatives and make a decision in a heated conversation when you decide to capitulate. Undercover work is 90 per cent acting, only 10 per cent observing. She needed me to be someone and I was going to be who she needed me to be, the man she wanted to see standing in front of her instead of the screwed-up brawler who just wanted his son back.

'What's your way?'

She jerked her head toward the closed door. 'First, tell me who is the charm school dropout?'

'Leonie. She's an information broker; she hides people who need to vanish. She lives under a false name because she's hiding from a guy named Ray Brewster; he's tied to the killers who are hunting you. She's done false documentation for Anna's kids, so Anna grabbed her kid to force her to help me find Jack Ming.'

'So since she *hides* people, they thought she could *find* Ming.'

'Yes.'

'They have both your children.'

'Yes.'

'Are you sleeping with her?' This was asked with a very slight tilt of the head. She gave me a look best described as halfway between horrified and amused.

Mila's bluntness: thank God you can't bottle it. 'None of your business.'

'Which means yes. And we have another complicating factor.'

I so did not want to have this conversation with her. 'We were exhausted and . . . upset.'

'A woman would have to be.'

I shook my head, gave a weak laugh. 'Is this what my life is going to be like once I find my kid and I'm working for you, still? Reporting on every detail of my life? Forget that.'

'I wanted to know.'

'Why?' Then I thought: wait, she can't care what I do. Who I sleep with. She'd never shown the remotest interest in me, or in anyone else. She was all ice except when she had a target. Then she was fire.

'You forget that we – my employers and I – have made a big investment in you.'

'Mila, go to wherever you go when you're not riding my ass. Go on a vacation. I'll either call you when this is all done or, if you don't hear from me, you'll know I'm dead. You don't understand our situation. What it's like to have a loved one taken and be at risk.'

She gave me a sad look. 'No one could understand your unique pain.' And something in the air shifted between us. 'You asked me why there is a price on my head.'

'I think it's your endless charm and witty banter,' I said.

She nodded toward the computer. 'I wrote it down for you. You read it. Then you decide whether or not to trust me with your child's life.'

PART THREE

TU MORI

63

Sam:
This is what happened, this is how I came to be.
– Mila

Harpă, Moldova
(My little town was named for a harp. Do you like that? But I do not play)

Three years ago. The children are done with their work and have escaped into the bright sunny afternoon; I mop up paint smears and bits of torn paper. The art supplies are a gift – from one of the families that runs Trans-Dniester, the sliver of Moldova that has declared itself free of the country. Aunt and Uncle say quietly at the Sunday lunch table that the whole region is ruled by crooks and outlaws. Not just crooked politicians but actual criminals – smugglers and Mafiya and drug lords who pour poisons west into Austria and Hungary and north to Moscow, Kiev and St Petersburg.

But let me be blunt: what do I care where the paints and papers come from? They are an extra to help my classroom. The children benefit and I don't care if a Mafiya bought crayons to ease his conscience. The towns of northern Moldova can barely afford to heat the school in dismal winter; I won't turn up my nose at free school supplies.

You are making a better Moldova, darling girl, Aunt tells me, and I want to shrug. No, I'm earning a paycheck and not having to be like my sister Nelly, casting her lot out into the distant world. I am a homebody who likes quiet.

After I gather up the scraps of supplies that can be used again, I take a rag and I dust the small TV, the old DVD player, the worn and loved books on the shelf. All again from the largesse of the criminal kings of Trans-Dniester, Uncle would say. But the machinery does not do evil and the books take no sides.

I dust and think Nelly would do a better job. Nelly the sunny one, Nelly the smiler, Nelly the adventurer. Nelly had shown me the brochure six months ago – the employment agency, based out of Bucharest in neighboring Romania, happy women in drab uniforms making military covers on hotel beds, serving food to smiling diners, filing papers behind a spotless desk with a computer resting on it, its plastics unyellowed by age.

'See, they need secretaries and waitresses and maids and nannies,' Nelly tells me. 'You could get a job with a computer that's new.'

I glanced at the marketing brochure. Moldova is the poorest country in Europe. These places all look better, sunnier, more hopeful. 'I don't want to move to Italy or Turkey or Israel. I don't speak their languages.'

'But your English is good. They'll always pay extra for English.' Nelly bites the eraser on her pencil. 'At a hotel I might meet a traveling businessmen from the West. Maybe America. A nice guy with a good job. Americans like eastern European girls. The supermodels have done at least that for us.'

'Americans don't talk to maids,' I say. I better spoil her

dreams right away, yes? That's what a good sister does. I hand her back the brochure. A hot beat of fear probes my chest at the thought of Nelly hundreds or thousands of kilometers away, working a job that gives her no time to come home.

'I could send money back to you and Aunt and Uncle,' Nelly said.

'No.'

'Well, I am not asking for permission.'

'Why start now?' I say and do a sister's roll of the eyes.

'Natalia went to Turkey and got a good job. There are no jobs here.'

'School teaching? Remember?'

'You better teach them well because they'll have to leave Moldova to get a job,' Nelly said.

And three weeks later, Nelly is gone. Teary hugs at the train station. She is taking a train to Chisinau, then onto Bucharest. Then a plane to Tel Aviv.

'I'll write everyday,' Nelly says, hugging Aunt and Uncle at once and looking over their heavy shoulders at me.

'No you won't,' I say. Nelly has always been the crier, not me. I am not about to start. But my heart shreds so much it turns into confetti.

'I will!' Nelly promises. 'I'll be bored. And I'll have to write to send you money.'

'Borrow the traveling businessman's BlackBerry,' I joke. 'And send us an email.' I have seen BlackBerries in movies. No one in Harpă owns one.

And then Nelly hugs me, smelling a bit of milk and goodbye cake, and is gone.

*

When I am done dusting the classroom I stop for a moment. The boys are playing football in the scrappy yard. My favorite student is the goalie. I watch the boys and remember playing on the scrubby grass with Nelly when they were young. Nelly complained I kicked the ball too hard, as though Nelly's legs were fashioned from porcelain. I did kick the ball hard. I was a good athlete, one of the best at our school.

Nelly's letters arrive regularly but there is no money in them, just brief words that she is well, in jagged handwriting that looks unhappy.

Nelly feels guilty about not sending money, I decide. But Nelly won't say so.

The classroom door behind me opens. I don't know the man standing there. He is tall, head shaved bald, a thick lacing of tattoo crawling out of the collar of his shirt. His eyes are brown and hard. He is the sort of man who makes you hold your breath for a moment. Not in a good, fluttering way.

He smiles. I know he is not a parent, not an administrator from the district. His clothes are too good, the suit Italian, the sweater underneath it silk, the watch ostentatious, a slash of steel on his gorilla's wrist.

He calls my name, like a question. I nod a yes.

'I'm a friend of Nelly's,' he says. 'You can call me Vadim.'

And my teacher's brain, used to the carefully built lies of children, notes he didn't say it was his name. It was what I could *call* him. What has Nelly gotten herself into, I think. What trouble?

A feeling of dread pierces my stomach. Vadim smiles. He steps inside the classroom. He shuts the door. The click is like a hammer hitting me in the silence.

'I bring you a message from Nelly,' he says.

Oh. All right, I think. Maybe he works with her in Israel. Maybe she actually met a traveling businessman, and here he is.

He holds up a DVD. He walks to the old machine and presses the power button, turns on the television. He ejects the DVD that's in there, a bootlegged PBS video with a bad Moldovan voiceover, a science show about the universe. I have been teaching the children about stars and planets. He glances at the bootleg, as if curious as to what useful lessons I might be teaching today's children.

He slides his disc into the machine and presses Play.

I stand, pierced, as my sister's face appears on the screen. Nelly is crying. Shivering. I have not seen Nelly cry this way since our parents died seven years ago. Her hair is different, dyed blonder, and bigger, as though a harsh wind has breathed it into place. A too-bright lipstick smears her mouth. Her eyes look dulled.

Nelly says my name like it's a foreign word. Then, on the tape, I hear a deep voice. Vadim's. Saying, 'tell her what you wanted to say'.

'I want to come home,' Nelly says. 'Help me come home.'

She's been a problem, Vadim says, in the detached tone of a mechanic discussing a faulty carburetor or a leaking gas line. She's a bit uglier than we thought she would be. The customers don't like her, she's not getting picked enough, she's just sitting on the couch.

'The customers?' I say. It's not a question, it's horror, bright in my heart.

Then a man's hand pushes Nelly back. Onto an unmade bed. The sheets are a bright, eye-burning aqua blue. The camera jars slightly. A man, heavy-shouldered, pale skinned, climbs on top of Nelly and begins after a moment, to thrust his hips. A thin, blonde anemic mohawk tops his head. Nelly doesn't scream, she doesn't fight. She simply endures.

The mohawk smiles back over his shoulder at the camera. Then he hits Nelly, a slap, and continues.

Vadim watches me for a reaction. Then he smiles. 'My boss, you see he likes her fine, but the customers are the ones who matter. I can arrange for Nelly to come home, if you like.'

If you like. If you like. I go hot and cold again. My throat feels broken. The searing feeling in my chest subsides. A fist of ice forms in its place.

My mind goes blank, for all of five seconds. Blank in a way it never has before.

It is all the shock I allow myself. There is no time for dismay or horror.

'What do you want?' I ask Vadim. 'Money?'

'I want a thousand euros. And I want three more.'

'Three more what?' I say. 'Euros?'

'Three more girls.'

The silence hurts like a knife sliding between my ribs.

'Recruit three more girls for me, to take your sister's place.'

I don't move, I don't speak.

'You're a schoolteacher. People trust you. You can do this easily. I prefer eighteen-year-olds.'

Sell three innocent girls into ... that. To save my sister.

My voice stays steady. How, I don't know because the shock is quickly fading in favor of another feeling I cannot describe, a heat in the heart that is beyond rage and fury. The heat of a decision, made. I shake. He smiles, like he thinks it is fear makes me tremble.

350

'And if I can't find three girls? Please, could I just pay you more money back to get Nelly?'

'I don't need money, schoolteacher. I need product.'

Product.

'All right,' I say. Too quickly.

He gives me a scowl. 'Don't bother going to the police. We own them. And you can hardly recruit girls if the cops know what you're doing.'

I believe him. I have no intention of going to the police. Right now I'm wondering if I murder him right here if I can clean up the blood so thoroughly that the children will not notice it tomorrow. Kids notice everything.

I swallow hard. Just to give a visible reaction beyond the overwhelming bitter, freezing hatred I feel for this man.

'How does this work?' My voice doesn't quite sound like mine.

'I'll be back in two months. You bring the three girls. They need to be no older than twenty-five. No older. You will send me their names and photos in two weeks and I'll arrange their passports. If they already have passports that's even better. You say nothing to them except that Nelly is really happy in her job working at a very nice hotel in Tel Aviv.'

'What if I can't recruit three girls?'

'Then little Nelly stays put. The brothel owner might sell her down the chain, to the cheaper houses. Either in Israel or over to northern Africa. Or,' he shrugs, 'he might kill her and dump her worthless ass in the Med. This is your one chance to get your sister back. Take it.'

'I'll do it. I'll do what you ask.' A shivery moan escapes my lips.

Vadim is happy. Message delivered, relative terrified, action promised.

He grins. 'Now you, schoolteacher, you're much nicer than Nelly. You could turn the money quite well.' He smacks lips at me. 'What is that old Van Halen song – hot for teacher?' He sings it in his bad broken English, off key. He pulls the tape out and considerately reloads the bootleg educational DVD and then he is gone. His expensive heels click on the worn tile down the hallway.

I go to the window and watch him walk past the boys playing their impromptu football game. The ball bounds toward him and he stops it with one Armani shoe. Gracefully. He aims a polite, perfect kick not to the closest child but back to the biggest, tallest player on the field. (Of course he would kick it to the biggest. He is that kind of showy asshole.) He walks to an Audi and consults a map and gets into the car and drives off.

A map. He had more places to go along the backwater roads, more people to see, perhaps more families to blackmail.

What will you do for your sister?

I move as if in a dream. I lock my desk. I gather up my lesson plans notebook and my lunchbox and my purse. I walk down the street, ten minutes to home.

At home, Aunt and Uncle cook dinner and watch television, a Romanian soap opera called *Only Friends* they say they don't care about but to which they are clearly addicted. I dutifully kiss the tops of their heads – Uncle's freckled, bald pate and Aunt's slightly greasy gray mop – and make a cup of black tea. I take it to my room, the one I'd shared with Nelly, and I shut the door.

I sit on the edge of the bed and drink the strong tea and I stare at a water spot above Nelly's bed. My sister always said the spot was shaped like France and I told her, no, it's a lion's

352

head. I lay down on the bed and, well, Nelly, was right, it sort of is like France. And a lion's head.

And I close my eyes and I think.

I think the problem through, with the care and patience of someone building a house of cards. When I see weakness, I tear the tower down with a flick of my mind and I start again.

The puddle of tea in my cup grows cold. I get up and I walk down to the hallway to the apartment at the end. I knock once and the door opens after a minute. It takes Ivan, with his one leg, a bit longer to get around, and he looks sleepy, as though he has dozed. I can hear an argument on his TV, he's watching *Only Friends*, too, the silly old soldier.

He smiles at me. We are only friends, too, but we are old friends. He invites me inside, asks if I would like tea, and I say no thank you.

'What brings you here?'

'Teach me, Ivan.'

'Ha, what can I teach the teacher?' the old soldier says.

I look at him.

He sees the unspeakable seriousness in my eyes and his smile fades.

'Teach me how to fight. Teach me how to kill.'

64

Harpă, Moldova

I follow Natalia from the market. Natalia is a petite girl and whenever I turned I could see the prominent heavy swell of her stomach. Pregnant. Natalia lumbers like pregnancy does not agree with her. She has no glow.

As Natalia reaches the edge of the market, I touch her elbow and the young woman turns. Recognizes me. And tries to smile, like smiling is a flexing of the face that she's forgotten.

'Do I know you?' Natalia says.

'You recruited my sister to be a prostitute for Vadim.' I see no point here in wasting time. She looks like she might explode with baby at any moment.

Every word detonates against the fortress of Natalia's smile. The woman's lips waver for barely a moment and the smile stays firm as brick. 'I have to go,' Natalia whispers.

I close a hand around Natalia's arm. I push the woman into a narrow alley between shuttered stores where For Rent signs hang in their windows like permanent fixtures. Broken glass from a beer bottle cracks under our shoes. I smell piss in the alley. Natalia tries to pull away but I am so much stronger. I ease Natalia up against the brick wall, where a graffiti artist has written unkind words about a rival football team.

'Where did they take her?' I ask.

'I don't know. Let me go.'

'Tell me, or I'll break your arm.'

'But I'm pregnant.' Natalia pales.

'Irrelevant. A broken arm won't hurt your baby. How does it work when Vadim gets the girls from here?'

Natalia doesn't answer and so I yank the girl's arm across my knee, begin to exert pressure on both sides. 'Let me assure you, I mean business.'

'But you're a *teacher*.' Now she remembers me.

'Yes, and I'll beat your ass with a ruler if you don't tell me what I want to know.'

354

Natalia's eyes widen. 'He'll kill Nelly if he knows you talked to me. Let me go, and walk away.'

My hands find the girl's ring finger and twist it savagely. Natalia cries out.

'You need to start taking this conversation seriously. How. Does. It. Work?'

Natalia gasps with pain. 'Okay. Vadim takes them to Bucharest. They are taken to a safe house there. They are then taken to Istanbul by car. There's another safe house. They stay there a while.'

'Why?'

'To . . . please don't make me say it.'

'Since you condemned my sister to it, you can say it.'

'Break them in.'

'Define.'

'They give them heroin. They . . . assault them. For days, until they're easier to manage.'

I made myself count to ten before I spoke. 'And then what?'

'They're – sold. To houses. Some in Turkey. To Israel, Albania, Italy. The prettiest ones go to Dubai.'

'Do you know where Nelly is?'

'There's nothing you can do for Nelly, except cooperate with them. They hold all the power.'

'If I can do nothing, then there's no harm in telling me.'

And then I see Natalia is not quite human any more. Natalia is not just flesh and blood but she is fear. She is ruled, shaped, made by fear. She is afraid of everything. This is what Vadim's forge has made.

Good.

'She . . . she is in Tel Aviv. I saw her there. I was there, too.

355

Lucky Strike Parlor. Above a pizzeria. There are eight girls there. Most from Moldova or Romania.'

'Is Vadim the pimp?'

'No. Trafficker. He just gets the girls to where they have to be.'

'There is a man with a blond mohawk. Who is he?'

'His name is Zviman. He owns the brothel, he inherited them from his father. He owns a whole bunch of them, around Africa, the Middle East, in Russia. You don't want to mess with him, he's a cold bastard. He'll kill Nelly and not blink.'

'Thank you, Natalia. You are keeping the baby?'

The shift in tone rocks Natalia and she blinks. 'Yes.'

'They didn't make you get rid of it?'

'They let me come home.' Now she glances at the floor.

'Oh, how generous of them.'

Natalia tries to nod but even that simple motion seems beyond her.

'How many girls did it cost to bring you home?'

She reacts as though I've slapped her. I wait. Finally she says: 'Five.'

'Including Nelly.'

Natalia can't look at me; I look at the broken beer bottles on the pavement. 'My mother got the replacements. She did it for me.' Now Natalia raises her face.

Replacements. The word twists like a knife in my gut. I realize I have bitten the inside of my cheek and I can taste the copper tinge of my blood.

'You're just a schoolteacher. You can't fight Vadim, he's greased every palm he needs between here and Istanbul. And if you cross him Nelly is dead. Get girls to replace her and forget about them.'

356

'I know your mother,' I say. 'I know where she lives, where she shops, where she likes to drink her wine.'

Natalia blinks, her vapid little mouth works in fright. 'Leave mama alone, please. Please.'

'You keep your mouth shut about our little talk. Or when I see Vadim next, I'll tell him you told me everything. He will regret his kindness to you then.'

She starts to pull away and I can tell it's not enough. She will warn Vadim. I grab her arm. 'And. If you talk to Vadim? I will kill your mother. I will walk up to her on the street and I will shoot her in the head. It's more of a kindness than what you and she did to my sister.'

Can you believe I said that, Sam? I said it. Me, the school-teacher. And you know I meant it.

My voice convinces. Natalia is pale with terror. I let her go and she stumbles away from the alley. I check my watch. Today Ivan is going to practice using the knife with me. We work in an abandoned winery a few kilometers from the ragged edge of town. No one is around to hear the ping of the bullets I put into the targets.

65

Harpă, Moldova

I find three photos of American girls on the web that look like ID or passport shots. It is at a website for people arrested for stupid crimes and the girls look attractive but rough, a bit down on luck. I assign three false names to them and email them to Vadim so he can craft fake passports.

I wait. I go out to the abandoned winery – there are too many of them in Moldova now – and Ivan and I practice what I am going to do.

'I wish you would let me help you,' he says. He is an old gentleman. He lost his leg in Afghanistan during the war, back when Moldova was Soviet. In recent years, when crime kept skyrocketing in Moldova, he taught me and Nelly both how to defend ourselves: how to kick, to punch with a fist, to gouge the most vulnerable areas: groin, throat, eye. Now I am taking everything he taught me before, everything I knew as an athlete, and I am trying to become a soldier in a matter of weeks. He corrects me gently when I aim the gun, when I draw the knife. This is a crash course and he says, more than once: 'Girl, I'm only preparing you to get killed. Please don't do this. You fail, *tu mori*.' It means *you die*.

'What should I do instead?' I say. 'Slave up some nice girls?'

'Go to the police,' Ivan says, but without much fervor.

I have already been on the computers, searching on the web for options. The United Nations has named Moldova as a critical point in human trade, with officials in the army, the police, and the government suspected of profiting from the slavery. Who am I supposed to turn to?

There is no one, I tell Ivan. Just me. And I have thought out my plan.

I was always good at lesson plans, and now I have a lesson for Vadim and the blond mohawk.

Ivan nods and then he tells me again: 'This is how you

strike with the knife, forward, lunge, no, not down like that, stay steady . . . '

Every time I begin to feel afraid I push the fear down. Nelly and I used to wrestle on the bed, and Nelly was all wriggling knees and elbows, easy to get giggling, and I would have to wrap my arms around Nelly until Nelly stopped laughing and squirming. So I hold my fear the same way, in a calm, sure grip until the fear is silent.

I hang the sacks two meters high in the dim glow of the abandoned winery. The rough figure of a man lies in black paint on the rough burlap. Light shines in bars through the worn slats. Ivan watches me work. Light begins to shine in the bullet holes I put through the painted men.

'Group of three,' he says, 'that's good. A triangle in the chest. That will put him down.'

I don't tell him I dream about shooting now, I dream about bullseyes, neatly patterned. He gets the ammo from a friend on the black market. I am eating up my savings; I don't want to waste expensive bullets. I still have to pay for my travel. I think Ivan is paying extra for me to have weapons and I will somehow pay him back. If I live.

When we finish, we catch the bus back into town. Weapons and targets in knapsacks. We look so harmless. But our time has come to an end.

'So you will see Vadim tomorrow?' Ivan asks.

'Yes.'

'Will I see you again?' His voice wavers. 'What will I tell your aunt and uncle?'

'You tell them I will be back. With Nelly.'

'I don't mean once you've . . . left. I mean if he kills you.'

'Tell them you weren't such a good teacher, then.'

I buy Ivan ice cream because he doesn't drink any more. We stand in the sunlight, him on his crutch, licking at the chocolate in a wafer cone.

Ready, I think. Ready.

66

Harpă, Moldova

'Where are the girls?' Vadim asks.

No hello. Vadim is a businessman. He has product to move. He is a busy professional with a jam-packed schedule.

Vadim and I stand in the quiet of a small café down from the train station. Natalia told me normally Vadim would meet the girls somewhere near the station, buy them a tea or coffee and a roll, be charming, show them their passports, offer an advance on two weeks' pay, say idle things about the fake hotel in sunny, delightful Greece where their non-existent jobs awaited. The coffee shop is warm but empty of customers, except for us. Rain hammers down, the sky looks chopped from lead.

'Olia and Lizaveta are in the ladies' room. Katerina is not here yet but she will be. She wanted to say goodbye to her grandmother,' I say. The lie is so easy. But I worry that my voice shakes. I cannot betray myself.

'You did well. The money?'

I hand him the envelope. He opens it, peels through the bills. The café owner, standing and brewing a fresh pot, does not look at me or Vadim as he refills my coffee and Vadim carefully counts the cash.

'Nelly,' I say.

'I'll bring her when I come back from Israel after delivering these three.'

'You could be lying to me.'

'I could. But I'm not.' He cranes his neck toward the back where the restrooms are. Eager to see the girls face to face, to take the measure of their worth to him, gauge their personalities and beauty, the gleam in their expectant smiles – and see if they're suspicious. That above all.

I glance at Vadim's messenger bag. The flesh trafficker carries a man purse. It doesn't make me laugh. 'Do you still have that DVD of Nelly?'

'Sure.' He flicks me a smile and I think: you really do have no soul.

'I'd like it back. I don't want it showing up on the internet.'

'Ah, schoolteacher. So proper. Ha. I wouldn't put it up on the internet.' He laughs. 'That stuff is free nowadays.'

The restroom door opens. He cranes his neck further – past my shoulder. He wants to see what he's buying.

I fling the hot coffee, kindly just poured into my cup, into his greasy bastard face. He shrieks and totters back in the leaning chair. Now he's flat on the tile floor. I stand and I fire the shot down into his knee. I thought long and hard about this in the quiet temple of the winery, discussing with Ivan how best to proceed. About whether I should kill him with the first shot or get him to talk. I decided on the knee.

A horrid tatter of a scream erupts from Vadim's throat. The café owner freezes. Then he tosses me a roll of tape from behind the counter. I catch it one-handed. The owner walks to the window, puts on the Closed sign, closes all the window

361

blinds, and he walks out the back, as though he has seen nothing, as though he is deaf to Vadim's shrieks.

He is Ivan's cousin and he can keep a secret.

I drag Vadim behind the counter.

He writhes on the ground, red welling from his leg in hot splatters, black fury and pain in his scalded eyes. Rage and fear, dancing together.

I push the gun up under his chin.

'Who do you meet in Bucharest?' I ask.

'Bitch, I'll kill you!' he screams.

'Give me the name.'

'You shot me! You shot me!'

'Give me the name.' I slide the gun, like a lover's hand, from his throat to his crotch.

'Boris! Boris Chavez!'

I search his pockets. Cell phone. Passport. Wallet. The train tickets for him and the three girls.

'You stole my sister.'

I stare at him, this nothing wrapped in human flesh. For a moment, the fear wins out in his eyes and I feel almost sorry for him. Then the moment vanishes. He made his choices.

'*Tu mori*,' I say. *You die*.

'You're dead, bitch! You're—' and I fire the bullet into his head. I don't pause. I don't think about it.

Do you think I am a bad person, Sam?

I walk out the back of the little café. I might be trembling. I don't stop to see if I am. I stroll to the train station. Ivan and his cousin are going to make sure that no one will find Vadim, no one will know.

I walk fast and I board the train and find a place to sit

362

alone. An old granny perches across the aisle from me and gives me a friendly smile. I nod back. I am such a polite killing machine. I take a deep breath. I will not falter. I cannot.

As the train pulls out for Chișinău (I will change there for the train to Bucharest), I find Boris's name in the call log in Vadim's phone. I go onto MySpace, using the cell phone to connect to the internet. Boris has a page. He is young, biracial, with a broad smile. He doesn't look like a slaver. But he is and now I know who to look for at the train station.

Hello, Boris. And, soon enough, goodbye.

67

Bucharest, Romania

Gray smears the sky like spilled paint but the sun has woven its light in patches through the clouds. The air in the train out of Moldova feels stale and cloying. No one else seems uncomfortable, though. People read their newspapers and eat their snacks and spin their gossip. I sit far away from everyone, in a corner, watching the countryside unfurl, watching the rain thin and die.

Ivan told me killing would make me feel funny. I do. Did it change you, Sam, after you first killed? You seem so normal, like other people, while I feel like the woman who is different, who is marked, who maybe has no shadow. Maybe I breathe differently now. I wanted to throw up about ten minutes after I put the bullets in Vadim. And every rattle and bump of the train feels like God thumping at me. But then the weirdness passes, because I have no choice. I have done this and I will do it again.

Boris looks for greasy Vadim and three fooled Moldovan beauties. He stands on the edge of the station, wearing clothes that slid out of fashion two years ago. Jeans too baggy, a Real Madrid shirt, a cap too big for his head. He's here to maintain control if the product gets antsy. I assume that he's armed.

I walk to a counter and buy a steaming cup of black tea. I make sure to stand near a column, so he can't see me watching him. Boris checks his watch, digs a phone out of the deep caverns of his pockets, thumbs the keyboard.

In my pocket Vadim's phone rings. It chirps a ring tone of a Kanye West song. 'Gold Digger'. How appropriate.

I answer it. 'Hello, yes, this is Vadim's phone.'

'Um, where is Vadim?'

'Oh. He is in the bathroom.'

'He's supposed to be on a train—'

'We missed the morning train to Bucharest, we're coming on the afternoon train.'

Boris gives an annoyed sigh. 'Well, he could have called.'

'Do you work with Vadim?'

'Yes. Who is this?'

'Olia. I guess I shouldn't answer his phone but he left it here on the table. He took us to lunch.'

Boris is already heading for the exits. I follow. He hangs up without another word and I switch off the phone. He walks to a nearby car park and gets inside a van, older, dusty, that hasn't been well cared for.

Of course, a van, I think, the product has to fit inside where no one can see.

I grab a cab and tell the driver to follow the van.

'You want me to follow someone? Like in a movie?' the cab driver asks. I am his most interesting fare all week.

'Yes, like in a movie.' I make it sound lighthearted. The cab driver is going to remember me now but that can't be helped.

We wind through the crowded streets of Bucharest, the cab driver running lights a couple of times to keep the van, a few cars ahead of us, in sight. I hope Boris is not going to a movie to kill time until the later train arrives. I have not been to Bucharest in years and the city seems so much bigger, so much more ... Western. I remember it was once called the Little Paris of the East, before Ceauşescu the maniac nearly destroyed its architectural beauty, its spirit.

I shiver again and think: I cannot be afraid now. I had Ivan's cousin to back me up before, I was on my own turf. This is entirely different, this is the dark unknown.

Boris drives and drives. Finally he wends the van through an older neighborhood on the edge of Bucharest. Cheap houses line the streets here, not apartments. Of course they would need a house. More privacy.

I shove a fistful of money at the cabbie and I get out, a block away. The tip is enough that the cabbie calls me kind miss and rewards me with a tea-stained smile.

I walk towards the house. A single light burns. I cut across to the side of the house and creep up to a window.

I hear the soft hiss of the television – a basketball game, Croatia playing Spain. I hear Boris clomping around in a household symphony: footsteps, refrigerator door, hum of its motor, click of it shutting. I hear the soft pop of a bottle opening. But I hear him. Only him.

I put my weapon into my hand. I go up to the front door. The doorbell is old and its light warms my finger.

Moldovan and Romanian are the same language – really the only difference is a political label dependent on borders. As he answers the door, I say: 'Yes, hello, I am here today to talk to you about our Lord Jesus Christ', and then I stop, with a firm, polite smile.

Boris holds his bottle of Noroc beer and because I am a harmless, petite girl he smiles at me, he hesitates before he would slam the door in my missionary's face.

Then I raise the Taser and fire.

Boris dances back, the needle-tipped wires jolting him, down into a quivering, tongueless heap. I step inside and I hit him again with the charge. He convulses and I close the door with my butt while he dances for me. The beer sprays across the hardwood floor, foaming into an ugly orange throw rug.

He's paralysed, helpless. I pull the plastic restraints out of my purse and I bind him, wrists behind back, ankles together so tight his feet will begin to swell.

Boris has a gun, a sleek Beretta lying on a kitchen counter. I check it. The clip is full, a round loaded. I pocket the gun in the back of my pants.

I move through the house. In one room there are two beds, unmade. They smell of dirty man. One bed has empty Noroc beer bottles by it and an unsettling stain on the sheets. Blood. A crescent of it, halfway down the mattress.

Heavy construction paper blacks out the windows, like the kind I use back in my classroom. Being a teacher feels like a thousand lifetimes ago. I can never go back.

I go through the rest of the house. Nothing, no one else.

But a door off the kitchen is locked. I scramble fingers through Boris's pockets and find the keys.

The door opens to stairs that lead down into a basement. The room is coal-dark. I find and flick on the light. Eight beds in the room. Three are occupied.

'Hello? Are you all right?' I call. First in Moldovan/Romanian, then in Russian.

Two of the girls moan, stir. On a table stand I see powder, syringe, candle, spoon – equipment for a horrible witchcraft. I hurry over to the young women. Track marks mar their pale, pearly arms; their flesh thrums under my fingertips. Chains bind them to the beds.

The third girl is dead. Eyes half open, showing a moon-sliver of white, throat choking with bile.

Another key on Boris's ring unlocks the chains and I get the two girls to sit up. They shudder and cry, lost in between the high of the cruel drug and the pain of what they've suffered. I find their clothes folded in a corner and get them dressed.

Natalia was wrong, or lied. This is where the women are broken and bent to force, not Istanbul. I wasn't expecting to lead a rescue mission; I was going to handle Boris like I handled Vadim, get the information on the next stage of the trafficking trail, move onto Istanbul. I lead the women up to the kitchen, reassure them all will be fine.

I talk to them in what I call my teacher-calm voice. The two girls stare at the dazed and bound Boris. They don't cry, they just stare at him, like I've dragged in the devil in chains to lay at their feet. I want to get them to safety – but I need information from Boris. The girls seem okay for the moment, just relieved to be free. I ask where they are from and both are from small towns in western Moldova. The dead girl was from Ukraine, they say.

Boris, gagged, stares up at me. I decide to risk more time under this roof. No one else is here. I tear the tape off his mouth.

'You fucking bitch we will kill you and your whole family you goddamned bitch' – and then I seal the tape back over his mouth. They are all so unoriginal in their name-calling. Then I tear off another strip. I play the sticky side of the tape against Boris's nostrils, like a teasing feather. His eyes widen and he kicks against the hard tile floor, trying to get away from me.

'Did he hurt you?' I ask the two girls.

One's too blissed out, riding a narcotic surf, to answer. But the other nods, hair hanging down in her eyes.

'Then I'm going to hurt him. Keep your seat if you want or go into the other room.'

The girls stay. The more sober one clutches her friend's arm.

I put my face close to Boris's. 'Six months ago. Moldovan girl named Nelly. Blonde. Do you remember? Nod yes or shake your head no.'

Boris nods. Vadim must have told him he was going to work Nelly's sister to get new recruits.

'Where is she?' Now I rip the tape free from his lips.

'Tel Aviv. A massage parlor called Lucky Strike, on Rehov Fin. It's above a pizzeria.'

This confirms Natalia's story. 'Who has her? The man with the blond mohawk?'

Boris hesitates and so I seal the tape back over his mouth. Then I stick the extra strip over his nostrils. I run a finger

368

along its edge. Boris begins to buck. His eyes roll and bulge in panic.

That's probably how the girls felt, like they had no control, no help, and they were going to die.

Boris screams behind the tape.

'Did you rape my sister? Did you pump heroin into her veins?'

He writhes, screams his throat raw. Begging now in his eyes as his body craves fresh oxygen.

I watch his face. I count to forty. He is a smoker and he didn't get a lungful before I sealed the exits. I tear the tape off.

Now Boris babbles: 'The man who bought her, there is a laptop upstairs . . .'

Tape really is the most useful tool around the house, I think. I put the tape back over his mouth but not his nose. I run upstairs. I find a file cabinet, a weathered desk spotted with beer bottle rings. And a laptop. I open it. It awakens from sleep; apparently Boris was web-surfing before he headed to the train station.

I pick through the hard disk. I open a folder called PROD-UCT. Each girl has a file. The top of the window tells me there are one thousand and thirty-six files.

I can't wrap my head around the number. Thinking about it is an ax to the brain. I search for Nelly. Sold, for a combination of heroin and $6,000, to a Yaakov Zviman in Tel Aviv. The notes in the file indicate she was auctioned off at a motel room in Eilat, five different bidders.

I try not to vomit at the thought.

I memorize the address. But I copy the entire folder to a disc and put the disc in my jacket pocket. I open the desk drawer and find rolls of money: euros, American dollars, Romanian leu, Turkish lira and Israeli sheqel banknotes. I scoop them all up, shove them into my pockets.

I close the laptop and head downstairs.

And hear the front door opening and a woman's voice, 'Boris, did you remember to feed the whores?', then 'What the hell?'

I run down the rest of the stairway and in the kitchen is a woman, standing over Boris's wriggling form. The woman is blonde, close to six feet tall, wiry, hair cropped short.

And this woman is pulling out a gun from the back of her jacket.

Mind goes blank – I forget I have the Taser – and I throw myself toward the tall woman. Like Ivan has taught me. I need a punching bag now. A rage fuels my blood. My fist courts her jaw. The blow, delivered, hurts my hand but the sheer force of my attack knocks the woman back into the refrigerator.

I hammer another fist, this time into her stomach. The woman swerves, shoving past me, trying to get room to fight back, gasping.

I step back and aim a hard kick at the woman's throat. I am too ambitious. I miss, hit low, the heel of my boot slamming into the woman's breasts, driving air from the lungs. The woman's gun clatters to the tiles.

The two captive girls stumble from the kitchen, one dragging the other, trampling over the bound Boris, who is trying to maneuver to his feet.

I throw the woman across the kitchen. She lands against the counter. Leftovers from breakfast lie by the sink. Coarse bread, mug of coffee. The tall woman throws the mug at me, it catches my temple, ice-cold, bitter coffee splashes in my eyes. I blink away the sting and then I see the sharp bread knife slashing toward me.

The tip of the knife catches me along the edge of the hand and it hurts, I cry out and the tall woman slashes back with the knife, an inch from my throat, the air singing. I can feel the whip of the blade, the slicing of air. Before the tall woman can slam the blade backwards in its arc – and I see her reverse her grip on the knife with a nimble strut of fingers – I grab the skillet, crusted with leftover egg, and slam it into the woman's face with the force of a tennis racket.

She howls. Blood flies from her mouth.

I crack the skillet against the woman's knife hand; the knife drops to the tile. It bounces, it gleams.

I use the skillet to batter the woman down, raining the blows. The final barrage sends her sprawling, bleeding, quiet at last.

The two girls are gone. I stand in the doorway and scan the street for them, flat of my hand against the sunlight, like a mama surveying the street for her kids.

Better this way, I think.

I have what I need. The disc, the address for Nelly.

I realize then that I'm hurt – cut across both sets of knuckles, another slash across my stomach. It doesn't hurt so much until I see the wounds; the blood brings the sharp sting.

I turn and Boris has staggered to his feet, hopping, and I pick up the skillet and I put him back down. Then I take the edge of the skillet and slam it into his crotch.

'*Tu mori*,' I say to him, but I don't think he's listening any more.

I turn to the stove. I crank on the gas on all the burners. I open a drawer and find foil and stick a wad of it inside the microwave and turn it on, set the timer to cook for five minutes. I run out the door, Boris screeching behind the gag, what sounds like a plea for mercy. He's a smart boy.

I'm not all the way down the street when the back of the house explodes outwards, the roof buckling, taking to air like untested wings.

I hear the debris crashing into the yard.

I don't look back. Sam, you cannot look back either.

68

Red-light district, Tel Aviv, Israel

It's been less than twenty-four hours since I left Bucharest. The bandages on my hands need a change and the pain from the knife cut surges up through my arm like a flickering torch. I had to leave the Taser and the guns behind – I could not have gotten them through Romanian or Israeli customs without extra forms and attention, and I don't want the Israeli authorities having anything in my file except arrival and departure dates.

I sit in the pizzeria. From this window I can see the men walking past the open door of the restaurant. I wear dark jeans, black untucked blouse, dark glasses. I order a steady supply of juice and food so the counter staff are not annoyed by me keeping a table. I have a notebook so they think I am a writer sitting and working. No Cokes, I cannot take caffeine on top of my nerves. I feel worn down, exhausted, as though I am getting sick. I eat a slice of vegetarian pizza. I don't have much appetite.

The brothel is above the pizzeria. The sidewalks on Rehov Fin – or, as it gets nicknamed, Rehov Pin, for 'penis' – are painted with red arrows that point to the peep shows and brothels. The windows on the second stories are barred. Signs show women, in silhouette, writhing in ecstasy, or bound, or beckoning to men with a curled finger. Club Joy. Sexxxy's Studio. Club Viagra. No, I'm not making that last one up, Sam.

I watch the men as they arrive and leave. Many are alone, and they are a mix: Jewish and Arab and Christian. Some look like businessmen or office workers, some like foreign laborers. Some are soldiers, in uniform. Apparently they rate a discount. Some are Orthodox Jews, stuffing their skullcaps into their pockets as they enter the doors. And pulling them out when they walk back into the accusing sunshine. Some are duos and trios of young men I am sure are Americans. College students.

What would their parents think, I wonder.

I want to storm the doors. But if my plan is to work, I must know how busy the parlor is, when it is at its least crowded. But I hate every second, knowing Nelly is inside.

I know what they will do to me if I am caught. They will kill me or try to break me like the girls back in Bucharest. Like Nelly.

So I force myself to watch, to find the pattern of scumball traffic that will allow me to get in and get out with the least violence. I see an older man leave, return with a bag of food. An employee. Probably there are at least two employees inside at all times. One to take payment, coordinate the visits. One for security, to make sure the girls can't leave and to make sure the clients behave themselves.

And maybe Mr Mohawk, Zviman, maybe he's inside. Him I long to meet.

I see that there is a sudden, noticeable drop in traffic before dinner time. Fine. I go back to a hotel, not the one that I am staying in, to get what I need.

Every hotel guard is armed in Israel. Ivan told me this; he'd read about it in an article covering a thwarted Palestinian attack where the guard shot down the suicide bomber. I approach a guard at a Marriott, fumbling with a Russian-language guidebook, confused look on my face, a wrongly folded map. Tourist from Moscow, I can almost see the thought flit across the guard's face.

I drop the map and jet the pepper spray I've bought into the guard's face, with a hiss of *sorry* on my lips. As he staggers, his hand going to the gun, I seize the weapon out of its holster.

And I run. I flee out of the hotel, through a shopping center, into a cab. The gun is cool against the flat of my stomach under my shirt.

I think about what to wear into battle. I expect I could die so I decide to splurge. Only the best for the crazy teacher, Sam. I know you have always admired my style, yes? The next afternoon I find a boutique at the very upscale Ramat Aviv mall and I buy black leather pants and a taut black turtleneck and a neat, fitted black leather jacket. It's as close as a girl gets to armor. Winter has passed so I get the gear on sale, but it still would cost a fortune back in Moldova. I use Boris's cash for the purchase. Thank you, Boris. The gun fits into the small of my back.

Back at my hotel room I get dressed and then I make a secret preparation, in case I am captured. A final revenge on

374

Zviman or his men. I check my gun. If I cannot get us out, then a bullet for Nelly and a bullet for myself.

I calm myself by applying my make-up – more than I would ever wear back home. I look like such a *bad* girl. Red mouth, cat eyes heavy on liner. I laugh to myself, thinking *girl now you have on your warpaint*. I feel like a different person. The schoolteacher is dead. The schoolteacher has killed three people and freed two slaves and blown up a house.

That was nothing to what I must do now.

I take a cab to the pizzeria.

It's still daylight, the sun sliding its farewell into the Mediterranean. It's the time of the pre-dinner lull I noticed yesterday.

A man catcalls me as I get out of the cab and tip the driver. I ignore him. I walk up the steps. Lucky Strike Parlor, the sign reads in both Hebrew and English. Whose luck? I wonder. I go up the stairs to a door that is blood-red, LUCKY STRIKE painted on it in cursive black letters.

I resist the urge to kick in the door. Instead, I open it like anyone else and step inside the parlor. The room is cool and smells of salt, of heavy perfume, of beer. I hear a whiny voice say, 'C'mon, baby, smile for me.' The voice has a New York crawl to it, like I have heard in movies and TV.

It is as if I have entered a stained dream. The lights in here are, yes indeed, a shade of red. A dim, bitter crimson. Low-grade electronica trance music plays in the background. I see a reception desk, an old man sitting there. He eats a cookie, with his mouth open. Behind him is what looks like a raised platform, two women sitting under sallow spotlights. They wear see-through clothing. Neither of them is Nelly. If they have heard the young man's plea they give no sign, no reaction. They sit very straight, and they do not smile. They could be mannequins.

I think: they are just waiting for the next bad thing to happen.

Lounging on a nearby couch are two college-age men, swigging Goldstar beers, wearing jeans, one in an American football jersey, the other sporting a sweatshirt that has a store name on it. The shirt is blood-red under the glow of the lights.

They are telling stupid jokes, in English, trying to get the girls to smile, like I know now tourists do in London with the British guards at Buckingham Palace. Either the girls are forbidden to laugh, like the guards, or they cannot. It strikes me that it might be dangerous for a girl here to laugh at a man.

Bubbles of hate rise in my chest. Bubbles, no, too soft a word, Sam. I must be honest: the hate fills me like a flooding river. I hate everything about them.

'Excuse me, miss?' the old man says in Hebrew. He is unsure – maybe I wandered in, he must think. He talks to me around the crumbs of his big cookie.

'Hello, there, you showing up for a shift, baby?' the boy in the store-name shirt calls. He raises the beer bottle toward me, like a welcoming toast.

'I am here to apply for a job,' I say to the old man, in English.

The old man is speechless, brow furrowing. He stands up, which is all I want him to do now that I see his hands are empty except for that fucking cookie.

I pull the gun out from the back of my leather pants and the bullet barks over the soft thrum of the bad disco music. The

376

old man drops, wordless, his chewing jaw gone. Him eating that cookie while those poor girls sit there waiting to be bought pisses me off.

The two Americans freeze in shock. The women on the platform stare, one of them stands, her chair tottering back to the floor.

'You're paying to rape,' I say to the guys. 'My sister is here and you are paying to rape her.'

'Now wait a minute, honey, wait—'

'We're Americans—'

I shoot them both, and, because they are stupid, thoughtless children, I fire into their legs. They jerk into screaming spasms on the floor. The blossoms of blood on their clothes are bright in the red lights. Their howls fill the room, broken by gasps of air.

'Go. Run,' I say to the tired, dull-eyed women. They run, in scanty lingerie, out and down the stairwell. But the fear on their faces, I think, it doesn't tell me that they're free.

Off the entrance parlor there's a hallway and in its curve I see a door open. A fortyish man, stumbling out, trying to pull up his pants, panic in his eyes. I see a glint of wedding ring on his hand. He charges toward me and I shoot him in both knees. He can explain *that* to his wife. He thunders to the floor, mewling and screeching. Behind him a woman screams.

I stop, yell at the woman in English, 'Get out! Run!' The woman doesn't. I repeat myself, but in Russian then Romanian. The young woman – younger than Nelly, bloodless with fright – hugs the wall, naked, too terrified to move.

Where is the guard?

Then I see a door yank open, two down and across the hall from the scared girl's room. The college boys keep shrieking and I hear one call out for his mama. Like Mama wants to see this.

No one exits the door.

I want to believe that it's Nelly, or some other girl too frightened by the gunfire, cowering in the doorway, unsure of what to do.

Too much hope in my heart. I call: 'Nelly? Nelly, it's me . . .'

Silence. Then a bear of a man charges around the open doorway toward me, a shotgun in his hands, leveled at me, and when he sees me – slip of a girl in black leather – a naked wave of surprise passes over his face. He hesitates.

I fire and a splinter of drywall explodes by his shoulder and I shoot again. He falls and fires as he ducks back and the pellets mist my doorframe into shreds. I throw a hand over my face and the adrenaline masks the pain, but I feel flesh pierced: ear, shoulders, back of the neck, by the flying debris.

I lie halfway in the room, my legs prone in the hallway and I freeze, my mind telling me to be still, I have baited a trap by lying here where he can't see I am conscious. Every fiber telling me to run, hide.

I stay still.

Wait. I steady my gun up at the shattered doorway. Waiting for him to creep into view. Playing dead. He can't see my gun until he's risked a glance around the peppered wall.

The man with the shotgun inches down the hallway. I hear the shuffle of his feet; weirdly, it sounds like Boris struggling to breathe. The Americans and the married man have either stopped fussing or have died. He sees my legs, I imagine, lying deathly still.

He turns into the doorway and I fire into his stomach. He screams and staggers back, the pain overriding his trigger finger. I stand and I kick the shotgun out of his hands. I think I break a toe. He screams and he falls, blind with pain. I pick up the shotgun.

What is strange now is my calm. The calm is a heaviness inside me, smothering the pain, the fear.

I leave him gut-shot. On his belt I see a baton of some sort. I pull it from his belt. There is a thumb control and it telescopes into a length. Cool. I like the weight of it in my hand so I take it, like a trophy. What is wrong with me? He has a knife, too. I tuck that inside my boot. Taking his weapons was like hoarding small treasures I had earned, Sam, isn't that odd?

No one else is rushing out to shoot me. I kick in the other doors. Mostly empty. No more men.

But none of the women are Nelly.

When the woman in the last room yells *please don't hurt us* in Moldovan, I lower my gun.

'Where is Nelly?'

'Working a party – for Zviman.'

Zviman. The mohawk. The owner. Smiling at me on the video, over his shoulder, raping and slapping my sister. I must pay my respects.

'Where is this party?'

'His house, I think, I don't know, I swear, please don't kill me.'

'What is the address?'

'I don't know. I don't know.'

I believe her. 'Run. This is your chance to get out. Now. Run.'

There are six women in the hallway and four of them flee immediately, hurrying down the stairs in their frilly lingerie.

The other two stay, as though frozen by the prospect of freedom as much as the certainty of peril.

'Run! What's wrong with you?' I know the police will be here in minutes and I don't have much time. I jab the gun into the face of the gut-shot man.

'Zviman! Where is he? Tell me and I'll call an ambulance for you.'

The man whispers an address and I whip him unconscious with his own telescoping baton.

'There's your ambulance. Consider it called,' I say. I shove the edge of the baton – it's a little bloody – against the wall to close it.

I herd the two reluctant women out, past the married client who has passed out from the agony of his broken kneecaps, past the mewling college boys. They're still alive, just quieter in their suffering. They try and crawl and hide from me, behind the couch, the little darlings. I am their lesson they will never forget.

Out on the street now, me and a gang of fugitive women.

'Are you stealing us?' one asks.

'What?'

'Stealing us to work for another brothel?'

Her question makes my heart hurt, Sam. 'No, honey, you are free.'

There is a hospital a few blocks away and I point them toward it. Police cars, summoned by the pizzeria owner, brake past them with sirens blaring.

I ignore the cars, the cops, the lights. I guess in my leather pants they think I'm one of the fleeing prostitutes. I herd them into the hospital emergency arrival zone and then I'm gone.

I have a man, or something that calls himself a man, to see.

69

Tel Aviv, Israel

The house is grand, overlooking the Mediterranean, sitting atop a flattening hill not far from Hatzok Beach on the city's north side. Pimping must pay awfully well. I thinks it looks more like the home of a legitimate businessman: perhaps belonging to a software maven, a real-estate investor, a well-regarded lawyer. A wall surrounds the house, with entrance gates. I climb over the gates. From inside the house I hear electronica music playing, the kind Westerners like and that sounds like a pulsing hump. It's not that different from the music inside the brothel. Are these men so pathetic, I wonder, that they need a dance beat for rape?

I step up onto a cool stretch of stone patio. Half-empty drinks line the table – red wine, empty Maccabee beer bottles, an ice-melted Scotch. The party appears to be over. Perhaps bad news has been received?

I try the door. Unlocked. The den is full of heavy leather couches. The scent of pepperoni pizza hangs kitchen-thick, the sting of marijuana touches my nose. I have only smelled it once, back at a party in Chişinâu when I was in school getting my teaching license.

I go down the hallway, gun at the ready.

I go past a darkened doorway and then I feel the cool of a barrel pressing into my hair.

I freeze.

'Drop the gun,' a voice says. In Russian.

I obey.

The gun guides me back out into the center of the hallway

and a man steps in front of me. Physically big, red-haired, with heavy lips and baggy eyes. 'I have her,' he calls in English. From the room down the hallway comes the man with the blond mohawk. It's not spiky, it's shaved down. He is as big as the Russian; you think he would have found a bigger body-guard. His face is unremarkable, his eyes a stone gray. He's dressed in a nice shirt, untucked, and jeans.

'Who else is with you?' he asks me in English.

'No one. Just me.'

'If you lying to me my friend will shoot off your ear.'

'I'm not lying.'

'Look at me, garbage.'

I look at him and he looks at me, scowling, then smiling. 'You come with me.' He takes the gun from the Russian and jabs it in my hair and pushes me along. 'You, you go check the grounds. See if she's really stupid enough to come here alone. Call the office, tell them she's here.' I hear the Russian huffing away, he's a mouth-breather.

At the end of the hallway is a slightly open door and in the dim light I see the edge of a bed.

On the bed, a pale, thin arm. My mouth dries. I used to see that arm, hanging from the tumble of sheets on the bed on the other side of the room.

I push open the door with my fingertips.

Nelly lies on the bed, sleepy, blinking like a child roused from dreams.

I forget myself for a moment and step forward.

Zviman shoves me against the bed. I twist, trying to escape and then a fist slams into my face. Once, twice, then a kick sledgehammers into my chest. His mouth is a curl of rage.

Nelly tries to sit up on the bed.

'You. Who are you?' Zviman asks me.

'Her sister.'

'This bitch is why you shot up my place?' His accent is heavy. He must have gotten news of the shooting at the Lucky Strike, sent his partygoers home. I wonder how he knows so soon. And then the thought occurs to me: anyone openly running a brothel owns himself some cops.

'Yes. Don't call her bitch,' I say.

He laughs. 'I apologize, bitch! I didn't know I hurt your feelings, bitch! Thanks for shooting my customers and releasing my whores, bitch!' He laughs again. Aiming the gun not at me but now at Nelly.

Nelly cowers, the gun lodged against her temple.

'The police will be here. I shot up your property. They'll want to talk to you.'

'No, they won't. There's nothing on paper to tie me to the Lucky Strike. Nothing at all.' He shrugs. 'I own the right people on the police force, anyway. All you've created is a mess that will take me about five minutes to clean up. But fuck, bitch, you got guts.'

I grit my teeth against the pain from the punches and kicks he gave me.

'Now. Who sent you?' he asks. Like we're going to have a real conversation.

'No one. I came on my own.'

'Don't lie to me. You work for who? Baran? Markov? The Nigerians?'

'I'm not lying. I'm her sister. Look at our faces, you can tell.'

He laughs, stops, stares hard at me. 'Tell me who hired you or you die.'

He just cannot believe I am here out of love. It tells me everything I need to know about how to kill him.

'Did you hear me? You die.'

'*Tu mori*,' I say back. He blinks at me.

I manage to stand. Grimacing, against the pain. 'I am her sister and I came for her.'

'Who do you work for?'

'No one. I just decided you and your people needed to die.' It is so simple, Sam, this decision. You know it and I know it.

He laughs at me.

Nelly opens her eyes and they slowly focus on my face. Softly Nelly murmurs: 'Mila?'

'Yes.'

'I'm dreaming. I don't dream any more.' Nelly's voice sounds like it lives at the bottom of a well.

'No dream. I'm here.'

'Big sister's going to work with you, Nelly, won't that be nice? I'm gonna sell you as a pair.' And I can tell that this Zviman, he thinks he's won. *He thinks he's won*.

I don't allow myself the smile.

He pushes the gun under my chin. He frisks me along the leather jeans, the tight turtleneck, the leather jacket. He lets his hands linger where he likes. He finds the guard's knife in my boot and tosses it to the floor. He takes the collapsible baton from my pocket.

'This is Natan's.'

'He loaned it to me,' I say. He tosses it in the corner.

'You are a stupid little girl, Mila. Look at me.'

I don't, not at first, frozen, and he puts the gun right over my shoulder, aimed at Nelly. 'I'll kill your sister if you fight me.'

So I look at him, waiting, and he punches me in the face. Once, twice. He kicks me in the stomach. Then he backhands me. I land on his expensive coffee table in the corner of the bedroom, scattering the sports magazines. I tumble into the space between chair and table. He seizes my hair, he hits me again. I stagger and he kicks me in the ribs.

I fall.

'You stupid Moldovan cow. You think you sweep in here and you ruin my business? What do I care that you shoot up a whorehouse? I have three dozen of them around the world. You can't even bloody my lip, bitch.'

I wanted to say, I killed Vadim. I killed your people in Bucharest. I set your prisoners free. But I don't, because I want him to treat me as he does every other woman.

He keeps the gun in my face as he kneels over me. I knew this could happen, I knew it, and I stamp down the terror that rises in me like fire. He unzips my leather pants and orders me to wriggle out of them or he'll kill Nelly. I obey him and the fear is hot and heavy in my throat.

'Get out of the jacket. The shirt. Naked, now, bitch.'

Shaking, I obey him. The tile floor is cold against my back.

'Don't, Yaakov,' Nelly murmurs. 'Please don't hurt my sister.'

He leans over and he slaps her hard. 'I'll do what I like and you keep quiet or she's dead.'

Nelly snuffles, mouths at me. *I'm sorry*.

Yaakov Zviman kicks out of his pants. He is a big man, at least 6 feet 2, meaty armed, legs thick from old work, a hard, flat stomach. On the lower part of his arm I see a weird tattoo: a sunburst in the heart of a stylized number nine.

He slips off his shorts.

I force myself not to close my eyes. I lie still.

He pushes the gun against my throat, surveys my body with a hunger uglier than lust. 'You look better than your sister, whore. Do you know how much you'll fetch in Dubai? Less because I might cut out your tongue. But still. A sister act.'

He puts one hand on my throat, the other down at his naked groin. He positions himself and slides into me – and screams, an incoherent shattering shriek of pure agony.

This is my revenge.

I did the unthinkable: I clutched his hips, twisting, and his scream rose beyond human hearing.

He writhed, trying to pull out of me and away from me and then froze, realizing that the horrific pain was only getting worse.

He dropped the gun, cringing like a kicked dog, trying to curl into a protective ball.

I shoved him free of me and he howled like a wounded beast. I felt blood – his – on my thighs. Hanging onto his penis, covering most of it, *clutching* at it, was a piece of rubber, blood now soaking its edges.

I slam a kick into his torn groin and he folds, sobbing, shattered by pain. I grab the gun and level it at him. My hand is steady.

I hear running footsteps. The Russian bodyguard, tearing down the hall toward me, drawing his gun. I have an advantage because the hallway narrows his options, but the advantage will be gone in six seconds and I aim and fire, like I'm aiming at the painted figures on burlap in the dusty air of the old winery. A triangle, like Ivan taught me. I hurt everywhere but my hand stays steady as a wooden beam.

The Russian crashes to the floor. He doesn't move or groan or keep living.

Zviman sobs, in hysterics, and clutches at his torn genitals. He huddles against a wall. 'Get it off me, how do I get it off me!' he screams.

'Nelly,' I say calmly, 'is anyone else here?'

Nelly stares at the wreck of Zviman. 'No.'

'Go get your clothes. Then go wait downstairs.' I'm using big sister voice now, no argument. 'You don't need to see what happens next.'

Nelly stares at the blood-smeared floor, at Zviman, curled into a ball. 'How did you?'

'Just do as I say. Here. Take this.' I hand her my gun. She stares at it and nods. She hurries down the stairs.

I stand above Zviman. Sweat pours around the blond strip of hair.

'Look at me, garbage,' I say, using his own words. I quickly get dressed.

I wait for him to look up into my face. 'It's an inverted rubber, lined with little serrated metal razors. They dig into the flesh and they don't let go. I got the idea from reading about deterrents to rape in Africa. Some women in South Africa make these to scare off attackers, or to mark them forever. You find the most interesting things on the web, you know.'

He gasps, sobs. He apparently is done with calling me names.

'Now, garbage. You want the razors out of you, yes?'

He makes a mewling noise.

'I can remove it without further harm. Where's your laptop?'

Zviman gags and points down the hall.

Gun on him, I force him to crawl down the hall and sit up into a chair. Blood and bile cover him.

'Disobey me, and I'll twist the knife, so to speak,' I say.

'Whatever you want. Please ... please ...' He can hardly speak the words.

'I want your bank accounts,' I say.

'What? Why?' The agony whittles his voice to little more than a whisper.

'Restitution. Give me access to the accounts or I'll twist the device and no doctor will be able to save your dick. Do we understand each other?'

He nods, disbelief and fury and agony all contorting his face.

I open a web browser and he murmurs the web address for a major Cayman Islands bank. He spits out his login and pass-word and I type them.

He has several accounts. I open balances on each. One holds seven million American dollars. In another, nine hundred thousand. In another, two million. The accounts in the bank total close to fifteen million US dollars.

'That's all I've got, the rest of the money goes back into the business. Please get it off me. Get it off me!'

'Don't be such a crybaby.' It's what I used to say to the children who whined, a million years ago, when I was a teacher. I push him out of the chair and do an e-transfer of funds into my own Cayman account, set up last week. I learned how to do it on the web. The Caymans are eager for business. I have set up instructions for that money, once deposited, to be instantly wired into a second account in Switzerland.

He will never find that money.

But I turn off the laptop, quickly strip out the hard drive, put it into my pocket.

'You're just a thief,' Zviman screams. 'Take it off me!'

'No. The women you've abused, they get this money. It can't make up for what you did to them but at least *you* won't have it.' Then I lean close and spit in his eye.

He cringes, rage and agony alternating on his face. 'You said you'd remove this . . . '

'So I did. Well, I'm not a doctor. The only way I know to get it off . . . is to yank.' I reach for him.

'*No! No!*' he screams, wriggling away.

'Fine, leave it on, it's a nice accessory. I'm sure the doctor will have to talk to the police, what with you being an assault victim.'

'My people will kill you for this.' He points at the tattoo of the sun inside the nine; blood dots the colors. 'They will kill you for this, they will kill you a thousand times, bitch. You're stealing their money, too.'

'I'm not sure you will still have people, if you can't pay them.'

I wish I had a camera for the shock on his face. He realizes without his money, he has no power. No empire. Nothing. I've burned him to the ground, Sam, and I am going to dance in the ashes. I even know which dance I will do.

'Let's do the twist.' I reach for the device. He screams again and lurches away. Blood leaks out of the contraption.

'No power. No hope. Knowing you've lost everything.' My voice is a steel whisper. 'That's how my sister and those women felt. Now that's you.'

He makes a broken sound.

I stand. 'You probably want to get to a hospital. You'll need to get the barbs loose from the flesh. It's going to take multiple surgeries. I'm not going to kill you. You alive and hurting and ruined is infinitely more interesting to me.' My voice is taunting now. I'd hurt him, I'd hurt him *so badly*. Every day would be a pain. Just like mine had been since Vadim walked into my classroom with his horrible images.

Gunfire. A scream downstairs. Nelly.

I rush toward the sounds, Nelly screaming my name and then a slicing boom of gun-thunder.

An awful silence, not even Zviman calling. Then he shrieks, 'I'm upstairs help me, help me, grab this bitch! She's stealing my money!'

I run halfway down the stairs and in the den I see a man, thick-necked, cheap-suited, holding an assault rifle, hurrying toward Nelly ... who lies in a crimson spread on the imported Italian tile, holding the gun I gave her.

The thick neck looks up at me. He fires and the stairs erupt around me and I flee.

'She doesn't have a gun,' Zviman screams, 'shoot her.'

The thick neck thinks he has all the advantage now. So he charges into the hall. I'm in a doorway, the telescoping baton firm in my hand, and I slash it down at the gun. The baton cracks his wrist but he keeps a grip on the rifle. I whip the baton across his face, breaking his nose. He staggers back.

I drop the baton and grab the gun. We struggle for it. But I have not had fingers and wrists whipped five seconds earlier.

I work a finger on the trigger and slam the hot barrel into his chest, kicking him against the wall.

The gun shreds him. Loudly, redly, and before he's dropping dead I'm running down the staircase.

I kneel by my sister.

Gone. Gone. I took my eyes off her for only a few minutes and—

I failed her. If I hadn't bothered with stealing his money, ruining his business, exacting my revenge, if we *just got out* . . .

Slowly, I don't know how much time passes, but I walk back upstairs.

Zviman is gone. A heavy smear of blood mars the wall and sill of one window. He's gone out onto the roof. I go to the window and the roof and the street and the yard are all empty. I pick up my knife and put it back in my boot.

I find Mercedes car keys in Zviman's abandoned pants and I gather my sister in my arms and I drive the Mercedes from the house, the empty grand home built on human suffering.

Nelly. I failed you. *Tu mori.*

Lesson learned, Sam: saving matters more than destroying.

70

Sydney, Australia

Sydney is a nice city. It has an endlessly beautiful harbor and excellent restaurants and the Australians are an astonishingly friendly nation. I go for long walks along the Rocks, the ancient – by Sydney standards – stretch of bayline where the convict ships dropped both anchor and prisoners, a miserable human cargo.

I am a miserable human cargo.

The breeze off the harbor is a near constant presence and I feel, standing still but leaning into the wind, as if I am running.

I am free, yet I am a prisoner.

I stop on my morning walk and across the stretch of water I watch tourists snap photos of the iconic Opera House. In a moment I have to go back to the house. Aunt and Uncle grow concerned if I am gone too long. Neither has good English and I slowly teach them. They are learning by watching Aussie soap operas, which are even juicier than their Romanian counterparts. I do not want to risk hiring an instructor. People talk. And I know there is the possibility that Zviman, with his diced-sliced penis, is looking for me and my family.

A well-dressed man, a bit younger than me, stands a meter away. He has dark, moussed hair, a quiet, composed face, gray slacks, a bright orange shirt that looks expensive. Not a businessman type, not exactly. More like a young man who wants to be an actor. He has a wry smile on his face.

'A cool million,' he says, as if speaking to the wind. His accent is British, educated.

I think he must be on a hands-free phone, or he is trying to impress me by randomly announcing a large sum of money. He looks like any of the men who approach me on the nights when I wander to the nicer bars to escape the prattle of Aunt and Uncle.

So I pay no attention to him.

'A cool million's the price on your head. It's a rather hefty incentive to find you. Just how you found Nelly. Usually such fees are reserved for heads of state, or particularly annoying warlords in backwater lands.'

Now I jerk a glance at him, fear a hot lump in my throat.

'Did you know,' he blows out a plume of Dunhill smoke, 'I've seen pictures of Zviman's, um, tattered sausage. Most difficult to get. Did you know he didn't dare go to a hospital to have your delightful mousetrap removed? Went to a very dodgy private clinic in Strasbourg, France, on a friend's private plane. I'm sure it was the longest flight of his life. I had to pay quite a horribly sizable bribe to said clinic for a singularly unappealing photo.' The young man gave a delicate shudder.

I don't walk around Sydney with a gun but I still carry the telescoping baton in my jacket pocket. 'You have me confused with someone else.'

'No, Mila, I don't.' He smiles. Not mocking. Friendly.

A million on my head. So I say: 'I didn't steal all his money, then.'

The young man clears his throat. 'Zviman did more than sex slavery, love. He was, well, still is, one of the biggest smugglers in the Mediterranean. Ordnance, drugs, military surplus. Even flowers and fish. You bloodied his nose and of course you bloodied his privates, and smartly done, that, but he's still operating. He runs with a dangerous crowd. You broke him, though, with the theft. It takes money to run smuggling routes. So he's gone under the radar, as they say. I've heard now he's trying to get into blackmail on a whole new scale, using computers to gather nasties about people. Blackmail's all about information and we live in an information age, don't we?'

'He sent you?' If they can find me here, they can find me anywhere.

'Ah, no. If his Tattered Dicklessness had sent me you'd be dead days ago and murking up the harbor, my sweet.'

'I'm not your sweet.'

'No, but a lad can dream.' He gives me a handsome smile.

'What do you want?'

'I want you. I want you to do something constructive with all that grief and anger.'

'I failed. My sister . . .'

'Mila.'

'I failed.'

'Mila. You are a schoolteacher from a little slice of nowhere, and you destroyed a major trafficking operation. You killed them and you stole a huge chunk of their money. Do you know how rare honest daring has become in our overcautious world? I want to toss diamonds at your feet, woman. You are incredible.'

I stare at him as though I would like to slap him. 'My sister is dead. Your praise is smoke to me.' Then I look at the cold steel of the harbor.

'What you did—'

'What I did failed.' I watch him. 'All I got was money. Is that why you're here? You want money for your silence?'

'No. Not everyone would have sent *Rolling Stone* magazine that database of trafficked girls, who their buyers were, and a bank account where Zviman's illicit money was. You created quite a little tempest from the shadows there, love. Dictating that the cash go to the women who could be found. Very generous. But you don't need to buy my silence, Mila. I mean you no harm. All I want is to buy you the best lunch in Sydney.'

'And a drink,' I say. I can use a drink, I think.

'Yes, love, what would you like to drink?'

'I don't have a favorite.'

'You look like a Glenfiddich girl to me.'

'That is what?'

'Whisky.'

I cross my arms. 'I have never tried it.'

394

'And after I have introduced you to the delights of a fine whisky, then I want to offer you a job.'

'I am in Australia under a false name, I don't have a work permit, nice man. Sorry.'

'You don't need a work permit. If I could find you, so can Zviman. And with a million dollars on that lovely pixie head of yours, it's only a matter of time.' He leans forward. 'We can hide your aunt and uncle better than you ever could. We can hide you. But I think you might go mad sitting around and reflecting about what happened to Nelly. You saved so many lives, Mila. You did good. You could do a lot more good. Or you can sit around with your aunt and uncle, watching Aussie TV to teach them English, and knowing that the man who destroyed your sister is still out there and is hunting you down.' He risks a smile. 'If you keep moving you'll be much harder to find.'

'What I did was crazy.'

'Decidedly.'

'I am only crazy when helping my sister.'

'On Zviman, did you see a tattoo? A sun, in the middle of a nine?'

I close my eyes. Remembering seeing it on Zviman's arm. 'Yes. I saw it. It was ugly.'

'You don't know how ugly. I think that tattoo is a mark, one that says he owes allegiance to something more than his own criminal ring. Something bigger, badder, than him.'

'That is not my problem.'

'No, your problem is that with a million-dollar bounty on your head, you are going to have every scumball hired killer hunting for you. Dozens of them, Mila. I can help you. Hide your family where they will always be safe. But you can't have a normal life, not until Zviman and his bosses are put down. They won't let you have a normal life.'

'Who are you with?'

'We're the opposite of Mr Zviman and his friends.'

'What are you? The police?'

He smiles.

'The CIA?'

He smiles again, shakes his head.

'The MI6?'

'Oh, Mila, those are all so twentieth century.' He laughs, and I decide I like his smile. 'The Round Table is so much more. Come to lunch with me. Let's talk.'

'What's your name?'

'You can call me Jimmy. And I'm going to be your best friend.' He held out his hand. And I, after a careful moment of consideration, took it.

71

The Last Minute Bar, Manhattan

I closed the file. Then I deleted it.

'I'm sorry,' I said to her.

'I know you are,' Mila said.

'Remind me never to anger you.'

'I have better control of my temper now, Sam. Yoga has worked wonders for me.'

'Zviman is Nine Suns. That's why you fight them.'

'Yes.'

'And Jimmy brought you into the Round Table, same as you brought me.'

She nodded. 'Ivan was my first teacher; Jimmy my second. You'll meet Jimmy one day. You and he will either like each other or kill each other.' She got up, walked to the window. 'You can understand my feelings on what you're going through with your son.'

I stared at her back. 'That you cannot save them.'

'An innocent caught up in this world, the odds are not good. And for a while, I thought you were lost to us, Sam. I meant what I said. They can control you forever with Daniel. They tried to control me with Nelly and you see what it got her. Dead. I was going to save her, I had saved her, and I got her killed.'

'You were alone. We have each other.'

'I was stupid.'

'But you had to try, Mila, same as I do. I can no more walk away from Daniel than you could from Nelly.'

'You misunderstand me.' She turned back to me, arms crossed. 'The man that shot Nelly? He wasn't even a guard at the house. He worked at one of Zviman's other brothels in Tel Aviv, heard about the shootings at Lucky Strike, came over to see if Zviman was okay. He sees a girl with a gun and he shoots her dead. He was what you call the anomaly that cannot be planned for. But such things always exist, they always come up. The unpredictable is what kills you. If I had been with her instead of stealing his money ... if we had just left the moment I had her ... she would be alive. But no. I couldn't just save her. I had to ruin Zviman. Rescue *and* revenge, no. You cannot do both.' She swallowed. 'You want to get Daniel and bring down Nine Suns. You cannot do both.'

'If I don't they'll never let me be. I am going to do both.'

She gave a long sigh. 'And I thought I could still be your teacher. You know what? They are going to catch me one day. As long as the million is hanging over my head, it will happen, Sam.' She sounded resigned.

'Not on my watch.'

'I might as well help you if you will listen to me.'

'How?'

'Zviman had a Nine Suns tattoo on him, although when I saw it I did not know what it is. He is part of it. We must draw in Zviman so he sees Jack is dead. We must convince him Jack is dead without killing Jack.'

'What about the notebook?'

'I find it fascinating that you never mentioned this red notebook when we first talked about the ransom.'

'I didn't know about it.'

'But it makes no sense that you kill Jack but leave damaging evidence behind. What if he hid it, then you never knew it was there. You think they would ask you to bring it to them after you kill Jack?'

'They didn't ask.'

'No,' Mila said, 'they didn't ask *you*.'

I glanced at the bedroom door. 'Leonie.'

'Perhaps. Maybe they told her to handle the notebook, same as telling you to handle the kill. Because no way could they trust you with that notebook.'

'She should have told me.'

'It is only a theory.'

The bedroom door opened. Leonie stood there. 'I have an idea on how to find Jack Ming,' she said.

'All right,' I said. 'We need to talk.'

'Then it's her turn to go.'

'I know I do not have a kidnapped child,' Mila said, 'but maybe you let me into your super secret club.'

'Don't you dare make a joke.'

'I wouldn't. I am helping you. It is decided.'

'No, it's not.'

'Yeah, it is.' I stood.

'We're supposed to work together,' Leonie said. 'Just us.'

'I am curious as to your objection,' I said. 'If she helps us kill Jack Ming, what do you care?'

'Is that what she's going to help us do? I thought she wanted to bring Nine Suns down.'

'The lives of your children trump my sense of revenge,' Mila said.

'Yes. We're sticking to the letter of what was demanded of us.' I glanced at Mila; she didn't look at me.

Leonie and she stared at each other, taking the measure. 'I am not comfortable with this, but, Sam, if you can control her and make her useful to us, that is fine with me.'

'Warmest greeting ever,' Mila said. 'I tingle.'

'Two guns are better than one, Leonie,' I said.

She looked at us both and then she surrendered. 'All right. Thank you, Mila. If we get Taylor and Daniel back I will be eternally grateful.'

'You said you had an idea on finding Jack?' I said.

'His phone number is the first step,' she said. 'If I can get that I can get his call log. I can start on that right now. Maybe I can find a way to see if any new numbers are calling anyone he knows, via his Facebook network or any of his family or other contacts.'

'All right.' I got up, somewhat painfully.

'Where are you going?' Mila said.

'I'm going to see if I can use an old friend.'

'Everyone can use a friend,' Leonie said.

'I mean literally use him, God forgive me.'

I walked downstairs, and I noticed the older, elegant, spare man in the corner drinking a pint. I noticed everyone but everyone else at a table was in a group. He was the only one flying solo. Someone who might want to observe the bar but garner less attention would not sit at the bar. You are kind of front and center sitting at the bar; everyone can see you and you craning your neck around to watch the rest of the room is noticeable. This may sound paranoid but this is how my mind works, especially with the thought that August might be watching the bar to see if I turned up here. I didn't like the look of him. He watched me, but in the mirrored back of the bar.

When I left The Last Minute, I waited at the next corner for him to exit. Five minutes. Ten minutes. He didn't. He wasn't tailing me.

I called Bertrand. 'The guy in the corner drinking his beer.'

'Yes.'

'Anything odd about him?'

'No.'

'Have you seen him before?'

'No, never. He has ordered one Harp and he drinks it slowly. He's not stirred from his table since you left.'

Well, then if·... Mila. 'Did Mila get here before or after he did?'

'Before.'

'We need to be very cautious of anyone alone watching for Mila or for me.'

400

'Go do what you need to do,' Bertrand said. 'Mila and I can handle any trouble that arises.'

'Well,' I said, 'are you sure?'

'Did she tell you about when we had the bathroom sound-proofed?'

'Uh, sort of. All right. I'll be back soon.'

I walked into the night.

PART FOUR

THE NURSERY

72

Ollie's Bar, Brooklyn

I sat on the crates of beer and when Ollie came in and switched on the light and saw me, he nearly had a heart attack.

'Jesus and Mary!' he yelled. Then he stared at me. '*You!* What the hell are you doing here?'

'I owe you a gun.'

'Christ almighty. You could have given me notice when you left.' A few months ago, when the Company decided to take me out of their private prison in Poland and dangle me as bait for Nine Suns, they'd gotten me a job bartending here at Ollie's. My decision to slip the Company's leash to go hunt for my wife necessitated I give Ollie no notice when I left my job. I had also stolen the gun from his safe, but, to my credit, I left an IOU.

'You know it hurts. It hurts to lose my only good bartender.' Ollie was famous for bemoaning the sad quality of his hired help. 'And for you to be a thief.'

'I left an IOU.'

'Which I believed, oddly,' Ollie said. 'I didn't call the cops on you.'

'The gun wasn't registered anyway, Ollie,' I said dryly. 'I lost it but I brought you a better one.' I handed him a sleek Beretta and a box of ammo I'd taken from The Last Minute.

'This is fancy,' he said. 'I'll never learn to shoot it.'

'You never learned to shoot the other one,' I said.

'True. Where did you go?'

'I went to go find my wife and my son.' For some reason I was done lying with Ollie. I'd answer a direct question as much as I could. He was a good man. Mila adored him, had wanted to buy his bar for years. She and I had first met here; she was scouting me as a possible recruit.

This confession made Ollie blink. 'Did you?'

'Yes.'

'That's good.'

'I'm trying to find August without using a phone,' I said. 'I thought you might be willing to pass him a message for me.'

'Are you allergic to phones?'

'No.'

'I hear they might cause brain cancer.' Ollie was happiest when worrying. 'He's out front and he's had a bit much.'

'Is he alone?'

'Yes, although there's a good-looking lady eyeing him up four stools down.'

'I am not one to interfere with the course of true love but do you think you could get him back here to talk to me without anyone knowing?'

'Why should I do you a favor, Sam? After how you treated me?'

'Ollie, do you want to retire?'

'Yes.'

'I will buy this bar from you when you retire. You don't have to worry about that, I'll pay a more than fair price.'

He blinked. 'Quit your joshing.'

'How many guys would come back and make stealing a gun right?'

'Not many, but could I get that in writing?'

'Like the IOU I was good for?'

'Yep.'

I tore a label off a case of Newcastle Brown Ale and wrote on the back: *I promise to buy Ollie's Bar at a fair price when he's ready to retire. Samuel Clemens Capra.*

'That's your full name? You poor kid.' Ollie inspected my handwriting for legibility and legal loopholes. 'Huh. I thought your answer would be because I'm a nice guy.'

'Well, that too.'

'Okay. I'll tell him I need him to help me move a beer keg. He's drunk enough it might work.'

'Thank you, Ollie.'

Two minutes later August came into the backroom. 'Oh, hell,' he said.

'Hi.'

He regarded me with a shake of his head and sat down on a stack of cases of Heineken. 'What the hell are you thinking? Well, taking you in with a broken arm should be easier.'

'You're not taking me in. We're not going to fight. We have to figure out a way to work together. Are you okay? I'm sorry I hit you.'

'I had to have three stitches.' He pointed at the back of his head. 'The Kum-ba-ya approach is a little late, Sam. You cost me my job today.'

I let ten seconds tick away. I couldn't tell if he was furious or numb. 'I'm sorry.'

'Well, that happens when you are supposed to pick up an untrained asset, who tells you to lose your tails because he's hacked the camera system following you, and you and your team can't subdue one ex-agent and you lose your asset.' His

407

voice rose in anger. 'I'm sorry. I know you are doing this for your kid but, hell, you can't do this, Sam. You're in my custody.'

'August. If you want your job back listen to me.'

'I think bringing you in will get me my job back.'

'It won't. Because something inside Special Projects is broken, and you know it.'

August frowned at me.

'You know Special Projects has been compromised. Either you have a mole, or your communications or networks are being monitored.'

'We've found nothing.'

'Jack Ming, in his old New York hacker days, his specialty was getting computer systems, as in printers, to send him information secretly. Tiny little sneaky bits of code that hide in other programs and harvest him what he needs. I'm pretty sure that's exactly what he wrote for Nine Suns, and they've been using these software spies to extort and control people in key positions in business and in government.'

August rubbed at his chin. 'Every traitor we've arrested since Lucy, they claimed they were blackmailed into doing this. We didn't believe them.'

'Either your systems have been compromised, or someone else has turned bad.'

'Hell.' August is not a big cusser.

'August, you're not the traitor, are you?'

'No.' He raised an eyebrow.

'Well,' I said, 'I had to ask.'

August tapped his foot against the concrete. 'Those women you killed, what do you know about them?'

'They were accused murderers, a sister act, who got a fresh

start and new names. A man named Ray Brewster hid them and used them as hit women for hire. The guy I killed in New Jersey, who kidnapped Jack Ming's mom, I think he might have worked for Brewster as well.'

'Someone who gives murderers and psychopaths fresh IDs and a job as hired muscle.'

'Do you know Ray Brewster?'

'No.' August shook his head. 'Do you know the name Lindsay Partridge?'

'No.'

'She's your red-haired sidekick.'

I waited.

'Ex-forger and counterfeiter, CIA informant, we paid her off well, then two years ago she vanished.'

'She gives people new identities now. Novem Soles has her kid, too.'

'Part of her file is locked. I can't open it, even with a Special Projects access. What's her secret?'

'I don't know,' I said.

'Who are these bastards?'

'One of them is a sex slaver named Yaakov Zviman. He seems to have moved into extortion as his mainstay, but he's the one who put the million dollars on Mila's head. I think he's a power in the organization. You ever hear of him?'

'No.'

'I think that whatever information Jack Ming has relates to whatever Zviman's doing now for Nine Suns. Maybe it's the list of people that they control. We get that, we cut off a major source of information for them. The kind of programs Ming wrote would give Nine Suns power over people who could help them profit.'

August ran a hand through his blond hair. 'Have you heard of Associated Languages School?'

'Yeah. The owners of the property where Mrs Ming was taken. Old abandoned house in Morris County.'

August stood and began to pace by the cases of beer. 'This fine language school also employs one of the dead women.'

'Meggie or Lizzie Pearson? Those were their real names. Lizzie struck me as a person who would not work well with others.'

'So they're Nine Suns?'

'Since they were trying to capture me, and I was Nine Suns' errand boy, I think not. I believe they are working for someone else who wants to collect the money on Mila. They talked about putting me in a cage and extracting information from me. Apparently kidnapping and interrogation were their specialties.'

'So we have Nine Suns after Jack Ming, and then a third party, and we don't know how and even if they're connected?'

'We do not.'

'I would love to have access to Special Projects files to see what we have on the women, but I'm supposed to go back to Langley next week and I'll be given a janitorial job. Or maybe fry cook in the cafeteria.'

'That's honest work.'

'Nothing wrong with it,' August said. 'My career is gone, Sam.'

I considered. 'Was your boss eager to get rid of you?'

'Not particularly. But today was a massive screw-up. A head had to roll and it wasn't going to be his although he could survive the bullet. He could survive anything.'

'Why?'

'He's retired officially, just brought back inside a couple of months ago to stiffen our backs and straighten our spines. Very old school, very much concerned about the honor of the Company, protecting its reputation. His name is Braun. Did you ever meet him?'

'No.'

'He retired before our time and came back after . . . after you left Special Projects.'

'If you came back to him with new information would he listen?'

'Maybe.'

'Is there anyone inside who would help you?'

August sat back down on the cases of Heineken. He looked more tired and frazzled than I'd ever seen him. 'Maybe Griffith.'

'Yeah, I kicked him kind of hard and I winged the other guy in the leg. Is he okay?'

'Yes. And you tried to murder Ming in front of him.' He shook his head. 'Why am I talking to you, Sam? We're done. We have to be done. I have to rebuild my career. I'm nothing without the Company, and, yes, I know that's pathetic, you don't have to tell me. I hope you find your kid, more than anything, I hope that. But I don't see how I can help you.'

'I can give you Jack Ming.'

'What?'

'I can give you Jack Ming.'

August stood up from the beer cases, then he sat back down. 'But you're going to kill him.'

'Yes, I am,' I said. 'And then I'm going to give him to you.'

411

73

The Last Minute Bar, Manhattan

Mila watched the man sitting at the corner table on the security camera. She had never seen him before. He ordered a small appetizer of tapas, slowly finished his pint of lager.

'Do you know this man?' she asked Leonie.

Leonie leaned over and studied the face on the camera. 'No. I haven't seen him before.'

Mila had stepped back from the monitor and watched Leonie: the lay of her gaze, the set of her shoulders, the curve of her mouth. 'I guess Sam was wrong, then.'

They watched the man in the corner get up and leave money for his tab and walk out.

'I don't think Sam is wrong about much,' Leonie said.

'So what is your plan?' Mila said. 'You and Sam get to save your babies and live an exciting, on-the-run version of *The Brady Bunch*?'

'I'm quite sure I'll never see Sam again when this is done. Does that make you happy?'

'Sam is only a friend. I am his boss. That is all.'

'Then I guess you'll never know what you're missing. That parkour running does hone a body. And he's been alone for so long, poor thing.'

'Alone I am sure you are not. For long. Ever.' Mila seemed to stumble over her English.

'Your jealousy translates clearly.'

'Do not confuse jealousy with concern for a friend.'

'I don't think I'm confusing anything, sweetie.'

Mila gave a thin smile. 'Do you know what I like about Sam?

He is clueless. He does not know he is attractive. He does not think about it and if you told him he is handsome he thinks you are just being nice. He is down on himself right now because he blames himself for Daniel being in danger. He loved Lucy very much and he doesn't trust his instincts now about women. He does not know he is a really good guy. So it is easy to take advantage of him right now.'

Leonie was silent for ten long seconds. 'He's not a fool and I'm not taking advantage of him.'

'I am sorry for what you are suffering. Your child being taken. I would not be myself.'

The sympathy seemed to take Leonie aback. 'I understand you want to help us, Mila. Thank you. I'm not exactly myself at the moment and maybe we'd get along fine under other circumstances. But Sam and I have to do what we're told and you will forgive me if the involvement of others makes me nervous.'

Mila's phone vibrated in her pocket. She gave Leonie a searching glance and then she answered her phone. She listened. 'This is a private call, sorry, do you mind?'

Leonie got up from the monitor. 'I need a cigarette anyway.' She retrieved her pack from the desk. 'I'll be back in a minute.'

Leonie walked downstairs. The bar was full, people milling about drinking, the music stopped. She stepped into the warm damp of the humid evening and lit her cigarette. The first two drags calmed her nerves. The man who'd sat in the corner of the bar now stood on the corner of the street. Watching her.

Did Mila have a camera on the front of the bar? She assumed there must be one. These people – whatever Mila and Sam were – were as organized as Nine Suns. She made a show of her pack being empty, shrugged in annoyance, and then she turned and walked in the opposite direction from the man.

She turned left at the light and walked down to the next corner. She stopped inside a store and bought a fresh pack of cigarettes. Then she stepped outside and fished one out and made a show of patting her pocket.

The man she knew as Ray Brewster stepped forward, offered her a light.

She glanced behind her, scared to see if Mila was following her.

He said: 'You look well, Lindsay. I'd like to say I've missed you but I don't care to start a chat with a lie. Not when we need each other.'

'Why are you here?' She managed to keep her voice steady.

'Two reasons.'

She waited.

'First. When you and your boyfriend kill Jack Ming, I want whatever evidence Ming has on the Nine Suns.'

'That's not possible.'

'You make it possible.'

'I can't steal it; I need it to ransom my child.'

'Then you are going to tell me where the exchange happens with Nine Suns. I want to know.'

'Why do you want it?' She drew hard on the cigarette. 'Have you switched sides?'

'No, sweetheart. I have just the one side, mine, as always.'

'I can't.'

'No, Lindsay, you will.'

She looked down the sidewalk again. No sign of Mila.

'And the other reason?'

'Have you seen a woman named Mila? She's connected to Capra.'

'Why?'

414

'I want her.'

Leonie drew on her cigarette. *One problem I can make go away*, she thought. Two words – *she's upstairs* – and Mila would cease to be trouble. She knew Ray Brewster well enough. That smarmy bitch would be as good as taken or dead as soon as she stepped outside The Last Minute.

But she knew she didn't want to be that person. She didn't want to be a traitor to Sam, no matter the acid dislike she felt for Mila. It gave her a momentary pleasure to deny him. 'I don't know any Mila.'

'Any woman who Capra works with? She's Moldovan, so she'd speak with an eastern European accent. She's petite, pretty, vicious.'

'No. He's not brought his friends around me. I have to go now.'

'This is my phone number.' He recited a number and she repeated it back to him. 'You get me that evidence and you give me Mila if she shows up, you and your child, if you get Taylor back, will be safe. From every threat.'

Her skin went cold. 'You know about Taylor?'

'Did you think you could hide from me? Really? That's awfully self-confident.'

'Why did you leave me alone, then, the last two years?'

'I didn't need you, Lindsay. Now I do. And if you don't do what I say, exactly, then I will make Taylor go away, and Leonie Jones will never see her child again.'

She wished she could stub the lit cigarette into his eye. 'And the line to blackmail me forms here. You're such an asshole. Can't you just leave me alone?'

'After what you did? No, sweetheart. I wanted you to feel nice and happy and secure until I could take it away from you. Nine Suns just beat me to the punch.'

415

She blew smoke into his face.

'You still forging? Identities, passports? Caring relationships?' He laughed. 'Really, the last is what you're best at faking.'

'That's a compliment from the biggest fraud of all.'

'You can't wound me. You already cut out my heart, Lindsay, and now I've got the knife at yours.'

She smoked in silence.

He tipped her chin toward him. 'What they know, I know. You really should give up smoking, sweetheart. When this is all done, you'll be the last one standing, alongside me. And then you can go take your fake self and live your fake life.'

He turned and he walked away from her.

She finished her cigarette. Horrible habit. She'd stopped now, twice before, and the thought brought her to tears. *Get a grip*, she told herself. She went back into the store, bought some chocolate M&Ms, and walked back to the bar.

Mila was off the phone and on the computer. 'Where did you go?'

'I was out of smokes.' She held up the candy from the store. 'And I thought I'd make a peace offering. Isn't chocolate the universal language?'

'Yes,' Mila said, 'I believe it is.'

74

Manhattan

The Watcher stood surveying the Manhattan skyline. He had spent the past twenty hours trying to suck every bit of information he could out of the extortion network. Before Jack Ming shut it down.

If they were unable to kill Ming and retrieve his evidence he wanted to sell to the CIA, then the Watcher was going to lose his entire power base among the Nine, and he would have to rebuild. It would be all right. He had rebuilt before after Mila stole most of his money. He'd fought and scrabbled his way back. But to lose the information feeds that had given him gold from Wall Street firms, from the White House, from Congress, from the British Parliament, from a good percentage of the Fortune 500, that would be devastating. The fearsome crime rings of the twentieth century – the Mafia, the Yakuza, the Colombian drug lords, the Mexican cartels – had never had their own spies, their own conduits to the highest powers in the land. This information had been oxygen to the blood of Nine Suns, knowledge that let them smuggle with impunity, keep the police at bay in a dozen countries, sell secrets to government and competitors and in turn own those buyers by virtue of their crimes. The extortion network that Jack Ming's software made possible had netted them tens of millions of dollars' worth of information in a matter of months.

And the Watcher needed to find something to replace that power base, and he had an idea.

His phone rang, and he answered.

'This is Jack Ming,' the voice said.

'My favorite person,' the Watcher replied.

'I want to make a deal with you.'

'With me? I doubt that.'

'No, I do. You wanted the notebook, I'll give you the notebook. I'll sell it to you.'

'I do not believe you.'

'I can't sell it to anyone else. Here's what we do. You deposit ten million in an account I provide. When I have the money, I will call you and tell you where to find the notebook.'

'How can I trust you?'

'Conduct a poll. I'm pretty sure I'll be seen as more trustworthy than you. Look, this is the deal, if you don't want it . . .'

'Why would you deal with us when we tried to kill you? Not to be overly blunt.'

'I will keep a few choice pages for insurance. If anything happens to me, they come to immediate light.'

'You could blackmail me again.'

'You could kill me again.'

'That's true. I thought you preferred to deal with the authorities.'

'They lost my trust.'

'Trust, so fleeting. All right, Jack. Where would you like to meet?'

Jack hesitated. 'We'll do it all by phone.'

'Are you going to fax me the notebook, Jack?'

'No.'

'Then we will have to meet.'

'And have your bitch Sam Capra show up and throw me off a building? No thanks.'

'Aren't you a smart lad?'

'And aren't you a right bastard, using his baby? Seriously.'

'Had a chat with him, did you?'

'I figure out things on my own, asshole. The notebook tells me a lot.'

'Oh, Jack,' the Watcher said. 'I look at you and I realize I mishandled the entire situation. I shouldn't have tried to get rid of you. I should have offered you a job. You're a smart, smart kid.'

'I'm smart enough to know I've got your golden goose here. I get my money, you get your notebook, and then we walk away.'

'You could have copied it.'

'And if anything happens to me, a nice copy of it will show up in the CIA's mailbox, along with a letter of explanation. So. You leave me alone and you have nothing to worry about.'

'So where shall we meet?'

'In Central Park. In the Ramble, north of the Bow Bridge. Tomorrow at three. When I've confirmed the money is safe in my account then I'll give you the notebook.'

'A lot of faith for me.'

'You want your notebook, don't you?'

'Yes, I do, Jack. Give me the bank account.'

Jack gave him the account for a Swiss bank. The Watcher wrote it on the palm of his hand.

'If you're one minute late, or I don't like the look of anything there, I'm gone and I'll just drive by Langley and toss the notebook on their front porch.' He hung up.

The Watcher clicked off his phone. Most interesting, that. Unexpected. Either Jack Ming had decided to bait a trap with himself or he'd decided that his need for money so he could vanish trumped all.

So. Should he have Sam Capra there to kill him? If Capra knew that someone from Nine Suns was meeting Jack Ming, he might try to seize him as a hostage to guarantee his son's release. But he wouldn't take the risk. That was the beauty of owning a child this way. The parent would never be able to cut the strings.

*

Jack Ming clicked off the phone. He sat on the edge of his bed back in his mother's apartment. It was the last place, he thought, that anyone would look for him. His mother was dead and his father was gone, and now he was truly alone in the world.

He walked to his mother's room. It was so spare, so absent of her, to be the place where she spent so much time. He had wept for his father for days, for weeks, but he could summon nothing for his mother except a promise: *I'm sorry I got you killed. I'm going to kill them for you, Mom.*

It would be so unexpected, he thought. Hackers hid in the shadows. They did not face threats in person; they lurked, they moved the intangible data, they did not cause bloodshed. Well, he was done with hacking. Tomorrow he would either die or he would kill. He didn't much care if he never saw a computer again. He had an identity and he could get a new one, Ricki could help him again, she had the contacts.

He wanted to cry for his mother, but he couldn't. Maybe later.

He picked up his cell phone and he dialed Amsterdam. It was very late there, actually early the next morning.

'*Ja?*' She sounded sleepy.

'Ricki. It's Jack.'

'Oh, my God, where are you?'

'It doesn't matter. I just want you to know that . . . I want to thank you. For helping me.' What was he going to say to her? My mom died, and, well, you're the only friend I have left. There wasn't much to say about him and his mom.

Ricki started to cry. 'I'm sorry, I'm sorry.'

'What?'

'They came . . . after you were gone. They came and they made me tell them where you went and they wanted to know what you knew about them. I'm sorry. They said they would kill me if I didn't talk.'

'It's okay, it's okay. Are you all right?'

'Not really. They . . . they took over my business. I have to work for them now or they'll kill me. They're taking all the money.'

'Oh, Ricki. Oh, God. I'm so sorry.'

She sounded as though she might cry but she didn't. 'I don't know what to do.'

'Listen. Tomorrow, I will either be dead or I'll have the money to vanish forever. Do you want to vanish with me?'

'What, go off with you? It . . . that is just stupid and crazy.'

'I like you that much,' Jack said. 'I'm sorry I waited until now to tell you.'

Ricki gave what sounded like a half-sob, half-laugh. 'Why would you trust me not to tell them? They own me now.'

'Because, well, I don't know. I do trust you. Do you want to come with me?'

'I would have to walk away from everything,' she said.

'It's not yours any more.'

She sniffed. 'True. Yes, Jack, I think I would like a new start.'

'Okay. I kind of love you a little.'

'I know. I've known for a while. I love you a little, too.'

His chest made a slight lurch. 'Okay, that's good then.'

'Well, don't die now,' she said. She started crying again.

'I won't. I won't. I'll call you back when I have the money and I'll tell you where to go. If I don't call, you figure out some way to get out from under these people. Just walk away if you have to, Ricki. You don't want any part of them.'

'I know.'

'I'm going to mail you a key to a locker. It has a copy of the notebook. If I die then it's yours, and you can do with it what you want. If you're too afraid of Nine Suns, then give them the key and they'll burn it, and I'll already be dead so I won't care. Or come to New York and get it yourself and give it to the police or to the FBI or sell it to the Brits or the French. I wouldn't deal with the CIA.'

'But if you're okay, then I'll be gone when the key gets here.'

'It won't matter. If I'm okay, I'll have the copy with me. You just be ready to get on a plane.'

'Okay. I wish I was there with you.'

'I do, too. I'll call you tomorrow night.'

'I'm going to be an optimist and pack my bag.'

'All right. I love you.' The three hardest, the three easiest, words to say.

'I love you, too.'

He hung up. If Ricki had kept her mouth shut his mother might be alive. But Ricki would be dead. He couldn't know how it would have turned out, and he couldn't hold it against her. If someone had said in his senior year of college he would get caught hacking, cause his father to have a heart attack, dodge arrest, hide out in Holland and fall for a Senegalese movie pirate, well, it wouldn't have ranked very likely in his mind.

Welcome to life. Life, something so sweet, something worth fighting for.

He had to get ready for tomorrow. He didn't have his gun any more. And he didn't know where he could get another one. You had to get close to hand over a notebook. A hand had to reach out to you.

His mother wasn't a great cook, but she'd loved having a gourmet kitchen.

In a drawer he found a pearl-handled chopping cleaver. He liked the unexpected.

75

The Last Minute, Manhattan

The bar was closed. Mila had vanished into whatever back corner of the night she lived. I was exhausted as I walked up to the apartment and reset the bar's alarm system.

Leonie sat at her computer. I couldn't be on a computer so much. I sort of hated them.

'Where have you been?' Leonie said.

'I'm not going to tell you, but it's going to get us our kids back,' I said.

She looked at me. And she said, 'All right.'

I went into the bedroom. I fell onto the bed. Bad day. Broken arm, missed the target, didn't get my son back. Exhaustion surged through me like a fever.

'We all looked at that man in the bar you thought was suspicious. He stayed another hour and ate some tapas and he left.'

'So maybe he was just a nobody,' I said. 'I know your name was Lindsay Partridge once.'

She sat on the bed's edge. Her back to me. I reached over and touched her shoulder.

'And who told you that?'

'Someone in Special Projects. The CIA has a file on you.'

'You know what I don't miss? Partridge Family or Partridge in a Pear Tree jokes. I don't miss those at all.'

'I think I'd still like to call you Leonie.'

'That's fine. That's my name now.'

'The CIA file on you has sections that are locked.'

'I can't imagine why. I'm just a soccer mom-wannabe who's good with computers.'

'I'd really like to know why you ran.'

'I needed a change.'

'Brewster has to be deep inside the CIA.'

'Or some group the CIA helps.'

'You were given a lot of money.'

'Yes.'

'To hide people off the books.'

'Yes.'

'That isn't in your file, so I'm told. So your file is about work you did for the CIA. Or for Brewster, on behalf of the CIA.'

She rubbed at her face. 'I think it's safe to say he did ... favors for the CIA.'

I didn't say anything to this. She had done dirty work, and doing it for Ray Brewster meant, like me, she was a CIA dirty secret. I felt her back tremble under my fingers.

'You went and talked to your friend August.'

'Yes. He got relieved of duty. We've declared a temporary truce.'

'So you can find Jack Ming.'

'Yes.'

'We're not going to be able to find him. They're going to kill our kids.'

'Listen to me. As long as we're chasing him, they have every reason to keep Taylor and Daniel alive.'

She seemed to decide not to cry. But I could feel the shudder under her skin, the tenseness, and I rubbed her upper back with my fingertips.

'One-armed man gives massage,' she said.

'House special,' I said.

'I should be tending to you. You're the one went off a building.'

'I don't make a habit of that,' I said. I dropped my hand from her back.

She looked over her shoulder at me. 'If Taylor dies my life is over. Done. I will have nothing.'

'Don't talk that way.'

'It's true.'

'It only feels true.'

'But there would be nothing left for me.'

'Revenge. If they hurt the kids–' I couldn't bring myself to say *kill* '–then I am going to hurt them, like they've never seen.'

'Revenge isn't a reason to live.'

'Mila once told me revenge is underrated. She might be right.'

'I don't think I could kill someone unless it was for Taylor.' Leonie stayed on the edge of the bed, I lay on my back.

'Well, if someone's about to kill me and you can stop it, feel free.'

She laughed. Not really a laugh, but a cross between a sigh and a smile. 'All right. Deal.'

'Even if Jack Ming is operating under a different name, he needs help. Resources. He can't access money in his name or his mother's right now. I'm sure August froze those accounts. So. Who are his friends? Who will he turn to? That's where we need to go.'

'Yes,' she said. 'So I checked his Facebook page. Not as Jack Ming, but back in Holland as Jin Ming. He only had ten friends on it. I imagine, posing as a Chinese student, he decided to keep a very low profile.'

'Ten is a nice workable number.'

'Now, in Holland, he's wanted for questioning about the death of that man in the hospital. So. It would have to be a good friend.'

I waited.

'So I got into his university records again. He had a majority of his classes with two of his friends. A Dutch kid and a Chinese kid. I checked their university email accounts and there was no sign that Jack has contacted them. But I found a photo of Jack with one of them on Facebook, and so I looked at all the photos of Jack on Facebook. The majority of the photos where he is tagged on Facebook belong to a girl named Frédérique Diagne, called Ricki for short. She's from Senegal but lives in Amsterdam. He is tagged in fourteen of her photos. Not in any others.'

'Girlfriend?'

'Hard to say. The most recent photo is from five months ago. They might have had a falling out. I asked around my hacker network and two of the guys told me there's a prominent female copyright pirate in Amsterdam. From Senegal. Her hacker code name is RT-Tavi.'

'What does that mean?'

'Rikki-Tikki-Tavi. It's a Kipling story about a mongoose that kills cobras.'

I remembered it now. 'You think this Ricki is RT-Tavi.'

'Yes. So I paid a guy to get into her phone log. She got a call about an hour ago from New York.'

'Jack.'

'It seems a distinct possibility. So I checked the line that called her. It has only called four numbers.' She showed them to me, written large on a legal pad with a black marker.

'One of those is August's cell phone.'

'And this is the main number for Central Park Conservancy.'

'The other two?'

'Ricki's phone in Amsterdam. And an unknown.'

'You can't trace it?'

426

'No. The last number is Israeli. I haven't been able to access a call log for it.'

Israel. Zviman was from Israel. But why would Jack Ming be calling the people who got his mother killed?

Because he wanted to find them and kill them himself.

'Do you want to call Ming?' she asked me.

'And what? Apologize?' I stared at the Israeli phone number.

Well, I could think of one good reason. But it was suicide for him, alone, to try and take them on.

'It fascinates me that he's calling Central Park. Why do you call an info line?'

'Maybe to get their hours, or to find out if there are events going in a certain section of the park.'

'You think he's meeting someone there.'

'Yes. It's open, it's crowded, he might feel comfortable meeting there.'

'To do what?'

'I don't know. But I do know what he's actually going to do tomorrow. He doesn't know it yet. But I do.'

I took a screen capture from the security monitor tape of the man in the corner. August didn't have a phone of his own; in Special Projects you are only allowed to have a phone that can be monitored by the group and he'd said he'd surrendered his to Braun. Unfair maybe but you give up a certain expectation of privacy when you do this work. If he had his own phone then I could send this to him. Tomorrow he'd get one. I'd send it then.

I stood and I winced. My body hurt. And I didn't want Leonie thinking much more about this phone number.

'Your arm is hurting. Let me get you a pain pill.'

'I can't be fuzzy. I have to be ready.'

'It won't make you fuzzy for tonight. Here.'

427

I grudgingly took the pill, swallowed it with cold water. 'You rest.'

I stripped out of my clothes, put on pajama pants I dug from a bureau, lay on the bed. I closed my eyes. I thought she would show more reaction when I knew her real name. But what, really, did it matter, when our children were in danger? I looked through the bedroom door and she sat at the computer desk. Looking at her picture of Taylor. The worn-with-love picture.

I closed my eyes again. Darkness fell on me.

Leonie awoke me when she slid into bed next to me. I raised my head up with a start.

'Is this okay?' she asked. 'I can sleep on the couch.'

'No, it's fine.'

I lay back down.

'Sam?'

'What?' I opened my eyes. I must have bruises going to the bone. I thought granules of sand had been driven past my clothes into my skin.

Leonie's face was close to mine. I blinked, hazy with sleep. The pain wasn't so bad; the pill must have taken off the edge.

'I feel sorry for you,' she said softly.

I don't do pity. I hate it. I got it from every kid who felt bad for me, always being the new kid in school, the new American who couldn't decipher the slurs or the name-calling in the native tongue. 'Well, don't.'

'You haven't even gotten to hold your child.'

I stared past her into the darkness. My skin itched under the cast, probably along the stretch of arm where Daniel should rest when I did get to hold him.

'Time will come,' I said.

'Yes. I want that for you, more than anything. It is the best feeling ever. Nothing matches it for love, for terror, for hope.'

'That sounds like a slogan for parenting.'

'And you and I can be the poster children for single parents.'

In the dim light from the street's glow I smiled. 'I shouldn't be on anyone's poster.'

She lay close, but not pressing against me. For a minute the only sound was our breath in the room, the soft grind of the air conditioner, the distant murmur of the city.

I turned my head to say something – I don't remember what – and she kissed me, softly, then more insistently, her mouth hungry, nipping at my lips. The kiss grew, deepened, her tongue tracing a delicious path.

The first time was from fear and stress. What was this? I was half dead but I felt my blood stir.

I tasted salt: the sting of her tears.

'I didn't mean to make you cry,' I said. I could smell tooth-paste on her breath; she'd brushed her teeth before she came to me.

'You didn't.'

'Why are you alone, with a child?'

'I wanted to be alone.'

'I never believe that. No one wants to be alone like that.'

Her hands had moved to my chest; her fingernails moved along my skin and my breath nearly left me.

'You don't have to use your arm, you know. I'll do the work.' She kissed me again. 'How sore are you?'

The correct answer was very, but I said, 'Not a bit.'

Probably people whose kids are in mortal danger shouldn't be having sex together. We're wrecks. It's not like this moment could bring intimacy or grace.

But there was none of that. Only an exhausting, fierce rawness of energy and anger and fury. At one point, her atop me and deep in her pleasure, she hammered at my shoulders, forgetting in the dark that I was a bruised beast. It was pain and glory all at once. That or she decided to fake an orgasm and beat the snot out of me at the same time.

She collapsed on me when we were both spent and her body was warm and wonderful and rich, lying against mine. Silence, only broken by breathing. I nuzzled her hair.

'That was good,' she breathed.

'Yes. Very for me,' I said.

'And very for me.' She cupped my face in her hands. 'We have to get them back, Sam. We can't fail.'

'I know. I know. We will.'

'Tell me what you're planning.'

'No. I can't.'

'Why?'

'Because if I do, you'll say no.'

'Don't . . . don't you trust me?' Her breath seeped against my throat, her nails traveled my chest.

'Yes.'

'So tell me.'

'Tomorrow Jack Ming goes down and our kids are going to be okay. All right?'

She lay next to me, not cuddling, but lying there. Present, our breath close together. I suspected she wanted to beat me to a pulp in her trembling anger, but she needed me functioning. So she let me keep my secrets.

While she kept all her own.

I got up while she slept, put on my clothes despite my exhaustion, and slipped out into the night.

76

Sam's phone, buzzing, woke Leonie. She groped across the empty bed for him; he was gone.

She sat up and grabbed for the phone.

'Yes?'

'Leonie. Let me speak to Sam.' She didn't know this voice. It was the phone Anna Tremaine gave them as the lifeline to Nine Suns, to get their instructions, but it was not Anna on the phone. A man's voice, crisp and precise and cold.

'He's . . . he's not here.'

'Where is he?'

'I don't know. I was asleep. Who is this?'

'This is the man who can have your kid killed with one phone call.'

'Please. Please don't.'

'I presume you are capable of taking a message?'

'Yes.'

'Tell Sam I will call back in one hour. I am not happy that he is not near this phone. What if I was calling him to tell him that I knew where Jack Ming was?'

'Then I'd go kill Ming,' she said. 'We already know where he's going to be tomorrow. Central Park.'

'Central Park doesn't quite narrow it down, does it?'

'We're finding out where, I promise . . .'

'Yes, I believe you would. You're an excellent mother. You just saved your child from unnecessary suffering.'

A flash of horror danced through her.

431

'I'll call back in an hour, and Sam better have a good reason for his absence.' The phone went off with a click.

77

Ming apartment, East 59th Street

The flame burst up from the pile of garbage bags across the street, drawing the night doorman out onto the sidewalk and hurrying over to the sudden, sputtering fire. He did not see me slip inside the lobby while his back was turned, while he had a cell phone pressed to his ear to summon the fire department. I spent six months of naughty teen years in Jakarta; kids there used to burn trash for fun, and they were most clever about how to torch with efficiency.

I took the stairs up to the Mings' apartment floor. I picked the lock to the apartment.

It was still and dark and airless but I could smell the odor of antiseptic cream and muscle rub. I turned on a light and Jack Ming lay huddled on the couch, curled up into a fetal position. I thought he would have been in the bedroom.

'Jack,' I said quietly. I moved toward him.

His eyelids snapped open – no one sleeps that great when they're on the run, trust me, I know – and a scream formed on his mouth.

He bolted from me, grabbed a ceramic tray off the coffee table, threw it at me. I dodged it.

'I'm not here to hurt you,' I said, calmly.

From under the couch cushion he pulled out a pearl-handled cleaver.

'I'm not armed,' I said. 'I just want to talk to you.'

He charged at me and he swung it at me. Twice. The blade made a sharp hiss in the air. Desperation and fear colored his face; he had no skill. I wasn't really comfortable fighting him with an edged weapon one-handed. So I kicked him, hard against the wall, and then slammed my foot against the wrist holding the cleaver, pinning his hand to the wall.

'I am not here to hurt you. I am here to talk to you.'

'I don't believe you.'

'I would have kicked you in the throat just now and broken your windpipe,' I said. I pressed harder with my foot. He winced and the cleaver clattered to the floor.

'I am not here to hurt you. I am here to talk to you,' I said again. 'I'm going to let you go now, so we can talk like adults. I have a proposition for you.' And I released his wrist. As a precaution I put my heel on the cleaver's blade.

He smacked a punch against my arm's cast and, yes, that did indeed hurt a lot.

I grabbed him by the neck. 'Jack. Please.' I was careful not to hurt him.

He grew still.

'May we talk?'

After a long moment he nodded.

'Can we go sit down in there and talk like two adults?'

He couldn't keep the surprise off his face. He sat on the couch; I sat on the leather ottoman next to it. I left the cleaver on the floor, but I was between it and him.

'Well,' he said. 'You don't appear to be killing me. Yet.'

'I have decided that even though I've been told to kill you, that is not how I am going to get my son back.'

He stared at me, his mouth working.

'Jack. Breathe. It's okay.'

'How . . . how did you find me?'

'I got hurt in the fall, I figured you did, too. And you lost your knapsack. You were back accessing your computer very quickly using remote software. Hard to download and install that on a coffee shop or library computer – and if I was hurt, I'd run home. No one would think you would come back here. But you could mend here, and have a computer, and call people who might help you and have a nice private conversation, and probably have an easier time accessing your mother's bank accounts and such. It was worth a try.'

Jack said nothing.

'I'm sorry . . . about today,' I said. 'I know I . . . scared you.'

'I do not accept your apology.'

'All right. I am very mindful that you could have shot me in that hallway rather than shooting the lock on the door.'

He rubbed his palms on his knees.

'The only way Nine Suns is going to leave you alone is if we convince them that you are dead. They have to believe you're gone for good for you to have a life. And for me to get my son back. Now. If we can make them think you're dead, then we both have a chance.'

He shook his head. 'I don't believe you.'

'Do you believe they have my kid?'

'Yes.'

'You said that there's something in the notebook about my son.'

'Yes.'

'What is it, please?'

'Where he was born. How much the doctor was paid, how much the forged documents cost to get him an American birth certificate. Who has him now: someone with the initials AT.'

434

Anna Tremaine. 'Anything else?'

He bit his lip for a moment, considering. 'No.'

'Where is the notebook?'

'In a safe place, and I don't care if we're new best friends now, I'm not telling you.'

'I want you to go to your computer's browser and enter in a web address.'

He didn't move.

'Go ahead. I want to show you something.'

Slowly he got up and went into his father's study. He sat at the computer; I gave him the URL; the prompt then asked for a password. He looked at me and I gave it to him.

He typed.

The webcam's screen opened. Lucy lay in her eternal bed, hooked to wires and tubes and a computer whose uncaring graphs and bars showed her lungs still breathed, her heart still pumped.

'You and I have nothing in common,' I said, 'except Nine Suns has destroyed our families. That is my wife. They took her and they made her into a person I never knew and then they put a bullet in her brain. Now they have my son. He is only a few months old. I have never seen him in person, never held him.' I pulled the photo from my wallet and I handed it to Jack. He looked at it wordlessly.

Then he gave it back to me.

'Your mother was killed by a stray bullet when I fought the guy who kidnapped her. If I could have saved her I would have . . .'

'Only to get her to help you find me.'

'No. Did I kill the men from the CIA who were supposed to protect you? I knocked them out of the fight but I didn't kill

435

them. Did I shoot down anyone who got in my way while I was chasing you?'

'And, what, you want a good citizen medal?'

'I held your mother's hand while she died, Jack. She asked me to help you. I had to lie to her then and say I would help you. I don't want it to be a lie.'

Jack closed the browser window; Lucy vanished. 'Why would you risk your baby's life to protect me?'

'Because I no longer believe they're just going to hand me my child. I know too much, I'm too big a threat to them. They have to be destroyed and you're the guy who can bring them down.'

'The notebook doesn't contain the names and addresses of Nine Suns. It gave me one phone number for one of them, the person who set up this extortion network. It mostly just names people that they're using.'

'People they've spied on using your software.'

'Yes.'

'Wouldn't it be nice if we could turn that around on them?'

Jack said, 'What do you mean?'

'Do to them what they did to these people. Spy on them, using your code.'

Jack Ming got up from the desk. I followed him into the living room. He picked up the cleaver off the floor, and I tensed. But he went into the kitchen and he set it on the granite counter top.

'And who gets the information? You?'

'When I get my son back, I'm done. If I don't, then I send them to hell, however long it takes.' I crossed my arms. 'I know you must think August Holdwine is a screw-up, but he's not. You can trust him. And he's being moved back to Langley, out of the group that was supposed to protect you. They've been dirtied. But he's clean.'

Jack Ming blinked at me, and I didn't blame him not trusting me. So cards on the table, so to speak.

'I know you called Ricki Diagne in Amsterdam. Maybe for help, maybe because she's someone special to you. If you don't trust the CIA, there is another group of people who could hide you. Think of them as the flip side of Nine Suns. My friend Mila works for them and I think they could hide you and Ricki, too, if you want, just about anywhere in the world. Especially if you could help them spy on Nine Suns.'

'Your friends are the Round Table.'

'Yes. Are they in the notebook?'

'There's reference to them.'

That made me uneasy. It could mean someone inside the Round Table had been compromised, maybe into giving up secrets.

He shook his head. 'Round Table. Nine Suns. Who the hell comes up with these names?'

'Every group needs a mythology. The Round Table was full of knights who wanted to do good. Nine Suns is from an old Chinese legend about the near destruction of the world. The names say a lot about each side.' I tried again: 'Can I please see the notebook?'

'No. You can't. I think you can understand that I need to keep a trump card to myself.'

The urge to ransack the apartment and find it was strong, but he needed to trust me, so I nodded.

The cell phone in my pocket rang. I answered it.

Leonie. 'Sam, Nine Suns just called on the iPhone Anna gave you. They want to talk to you and they want to know where you are.'

'All right, I'm on my way back.'

'Where are you?'

'I needed some air.'

'Sorry you couldn't get that here with me.' Just a dash of bitter.

'I'm on my way.' I turned off the phone. 'They're calling me with instructions on your meeting, I suspect. So I can ambush you.'

Jack's throat worked. 'So. How do we do this?'

'You're in?'

'You made your point. Plus, what if I say no? You kill me then, right. You have no choice.'

'I always have a choice. So do you.'

'I want them taken down. I can't do it alone, I know that.'

'Will you trust August?'

I could tell it wasn't an easy decision. But after thirty seconds Jack said: 'All right.'

'Fine. Sit down. Here's what we do.'

78

The Last Minute Bar, Manhattan

'You're going to kill Jack Ming.' The man's voice was slightly accented. Israeli. I felt sure this was Zviman, the man who'd nearly killed Mila, who she had emasculated and enraged, the man responsible for the horror that Mila's sister endured, the man ultimately responsible for Nelly's death. 'At Central Park, in the Ramble. It's heavily wooded, not one of the busiest sections. This afternoon, a bit before three.'

'All right,' I said.

'He and I are going to meet north of Bow Bridge. It will be crowded. He won't be willing to step into any more private areas of the park. So he has to go down without drawing attention.'

'You're not from here, are you? I can't kill a guy by Bow Bridge and not have it go noticed. Look, you've drawn him to the park. You get whatever you're buying from him and then he's my problem.'

'I'm not funneling him money. He's dead before then and then I get what he's carrying.'

Which meant he would want to see the notebook.

'Kill him quietly. Break his neck or use a knife,' the man I believed to be Zviman said. 'Don't think for a second you can skimp on the job.'

'I don't ever think for a second,' I said.

I clicked off the phone. Leonie lay on the bed.

'Did he tell you what to do?'

'Yes.'

'But you're working a scam. Don't bother to lie.'

'Yes.'

'All right,' she said, and I could hear the tone of surrender in her voice. 'What do you want me to do?'

79

The Ramble, Central Park, Manhattan

A guy with a broken arm in a fiberglass cast just doesn't look threatening. Ted Bundy and Buffalo Bill in *The Silence of the Lambs* used arm casts as camouflage to lure in women to help them so they could commit abduction. Then they turned the casts into weapons. Of course, they didn't actually have broken arms. I did.

It's hard enough to kill someone when you've got two good hands. I was only going to get one chance.

I sat on a bench north of the beautiful iron-built Bow Bridge, a book in hand, a Yankees cap pulled low over my head. Waiting. I was on the edge of the Ramble, a dense, wooded area planted by hand well over a century ago, now mature woodland, with a maze of walkways cut through its growth. I saw at least four different passersby with binoculars and field guides: this was a prime birding spot. I also saw teenagers who looked like they might savor a bit of privacy. But this stretch of park, at least this afternoon, wasn't quite as busy as the Zoo or the playgrounds or the Mall. Now and then a family milled by, joggers jogged, a pair of lovers leaned into each other, walking hand in hand. I still don't like to see couples. Nothing against them. I'm all for love and commitment. It just reminds me of what I thought I had, and never truly did, with Lucy. I thought we would grow old together. I thought we would be grandparents together, Daniel bringing us his own children to spoil and love. We should have had years to spend in parks, tossing crumbs, hearing the lull of the breeze in the trees, watching the sunlight shift its mosaic on the grass.

Now I sat alone on a park bench waiting to murder someone.

My orders were explicit. When the Nine Suns contact – I knew it was probably Zviman but I wasn't going to admit to him I knew who he was – walked away from Jack Ming, I would intercept and kill Ming. I didn't believe for a second that Ming's bank account would go unhacked; Nine Suns wasn't going to give him ten million dollars.

The day was grayish, clouds grappling with sun for a momentary dominance. I sat, with my sunglasses and my book. I checked my watch. Time. On the under side of the bench I groped and my fingers found tape. I pulled the tape free. In my hand was an earpiece. I thumbed it into place.

'Hello, Sam,' the voice slipped into my ear.

I said nothing.

'Cat got your tongue?'

'No. I just have nothing to say to you.' I put my gaze back to my book.

'I have taken precautions. If I do not call in to a number and give a correct passcode, your son dies. Don't decide you can kill both Ming and me, or take me hostage for your son.'

'I can follow orders.'

'I played with your son the other day,' Zviman said.

My blood went cold.

'He's very responsive for a child. I don't know a lot about babies, but your little lad looks you in the eye. I enjoyed getting to hold him.'

Wordless rage.

'I know you'll do a first-rate job. Then you'll get to see your son. I hope I don't cry. Family reunions make me tearful.'

I saw a man move from the walkway to a dense copse of black locust trees, a good thirty feet off the path. He stood in their shade, and produced a smartphone from his pocket. The blond mohawk was a trimmed, ghostly strip of hair. I knew his face from Mila's description. It *was* Zviman. He didn't walk funny, though. I didn't look at him but I felt quite sure he looked at me. I kept scanning the approaches.

Then I saw Jack Ming. Dressed in jeans, and a Giants windbreaker, and a Giants baseball cap.

He was holding the red notebook in his left hand, and had his right hand in his pocket.

The stiletto I had hidden in my cast felt heavy. The handle of the blade I'd cut down to conceal it rubbed against my wrist. Bertrand has an interesting collection of knives at The Last Minute.

'Here he comes,' I said.

'I see him,' Zviman said. 'Look at him, he thinks he's tough. I wonder how he thinks he got tough sitting at a keyboard all day.' The hatred in his voice was thick.

I glanced around. Two people, binoculars up, looking the opposite way, focused on their birding. A couple and a single man heading toward Bow Bridge. A young woman, iPodded, lost in her music rather than birdsong and park noise.

Ming had his back to me.

Jack Ming stopped and glanced around. Then he looked right at Zviman. And he walked to the tree.

I waited.

80

The Ramble, Central Park, Manhattan

Courtesy of Zviman's earpiece I could hear the conversation.

'Hello, Jack.'

'Let's set the conditions. If I don't come back from this meeting, a friend calls the police and gives them your description. He already took your photo with a telescopic lens.' Jack's voice was steady. 'I think you'd have to shave off that Velcro strip on your head and wear a wig to make it out of the city.'

'Jack, please don't insult me.' Zviman's voice was kind. 'I'm a businessman. I'm here to make a trade. We both end up happy.' He shrugged. 'Look, I'm not unmindful you wrote the code that let us steal the secrets. I respect that what you're getting could be considered a fair cut.'

'Move the money.'

Zviman held up his smartphone so Jack could see its screen. He keyed in the account transfer code and kept the phone raised so Jack could see the blue progress bar fill as the dollars and cents jumped from an account in the Caymans into a Swiss account. Silence between them.

'Done. Check it for yourself if you like,' Zviman said.

At the word *done* I stood. Jack Ming still had his back to me. I moved forward, silently across the grass, weaving in between the trees, my hand on the hidden stiletto handle in the cast.

Jack brought a cell phone up from under the red notebook. He kept his right hand in his pocket. No one watching would like that. He'd apparently preset the phone's browser to his bank account and he hit a refresh button.

I kept approaching, keeping the center of his shoulders as my axis of approach. I moved quickly and quietly across the damp grass.

'The page isn't loading,' Jack said, a tinge of nervous frustration in his voice.

'The internet. So unreliable.'

He thumbed a button again. 'Still locked up. I'm not giving you the notebook until the money's in my balance.'

Zviman smiled with infinite patience. 'That's fair.'

I was twenty seconds away.

'You're trying to cheat me,' Jack said. And he pulled the gun from the pocket of the windbreaker.

I was still ten feet behind him but now running at full force, no attempt at stealth. Jack jabbed the gun toward Zviman, as though counting on his target's own flesh to muffle the sound of the shot. Zviman jumped back, wrenching Jack's arm up, and by then I slammed my cast into the side of Jack's neck. He staggered and I yanked him backward, away from Zviman, and he tried to aim the gun at me. I folded his elbow back toward him and he made a little mewling protest as the gun's barrel touched his stomach. He bent and I got a hand on the trigger and the shot wasn't as loud as it could have been. I moved the gun to the chest and pulled the trigger again and he fell to his side, two small, bright blossoms of blood on his shirt. He gave a hard, wet cough of red and then he lay still among the trees.

I pulled him back against the trunk of the tree and zipped up the Giants windbreaker to cover the blood. 'Make it look like he's sitting. He won't draw attention that way.'

Zviman moved away from me, staring at Jack. 'The stiletto. Drop it.'

'What?' I was trying to raise and settle Jack's head so it didn't loll and I couldn't get the angle right.

'You didn't need the knife. But you're not getting armed into a car with me.'

I dropped the stiletto to the ground, kicked it behind the tree.

'Hey, hey!' A tall black man, with a birding book and binoculars, had wandered closer to us, directing his shout to a bird in a distant tree, but he seemed absorbed in his lenses. Which were aimed in the sky above our head. He could notice Jack, or us, at any moment and I heard Zviman suck in a hiss of breath.

'Go. Walk. Now. Before he sees the blood.' I used my sleeve to wipe Jack's mouth blood away.

Zviman knelt, picked up Jack's phone – and the red notebook. It was one of those classic leather-covered ones, with an elastic band to keep it closed. It was smaller than I thought it would be. He started hurrying away from the body, flipping the pages.

'Don't run,' I said to him. 'Keep walking normally.'

He glanced back. The tall black man still studied the sky, then glanced at his birding book, then at the treetops again.

Zviman and I continued our steady walk.

'Where are the children?' I asked.

'Wait, we're not clear yet.'

We cut across Bow Bridge, silent with each other, and headed down to the 72nd Street Transverse that sliced through the park. Zviman hurried to the street and raised his arm for a cab. Well-dressed guy, moneyed – a cab stopped within thirty seconds, releasing a pair of tourists clutching Beatles memorabilia who looked like they intended to go pay tribute to John Lennon over at Strawberry Fields. New York luck. We both got inside.

Zviman gave the cabbie the address of a parking garage a dozen blocks away. He raised a finger toward his lips, like I was stupid enough to speak in front of a witness. He flipped through the pages of the notebook, shaking his head. 'Little bastard,' he said more than once. 'Little, rotten bastard.'

We got out of the cab, he paid. We took an elevator up to the ninth floor and I followed him to a black BMW sedan.

'Where is my son?'

'I will take you to him, right now.'

'Anna told us the children would be left at a church and we could collect them. I don't know where the hell you are taking me.'

'I am taking you to your son, Mr Capra, and you can either get in the car or not. Your choice.'

I got into the BMW. He wheeled back toward the park, driving with confidence and not a little verve. He held on tight to the red notebook.

At the south-east edge of the park, he pulled up to the curb. Leonie stood waiting on the sidewalk. So far no distant cry of siren or ambulance.

She saw me in the passenger seat and she got into the back seat. 'Is he dead?' she asked.

'He's dead. Practically killed himself,' Zviman said. He glanced back at Leonie, gave her a nakedly appraising look. I wanted to say: isn't that wasted on you? But I kept my mouth shut.

He pulled away from the curb, punched a button on his phone.

'Cleopatra.' I guessed it was his code to say all was well. 'Ming is dead, I have the notebook, and I'm bringing the happy parents to the nursery. Get the kids ready.' He clicked off the phone. 'And then I call again in thirty minutes, with a different passcode, to let her know that you haven't tried to hijack the car. If she gets the least bit suspicious that you've betrayed me en route, the kids will suffer. Guaranteed. Sit back and enjoy the ride.'

Behind me, Leonie made a noise in her throat. Zviman smiled at her in the rear view mirror.

'All right, Mr Capra, Ms Jones, let's go get your children.'

81

'Don't move,' the tall black man said. 'They could drive back by to see what's going on.'

Jack Ming left his eyes half open. 'He bought it,' he mumbled through closed mouth.

'It helped that you pulled and died by your own weapon. I

think it worked, yes. He wants you dead and sometimes the eye sees mostly what it wants to see. My name is Bertrand. I'm a friend of Sam's. We're going to get you to safety.'

Jack stayed still. Through his half-mast eyes he could see a woman standing behind Bertrand, holding a video camera. 'When it looks like you're shooting a YouTube video, no one thinks you were actually shot,' Bertrand reminded him. The woman was a small pixie-faced type, very pretty, with big sunglasses shoved up to her dark hair.

Ten, twenty minutes passed. A couple of people strolling by gave them curious glances, but the presence of the woman shooting video answered unasked questions. 'Okay, get up,' Bertrand said. 'We walk. Quickly.'

The woman murmured to Bertrand, he couldn't quite hear what, but her accent sounded Russian or something.

Bertrand said, 'Good luck and be careful.'

He and Bertrand headed one way, the woman the other.

And if they're watching us right now, if this wasn't enough, Sam is a dead man, Jack thought, and I've given them back what they wanted most, and my mother died for nothing.

Bertrand hurried him through the park; they went in the opposite direction of Zviman and Sam, toward Belvedere Castle and the 79th Street Transverse.

'Wait,' Bertrand said. 'Wait.' Jack thought his heart would explode, suddenly scared that their ruse had been discovered.

A Ford sedan pulled up next to them. At the wheel, August of the CIA.

And in the back seat, *impossibly*, Ricki.

'We thought it best to get her to safety,' Bertrand said, 'but I didn't want you distracted by knowing she was close. Sorry. We have a private jet . . .'

Jack hardly heard him. He was in the back seat, embracing Ricki, who kept covering his face with kisses. Safe. She was safe.

The car pulled away. Bertrand gave a quick wave and vanished back into the park.

'Thank you, thank you,' he said to August.

'Thank Sam and his friends,' August said.

He thought of that crazy Sam Capra, and his baby, and Jack's heart felt heavy.

'Jack, we're going to get you and Ricki to Langley. You'll be safe there. And I understand you made a paper copy of the notebook . . .'

'Yes,' he said. 'But you can't have it. Not yet.'

The car stopped. August turned. 'Are you serious?'

'Sam promised to give you me, August,' Jack said. 'Not the notebook. He needs the original notebook to get his son back. If he makes it back with his son, you get the notebook. If he doesn't get his son back, then the copy I have is his, to do with what he wants.'

August stared.

'Think of it,' Jack said, 'as the map of Sam's revenge.'

82

Parking garage near Central Park

Mila put the camera in a bag in the back of the van. She pulled off the dark wig she'd worn under a stylish hat, shook her sweaty hair free and pushed the black sunglasses back on her head.

Now. Sam had forgotten for a moment that he worked for her; he had forbidden her to come after them. Ridiculous. He could not go off with a man as evil as Zviman and expect to have an exchange go smoothly. And she did not trust Leonie. And although Sam had been clever enough to slough off her tracking chip the other night, Leonie was not. The chip went into the pocket of the light jacket Leonie wore, that Mila had lent her from the apartment over The Last Minute.

From the back of the van – the same one she and Bertrand had used to move out the corpses of the bodyguards, what felt like a thousand days before when she and Sam had pretended to be baby buyers – she pulled out a GPS device. A slight red gleam showed her Leonie's position. She could follow, unseen, at a distance.

She heard the footsteps behind her as she shut the door. She turned and the Taser needles hit her. Shocking her. Then a tall, spare man stepped forward and closed a damp cloth over her face.

The man who sat at The Last Minute, the man Sam thought suspicious.

'You're my million-dollar baby, Mila,' he said to her, before the darkness closed in.

Braun handcuffed Mila, all with the van doors closed. He heard the laughter of children, a family walking past the van as he worked. He made sure she was secure: he had no intention of underestimating her. He relieved her of the knife in her boot and the gun at the small of her back. He bound her feet with rope.

He examined the GPS reader. Clever. Either Lindsay or Capra were tagged, and Mila was going to follow them.

He could see that they were now off Manhattan, heading north into Westchester County. A cold tingle touched his spine. No. Surely not. Surely Zviman was not taking them *there*.

He took the keys from her pocket. He opened up his phone. He sent a text message to the email address where the reward had been posted. *I have your Mila and I want to collect the million. Caught her trying to help your friends in the car. May I make your day and bring her to you?*

83

On Highway 87 North

We headed north and east, leaving the city well behind, cutting up past Irvington, heading on 87 North. I wondered where we were headed. Peekskill? Albany? The Catskills? A silence filled the car because Zviman said, 'No talking.' Zviman put on the satellite radio and tuned it to the alternative classics of the eighties. He even sang, very softly, under his breath, barely audible. The Cars, Elvis Costello, and, God help us, Katrina and the Waves.

I did not trust this man in a good mood.

No one spoke for an hour at least, and, as we passed Newburgh I couldn't contain myself further. 'Where are our kids?' I said.

'At a safe place,' Zviman said. 'I'll take you there and then you may have this car to go where you please. Considering you killed a man in the park I wouldn't return to New York for a while. I'm sure Ms Jones would like to get home to Las Vegas.' He sounded so calm, so reasonable. I felt like I was going to jump out of my skin.

'You're probably thinking, Sam, that you're surprised we struck you a deal.'

'Very.' I wasn't thinking he wanted to let me out alive. Now I was going to have to fight my way out, I felt sure, and I didn't know how I was going to do that while holding a baby. The obvious answer was Leonie. Have her run to safety with the kids, if at all possible, and leave me to deal with Zviman.

'I don't think the CIA will be offering you a job again,' Zviman said. 'Now that you killed their prize asset. Of course, they didn't see you kill him, but you'll be the prime suspect. Unless you could convince them that you weren't trying to kill him but protect him from a danger within the CIA.'

'I should update my resume,' I said. 'And I'm not that good an actor to pull off that lie.'

'In fact, with Jack Ming dead, they'll be hunting for you. If you gave them someone else as Ming's killer, well, you might be in the clear with them. Nice for you, that would be, for you and your son.' His voice was like a knife.

'Why are you so concerned about what happens to me?'

'We made a deal and I intend to stick to it. What, you think I'm going to kill you?'

'I think you're going to try.'

'That would undo all that's been done.'

'Done?'

'To make you who you are, Sam,' Zviman said. 'You've been a long-term project for us. You could still be of value to us. We've watched you for years now. We've been interested in you for a long time.'

451

I stared at him. He didn't look at me. He almost smiled as he drove. How could I have been a long-term project for a bunch of criminals? 'That . . . that doesn't even make sense,' I said.

'Of course it does,' he said. 'We think long term. You've been thinking in terms of hours, days, weeks: how do I find my wife, how do I get my son back? Small problems. We think in terms of years. You have gone from being a problem for us to becoming useful to us. We were willing to sacrifice your usefulness because you could kill Ming for us, and he was a tremendous threat. But no one can *prove* that you killed him. You could still serve a purpose.'

I had a sudden, weird sense that I was a piece on a chess board, not the king, and some giant hand had flicked me around the squares. 'I have no interest in being useful to you. I want nothing to do with you. I am getting my child and then we are done.'

'I never had the pleasure of meeting your wife,' he said. 'But I think we all felt her loss.'

This is to make you snap, I thought. He wants to worm under your skin, get you off your game. Nothing but lies and distraction. 'I'm not discussing my wife with you.'

'You're ready to quit the battlefield.'

I stared straight ahead.

'You said, more than once, I think, when the Company kept you in their private prison and you slept on stone floors, and that the world believed that you were guilty, that all you wanted was your old life back.'

'My old life is gone.'

'No it's not. Not exactly,' he said. 'Now be quiet. We'll have plenty to say when we get where we're going.'

452

84

Along Highway 87 North

Leonie had wedged the cell phone in the calf-high boot she wore. She kept her eyes ahead, occasionally glancing out the window, trying not to appear as though she were listening to the awkward conversation.

To Ray Brewster she texted: north on 87, past Kingston 5 min ago.

She turned off the phone and she slid it into her boot.

The two men in the front seat, locked in their discussion, locked into their anger and mistrust, did not notice.

Braun drove aggressively and fast, and closed the distance between himself and Zviman's car to ten miles. He glanced at the text message.

He was entirely sure of their destination. All stories, he thought, come back to their beginning, all circles must close.

85

Zviman opened his phone, as he had done every thirty minutes for the past two hours. He pressed a number. When Anna answered he said, 'Pericles. Yes, all is well.' He clicked shut the phone.

My fist slammed against him hard, then I grabbed his head and pounded it against the steering wheel.

Leonie screamed, 'What are you doing, what are you doing?'

The BMW veered across its lanes, narrowly missing a semi that laid on its horn like a stuttering war cry. It is very hard to fight a man one-handed.

'I know where we're going,' I yelled at her. 'He can be our hostage to get the kids.'

Then she understood. Leonie snaked her arm around Zviman's throat and levered back. He gagged and spat, arching in the seat. I hit the brake with my foot and levered up the parking brake. The BMW howled and bucked but we stopped. I took my good hand and pounded five blows into his sorry face. It felt good. He finally sagged, beaten, out.

'Oh, God, oh, God,' Leonie said. Panic jagged her voice.

'Listen to me. I know where we're going now. The company that was a front for the sisters, for the house in New Jersey. I looked them up. They owned another retreat off this highway, about five more miles up. That's where we're going. And now we can trade the kids for him.'

'What if you're wrong?' Leonie said. 'Oh, God. What if you're wrong?'

I hauled the unconscious Zviman into the back seat. 'Drive,' I told Leonie. I accessed the Associated Languages School website. 'North about four miles, then turn onto Mountain Bridge Road.'

'If we drive up into a bunch of execs learning Spanish, I'm going to kill you, Sam.' Her voice was a ragged, broken shock.

'I'll kill myself,' I said.

86

Associated Languages School, near the Catskill Forest Preserve, New York

The building was a long, low affair, hidden in the dense growth of red cedars and sugar maples, with a curving gravel driveway before it. It looked like a grand mansion, one perhaps left over from the Catskills' Borscht Belt days, a shrunken resort. A toy, ignored and misplaced in the heavy forest. The windows were boarded. The grass around the building needed cutting. Abandoned, like the house in New Jersey. Or, if not abandoned, then not in use to help tourists conjugate their French verbs or contract out to business employees who needed to master Spanish or Farsi in between shuffleboard and trout fishing.

'What do we do?' Leonie said as she pulled up to the shuttered house.

'We trade him for the kids and we get the hell out of here.'

'Sam . . .'

'We did what they wanted but we're done playing by their rules,' I said.

'What about what he said . . . about you being some kind of project . . . ?'

'Ignore him,' I said.

No one emerged onto the porch.

I opened the car door, got out. Put both hands on Zviman's head, one along the jaw, the other on the throat. 'Honk the horn.'

Leonie hammered twice on the horn. It sliced through the hush of the woods.

A moment later the door opened. Anna Tremaine stepped out onto the porch. She wore a cream-colored T-shirt and green cargo pants. She was pale and did not look quite so confident as she had a million years ago in Las Vegas.

She held a gun in her hand.

'Hello,' I said. 'We're here to pick up our kids.' My voice rose. I didn't sound quite human.

'So I see.'

'Who else is inside, Anna?'

There were no other cars parked in the lot. She just stared at me.

I held Zviman up. 'Answer me, or I break his neck.'

'Let him go.' Now she raised the gun. Toward Leonie.

'No.'

'I'll shoot her.'

'And I'll snap his neck. Answer me. Who's inside.'

'No one.' She could be lying. It's what I would have said, if there was a full house of guards.

'Okay, drop the gun.'

'I don't believe you can break his neck,' she said. 'With your arm in a cast.'

'It's all in the fingers and the biceps, baby, and those are working just fine.' I strangled Zviman more than a little. He obligingly purpled and gagged for me. I thought about what he'd tried to do to Mila, and what he'd done to Nelly, and it took control not to crush the life out of him.

'Okay, Sam, let's talk.'

'My friend already maimed the son of a bitch. I will be happy to finish him off.'

'Please, Sam, let him go,' Anna said. 'Let's all calm down and . . .'

'I am done negotiating with you!' I screamed at her. I'm not sure I'd ever quite heard my voice sound this way. 'This is what is happening. Either you drop that gun right now, or the next sound you hear is his vertebrae snapping. This! Is the extent. Of. Our. Talking!'

Then silence, the wind crying in the trees.

Anna's gaze went to Zviman's purpling face, and she dropped the gun. I doubted he would have done the same for her.

'Leonie, go get it,' I said.

Leonie hurried up to the porch. She took the gun, eased it away from Anna.

'Okay, stay calm.' Anna tried to smile at Leonie. 'Leonie, I want you to know, I've taken good care of—' and Leonie shot her, in the heart. A curl of smoke, a flower of blood on Anna's T-shirt, and then she fell wordlessly.

Leonie ran inside the house.

Damn it. I hammered a fist into Zviman's face and dropped him to the gravel. I tore into the house after her. The house was old, perhaps a grand country estate built back in the early 1900s. The entranceway was hardwoods, with a large staircase leading up to a mezzanine on the second floor. Sheets covered most but not all of the furniture. Leonie ran, searching, through the adjoining rooms: study, library, dining room, kitchen.

'Leonie, come back here,' I yelled at her. Hell, if Anna was lying, we could be gunned down. And she had the gun, not me.

'Taylor!' she screamed.

I lost her, then heard footsteps caroming up a flight of stairs I couldn't see. I followed the noise through the kitchen. A bottle was warming on a stove. I saw a formula box on the kitchen island, the remains of a grown-up's meal of steak, salad and French fries.

A couple of soiled bibs. A noise between grief and joy surged in my throat.

Beyond the main room of the kitchen was a servants' staircase. She had already run up to the second floor.

'Daniel!' I screamed. Like he was going to answer. But my mind was shuttered or sharpened, I'm not sure which. On the second floor I saw a hallway of rooms, one of them open.

I ran into the doorway. Leonie, standing at a crib, picking up a baby, holding the child close to her shoulder in a mother's embrace, nearly weeping in relief. I looked around the room.

There was only the one crib.

I bolted down the rest of the hallway, opening every door. Next was an empty bedroom, a woman's clothes tossed on the foot of the bed. No crib. Anna's room.

The next was another room, men's clothes littering the floor. Where Zviman had stayed.

The other rooms were empty.

'No, no!' I screamed. 'Daniel!'

I ran back to the first room. Leonie stood there, holding the baby, cradling its blond hair against her shirt.

Blond hair. I remembered the weathered picture, handled with love. The smiling dark-haired girl. Taylor was a bigger baby, and brown-haired.

'Sam,' Leonie said, and her voice turned into a broken sob. 'Sam. I'm sorry.'

And she pointed the gun at me.

87

In the back of a van

This was how Mila thought it might end: bound and hand-cuffed, riding in a bounty hunter's car, to be delivered to her fate, because Zviman wanted her alive.

Six had tried in the past three years, and six had died. Two had come closest, handcuffing her (which she respected: it was much quicker than tying her with rope or even plastic cuffs) and binding her feet. The first of the two were ex-IRA, seized her outside The Adrenaline Bar, the Round Table-owned drinking spot in London, in the hipster Hoxton neighborhood. Kenneth, the manager of (now) Sam's bar in London saw her grabbed, injected in the neck with a sedative, and forced into an Audi's trunk. Kenneth had caught up the kidnappers on the A5 and shot the driver through the car window. The car crashed and Kenneth shot the other kidnapper, then politely carried Mila out of the trunk. She was grateful, of course, but humiliated to be saved.

The second time was barely three weeks ago, two Filipinos trying their luck. They had gotten her handcuffed in her apartment but before they bound her feet she had, to put it bluntly, kicked and stomped the two of them to death. The unpleasantness made for a gruesome evening, when all she'd been in the mood for was a nice Thai green curry for dinner, a cold bottle of lager and watching *Emmerdale* on TV. But both times she'd had to have Kenneth slice the cuffs off her. Then, of course, she had to vanish and get an entirely new apartment, under a different name, on the other side of London. Very inconvenient. It made her think.

Those were the last two attempts: word had spread among the shadowy vines that connected hired killers that she was very dangerous. Kill four people who come after you and everyone recalculates the value of hunting you down.

She blinked back slowly from the chloroformed unconsciousness. Her nose ached and her lips were thick where he'd hit her. She could see, on the van floor, splinters from the boxes where she and Bertrand had loaded in the dead guards she and Sam had killed when they got the best lead on Anna Tremaine and Daniel. She should have swept it more thoroughly.

Why are you in New York? Sam had asked her when he'd come to The Last Minute after leaving Las Vegas, and she answered, with a smile: *shoes.* He thought she was being Mila, joking, parrying his question. But what Sam had not quite learned was that she spoke the truth more often than not.

She had indeed gotten shoes in New York. Custom-made boots. She eased the back of her heels closer to her hands. On the left boot she maneuvered her fingertips into place and gave the heel a slight twist and push all at once, like on a medicine bottle. The right heel popped off. Embedded in it was a handcuff key. A universal key, especially made for her by a master locksmith who had once been the KGB's finest lock designer. She freed the key from the heel with a finger flick, and then repositioned herself gently, trying to ease the key into the lock.

'I can hear you, you know,' the man driving the van said. 'Nice sleep?'

'I had bad dreams.'

'Baby, you're about to have much worse. But then your dreams will end.'

'You have a poetic soul.'

460

'I have received many compliments in my life but that is a first. Thank you, Mila.'

'What is your name?'

'Oh, I should keep some secrets. I'm just a nobody.'

'I have seen your face on a camera. A picture I think Sam will send to the CIA.'

Silence.

'Ah. You do not like that,' Mila said. 'You are a nobody they will know, yes?'

'My name is Braun.' He said it with pride. 'I want you to know who's beaten you after others have failed.'

'Well, Mr Braun, I will pay you more than a million dollars to let me go.'

'Tempting. But this isn't about money. It's about cleaning house. Setting a mistake to right. I understand that's how you got your start, setting a mistake to right.'

'It's hard to be the star of your own legend.'

'I find your confidence in the face of death charming. I like you. If Mr Zviman wasn't so specific about getting you alive and in a state to be tortured, I might give you a mercy bullet.' His voice sounded almost merry. 'Out of respect.'

'I am curious . . .'

'Why would you be, when you're about to die? I wouldn't bother learning new facts. I would be reflecting on all the old choices that brought me here. We have a duty to learn more from our mistakes. I mean, you're one of my mistakes, and I'm learning from you. I would have liked to have dinner with you, Mila. Talked to you. You fascinate me. Both you and Zviman.'

He wasn't talking about her but she wanted him to keep talking. He would be less likely to notice anything she did.

'I am not sure how I am your mistake,' Mila said. The

461

handcuff pick slid home. Now, if it would work. It better. She had paid very good money for it.

'You. Zviman. Two sides of the same coin, my dear. I mean, there's an irony that I'm going to profit from my mistake. But after all I am cleaning up the mess. I was retired. I had a place to live in Florida. I was going to focus on golf and fishing. Mistakes shouldn't come back to haunt you at that point in life. Mistakes should die first and then let you die.'

This Braun was a crazy man. The handcuff opened. She gave out a little sigh.

'I do not know what you mean. I am not a coin.'

'No, Mila, you're a jewel. But you are worth a great number of coins. Retirement doesn't go as far as it used to.' He gave a sigh. 'Now I can retire in peace, knowing my past mistakes are rectified. It should really help my golf game.'

She eased a wrist free. She was careful not to make a clicking sound.

Now the other heel. She loosened it and wedged in the heel was a small, sheathed knife. She flicked off the sheath and the knife, forged from Japanese steel, rested in her hand. It was actually harder to cut the ropes around her feet than open the cuffs; it required more movement to saw through the fibers.

'Well, I find it odd that I am your mistake when I have never seen you before. Are you my long lost father, Mr Braun?'

'Not biologically, but, yes, I am your father, in a manner of speaking.'

Okay, she thought, entirely crazy. 'You cannot answer straight questions,' she said. 'You must have been CIA. You talk all vaguely, just like Sam.'

'Yes, he's the problem, isn't he? It all comes back to him.'

She felt the van slow, make a turn. They had been driving

462

north in a relatively straight stretch; she couldn't see, but she assumed he had the GPS monitor up in the seat with him.

'We're here, Mila. Here where it all began,' he said. 'Where it was all born.'

He stopped the van.

'Well, that's not good,' he said. 'I better not be too late.'

And then he got out of the van and slammed the door.

Mila writhed, slashing at the ropes. She had maybe eight seconds before Braun opened the van's rear door.

Not enough time.

88

The Nursery

'Leonie.' My glance kept flickering between the gun and the baby. 'What are you doing?'

She wept, tears bright on her cheeks. 'I'm sorry. I can't let you take him.'

'That is Daniel. Where is your child?'

She glanced at Daniel. He cooed and moved against her, gently. As though he knew the smell of her skin, the swell of her breast.

I shook my head. 'No. No.'

'He's mine. I'm all he's ever had, all he's ever known,' she said. 'He's not yours any more. His name is Daniel Taylor Jones. I sometimes call him Dat. Like in a peek-a-boo game, I go who, then I go dat, and he laughs.' Fresh tears, but her mouth curled into a twist of resolve.

'He is my son,' I said and she steadied the gun. 'Okay, okay,' I said. I raised my hands. 'Leonie. We can talk about this.'

'No. No talk. I am leaving. With *my* son.'

'The child in the picture you showed me . . .'

'That was my first child. My daughter. I had to leave . . . Ray Brewster when I got pregnant. I didn't want him to be the father. He wouldn't have let me be tied down with a child; in case I ever had to run with him. Children complicate everything. So I went.' She steadied her voice. 'I would have liked . . . someone like you, Sam, I so don't want to hurt you. I don't want to. I will keep him safe in a way you can't, not with the life you lead, the enemies you have. So move to the wall, and keep your hands up, and let me leave.'

'What happened to your daughter?' As long as she was talking, she wasn't shooting me or leaving.

'She died. She died.' And I thought the grief would make her body fold. 'Meningitis. It takes them so fast. She . . . I had done work for Anna. On the babies' new identities. She gave me Daniel. She said . . . he could be mine. A replacement, but he's not. I loved Taylor just as she was, she was the greatest, Sam . . . oh, God . . .'

'I bet she was.' My own face felt hot and heavy. 'Leonie, please.'

'. . . but . . . but she gave me Daniel and I love him just as much . . .' her voice broke to a whisper. 'And you are not going to take him away from me.'

I could see how Zviman and Anna had planned this ending. I, the ex-CIA, killed Jack Ming, the one man CIA Special Projects wanted more than anyone else. Then I died, at Leonie's hand, when my defenses were down, when victory was in my grasp. Leonie as a partner would ensure that I would not betray or move against Nine Suns, and, if I did, she had every reason to kill me.

Leonie would have a bigger motive for wanting me dead than anyone in Nine Suns. I could take away the thing most precious in the world to her.

'Give me my son,' I said. I opened my hands toward her.

'He isn't yours. I'm his mother. I'm the only mother he's ever known. That ... that ... traitor you married, she gave him up, *she gave him up* ...'

'I never did,' I said. 'You know how hard I have fought to find him—' And then I heard it.

'You!' she screamed, and the sympathy she seemed to feel for me turned instantly to venom. 'I have fought a thousand times harder ...'

I raised a finger to my lips. 'I heard something. Downstairs. Someone's here.'

She shook her head. 'You're trying to scare me or trick me ... you want to go down there and get a weapon because I've got the gun ...'

'Leonie!' I hissed. '*Someone is downstairs.*'

She shut up, my tone slicing through her fury. Listening.

I held out my hand for the gun. After a moment she stepped forward, hand shaking, and gave it to me.

'Hide,' I whispered. And she nodded, my son gurgling against her shirt. I looked at him for one second. His eyes met mine, his little mouth parted and a spit bubble formed and burst like a flower given a five-second life. I have never wanted to hold another human being so badly in my life.

Instead I checked the gun for the remaining clip and I eased onto the mezzanine.

89

But, to Mila's surprise, Braun didn't come around the van's back door.

He walked away from the van. She could hear the soft hiss of his footsteps on the gravel.

Unloading his prisoner wasn't a priority. Fine by her. She risked a glance out the front window. Braun stood by a BMW, looking down at the ground. *Talking* to the ground.

It must be someone lying next to the car.

Then Braun shook his head and he walked into the grand house, a gun in his hand.

She sliced through the remaining ropes, kicked them away. Her hand went to her watch. The garrote's wire was inside, just as when she had used it against Anna's men in New York. She palmed the heel of her boot, with the miniature Japanese knife. The blade protruded between her ring and middle finger. Two small weapons. She hoped they would be enough.

She let herself out of the van through the driver's door and dropped to the ground. She looked under the van to see if she could spot who was lying by the BMW. She saw legs, but they were upright now. Gray pants, nice shoes.

She heard a trunk open. She peered around the van.

The blond mohawk. Yaakov Zviman. He looked up toward the house and she saw a rising bruise on the side of his face. Sam hit him, she thought.

Zviman hoisted an ax out of the BMW. He took two steps toward the house.

Then he stopped.

She ducked back around the van, cursing the gravel. It made a whispery noise that was unavoidable. She froze.

He couldn't resist. Surely Braun had told Zviman his prize was in the van and he, instead of going inside to help Braun, he was coming here to gloat. To make sure it was her.

Because it would only take a second, he must have thought, and he was a weak man. And she knew he thought it would strike blind terror into her heart to see his face, her being bound and helpless. And it would have. She knew what kind of revenge he would take on her for her maiming of him. The cruelty of it would be all but unimaginable.

'Oh, baby,' he called to the closed rear door of the van. 'I don't have the hours it will take to do you properly, not right now, but in a few minutes. I'm going to slice you up good in front of your friends and if you scream I cut a piece off them. Then I'm going to kill them in front of you—' and he swung open the van door and it was empty. Just the sliced ropes and the unlocked cuffs. She could hear his suck of surprised breath.

Let him be scared for one second, she thought.

She rounded the van's back door and she aimed a hard punch at the side of his neck with the blade extending from her fist. She wanted an artery. She missed as he jerked back but the knife scored north of his jaw, a hard puncture into cheek. The blood welled up; she aimed again at his eye.

He ducked, she missed, and, grunting with pain, he swung the ax. But he was off balance and no muscle behind the swing, and the edge bounced off the van's door, four inches from her head. He nearly dropped the ax.

She swung her fist again, looking to slice his throat, but he kicked her midsection. She stumbled back and now he had both

467

hands on the ax, and momentum and balance. Her blade was a sting, his ax a missile.

'Oh, bitch, dream come true,' he said. 'I've waited for this. I've so waited to feel you die.'

'Really?' she panted. He had a rage, she remembered. Make it work for her. 'Does the thought of hurting me make you hard? I mean, what's left of it?'

He swung the ax, viciously, in an arcing trace. He missed her by inches. Then swung it back, the blunt edge catching her hand when she made the mistake of a panicked slash. The heel blade flew out into the gravel.

'I don't even know what I'll do first to you,' he said. 'I made a list once. It ran to three pages.'

'Go get your list, raggedy man. I'll wait.'

At her words he stopped swinging wildly at her. His grin was inhuman, the stuff of a leering boogeyman. He steadied the ax, and they did a little dance on the gravel, back and forth. She badly wanted to run. But her shoes were awkward without the heels and he could throw the ax into her back. Better to keep her face to him.

This went on for thirty long seconds. He wouldn't quite commit. She realized, even as he choked with rage and spite, that he was afraid of her.

'Wow, raggedy man. Wielding an ax against an unarmed woman. And still you won't fight.'

He snarled and chopped at her. Missed. She'd had an idea and she circled back toward the van. He stepped in too close and she got a grip on the handle, trying to pry it from his fist. He shoved her against the side of the van, and powered a mighty blow.

The ax slammed into the steel side of the van, perforating the metal. It missed her head only because she fell, her heeless boots slipping and skidding out on the gravel.

He grunted as he tried to pry the ax out. It was stuck.

She would not get another chance. She pivoted out from under the handle, turned and pulled the watch's face free. The garrote's wire glinted in the fading, dusky light. She looped the wire over his throat and threw herself onto his back. Then she pulled.

Yaakov Zviman tried to pry fingers under the wire but she tightened it too fast. He tried to throw her free; she wrapped her strong, lithe legs around him, ankles crossed above his ruined crotch. She thought of his wicked, smiling face, looking back over his pimpled shoulder while he raped her sister. She thought of Ivan, teaching her in the dusty, broken light of the winery how to fight, how to kill. She thought of Nelly, lying in surprised blood, the last of her life pulsing out of her.

And she pulled tighter.

He made noises no human should make. He threw himself against the van, trying to scrape her off.

'*Tu mori*,' she gasped, '*tu mori*.'

He fell, face down into the gravel. She felt the wire slice her own flesh on her fingers, the side of her hand. She drove her knees into his back.

The handle on the fake face of the watch broke. She felt it give. The garrote would not work.

She didn't look to see if he was even still breathing through the compressed wreckage of his throat. With a shuddering moan she kicked against the van, levered the ax out of its torn side with a rush of strength, and she avenged her sister with a final downward blow.

469

90

Where it all began

I took the gun and inched toward the mezzanine's railing.

'Sam?'

A voice calling to me. I didn't know it. So I didn't answer.

'Sam, I've brought your friend Mila.'

I stopped. I thought he was in the foyer, walking along the hardwoods in the entrance.

'Now if you don't come out, she's going to get hurt.'

If that was true, Mila was going to get hurt anyway with Zviman around. His threat wasn't going to flush me out.

'You're not being a gentleman,' he said with disapproval in his tone.

I got still. I listened. And then, muffled, I heard Daniel begin to cry.

'That's the future crying,' he said. He started coming up the stairs. I heard the creak of the wood against his heels. Outside I heard – noises of struggle, a fight. Zviman might be functional. And he was out there, with Mila as a prisoner.

Oh hell.

Now he walked into sight. We kept guns raised at each other. The man who had sat in the corner of the bar, nursing his pints. Ray Brewster.

'I don't want to hurt you,' he said.

'That must be why your limo driver and your psychotic sister act tried to kill me, Mr Brewster.'

'Ray Brewster was just an alias. My name is Ricardo Braun.'

Braun. August's boss. The un-retired head of Special Projects.

Braun shrugged. 'Kill Jack Ming, that was fine. I didn't need him exposing the truth. You, Sam, you were different. You were the bridge.'

'I don't know what you mean.' At this distance we couldn't miss each other. He kept heading toward the top of the stairs, I kept moving toward where stairs met mezzanine.

'You're the bridge between Special Projects and our biggest mistakes. You being that bridge, well, I could let you and your child live.'

'Mistakes . . .' I fell silent. 'Nine Suns. Nine Suns was started by Special Projects.'

'Yes, years ago. May I explain?'

'Why? So I'll pretend to listen and you'll get a chance to shoot me?'

'No. Because you have a role to play, Sam, if you dare.'

I was silent.

He cleared his throat. 'The CIA had a long history of dealing with questionable sources. People who were criminals. Often they were heads of state. You develop a high tolerance for holding your nose. But we thought – I thought, it was *my idea* – what if criminals, carefully selected, could be put to use by the CIA. They know about dark corners of the world. They could help us insert people into situations where we never could have access. They could give us information and people we could never find on our own.'

'And why?'

'We would protect them and their interests. Really, no different than propping up a brutal but pro-Western government in the old days. So we researched them, people in positions of power in criminal rings from around the world, and we brought nine of them here. Here, to this house. The language schools are an old Special Projects front.' He laughed. 'You know how the CIA is, once they buy property they never want to sell it. They're always afraid some secret has been left behind, hidden in the woodwork.'

'They came willingly?'

'Not exactly. Kidnapped them. But treated them with dignity once they were here, in the lovely Catskills. I explained to them the ... opportunity. They embraced it. What we couldn't have foreseen was – they bonded. As a group. I didn't anticipate they would think if they didn't cooperate, they would lose a competitive advantage. They understood each other. They respected each other and since all nine were scattered about the world, they weren't, well, natural enemies. These were men and women on the edge of the powerful rings, ambitious and looking for a way to the top.'

'Like Zviman out there.'

'Yes. I recruited his father, he stepped in after his dad died. They went from being whoremasters – who are a very useful source of information – to smugglers to a supreme extortionist and spymaster.' He flexed a smile, almost of pride. 'I chose well with my recruits. The Suns, they took what I taught them about tradecraft and stealing secrets and they, well, formed a gang beyond a gang. A meta-gang. To grow their own power and profit. With an eye, I think, on becoming the most powerful criminal syndicate in the world. They stopped doing exactly what the CIA asked for. It was harder for me to shield them. I retired. They broke away; but kept their own alliance.'

'Nine Suns.'

'There were leftovers, of course. People I recruited who were criminals but not parts of rings. Individuals working alone for Special Projects.'

'Such as the limo driver. The sisters. The people that Leonie hid for you.'

'Yes. Odd, that the psychos were more loyal than the sane criminals for me. But the psychos prefer the attention and support.'

'Your group inside the CIA gave birth to the most powerful and ambitious criminal ring in history,' I said. 'One that just tried to commit a mass assassination against our government.'

'You don't want to see those words in a news report,' Braun said. 'It would have been devastating. CIA in bed with renegade Russian Mafiosi and Japanese Yakuza and Israeli racketeers.' He flexed a smile; he held up the red notebook. 'There's a picture of me, in here, with two of the Suns. Two of the ringleaders. I can't have that. I can't have what they've done tied to the CIA. I can't be disloyal to the Company that way.' He pointed down to the foyer. 'Right here's where they got their name. There was a tapestry, hanging in the library here, a Chinese tapestry that showed the legend of the Nine Suns. I think an agent had been given it as a gift from someone we'd smuggled out of mainland China. One of the criminals noticed there were nine suns, and nine of them. They picked the name, almost as a joke, while they sipped cocktails and I explained how the CIA could protect them if they helped us. I got them to use the Latin form because I thought it would sound like a religious order. I was worried someone in the Company would hear of them and see the tapestry. The Company uses this facility, still, now and then.'

'So. You came back to Special Projects after Nine Suns tried their assassination plot to clean up the mess.'

'I can't destroy them. But I can keep the Company's role in creating them from being exposed. That's all I can do. Oh, I'll kill Zviman, and any other Nine Suns bastard I find because it tells the others to remain silent. I don't mind waging a private war, that's what Special Projects is going to have to do now. That's why I wanted you.'

'Me.' Maybe now I'd know why he told me all this instead of just shooting at me.

'I tried to cover all my bases.' He cleared his throat. 'Criminals to give me information. Corporations to give me information. Just as I found criminals who were too ambitious for their own rings, I found . . . certain people, successful people, who were idealistic and had money to burn and were willing to . . . back another idea of mine. A way to fight back against the Suns.' He flicked another smile.

I felt the world drop out from under me. 'The Round Table. You started them, too.'

'They didn't gel quite as fast as Nine Suns did, but they provided a lot of good information. But these were either people who had inherited vast sums, or made vast sums at young ages. They didn't relish taking orders from me. They don't like or trust bureaucracy. So. They split off. There wasn't anything we could do to stop them. They weren't going to be an embarrassment the way Nine Suns would be. But still. We created two sides and then we left them to fight it out.'

'Because they began to encroach on each other.'

'After 9/11, no one cared what Nine Suns was doing. Punk-ass criminals with delusions of grandeur? Please. But now. They're a serious threat; they've realized that an undermined social order, a chaos, is where they can consolidate power and profit. Look at the areas of the world that are ruled by criminals: parts of Latin America, Moldova, parts of Africa, and those are the testing grounds for Nine Suns' vision of the world. Which is why I want to talk to you. I can offer you amnesty, Sam. That's why I told Zviman to bring you here. I'd worked out a deal with him. Mila for you. He wouldn't kill you if I brought him Mila.'

I shot him. I was tired of him and his excuses. The bullet hit him in the shoulder, in the gun arm, and he staggered and screamed and clutched at the wall. His gun clattered down the stairs.

What did Mila say? The unpredictable is what killls you. Well, that cut both ways. I was done with Braun.

'You . . . goddamn it, let me finish! Come back and work here. You can tear them both down. Nine Suns and Round Table.'

'Project A and Project B. I'm not interested in being the consultant who fixes your mistakes.'

'You . . . do you think they'll let you out of prison? You killed the guy Special Projects wanted. You attacked a CIA team and nearly exposed them. I'm your only choice, Sam. I'm the only way to keep your freedom and have your son.'

Braun sagged on the wall.

'I am done,' I said.

'Your brother. In Afghanistan. Wasn't a bunch of Taliban hash smugglers that killed him. It was a Nine Suns job. Initiation . . .'

His gasp echoed in the foyer. 'Now you're just desperate. Desperate.' I shook my head. 'I'm not getting played by a loser like you.'

'Your brother's execution wasn't what it seemed.' He laughed. 'Do you think it's just coincidence that Lucy betrayed you? They aimed her at you. They've watched you ever since you went into the CIA. They've wanted to bring you to them. Both sides.' He stuck fingers along his bloodied shoulder. 'Christ. I need a doctor.'

'Did you know, as a CIA officer, that my son was being held here?'

475

His mouth moved.

'You've run and profited from your own little fiefdom.'

'Yes. But I'm retiring. I want you to have it. You to take it over. At least I did before you shot me.' He spat at me.

'And Leonie?'

'Lindsay. Ah. Don't trust her. She'll leave you.' He coughed blood.

The father of Nine Suns, and the father of the Round Table, sitting before me, giving me the perfect excuse to go back to the CIA and get my old life back, with a new mission. What was I going to do with him?

The front door clanged. Mila walked in, dragging a bloodied ax. Always a good sign.

'You okay?' I called down to her.

'Yes. Is Daniel here?'

'Yes.'

'Safe?'

'Yes.'

She looked up the stairs at Braun and pointed. 'This man is crazy. He thinks he is my father. I assure you my mother had much better taste.'

'He invented Nine Suns. And the Round Table.'

'Both?'

'Both.'

Mila stared at him. For one second, ax in hand, she started to step up the stairs. Then she stopped. 'You should have picked a side.' She dropped the ax. She picked up a bloodied, slightly mangled notebook that he had dropped when I shot him.

I could hear the hiss of Braun's breath. He wanted it. Whatever Jack Ming had found, it had to contain threads that led back to the CIA. Otherwise he wouldn't have cared; he'd not chased after his Frankenstein monster before. Nine Suns wanted Ming dead because they didn't want to be exposed; Braun wanted Ming dead because he didn't want the CIA exposed.

So drag his ass out into the light.

'Good luck, Braun. I'm not going to kill you. I'm going to let you sit and bleed on those stairs, in the place where you had so many clever ideas that have come back and bit you in the ass, and I'm leaving. If I ever see you again . . .'

'Sam. You said you wanted your old life back. It's been your mantra, from what I understand. I am offering you your old life. All you have to do to get back into the CIA is help me clean up this mess. You get what you want and so do I.'

'I'm not giving the CIA my friends in the Round Table. I'm not giving you Mila. And I'm not helping you.'

'Your old life,' he said again. 'Yours. They will give you no peace. All I'm offering you is your only chance to regain what you lost. Your child, your career.'

'My wife?'

Braun swallowed. 'I can give you back what can be given. What sort of life will you have with your son now? Do you think Nine Suns will give you peace? My offer is the only one that makes sense for you.'

'All you are offering me is a chance to be you. Which is less than nothing.'

'This is a very good offer I am making!'

' . . . if I ever see you again, or you come near Mila, or Leonie, or my son, I will kill you. If you ever try to harm August, I will kill you.' I almost mentioned Jack Ming but perhaps better if he thought Jack Ming was dead. 'If I think you're thinking about me, I will kill you. Go retire. Just . . . go away.'

'I'm not lying. About your brother. Lucy always said that was why you joined, to get your revenge . . .'

'And that's why you'd lie,' I said. 'Think about it. You're bragging you founded the group that killed my brother? I really would shut up now.'

I turned and went back down the hallway. I found Leonie and Daniel hiding in a closet.

'It's all right,' I said. 'We're all leaving. Together.'

She clutched Daniel close. She had held him for several minutes, and her closeness calmed him. He looked up at me. Blinked, disinterested. Then looked at me again, one little fist raised toward me.

I took him from Leonie; I did not ask. She did not fight me. He was hers in a way but he was mine. I tucked his little head under my arm, like I'd seen the fathers on television do, and I could smell his warm milky breath. The soft weight of him. The miracle of him.

He raised his little fist again, and I kissed it.

91

The Bahamas

Daniel was afraid of the water.

I held him close to me. I found it hard to let him go at times, it was almost as if I needed to drink in his touch. He had grown used to me, in the past several weeks, and I liked to tell myself that my absence in the first months of his life was not impossible to overcome. That being apart from me for so long at his life's beginning wouldn't scar him. I read obsessively about the topic of parental separation on Google. It didn't matter what the experts said.

I would make it right.

We walked in the surge of the tide and he stared down at the waves eddying around my calves. I timed it carefully with the surf and after a healthy wave passed I dipped his feet in the cool. He giggled. As the next wave surged forward I hoisted him high out of its path and he loved being raised toward the sky. We played the game, him laughing, until I miscued and the top of a foaming wave crept up past his swimsuit to splash his chest. Then he howled in dismay. Daniel, I had learned, liked his comforts.

Leonie had taken good care of him.

With my fussy boy fussing, I walked back up to the beach cottage. I thought Leonie would be inside, fixing lunch, but instead Mila sat at the table.

'Hello,' I said. I made Daniel's hand wave. 'Hello, Mila. I went surfing with no board.'

'Please,' Mila said. 'Do not treat that beautiful child like a puppet.' She got up and tapped his nose playfully with her finger. She frowned. 'He is like a greasy pig.'

'Sunscreen.'

'Did you dip him in it?'

'I don't want him to get sunburned.'

'Amazed you could maintain a grip.'

'Do you want to hold him?'

'Linen,' she said, pointing to her blouse. 'I don't want to risk a massive oil stain.' But she waved her greasy finger at the yawning Daniel and smiled a grin that seemed too bright for the Mila I knew. 'Hello, *puişor*,' she chimed. I had learned this meant 'little birdie'. Daniel gurgled back. He seemed a bit uncertain about Mila.

'I think you're a bit ambivalent about babies,' I said, settling him into a chair and wiping his hands clean. An ocean explorer deserved a snack. I opened a bottle of organic pureed pears. I sat down and spooned the fruity mush into his mouth. Daniel gobbled.

'Humans are much more interesting when they reach school age. Then I like them much better.' She glanced at me. 'Maybe by then I will retire and be a teacher again. Just for Daniel. Perhaps I will open an exclusive language school.' She made a face. 'I hear they are hiring.'

'Uh oh.'

'Ricardo Braun is now a big hero. I heard that he broke up a criminal ring here that was spying on American citizens and government and companies. He killed the two ringleaders: an Israeli man, a French woman.'

'Of course he's a, and I quote, "hero".'

'Wounded in the line of duty. Retired with honors. No farewell cocktail party, though. Went back to Florida. Living very quietly.'

'So giving August the notebook was the right thing to do. That picture of Braun with two of the Suns sunk his comeback.'

'The lovely red notebook can't hurt us.' Mila shrugged. 'I tore out the pages of interest to me.'

'The ones about the Round Table?'

'Very few. But there are some useful people in the missing pages of the little red notebook. I say give them a chance to redeem themselves helping us rather than being blackmailed by Nine Suns.'

I shook my head.

'On a voluntary basis,' she said, with a cough.

'The CIA has more resources than we do to bring down Nine Suns.'

'And they will bring down at least a few of them that they can tie to the blackmail ring. The CIA will identify some of their plans. But, Sam, Nine Suns, they will not go away. Some fall, they will be replaced. Your friend Braun created too good and useful a template. They have made too much money, accrued too much power. They won't give it up.'

'I keep wondering if I should have killed him.'

'You must not talk about killing people in front of *puişor*,' she said. 'It is bad for child development. You need boundaries.'

'So Braun's not running Special Projects.'

'No.'

'Who is?'

'One of the few big secrets I do not know.'

'You really don't know?' I hoped August got the job. He'd brought in Jack Ming, after all.

'I really don't know, don't care. You. You are my problem.'

'How so?' I knew what was coming.

'We gave you many bars to run.'

'Yes. Thank you.'

'Bars to serve as a cover for you, so you could do jobs for us.'

'Ah.'

'I don't believe you are going into fights with *puişor* strapped to your back.'

'No.'

'So. May I have the bars back?' She was asking so politely.

'No.'

'I do not understand.'

'Well, the Round Table still needs the bars run, right? And any other employees such as yourself need to avail themselves of the bars as safe houses, yes?'

'Yes.'

'So let me run the bars. I'll make sure they turn a tidy profit.'

'And that will be enough for you.'

'For now.'

Mila drew her knees up to her chin. 'And what about what that old asshole said about your brother's death?'

'I have Daniel. I'm not interested in the revenge game.'

'May I be honest?'

'You're still my boss.'

'I forgot momentarily. Right now you are captivated by this greasy child. You will want to be a good and present father. But you will get restless, bored.'

'Never of him.'

Mila nodded. 'You will get bored of not knowing.'

'The truth?' Nine Suns had a plan for me, according to Zviman. One cultivated over the years. I still didn't know what that plan was. Did I want to?

'No, you will want to know what these jerks are doing,' Mila said. 'You and Jack Ming destroyed their main source of information. Now. Extortion does not have a long life anyway. But they will replace Zviman in their constellation of assholes, and they will find new mischief. New ways to earn profits or grab power. Or there will be some other jerk to fight because no one else knows that he is a threat, or no one else will dare to fight him.'

'Not my problem,' I said carefully, 'until it is.'

'Ah. My glimmer of hope. Therefore you may keep the bars. For now. Run them at massive profit or I will bring Barney DVDs for Danny boy.'

'Leonie calls him Dat.'

Mila made a face. 'For a woman who invents names she has horrible taste.' She jerked her head toward the sliding glass door. 'She left when I came here.'

'Your charm is contagious.'

'Why is she still here?'

'For Daniel.'

'How convenient his nanny is a master forger. No doubt she can teach him to copy your signature on excuses for his teachers.'

'She's not his nanny.'

'Well. She is not his mother, she is not your wife, what is she? Aside from a champion liar?'

'We're deciding.'

Mila watched the pear ooze past Daniel's lips. 'I noticed there were three bedrooms here. All used.'

'You can count.'

'Sam. She has no claim on your child. Her adoption was both illegal and immoral. Don't reward her. Don't let . . . this woman into your life.'

I glanced up at her. 'Do you think I want to send someone who loves Daniel, who would have died for him, to jail?'

'No. You can't expose yourself that way, either, to police questions as to where you were when Daniel was born.'

True.

'It's done,' I said, 'and it's my business, not yours, and . . .'

'And I will let it go,' Mila said quietly.

I decided to change the subject. 'Did your CIA source have anything new on Jack Ming?'

'Yes. He and his girlfriend have new names, new city, new jobs. They have a brand new start.'

New start. Didn't everyone deserve one?

I left Mila considering whether a towel would protect her

from Daniel's oily embrace and walked along the sand. Leonie stood at the water's edge. The ocean surged then retreated around her feet. Tides. Where one world ends, another begins. I had loved when my parents, in their globetrotting do-gooderness, were assigned to coastal areas. Beginnings and endings, on the sand, the water erasing and renewing, all at once. She stood in a yellow sundress, a big floppy hat.

'You saw Mila arrived,' she said as I joined her.

'Yes. We had a nice chat.'

'She still hates me.'

'She hates most people. Except Daniel.'

'Her one redeeming feature.'

'I'm keeping the bars,' I said.

'Oh. So. I guess Daniel will be traveling with you.'

'I'm not sure I'd wish my vagabond childhood on him.'

She looked out at the boats skidding across the sea, then back at me. 'What does that mean?'

'It means I travel and then I have a home. Where Daniel is. Where I will need help.'

'Are you offering me a job?' Her voice sounded cold.

'A job, no. You're the only mother he's known, Leonie. I cannot take him from you, I can't take you from him.'

Her lips narrowed. 'If you are going to do that someday, Sam, do it now. Now is easier.'

'No. I know you love him.'

'And my legal standing with Daniel?' she asked in the barest whisper, a question she almost couldn't risk.

'None, right now. This is a test drive, Leonie. We'll see.' I did not feel the need to say that if she ran with Daniel, she couldn't run far. Not with me and Mila and friends looking for her.

She scratched at her lip, considering.

We were silent for several moments, watching the water wipe the sandy slate clean.

'Thank you,' she said. 'I accept.'

'I might be at home a lot, I might have to travel. I plan on staying well clear of trouble.'

'Man plans, God laughs.' She crossed her arms. 'You know I didn't sleep with you because . . . I did it because I wanted you.'

'I know. I wanted you, too.'

'But.'

'But. We were both in an extreme mental state. It's too soon for me, after Lucy. I'm sorry.'

She steepled her fingers before her face and studied me. 'And the future?'

'I don't know. I won't promise something I can't keep. I've had enough of that in my life.'

'All right. So what city? Las Vegas or New York?'

'Do you want to go back to art school?'

She looked genuinely surprised. 'I . . . I hadn't considered that as a possibility.'

'Well. If you want, pick a good one. I'll pay for it. Or I'll get you a studio, if you don't want to go back to school. I would rather you be back at art than forgery.'

Delight played across her face. Art school and Daniel: that was heaven. 'You don't have any preference for a city?'

I shrugged. 'My folks live in New Orleans, but I don't really talk to them. I think, with Daniel, now maybe I should mend that fence. I can't teach him the value of family if I'm too distant from my own.'

'Yes, show up with your new son and your non-girlfriend who's not a nanny and takes care of the kid. They would love that, I'm sure. Where else?'

I bit my lip. The wanderer gets to choose a home. 'I like Austin. I like Savannah. I like Boston and Nashville. I like London and Paris and Dublin.'

'I like all those choices,' she said.

'Then you decide.' And I meant it. I didn't care where we lived. I was getting a new start. So was she, so was Daniel. So, even, was Mila. Wind, lift me, take me, then settle me down. I'd lived so much of my life planned out and I was ready for a jolt of spontaneity.

'Okay. I'll decide,' Leonie said, and we walked back to the cottage.

But in the end, Daniel chose, that night. Leonie had written down a bunch of cities on slips of paper, tossed them into a rainbow knit hat she'd bought down on the beach. She couldn't decide and had thought she'd have me draw a city from the hat.

Daniel, holding onto the coffee table, pulled himself standing. He knocked over the hat and shook it and to his delight the scraps of paper spilled loose.

He grabbed one and tried to stick it in his mouth. I pulled it from his little fist and uncurled the damp strip. Held it up for Leonie to see. She laughed and said, 'Sold.'

'Good choice, Daniel,' I said. He offered up a hand and I gave him a gentle high-five.

He plopped on his butt and began to fuss and then he reached up for the comfort of my arms.

Acknowledgments

I would like to thank Mitch Hoffman, Daniel Mallory, Peter Ginsberg, Shirley Stewart, David Shelley, Jamie Raab, Ursula Mackenzie, Thalia Proctor, Kim Hoffman, Dave Barbor, Holly Frederick, Nathan Bransford, Sarah LaPolla, and the amazing teams at Little, Brown UK and Grand Central Publishing.

Also thanks to Kevin Casey, Steve Basile, Dan Edwardes, James Whitaker, and special thanks to Leslie, Charles, and William, as always.

Sharon Sulzburg

* Sylvia Borstein   Spirit Rock